All about Skin

All about Skin

Short Fiction by Women of Color

Edited by
Jina Ortiz
and
Rochelle Spencer

The University of Wisconsin Press

Publication of this volume has been made possible, in part, through support from the Anonymous Fund of the College of Letters and Science at the University of Wisconsin–Madison.

The University of Wisconsin Press
1930 Monroe Street, 3rd Floor
Madison, Wisconsin 53711-2059
uwpress.wisc.edu

3 Henrietta Street, Covent Garden
London WC2E 8LU, United Kingdom
eurospanbookstore.com

Printed in the United States of America

Library of Congress Cataloging-in-Publication Data

All about skin: short fiction by women of color / edited by Jina Ortiz and Rochelle Spencer.
pages cm
ISBN 978-0-299-30194-1 (pbk.: alk. paper)
ISBN 978-0-299-30193-4 (e-book)
1. Short stories—Women authors. 2. Short stories—Minority authors.
3. Minority women in literature.
I. Ortiz, Jina, editor of compilation. II. Spencer, Rochelle (Writer), editor of compilation.
PN6120.92.W65A45 2014
823′.01089287—dc23
2014007452

The stories I have chosen are simply those I loved above all others given to me for consideration.

Amy Tan,
"Introduction," from
The Best American Short Stories, 1999

Contents

Foreword

Helena María Viramontes

It is the Afterword that'll count.

Toni Cade Bambara

In the years charting the cultural shifts forced upon the country by the waves of activism and political movements of the sixties and seventies, we women writers of color came to understand that publishing houses remained slow in capturing the ever-changing, ever-inquiring flux of the times, nor were they interested in publishing our blooming *flor y canto* of resistance—our lyricisms performed in revolutionary celebration, our artistic offerings of flowering hope. In those years, one could hardly find a collection of women short fiction writers, much less women writers of color. Case in point: On my book shelf, I have two collections discovered and purchased as a feminism student and undergraduate attending Immaculate Heart College, the first one titled *By and about Women: An Anthology of Short Fiction*, edited by Beth Kline Schneiderman and published in 1973. Of the nineteen fine women writers selected for inclusion, only one, Gwendolyn Brooks, is a writer of color. Also published in 1973 was the collection *No More Masks! An Anthology of Poems by Women*, edited by Florence Howe and Ellen Bass, which was more inclusive, with a number of African American poets selected for inclusion, undoubtedly reflecting the black/white racial representational binary of the times. I did not fault these editors, and in fact pay tribute to their efforts. In 1973 I was extremely content to have discovered these books and was grateful for such important contributions to my well-being as a woman beginning her overtures into literature.

And yet . . .

Where were the others of color? In those years of erasure, we women writers wrote poems on the backs of market receipts in the privacy of a bathroom, mimeographed stories to mail to one another, developed support groups for self-expression with such seriousness we bent our lives into midnights so as to light our world with words, because most of us believed, especially we writers of color, that our lives depended on it. This has surely become a cliché, but people, many of them women, were being beaten in the streets, stripped of their dignity, spit upon with unashamed hatred, bludgeoned with unfair laws, yet maintained a profound belief in our ability to change our cultural, racial, sexual, economic, and judicial injustices with words and practice. Since telling stories was our first engagement in democracy, we women writers of color are, have been, and will continue to be instrumental in the public area of labor strikes and civil rights; we maintain half of the ethnicity-identified self-determination and continue to fearlessly challenge the inhospitable heterosexual norms, providing consciousness-raising empowerment for past, present, and future generations. Little wonder why the seminal and game-changing collection edited by Cherríe Moraga and Gloria Anzaldúa was titled *This Bridge Called My Back*. For we knew, we women writers of color, that we could create the bridge and have the resiliency to brave the treacherous accountability for the spiritual health of our neighborhood, our community, our country, and our planet.

I am pleased and profoundly excited by another seminal and game-changing collection edited by Rochelle Spencer and Jina Ortiz and titled *All about Skin: Short Fiction by Women of Color*. Not since D. Soyini Madison's *The Woman That I Am: The Literature and Culture of Contemporary Women of Color* (1994) has there been, for me, such a remarkable and wonderful collection of mostly younger, vibrant, and astonishing voices aptly deserving of their many awards and recognition. I am so very proud and honored to be a small part of this oasis of literary work, one that cannot, will not, be permitted to be ignored, erased, or forgotten.

Many of these stories are written from the fringes of life and time with such searing imagination, it is a testament to the talent of these women writers of color—they know how to solder their words into steel girders. Through their stories, they make us live in another's *feel* of life, in another person's shoes, because they invest the inertia of words with active meaning so as to experience an empathy crucial for our survival. They are talented writers who build on sensory architecture, of the divine detail, of the forensic historical research with an ice axe of language intent on shattering Kafka's frozen seas, creating an intimacy like no other. Here Paul Auster's observation of fiction is useful: "Every novel is an equal collaboration between the writer and the reader, and it is the only place in the world where two strangers can meet on terms of absolute intimacy." Empathy is the glue that makes the words of a writer stick to the reader, and in this era of globalization, understanding and feeling the life of another through narratives is a nonviolent act of sheer humane importance. That these women writers of color are brave enough to open up to others with their stories—opening up to those who are different from us, those we do not know or who cannot recognize our cultural terms—is also apprehending that these others, the readers, are themselves open to intimate interactions. We need to imagine so much more of this. To share stories then, imbrications then, pain and suffering then, but also hope then, in life as in art, is what these wonderful women writers of color celebrate with fearlessness, audacity, and beauty.

Preface

Rochelle Spencer

Short stories are not mini-novels. The condensed nature of the short story forces us to focus on a single moment in time, and if a story soars or falters, its achievement lies in its ability to capture a moment of understanding, that moment when the story's protagonist (and subsequently, its reader) becomes wise yet vulnerable—and breathtakingly lucid.

This isn't easy. The contrasting tensions inherent in the short story—a tightly controlled text that explores the human experience in one ephemeral moment—mean that it seldom reads like a novel. A genius (see Toni Morrison's "Recitatif," Louise Erdrich's "Shamengwa," or Paule Marshall's "Reena") may produce a short fiction that spans multiple years and generations, but for most writers, the short story is a narrow, highly specific genre. Short stories are not mini-novels; they are little moments of grace.

As MFA programs proliferate, short stories' tightness and complexity have made them the dominant form for teaching fiction. Seemingly, the relative ease of writing a short story, as compared with that of writing a longer work, would make it a good choice for the working-class writer. Yet, because it is notoriously difficult to sustain a career writing short fiction, achieving mastery at the short story has become almost a luxury. In the 1970s, Toni Cade Bambara, author of the brilliant short story collection *Gorilla, My Love*, spoke often of the pressures she faced to complete her novel *The Salteaters*; more than thirty years later, the sundry writers publishing short fiction on personal blogs and websites have made it even more difficult to achieve acclaim as a writer of short stories.

Complicating matters even more for emerging short fiction writers is the fact that being anthologized is a common way of gaining recognition, and spaces in these anthologies are, of course, limited. Toni Morrison's essay "Black Matters" from her landmark study *Playing in the Dark* suggests not only that writers write about people like themselves but also that readers are drawn to protagonists who look like them. And, in a society that isn't yet postracial, this often leaves writers of color in marginalized spaces.

These odds are even more daunting for women writers of color, as traditionally, women writers have also received less attention than have male writers. (Every year, the website Vidaweb.org's "The Count" has regularly pointed out the disparity of women authors who are reviewed or published in prestigious outlets such as the *New York Review of Books*, *The Atlantic*, and *Harper's*.) Thus, because of limited places for publication, an anthologized story written by a woman of color is often left with the burden of representing an entire population.

Jina Ortiz and I have seen up-close how damaging this "single story" phenomenon can be. Years ago, as a young writing instructor at Spelman College, a historically black women's college, I heard a student complain that "all black women writers write the same story." My student's attitude wasn't unique; many of her classmates felt the same way: they truly believed that there really *was* one black experience or one woman experience worth writing about, for in their high schools, that was all they had been taught. Despite being female and of color themselves, they had rarely been exposed to multicultural writing by women authors.

As new writing instructors, Jina and I found ourselves looking for anthologies featuring the short fiction of contemporary women writers of color and were at a loss. We knew meaningful fiction was being written—and garnering prizes (we were acquainted with two young writers, Emily Raboteau and ZZ Packer, whose short stories had been reprinted in *Best American Short Stories*)—but it was difficult to locate this work in one anthology.

It is one thing to complain about a problem, but it's another to do something about it. On a sleepy Saturday morning, Jina and I made a list of both brilliant women of color who were in love with the short story and the publications that rightly championed their work. We e-mailed these people and places and asked them to send us work that was contemporary, exciting, and a celebration of the short story's revelatory nature.

And so *All about Skin* was born.

Acknowledgments

Special thanks to Opal Moore, Maria Acosta Cruz, Sandra Govan, Veronica Watson, Sharan Strange, Winston Napier, Kathleen Cleaver, our parents, our mentors from our MFA programs (Solstice of Pine Manor College and New York University), and to the following publications:

Epigraph: "Introduction," copyright 1999 by Amy Tan, from *The Best American Short Stories* (Houghton Mifflin Harcourt, 1999). Reprinted by permission of Houghton Mifflin Company Publishing Company. All rights reserved.

"Aida," copyright 2012 by Patricia Engel. First published in *Harvard Review* 43 (Winter 2012).

"Fairness," copyright 2012 by Chinelo Okparanta. First published in *Subtropics* 14 (Spring/Summer 2012). Reprinted in *Happiness, Like Water*, copyright 2013 by Chinelo Okparanta (Houghton Mifflin Harcourt, 2013). Reprinted by permission of Houghton Mifflin Harcourt Publishing Company. All rights reserved.

"Pita Delicious," originally published as "Gideon," copyright 2007 by ZZ Packer. First published in *The Book of Other People*, edited by Zadie Smith (Penguin Books, 2007).

"Candidate," copyright 2012 by Amina Gautier. First published in *Crazyhorse* 82 (2012).

"How to Leave the Midwest," copyright 2009 by Renee Simms. First published in *Oregon Literary Review* 4, no. 2 (Summer/Fall 2009).

"A Different Story," copyright 2010 by Ivelisse Rodriguez. First published in *Quercus Review* 10 (2010).

"American Child," copyright 2006 by Manjula Menon. First published in *North American Review*, March/April 2006.

"Sirens," copyright 2013 by Joshunda Sanders. First published in *Bellevue Literary Review* 13, no. 2 (Fall 2013).

"Just the Way She Does the Things," copyright 2010 by Jennine Capó Crucet. First published in *Los Angeles Review* 8 (Fall 2010).

"The Rapture," copyright 2013 by Emily Raboteau. First published in *Creative Writing: Writers on Writing*, edited by Amal Chatterjee (The Professional and Higher Partnership Ltd, 2012). Reprinted by permission of the publisher and editor.

"The Lost Ones," copyright 2011 by Aracelis González Asendorf. First published in *Kweli Journal*, December 2011.

"Noelia and Amparo," copyright 2013 by Glendaliz Camacho. First published in the *Southern Pacific Review*, July 4, 2013.

"A Strange People," copyright 2008 by Mecca Jamilah Sullivan. First published in *Crab Orchard Review* 14, no. 1 (Winter 2008).

"Beautiful Things," copyright 2004 by Jacqueline Bishop. First published in *Margin: Exploring Modern Magical Realism* (Spring 2004).

"Lady Chatterley's Mansion," copyright 2008 by Unoma Azuah. First published in *The Length of Light: A Collection of Short Stories* (VDM Verlag Dr. Müller, 2008). Reprinted in the *New Black Magazine*, May 1, 2010.

"All about Skin," copyright 2012 by Xu Xi. First published in the *Kenyon Review*'s KROnline 9, no. 2 (Spring 2012).

All about Skin

Introduction

The subtitle of this anthology includes terms that have become loaded with meaning in contemporary society: "women," "color," "fiction."

In a world that has grown increasingly knowledgeable about the complexity of gender identity, we can wonder what it means to declare oneself "woman"; we can also debate what it means to identify as a "person of color" in the United States, where the Pew Center reports that in the last decade, "racial and ethnic minorities accounted for 91.7 percent of the nation's population growth." Finally, twenty-plus years of postmodern theory have dismantled traditional ideas about authorship and truth, and so we may very well ask ourselves: what does it mean to write fiction?

Nearly thirty-three years after the publication of Cherríe Moraga and Gloria Evangelina Anzaldúa's landmark anthology *This Bridge Called My Back: Writings by Radical Women of Color*, the popularity of Twitter hashtags such as #notyourasiansidekick, #solitaryisforwhitewomen, or #blackpowerisforblackmen reveals that contemporary discourse continues to focus exclusively on one's gender or race but rarely on both. Today, women writers of color are not "unlikely to be friends of people in high literary places," as Anzaldúa would put it, but several flourishing new talents still deserve much greater attention. To that end, we decided that the usefulness of acknowledging the work of these gifted individuals justifies the use of the term "women of color"; furthermore, we felt that whatever the emotional truth in their writing, these writers' abilities to imagine entirely new worlds necessitates the use of the word "fiction."

Short fiction, in particular, creates a unique challenge for writers; short stories can be difficult to publish and produce few financial rewards, so prose writers of limited financial means often turn to the more lucrative novel or autobiography. The financial obstacles associated with publishing short fiction are a reality for contemporary writers, but they were especially harsh for early twentieth-century women writers of color. In the United States, a lack of economic or educational opportunities severely limited these writers' literary production, and the writing that was produced was mainly autobiographical in scope. Prior to the 1920s, formerly enslaved African American women such as Harriet Ann Jacobs (Linda Brent) and Hannah Bond, and Harriet E. Wilson, a mixed-race indentured servant, wrote either autobiographies or autobiographical novels that focused on gendered racial oppression. Effie Waller Smith, an African American woman whose short fiction appeared in *Putnam's Magazine* in the early 1900s, is an example of the rare woman of color who was able to publish short stories, but even still, Smith stopped publishing at the tender age of thirty-eight (though she lived to be eighty).

Latina and Asian writers also faced discrimination. In the early nineteenth century, Puerto Rican activist-writer Luisa Capetillo published short fiction in between campaigning for suffrage for women and for better work conditions for laborers. Capetillo, the author of *Mi opinión sobre las libertades, derechos y deberes de la mujer* (My opinion on the liberties, rights and duties of the woman) and *Influencias de las ideas modernas* (Influences of modern ideas), wrote essays, plays, poems, and short fiction.

Three years after Capetillo's birth, the Chinese Exclusion Act (1882–1943), which prohibited Chinese laborers from immigrating to the United States, became federal law. Still, despite the racial oppression that Chinese Americans faced, two sisters of Chinese and British heritage—Edith Maude Eaton and Winnifred Eaton—became noteworthy writers. Edith Eaton published *Mrs. Spring Fragrance* (1912), a collection of short stories, while Winnifred Eaton (Onoto Watanna) authored a series of successful novels and saw the publication of her short stories ("Maneuvers of O-Yasu-san," "Delia Dissents") in the *Saturday Evening Post* and in *Harper's* ("The Wrench of Chance").

The 1920s brought women's suffrage and a short-term economic boom; the resulting financial opportunities produced the Harlem

Renaissance, a black literary movement, and allowed African American–focused magazines, such as *Crisis* and *Opportunity*, to flourish. The women publishing short fiction in those magazines include the multiracial writers Angelina Weld Grimké (whose father was biracial and whose mother was European American) and Nella Larsen (who was of Afro-Caribbean and Danish descent), as well as African American writers such as Jessie Redmon Fauset, Dorothy West, and most notably Zora Neale Hurston, who published several short stories in addition to her masterpiece, *Their Eyes Were Watching God*.

The Great Depression that followed the roaring twenties made survival, let alone literary production, challenging for an artist of any race, but particularly so for a woman artist of color. The world had to wait until after World War II to read work by women writers of color, and World War II revealed increasing discrimination against Japanese Americans. Japanese American writer Hisaye Yamamoto and her family were held in an internment camp. After her release, Yamamoto's fiction appeared in a number of literary magazines, with three stories ("Seventeen Syllables," "The Brown House," and "Epithalamium") being declared "Distinctive Short Stories" by the *Best American* anthology series, and her short story "Yoneko's Earthquake" receiving recognition as one of the *Best American Short Stories* of 1952. The post–World War II period also saw the emergence of Ann Petry, the first black woman to write a best-selling novel, *The Street*. Today, Petry is still best known for *The Street*, but she also published several short stories, which have been the subject of recent critical attention.

Still, it wasn't until the 1970s and 1980s that readers could finally enjoy a large outpouring of short fiction by women writers of color. In 1983 African American writer Alice Walker received the Pulitzer Prize for her novel *The Color Purple*, but in the early 1970s and 1980s, she also published short fiction, including the collections *In Love and Trouble: Stories of Black Women* (1973) and *You Can't Keep a Good Woman Down: Stories* (1981). During this time period, other African American writers also received a great deal of critical attention: Toni Cade Bambara received acclaim for her 1972 short-story collection *Gorilla, My Love* while her famous editor, the Nobel Prize winner Toni Morrison, who published her widely anthologized short story "Recitatif" in 1983, is more widely known for her novels than her short stories.

During the 1970s and 1980s, several contemporary Latina short-fiction writers also began publishing. Nicholasa Mohr's collection about Puerto Rican children living in the South Bronx, *El Bronx Remembered: A Novella and Stories*, was awarded the New Times Outstanding Book Award in 1975, making Mohr its first female Hispanic recipient. Judith Ortiz Cofer, who in 1994 would become the first Hispanic to win the O. Henry Prize (a prize for short fiction), published *Pegrina* (1986), a book of poetry, and *The Line of the Sun* (1987), a novel, during this era.

Mexican American writers Helena María Viramontes, Sandra Cisneros, and Denise Elia Chávez also published well-received collections of short fiction. USA Ford Fellow in Literature Viramontes published *The Moths and Other Stories* in 1985 while Sandra Cisneros's novel-in-stories *The House on Mango Street* (1984) garnered the American Book Award and her collection *Woman Hollering Creek and Other Stories* (1991) received the PEN Center West Award for best fiction. Denise Elia Chávez, who would win the American Book Award in 1995, published her short-story collection *The Last of the Menu Girls* in 1986.

Asian American writers, such as Amy Tan and Maxine Hong Kingston, also received more attention in the 1970s and 1980s. In 1975 Maxine Hong Kingston published her best-known work, *The Woman Warrior: Memoirs of a Girlhood Among Ghosts*, a book of creative non-fiction that combines memoir with the elements of short fiction; fourteen years later, award-winning author Amy Tan released *The Joy Luck Club*, a collection of linked short stories that became a bestseller.

The 1990s and early 2000s witnessed the births of several exceptional writers of short fiction. Dominican writer Julia Alvarez published the critically acclaimed *How the García Girls Lost Their Accents*, a novel-in-stories that inspired fellow Dominican writers Angie Cruz and Nelly Rosario. In addition, Haitian American writer Edwidge Danticat, Chinese American writers Gish Jen and Lan Samantha Chang, Indian American writers Chitra Banerjee Divakaruni and Jhumpa Lahiri, American Indian writer Louise Erdrich, and African American writers Danielle Evans, Carolyn Ferrell, and Roxane Gay have all been featured in *Best American Short Stories* and won several other prestigious prizes.

As more educational and economic opportunities open up, women writers of color continue to make strides. In *All about Skin*, we wanted to celebrate these writers and also help readers to gain a better understanding of some of the common challenges facing writers whose voices are outside the mainstream. For instance, coming-of-age, reinventing oneself, and living with various culture borders—in an often hostile or indifferent world—seem to be ongoing themes in the fiction of several women of color. For instance, we can compare Toni Cade Bambara's classic short story "Gorilla, My Love" (1972) to a new story featured in *All about Skin*, Renee Simms's "How to Leave the Midwest." Both "Gorilla, My Love" and "How to Leave the Midwest" celebrate coming-of-age and African American girlhood, but they also remark on its challenges: the difficulties of fitting in and finding ways to let your voice be heard. Likewise, we could also discuss how the lyrical voice in Helena María Viramontes's "The Moths" (1985) compares with the melancholy tone in Patricia Engel's "Aida." Viramontes's and Engel's stories, which explore adolescent girls dealing with the loss of a relative, suggest both the deep connections between women and also how quickly girls in working-class communities of color may have to mature and reinvent themselves. We can compare how Amy Tan's "Rules of the Game" (1985), like Manjula Menon's "American Child," explores ideas about assimilation, tradition, and dual identities.

All about Skin: Short Fiction by Women of Color features women writers who have received or have been nominated for prestigious prizes including the Pushcart Prize, the Iowa Short Fiction Award (Jennine Capó Crucet is, in fact, the first Latina to win this accolade), the National Endowment for the Arts Award for Fiction (Patricia Engel), the Caine Prize for African Writing (Chinelo Okparanta was short-listed for the 2013 prize), the AWP's Grace Paley Prize for Short Fiction (Ramola D), and the Flannery O'Connor Award for Short Fiction (Amina Gautier is the second African American writer to win this award). In addition, these writers have been included in such prize-winning collections as the *O. Henry Awards* (Xu Xi, Jennine Capó Crucet) and the *Best American Short Stories* (ZZ Packer, Emily Raboteau) anthologies. Many writers selected for *All about Skin* have also received fellowships from organizations such as Yaddo, VONA, and Cave Canem, and from top MFA programs.

Still, despite our writers' many publications and prizes, our chief qualification was that the writers present interesting, well-crafted stories, and the stories we have selected are purposefully diverse. The stories in

All about Skin represent the myriad ways women of color are approaching short fiction, and we've included stories that are grimly realistic (Joshunda Sanders's "Sirens"), brilliantly comic (Emily Raboteau's "The Rapture"), and delightfully surreal (Xu Xi's "All about Skin," from which our anthology takes its title).

Readers often complain that we need new voices. But, with more than twenty stories by women writers of Asian, African, Latin, and mixed-race descent, we feel *All about Skin* acknowledges the diverse voices that already exist, ready to be heard.

Part 1
Coming-of-Age

Several writers of color, both female and male, have written well-received novels about a young protagonist's coming-of-age. From Zimbabwean writer Tsitsi Dangarembga to Puerto Rican author Nicholasa Mohr, the coming-of-age novel or bildungsroman, when written by someone whose culture is outside the mainstream, often explores not only how one develops an individual identity but also how one does so when facing a harsh or indifferent environment.

The stories in this section are like the traditional coming-of-age narrative in that they feature protagonists who are relatively young and at a crucial point in their careers, romantic relationships, or self-development. However, the stories found here—such as Amina Gautier's "Candidate," in which a young woman embarks on an academic career, or ZZ Packer's "Pita Delicious" and the world the narrator encounters as she enters her first real romance, or Ramola D's "The Perfect Subject," which examines a woman's relationship with her parents' traditions—provide an idea of how race and gender complicate the traditional "growing into adulthood" narrative.

Aida

Patricia Engel

The detective wanted to know if Aida was the sort of girl who would run away from home. He'd asked to talk to me alone in the living room. My parents stood around the kitchen with the lady cop and the other detective, an old man who looked to be on his last days of the job. They were telling my parents Aida would walk through that front door any minute now. She probably just got distracted, wandered off with some friends. Our mother wasn't crying yet but she was close. I sat in the middle of the sofa, my thighs parting the cushions. The detective sat on the armchair our mother recently had re-upholstered with a *fleur-de-lis* print because the cat had clawed through the previous paisley.

He looked young to be a detective. He wore jeans with a flannel shirt under a tweed blazer even though it was August. He wanted to know if Aida ever talked about leaving, like she had plans beyond this place, something else waiting for her somewhere.

I shook my head. I didn't tell him that since we were eleven, Aida and I had kept a shoebox in the back of our closet that we called our Runaway Fund. The first year or two, we added every extra dollar we came across and when our piles of bills became thick and messy we took them to the bank and traded them for twenties. We planned to run away and join a group of travelers, sleep under bridges beside other refugee kids and form orphan families like you see in movies and Friday night TV specials. Those were the days before we understood how much our parents needed us. Aida insisted on taking the cat with us. Andromeda was fat but could fit in her backpack. Aida had lied to our parents and said she found the cat alone one day by the river behind the soccer field but she'd really bought her at the pet shop with some of our runaway savings. I didn't mind. The cat always loved her more than me though.

"Does she have a boyfriend? Somebody special?"

She didn't. Neither did I. Our parents told us boys were a big waste of time and we kept busy with other things. School. Sports. Jobs. Painting classes for Aida and piano lessons for me. Our parents said just because we were girls who lived in a small town didn't mean we had to be small-town girls.

"Did she have any secrets?"

"Not from me."

"Even twins have secrets from each other."

He made me tell him all over again what happened even though I'd gone through it several times in the kitchen while the old man detective took notes and the lady cop leaned against the refrigerator, arms folded across her blockish breasts. The young detective said he'd keep whatever I told him in the strictest confidence. "If there's something you left out because your parents were around, now is the time to tell me, Salma."

"There's nothing," I said, and repeated all I'd already told them. How Aida was coming off her summer job as a gift-wrapper at the children's department store at the bottom end of Elm Avenue, while I was sweeping and cleaning the counters before closing at the coffee shop on the top end where I worked the pastry case. We had this routine: whoever finished their shift first would call to say they were on their way to the other. Or we'd meet halfway at our designated third bench on the sidewalk in front of Memorial Park and we'd walk home together. That night, a little after seven, Aida had called and said, "Sal, I'll come to you." When she didn't show up, I took my purse and walked across the intersection to the park. I sat on our bench for a few minutes before walking the periphery of the park to see if maybe she'd run into some kids from school. Aida was friendly with everyone. Even the dropouts most everyone in town avoided though they hung around the bus station and liquor store and you couldn't walk through the park without getting a whiff of their weed. Aida had a smile for everyone. People liked her. Sometimes I got the impression they just tolerated me because we were a package deal.

I called her phone but she didn't answer, then I tried our parents to see if they'd heard from her. It started from there. The calling around.

Probably for the first time ever, the town employed that emergency phone chain where each person is assigned five others to call, to see if anyone had seen Aida. Around here, you can't get a haircut without it being blasted over the gossip wires, but nobody knew where she was. This is a town where nothing terrible ever happens. There are perverts and creeps like anywhere else but never an abduction or a murder. The worst violent crime this town ever saw beyond an occasional housewife wandering the supermarket with a broken nose or split lip was back in 1979, when one sophomore girl stabbed another with a pencil in the high school cafeteria.

The old man detective reminded us we had the good fortune of living in one of the safest towns on the East Coast. "This isn't some third world country," he told our mother. "The likelihood that your daughter was kidnapped is extremely remote." He told our parents it was common for teenagers to test boundaries. If he only had a dollar for every time a parent called looking for a kid who it turned out had just taken off to a rock concert at the Meadowlands or hopped in a car with some friends and headed down the shore. And it'd only been four hours, he emphasized. Aida couldn't have gotten very far. Our mother argued that four hours could take her to Boston, to Washington, DC, so far into Pennsylvania that she might as well be in another country. Four hours was enough to disappear into nearby New York City, her dark pretty face bleeding into millions of others. But the old detective insisted, "Four hours is nothing, ma'am. You'll see. You'll see."

▩

Our mother and father arrived late to parenthood. Our mother was a spoiled Colombian diplomat's daughter who spent her childhood in Egypt, India, Japan, and Italy. She never went to university but was a dinner party scholar, a favorite guest, and indulged her international friendships for two decades of prolonged escapades in Buenos Aires, Los Angeles, London, Marrakesh, and Barcelona. She had many boyfriends, and was engaged three or four times but never married. She was a painter for a while, then a photographer, and an antique dealer. She sometimes worked in boutiques or found a man to support her, though she never wanted to be tied down. She was thirty-eight when she met our father in a Heathrow airport bar. He was a shy history professor from Marseille who'd written three books on the Marranos of the sixteenth century. She thought he was boring and lonely yet stable, tender, and adulating, everything she needed at that particular moment in her life. They married and tried to have a baby immediately but our mother had several disappointments until she received the good news of twin girls at the age of forty-four. We were born during our father's sabbatical year in Córdoba. Our mother said those prior broken seeds had been Aida and me but neither of us was ready for our debut.

"You were waiting for each other," she told us. "You insisted on being born together."

Our father never liked when she talked that way. He said she was going to make us think we had no identity outside our little pair. Our mother insisted this was the beautiful part of twinship. We were bound to each other. We were more than sisters. We could feel each other's pain and longing and this meant we'd never be alone in our suffering. When Aida was sick, I'd become sick soon after. Our father blamed it on practical things like the fact that Aida and I shared a bedroom, a bathroom, and ate every meal together. Of course we'd pass our germs around, be each other's great infector. But our mother said it was because we were one body split in two. We'd once shared flesh and blood. Our hearts were once one meaty pulp. Our father would scold our mother for her mystical nonsense and our mother would shoot back that he was always dismissing her; just because she didn't have fancy degrees like he did didn't make her an idiot. She'd cry and it would turn into the song of the night with our mother locking herself into the bathroom and our father calling through the door, "Pilar, don't be like that. I just want them to know that if anything should ever happen, they can live without each other."

He wanted us to be individuals while our mother fought for our bond. We knew we held a privileged intimacy as twins but Aida and I were never exclusive. We had other friends and interests away from each other yet it only made our attachment stronger, and we'd run into each other's arms at the end of each day, reporting every detail of our hours apart.

Ours was a brown Tudor house on a slight hill of a quiet block lined with oaks. Aida and I lived in what used to be the attic. It was a full floor room with slanted ceilings and strange pockets of walls so we each had niches for our beds, desks, bookshelves, and dressers, with a small beanbag area in the center. There was an empty guest room downstairs that either of us could have moved into but we didn't want to be separated, even as Aida's heavy metal posters took over her half of the walls and she started to make fun of my babyish animal ones. We liked living up there even though it was hot in summer and cold in the winter. We couldn't hear our parents' late night fights once we turned our stereo on. Every now and then we'd lower the volume just to check in, see how far into it they were so we could gauge how long before we'd have to go downstairs to help them make up.

Aida and I considered ourselves their marriage counselors. It was like each of our parents had an only child; I was my father's daughter and Aida belonged to our mother. When the fights became so bad we weren't sure they could make it back to each other on their own, Aida and I would assume our roles. I'd find our father alone in his study hunched over his desk or slumped in the leather reading chair staring out the window at nothing. Aida would go to their room, where our mother was always on the bed lying fetal in her nightgown. Aida would tell me that our mother would often ask her who she loved best, and Aida would declare her devotion to our mother and say that if our parents ever split, Aida and our mother would run off together to Paris or Hong Kong. Aida would always tell me this part laughing because we both knew she would never leave me, and I would never leave our father. That was our trick. That's how we kept our family together.

▪

Flyers of Aida's face went up on every telephone pole and shop window in town. Though the detectives briefly tried the idea that she'd run away, it was a Missing Persons case. The police searched the town. The detectives made rounds of the homes of all Aida's friends. They focused on the boys, especially the ones with cars. But Aida wouldn't have gotten into a car with someone she didn't know. Our mother was mugged in Munich in the seventies and sexually assaulted behind a bar in Majorca in the eighties. She raised us on terror stories of vulnerable wandering women being jumped by aggressive, predatory men. We were each other's bodyguards, but when alone, which was hardly ever, we were both cautious and sensible, even in this stale suburban oasis. If held at gunpoint, Aida would have run. She had long, muscular legs, not at all knock-kneed like me, and the track coach was always trying to get her to join the team. Aida was a brave girl. Much braver than me. She would have screamed. She would have put up a fight. She would not have simply vanished.

A group of local volunteers quickly formed to comb the grass of Memorial Park, hunt for witnesses, go to every apartment and storefront with a view of the avenue and back alleys. The story made it to the evening news and morning papers, and a tip line was set up for people to phone in. Our parents didn't leave the kitchen. Our mother waited, an eye on the front door, for Aida to show up in yesterday's clothes. Several people called and said they'd seen her the night before just as the summer sky began to darken. She was in cut-off shorts, brown leather boots, and a white peasant blouse that had belonged to our mother. They'd seen her at the bottom of Elm and someone else had seen her further up, approaching the park. She was alone. But someone else saw her talking to two young guys. Someone saw her later on. A girl in cut-off shorts and brown boots walking along the far side of the park across from the Protestant church. But she was in a blue shirt, not a white one. That girl, however, was me.

Aida and I hadn't dressed alike since we were little girls and our mother got her fix buying identical dresses to solicit the compliments of strangers. But the day she disappeared we'd both put on our cut-offs, though every time we wore them our mother warned we'd grown so much they were pushing obscene. We'd also both put on our brown gaucho boots, sent to us from one of our mother's friends from her bohemian days in Argentina. We were both running late for work that day and that's why neither of us decided to go back upstairs to change.

One of the volunteers found Aida's purse by the Vietnam veterans' monument in the middle of the park. Her wallet was inside, though emptied, along with her phone, the battery removed. Our mother wanted to take the bag home but the police needed it for their investigation. The only other things they found were her lip gloss and a pack of cigarettes, which was strange because Aida didn't smoke. Chesterfields, our father's brand, probably swiped from the carton he kept on top of the fridge. The box was almost empty. I would have known if she'd been smoking, and our parents wouldn't have particularly minded. They were liberal about those sorts of things: a benefit of having older parents. They served us wine at dinner and spoke to us like colleagues most of the time, asking our opinions on books or art or world events. They'd trained us to be bored by kids our own age and to prefer their company over that of anyone else. We had no idea how sheltered we really were.

■

In the days that followed, there were more sightings of Aida. Somebody saw her cashing a check at the bank. Somebody saw her cutting through the woods along the train tracks. Somebody saw her by the river behind the soccer field. Her long, dark hair. Her tan bare legs in those same frayed shorts, though this time she was wearing sandals. And each time our parents would have to tell them it wasn't Aida they'd seen. It was her twin.

Three different people called to say they'd seen her, the girl whose photo they recognized from TV and the papers, hitchhiking on a service road off the turnpike near the New York State border. Someone else had seen her at a rest stop a few miles down. A woman had even said she'd talked to Aida at a gas station in Ringwood and only realized it was her after she caught the news later that night. She'd asked Aida where she was headed and Aida had said north, to Buffalo.

Aida didn't know anybody in Buffalo and she'd never take off. Not like that. She worried about everybody else too much. When we were little she would say good night to every stuffed animal in our room before falling asleep, without skipping a single one so she wouldn't hurt anyone's feelings. She wouldn't leave the house without letting everyone know where she was going. I'd joke that she had separation anxiety and she'd say, "No, that's just love, you moron." Even so, after I heard the bit about Buffalo I went up to our room and knelt on the closet floor until I found our old shoebox under the dusty pile of plush animals. It was empty but I knew she couldn't have taken our money with her. Two years earlier we'd used the savings to buy our parents an anniversary gift of a sterling silver frame for their wedding picture. We'd depleted the funds but started adding money to the box again. Not much. Just dollars whenever we had some to spare. We didn't think of it as our Runaway Fund anymore but as our Petty Cash. Maybe she'd used it for something and had forgotten to replenish it.

In Aida's absence, Andromeda howled around the house the way she had before she got spayed. She slept in Aida's bed next to her pillow as if Aida were still there, nestled under the covers. She purred against my knee and I ran my hand over her back but she stiffened and looked up at me, hissing and showing her teeth before running off, and I knew she, too, had mistaken me for my sister.

▩

Aida and I turned sixteen a month before she disappeared. The other girls in town had lavish Sweet Sixteen parties in hotel ballrooms or in rented backyard tents. Aida and I didn't like those sorts of parties. We went when invited and sometimes danced, though Aida always got asked more than me. We were identical, with our father's bony nose and our mother's black eyes and wavy hair—tall, dark, and Sephardic all over, as our parents called us—but people rarely confused us. Aida was the prettier one. Maybe it had to do with her easy way. Her trusting smile. I've always been the skeptical one. Aida said this made me come off as guarded, aloof. It made boys afraid to get near.

We were both virgins but she was ahead of me by her first kiss. She'd had it right there in our house during a party our parents hosted when our mother's jewelry collection got picked up by a fancy department store in the city. She could call herself a real designer now, not just a suburban hobbyist, selling her chokers and cuffs at craft bazaars. One of her friends brought her stepson, who'd just failed out of his first semester of college. Our father was trying to talk some wisdom into the kid, whose name was Marlon, and inspire him to go back. Later, Aida arrived at Marlon's side with a tray of crudités. For a virgin, I'd teased her, she had her moves. She brought him up to our attic cave and he'd gotten past her lips to her bra before our mother noticed she was gone from the party and found the two of them unzipped on our beanbags. A minor scandal ensued. Our mother called him a degenerate pedophile in front of the whole party and his stepmother said Aida was too loose for her own good. After all the guests had left, our mother sat us down at the kitchen table and warned Aida and me that the world was full of losers like Marlon who'd come along and steal our potential if we weren't careful, while our father just looked on from the doorway, eyes watery for reasons I will never know.

Neither of us was ever interested in the boys at school though. Sometimes we'd have innocuous crushes, like Aida's on the gas station attendant up on Hawthorne Avenue or mine on the head lifeguard at the town pool, boys who were just out of reach. But our parents had always told us we were better than the local boys, suburban slugs who would peak in their varsity years and come back to this town to be coaches or commuters. We, on the other hand, were sophisticated gypsies, elegant immigrants, international transplants who spoke many languages. We had our mother's inherited Spanish, Italian, and quasi-British private school inflections, and our father's French and even a bit of his father's Turkish. The fact that we'd settled here was incidental, temporary, even though Aida and I had been here all our lives.

"You're not like them," our mother would say every time we were tempted to compare ourselves to the local crowd.

▩

For our sixteenth birthday our parents took us to the Mostly Mozart Festival at Lincoln Center. It was a warm July night. During the intermission we went out to the fountain so our father could smoke a cigarette and Aida and our mother drifted up toward the Opera to look at the hanging Chagalls. I stayed with our father. I asked him to let me have a smoke too, like I always did, because it gave him a laugh, though he never gave in. But that night, even though we were supposed to be celebrating, he was somber.

"I don't want you to pick up any of my bad habits, Salma."

Sometimes our father put things out there, like he wanted me to push him to say more, but I wasn't in the mood.

I'd always been his confidant, like Aida was our mother's. For a while now, he and our mother had been doing well, hardly any fights. Aida said the Angry Years were behind us. The crying, the oversensitivity, the accusations, the hysteria. Aida said our mother was too romantic for our father. He didn't appreciate her capricious moods and found them unnecessary. Aida said it had nothing to do with our father's affair, but something deeper between them and that our mother was too progressive to get hung up on infidelity. She'd found out the usual way when the girl, one of our father's students, called our house and told her she was in love with her husband and that he wanted to leave her.

I'd had my suspicions since the day our father was promoted to chair of his department and our mother decided this was our father's way of undermining her intelligence yet again. She'd locked herself into their bedroom but instead of pleading to her through the door, our father went out to the backyard to smoke, and when I arrived at his side he looked at me and said, "Can I tell you something, baby?"

He only called *me* baby. Never Aida, whom he called darling. "I don't love your mother anymore."

"Yes, you do."

He shook his head. "No, I don't."

I never told Aida. She thought she had our parents all figured out. When we later discovered love notes in his briefcase from his college girl, Aida said it was probably just a crush gone wrong. It would pass, she said; our parents were too old to leave each other and start new lives. They'd eventually accept that this marriage was the best they could do. I let her have her theory. But I knew my father truly loved that college girl, even if just for a moment, and even if it had nothing to do with who she was, but who she wasn't.

■

It was the end of the summer. Another week until I started eleventh grade and our father was due to go back to the university for the fall semester. Our mother said I didn't have to go to school anymore. I could be homeschooled, work with tutors, and spend my days in the house with her. Watching. Waiting. She hardly ate. She drank sometimes. Just a bit to wash down her Valium, which she hadn't taken in over a decade, but one of her Manhattan friends showed up with a vintage vial for the rough nights. Our father didn't try to stop her. He was drinking and smoking more than usual, too, as if with Aida gone we'd become short-circuited versions of ourselves.

I wasn't sleeping so much as entering a semiconscious space where I'd talk to my sister. Our mother believed someone was keeping Aida prisoner. In a shed. A garage. A basement. In a wooden box under a bed. I tried to picture her in her darkness. I knew wherever she was she'd be able to hear me speak to her in my mind. Our mother used to buy us books on telepathy. She said it was one of our special twin gifts. We'd play Read My Thoughts games in our bedroom every night. We learned to speak to each other silently from across a room and know what the other was thinking. In seventh grade, when Aida fell off her bike, I knew it before the neighbor from across the street spotted her hitting the curb.

I'd felt her fainting, her fall, the impact of the sidewalk hitting her cheek, the sting of broken skin and warm fresh blood.

I waited for the pain. Something to tell me what was happening to Aida. I tried to feel her. I wanted to make our bodies one again. Remember that her veins were once my veins and her heart was my heart and her brain was my brain and her pain was mine. I waited for the sensations. I wanted them to hit me and within them I'd be able to know the story of her disappearance. I'd know who stole her. What they were doing to her. How they were punishing her.

I knew she was alive. Otherwise something in me would have signaled her death. If she'd been hurt or tortured or even killed, my body would have turned on itself. One of my limbs would have blackened. My fingers and toes would have contorted or my skin would have bubbled up in boils and cysts. I didn't dare consider the possibility that I could be like the starfish, a self-healing amputee capable of regeneration.

I heard the phone ring downstairs. Aida and I had our own line in our room but it hardly ever rang. The family line never quit until night, when the calls cooled and our house fell into a cemetery silence. I heard footsteps and knew it was our father. Our mother hadn't been up to our room since the day Aida went missing, when she searched her drawers for a diary, photographs, or letters. I think our mother was hoping Aida wasn't as good as we all thought she was. She searched for evidence, anything that would give her a suspicion, a place to look. I watched her rummage through Aida's drawers and even accuse me of hiding things, but I told her, just like I'd told the detective, Aida didn't have a secret life beyond the one we had together under those lopsided attic walls.

Our father pushed the door open. I never bothered closing it all the way. His eyes avoided Aida's half of the room, and he settled onto the edge of my bed. I was lying above the covers with my day clothes on even though it was close to midnight. I thought he was just coming in to check on me since I hadn't bothered saying good night. He wouldn't look at me, his chin trembling.

"They found her shirt." He folded over and cried into his hands.

I sat up and put my arms around his shoulders as he choked on his breath.

Later I'd learn that her shirt was ripped almost in half and was found stuffed into a bush behind the high school parking lot. I, however, took this as a good sign. A sign that Aida was real again, not the lost girl in danger of becoming a legend, the girl people were starting to get tired of hearing about because it made them scared and nobody likes to feel scared. A ripped shirt meant she'd resisted. But it also meant she was up against someone brutal. The high school parking lot meant she'd been close to us that first night. So close we might have even passed by her when I went out with our father in his car to retrace her steps and mine to every familiar place. The school grounds were empty that night. I'd stood out by the bleachers and called her name. I'd felt a lurch inside my chest, but around me there was only silence, wet grass, a low moon. On the ride home our father had driven extra slow while I stuck my head out the open window hoping to see her walking on the sidewalk or under the streetlights, making her way home.

"We moved out here because we thought it would be safer for you girls," our father had said as if to both of us, as if Aida were curled up in the backseat.

We took a long time to get out of the car after we pulled into the driveway. Our father turned off the headlights and kept his fingers tight around the wheel. I wanted to tell my father it would be okay. We'd walk into the house and find Aida sprawled across the sofa just like last night when we sat around together watching dumb sitcoms. I wanted to tell him Aida had probably gone off with other friends. I didn't mind that she'd forgotten about me. My feelings weren't hurt. I wanted to tell him we shouldn't be mad at her for making us all worry like this. I wanted to tell him nothing had changed, everything was just as it had been the day before, Aida, guiding our family like the skipper of a ship through choppy waters, reminding us all to hold onto each other.

▒

I didn't go back to school right away and never went back to my job at the coffee shop. Our friends came by less and less and I understood it was because there was no news. Our father went to work but I spent the days in the house with our mother. I followed the home school program and did my assignments with more attention than I'd ever given my studies before. Aida was always the better student. It took some of the pressure off. When I wasn't studying, our mother and I orbited each other with few interactions. Sometimes I'd suggest we do something together. Go to a midday movie or watch a program on TV. Sometimes

I'd bring up a book I knew she'd read just to give her the chance to talk about anything other than Aida, but she never took me up on any of it. She spent most afternoons in a haze, drifting from bed, to kitchen, to sofa, to bed, taking long baths in the evenings when I thought she might drown herself accidentally or on purpose. The people in town were still holding candlelight vigils at the Memorial Park every Friday night in Aida's honor but our mother never went. I went twice with our father but we agreed turning Aida into a saint wasn't going to bring her home any faster.

The vigils continued though, and the volunteers kept searching the wooded areas around town, the shrubbery along the highway, the vacant buildings and abandoned lots next to the railroad tracks. The reporters kept the story in the news and when they found her shirt, the TV stations wanted a statement from our parents but they were too broken down to talk so our next-door neighbor whose dog once tried to eat Andromeda spoke on their behalf. The police wouldn't let me do it because they didn't want whoever had Aida to see me and know there were two of us out there.

Sometimes people brought us food. Casseroles, lasagnas, hero sandwiches. The church ladies dropped Mass cards for Aida in our mailbox. The department store where she worked set up a fund in Aida's name to help send some kid to art school, and there was a community initiative to raise money to contribute to the reward my parents had already publicly offered for Aida's safe return or information about her disappearance. Our father said we should be grateful to live in such a supportive and generous town but our mother resented it. She hated that she was the one: the mother who'd lost the daughter. She hated that her life, which she'd curated so meticulously, had become something else. Her Aida was no longer her Aida but a story that belonged to all of them now. But our father didn't want us to come off as unappreciative so he took me aside and told me I was in charge of writing thank-you notes, and on every note I was to sign our mother's name.

▒

Aida and I had a plan. After high school, we'd go to college in Manhattan. I'd go to one of the universities and study history and she'd go to one of the art schools. We'd share an apartment and get jobs near each other so we could see each other for lunch or meet after work like we did here in town. We'd make extra money by signing up for twin research studies like we always wanted to do though our father never let us. We'd never live apart. We'd have to meet and marry men who could get along like brothers and tolerate our bond with good humor. If not, we'd be happy to live as a twosome forever. We'd move back in with our parents and look after them in their old age. It wouldn't be so bad.

Our mother liked to think she raised us to live in a bigger world, but Aida and I only wanted a world together. Our father tried to undo this attachment early on by sending us to separate summer camps, but Aida and I protested until they finally let us go to one in New Hampshire together. It didn't become a trend though. Aida and I quickly figured out that our absence had led our parents to the brink of divorce. When we returned, our father was sleeping in the guest room. I urged him to offer endless bargain apologies, for what, I had no idea, and Aida encouraged our mother to forgive, and after she was done forgiving, to forgive some more.

I often wondered how our parents survived six years alone together before our birth when they had so little in common. "It's just love," Aida would say, as if that explained everything. She always had more answers than I did about why things were the way they were, so one day I asked her if she would love me this much if I wasn't her twin and she didn't hesitate before telling me, "It's *only* because you're my twin that I love you this way."

▒

The night our mother caught her on our beanbag with Marlon, Aida told me that being kissed for the first time was like being shot in the chest. I said that doesn't sound very nice but she assured me it was, the feeling of being ripped apart followed by a beautiful hot internal gush. In the early days of her disappearance, our mother's suspicions had gone straight to Marlon. His father and stepmother lived a few towns over and he hadn't yet gone back to school. The police looked into it. Marlon admitted that after their encounter he and Aida had called each other a few times, which I never knew, but he insisted they'd never seen each other again. He had a solid alibi for the night Aida disappeared in his stepmother, who said he'd been home watching television with her. As the months passed, our mother became obsessed with him, regularly phoning his stepmother to call her a liar and Marlon a monster, until the lady filed a complaint and the police told our mother she had to stop harassing them or else.

▩

Every now and then we'd get word of another sighting. Someone saw Aida in Texas the same day she was also seen in Seattle. There was a spotting in the next town over, down the shore, up in the Ramapo mountains, and down by the reservoir. The police followed these leads but they all led to nothing. Even as the reward money increased, there was no solid theory for what might have happened to her. The locals started worrying maybe there was a serial killer on the loose, but that would suggest Aida was murdered and there was no body. The reporters liked to say that for the missing girl's family the worst part was not knowing, but our mother always said not knowing preserved hope that Aida would soon come home, and hope is never the worst thing. Our mother warned the police and detectives not to use words like *homicide* in our house. Aida was alive. She might be half-dead, broken apart, mutilated, and of course, she would never be the same, but Aida was alive and unless the police could present her cadaver as proof, we were not allowed to think otherwise.

At dinner, our mother pushed her food around her plate. We didn't bother nagging her to eat anymore. Her hunger strike was for Aida, who she was sure was being starved in some psychopath's home dungeon. Sometimes she had visions. She saw Aida chained to a radiator crying out for help. She saw her bound and gagged in the back of a van, being driven down some interstate far from us. She saw Aida drugged, captive in a dingy den, man after man forcing himself onto her.

Our mother never left home, in case Aida returned after escaping her captor, running to our house, where she'd find the door unlocked, our mother waiting with arms open. Even at night, our mother insisted on keeping the door ajar. Our father told her it was dangerous but she said she feared nothing now. Everything she loved had already been taken from her.

▩

A few days into December we got the call that a hiker up in Greenwood Lake found Aida's boots. They were ruined from months of rain and snow but the police took them for analysis. Just like with her purse, there were no discernable fingerprints, but Aida's blood was found in trace amounts. It could have been from before. A cut. A picked-over bug bite that left a smudge of blood on the leather. After all, our mother offered, Aida had that terrible habit of scratching an itch until it became an open sore. Or, the blood could have come after. I slept with my identical pair of boots for weeks after that. I held them into my chest and closed my eyes waiting for images to burn across my mind, but they never came. I spent hours in bed staring at Aida's half of the room, still afraid to cry because I told myself you only cry for the dead.

▪

That Christmas passed like any other day. The year before, Aida and I had helped our mother with the cooking while our father fumbled with the fireplace and played old French records, but this year there was no music and the three of us ate reheated food delivered by the townspeople. Our parents floated around the house avoiding each other while I divided my time between them, then alone upstairs in our room with Andromeda. Days earlier, a documentary-style crime show called asking if they could do a one-hour special on Aida's disappearance with family interviews and all. They assured us it wouldn't be tacky or macabre, and said that in a few cases, their shows had helped witnesses to come forward with information about the disappeared. Our father had agreed but when he told our mother I could hear all the way in the attic as she cried out, "What do they want from me? There's nothing left for them to take."

Our father thought publicity would be good for Aida's case. The campaign to bring her home, like some POW, was down to its final embers, and the detectives had recently come by to warn our parents with weak, well-meaning smiles that there was a good chance we might never know what happened to her. They encouraged us to join a support group and gave us a list of all sorts of networks for families of missing people. But our mother insisted that because Aida was alive, that kind of publicity would force whoever had her to cause her more harm or finish her off out of fear of being caught. She didn't trust the media, believing their stories on Aida were meant to sell papers rather than find her. She regularly accused the detectives of incompetence, calling them small-town sleuths who never investigated more than a stolen bicycle and who secretly wanted to abandon Aida's case because it tarnished the town's "safe" image. She considered all the neighbors suspects. Every man who'd ever met Aida was a potential kidnapper or rapist, and every woman, a jealous sadist. It was a community conspiracy. It was because we were outsiders. It was because Aida was so perfect that people wanted to hurt her. It was because we never belonged here that they wanted to hurt us. Our father didn't disagree with her anymore. I wondered if it was because he'd given up trying to reason or if it was because he was starting to believe her.

▩

I celebrated our seventeenth birthday twice. Our mother was finally willing to leave the house for hours at a time so she took me to dinner at an Indian restaurant in town. For dessert, the waiter brought me a mango mousse with a candle jammed into its gooey surface. I smiled at our mother. I knew she was making an effort. She held my hand as I blew out the candle. It was strange to see her thin finger free of her wedding band.

When we walked back to the car a group of kids driving fast down Elm shouted, "Hi, Aida!" They did this sometimes when they saw me around, whether it was a sincere error in recognition or just to torment us, I never knew. Our mother pretended not to hear them. She was getting stronger about these things.

That weekend I celebrated again with our father. He took me to Mostly Mozart again and this time, he offered me a cigarette by the fountain. He'd moved out two months earlier. He swore to our mother it wasn't for another woman but because he just needed to be on his own, to discover who he really was. Our mother turned to him with a stare that was somehow vacant while containing the sum of her life.

"If you don't know who you are by now, my love, not even God can help you."

He rented a small, dark studio near the university. It had an interior view, a Murphy bed, and a kitchen with no stove. It was all he could afford as long as he was still paying the mortgage on our house in the suburbs, and there was no way, as long as Aida remained unfound, that our mother would let him sell it.

He admitted to me that he'd been planning to leave our home since long before we lost Aida. He loved us, he said, but he always felt wrong among us, out of place, as if he'd made a wrong turn somewhere. He said there was a time when he thought he and our mother would grow closer from the pain of Aida being gone but he was tired of trying and tired of hoping.

"You understand, baby," he said, and I was embarrassed to tell him I didn't.

"You're all grown up now. Only another year and you'll be off to college. There will be new beginnings for all of us."

We still didn't know how to talk about Aida. I asked him, because I knew he would tell me the truth, if he thought we'd ever find her, or at least know what happened to her.

"No. I don't."

Just like our mother couldn't go on without Aida, I knew the only way our father could hold on to her was by letting go.

▪

Later that summer, some teenagers getting high up on Bear Mountain came across what they thought was a deer carcass, and started poking around until they spotted a human skull. When the forensics results came back conclusive the newspapers decided, as if they were the judges of such things, that our family could get closure now, find some peace in knowing the search was over, and Aida's broken, abandoned body could finally be laid to rest. The community held a big public memorial at the same spot in the park where they'd held all their vigils but our mother insisted Aida's funeral service be kept private. And so we sat on a single pew before the altar watching a priest who never knew her bless my sister's pine casket, the four of us together in an otherwise empty church for the first time since our tandem baptism, though our family was far from religious and, if anything, Aida and I were raised to believe in only what is seen.

A few days before Aida's remains were found, I walked slowly through the park on my way home from school the way I often did in a sort of meditation, whispering her name with each footstep, wondering what would become of us, what would become of me, all those empty years spread out ahead in which we were supposed to go on living without her. Across the brick path, I saw a pair of kids chasing pigeons and I thought of my sister, the way she would have walked over to them and explained with her boundless patience that it was wrong to scare helpless animals, that they belonged to nature just as much as two-legged wingless folk did and had the right to live without fear of unreasonable human violence. And then I heard her call my name, loud, with laughter just beneath it, the way she would call to me when we'd meet each other halfway after work, her airy voice rushing through the mosaic of dried leaves on the wilting grass, shaking the naked branches overhead, then departing just as quickly as it came, leaving the park and every breath of life within it entombed in stillness. Anybody else would have called it the wind, but me, I knew it was something else.

Fairness

Chinelo Okparanta

We gather outside the classroom, in the break between morning and afternoon lectures, all of us girls not blessed with skin the color of ripe pawpaw. We stand there, on the concrete steps, chewing groundnuts and meat pies, all of us with the same dark skin, matching, like the uniforms we wear. All of us, except Onyechi of course, because her skin has now turned color, and we are eager to know how. It is the reason she stands with us, though she no longer belongs. She is now one of the others, one of the girls with fair skin.

Clara looks at Onyechi, her eyes narrow, a suspicious look. Boma chuckles in disbelief. She claps her hands; her eyes widen. She exclaims, "*Chi m O!* My God! How fast the miracle!" Onyechi shakes her head, tells us that it was no miracle at all. It is then that she tells us of the bleach. Boma chuckles again. I think of Eno, of returning home and telling her what Onyechi has said. I listen and nod, trying to catch every bit of the formula. Clara says, "I don't believe it." Onyechi kisses the palm of her right hand and raises it high toward the sky, a swear to God, because she insists that she is not telling a lie. Our skin is the color not of ripe pawpaw peels but of its seeds. We are thirsty for fairness. But even with her swearing, we are unconvinced, a little too disbelieving of what Onyechi has said.

Hours later, I sit on a stool outside, in the backyard of our house. I sit under the mango tree, across from the hibiscus bush. Ekaite is at the far end of the backyard where the clotheslines hang. She collects Papa's shirts from the line, a row of them, which wave in the breeze like mis-shapen flags. Even in the near darkness, I can see the yellowness of

Ekaite's skin. A natural yellow, not like Onyechi's or some of the other girls. Not like Mama's.

Eno sits with me, and at first we trace the lizards with our eyes. We watch as they race up and down the gate. We watch as they scurry over the gravel, over the patches of grass. When we are tired of watching, we dig the earth deep, seven pairs of holes in the ground, and one large one on each end of the seven pairs. We take turns tossing our pebbles into the holes. We remove the pebbles, also taking turns. We capture more and more of them until one of us wins. The game begins again.

The sounds of car engines mix with the sounds of the crickets. It is late evening, and the sky is gray. Car headlights sneak through the spaces between the metal rods of the gate. The gray becomes a little less gray, a little like day. Still, mosquitoes swirl around, and I slap them, and I slap myself, and Eno stops with the game, unties one of the two wrappers from around her waist, hands it to me.

At the clothesline, Ekaite is slapping too. She is slapping even more than Eno and I. Her skirt only comes down to her knees; she is not wearing a wrapper with which she can cover her legs.

I say, "They bite us all the same."

Eno says, "No, they bite Ekaite more. Even the mosquitoes prefer fair skin." The words come out like a mutter. Her tone is something between anger and dejection. I imagine the flesh of a ripe pawpaw. It is not quite the shade of Ekaite's skin, but it, too, is fair. I throw Eno's wrapper over my legs.

Emmanuel walks by, carrying a bucket. Water trickles down the side. A chewing stick hangs from the side of his mouth. His lips curve into a crooked smile. He stops by Ekaite, maybe they share a joke, because then comes the cracking of his laughter, and then hers, surging, rising, then tapering into the night sounds, at the very moment when it seems that they might become insufferable. I look at Eno. Eno frowns.

Emmanuel pours the water out of the bucket, at the corner of the compound where the sand dips into the earth like a sewer. The scent of chlorine billows in the air, and I think of Onyechi and her swearing. I exhume the memory of the morning break, toss it about in my mind, like a pebble in the air, as if to get a feel for its texture, its potential, its capacity for success. And then I tell it to Eno.

▩

When the sky grows black, I hand Eno back her wrapper, and we enter the house. We go together to the bathroom. First we pour the bleach into the bucket. Only a quarter of the way full. Then we watch the water bubble out of the faucet. We inhale and exhale deeply, and the sound of our breathing is weirdly louder than the sound of the running water. We caress the buckets with our eyes as if we are caressing our very hearts. The bucket fills. We turn the faucet off and gaze into the tub. We are still gazing when Ekaite calls Eno. Her voice booms down the corridor, and Eno runs off, because she knows well that she should not be in the bathroom with me. Because Eno knows that she must instead use the housegirls' bathroom, outside in the housegirls' quarters in the far corner of the backyard. But mostly, when Ekaite calls, Eno runs off, because dinner will be served in just an hour, and Eno will have to help in the preparation of it.

At the dining table, Papa sits at the head, Mama by his side. The scent of *egusi* soup enters through the kitchen. Mama picks up her spoon, looks into it, unscrews the tiny canister, still with the spoon in her hand. It is lavender, the canister, and the lipstick in it is a rich color, red like the hibiscus flower; and it rises from the container, slowly, steadily, like a lizard cautiously peeking out of a hole. Overhead the ceiling fan rattles and buzzes. The air conditioner hums, like soft snoring. In the kitchen we hear the clang-clanging of Ekaite's and Eno's food preparation: of the pestle hitting the mortar, yam being pounded for the soup. Off and on, there is the sound of the running faucet. We listen to the clink of silverware on glass. I imagine the plates and utensils being set out on the granite countertop, and then I hear a sound like the shutting of the fridge, that shiny, stainless steel door all the way from America. And I wonder if Ekaite ever takes the time to look at her reflection in the door. And if she does, does she see herself in that superior way in which I imagine all fair people see themselves?

A bowl of velvet tamarinds sits at the center of the table, a glass bowl in the shape of a dissected apple, its short glass stem leading to a small glass leaf. Mama got it on one of her business trips overseas. She returned from that trip with other things too—silk blouses from Macy's, some Chanel, bebe, Coach, some Nike wear. The evening she returned, she tossed all the items in piles on her side of the bed. She tossed herself contentedly, too, on the bed, on a small area on Papa's side, the only remaining space. She held up some of the overseas items for me to see. One blouse she lifted up closer to me, held it to my chest. It was the yellow of a ripe pineapple. "Will lighten you up," she said. She tossed it to me. I didn't reach for it in time. It dropped to the floor.

The first magazine arrived two weeks later, *Cosmopolitan*, pale faces and pink lips decorating the cover, women with hair the color of fresh corn. Perfect arches above their eyes.

Next was *Glamour*, then *Elle*. And every evening following that, Mama would sit on the parlor sofa for hours, flipping through the pages of the magazines, her eyes moving rapidly over and over the same pages, as if she were studying hard for the JAMB, as if there were some fashion equivalent to those university exams.

■

I stare at the dissected apple, at the velvet tamarinds in it. I imagine picking one of the tamarinds up, a small one, something smaller than those old kobo coins, smaller than the tiniest one of them. Ekaite shuffles into the dining room, Eno close behind. They find themselves some space between me and the empty chair next to me. Ekaite sets the first tray down, three bowls of pounded yam.

She lifts the first bowl out of the tray. She sets it on the placemat in front of Mama. Mama smiles at her, thanks her. Then, "*Osiso, osiso*," Mama says. "*Quick, quick*, bring the soup!" Ekaite hurries back to where Eno is standing, takes out a bowl of soup from Eno's tray, sets it in front of Mama. Mama says, "Good girl. Very good girl." The skin around Mama's eyes wrinkles from her deepening smile. Ekaite nods and does not smile back. Eno, by my side, is more than unsmiling, and I can hardly blame her. But then I remember the bucket in the bathroom, and I feel hope billowing in me. Hope rising: the promise of relief.

It is Eno who serves Papa and me our food. She puts our dishes of pounded yam and soup on our placemats, still unsmiling. Papa thanks her, but it is a thank you that lacks all the fawning that Mama's for Ekaite had. He thanks her in his quiet, aloof way, as if his mind is in his office, or somewhere far from home.

Mama waves Eno away. I watch her hand waving, the gold rings on her fingers, the bracelet that dangles from her wrist. I take in the yellowness of her hand. I think of the bucket in the bathroom, and I feel that hope again in me.

▩

"Uzoamaka," Mama says, when Eno and Ekaite have disappeared into the kitchen. "You are looking very tattered today."

Papa squints at her. I don't respond.

"It's no way to present yourself at the dinner table," she says. The words tumble out of her mouth, one connected to the other, and I imagine rolls of her pounded yam all lined up on her plate, no space between them. Like her words, I think, that American way, one word tumbling into the next with no space between.

Papa looks at me for a moment, taking me in as if for the first time in a long time. "How was school today?" he asks.

"Fine," I say.

Mama says, "A good week so far. A good month even. Imagine, an entire month and no strike! Surprising, with the way those lecturers are always on strike."

"No, no strike so far," I say.

"In any case," Mama says, "not to worry." She pauses. "Arrangements are already being made."

Papa shakes his head slightly, barely perceptibly, but we both see, Mama and I.

"She needs a good education," Mama says to him, as if to counter the shaking of his head. She turns to me. "You need a good education," she says. It is not a new idea, this one of a good education, but she has that serious look on her face, as if she is weighing it with that thoughtfulness that accompanies new ideas. "That is what America will give you," she says. "A solid education. And no strikes. Imagine, with a degree from America, you can land a job with a big company here, or maybe even remain in America. Land of opportunities." She smiles at me. Her smile is wide.

Papa stuffs a roll of soup-covered pounded yam into his mouth. He keeps his eyes on me. Mama turns back to her food. She rolls her pounded yam, dips it into the bowl of soup, swallows. For a while, no one speaks.

"In the meantime, you can't walk around looking tattered the way you do, shirt untucked, hair unbrushed. As for your face, you'd do well to dab some powder on. It will help brighten you up."

Papa clears his throat. Mama turns to look at him. His eyes narrow at her. She starts to speak, but her words trail into a murmur and then into nothing at all.

There is another silence. This time it is Mama who clears her throat. Then she turns to me. She says, "Even Ekaite presents herself better than you do. The bottom line is that you could learn a little something from her. Housegirl or not."

I roll my eyes and feel the heat rising in my cheeks.

"Very well-mannered, that one. Takes care of herself. Beautiful all around." It is not the first time she is saying this.

I roll my eyes like I always do. "Eno is pretty too," I counter. It is the first time that I am countering Mama on Ekaite. I only intend to mutter it, but it comes out louder than a mutter. I look up to find Mama glaring at me. I catch Papa's eyes on me, a little sharper than before.

"Eno is pretty, too," Mama repeats, sing-songy, mockingly. "Foolish Eno. Dummy Eno." She has to say "dummy" twice, because the first time it comes out too Nigerian, with the accent on the last syllable instead of on the first. She tells me that Eno is no comparison to Ekaite. Not just where beauty is concerned. What a good housegirl Ekaite is, she says. She adds, an unnecessary reminder, that when Ekaite was around Eno's age, which is to say fourteen, the same age as me, Ekaite already knew how to make *egusi* and okra soup. And what tasty soups Ekaite made as early as fourteen! Even Ekaite's beans and yams, Mama continues, were the beans and yams of an expert, at fourteen. "The girl knows how to cook," she concludes. "Just a good girl all around." She pauses. "Eno is no comparison. No comparison at all."

Papa clears his throat. "They're both good girls," he says. He nods at me, smiles, a weak smile. In that brief moment I wonder what he knows. Whether he knows, like I do, that it's only bias, the way Mama feels about Ekaite. Whether he knows, like I do, that the reason for the bias is that Ekaite's face reminds her of the faces she sees on her magazines from abroad. Because, of course, Ekaite's complexion is light and her nose is not as wide and her lips not as thick as mine or Eno's. I look at him and I wonder if he knows, like I do, that Mama doesn't go as far as saying these last bits because, of course, she'd feel a little shame in saying it.

He dips his pounded yam into his soup. Mama does the same.

I don't touch my food. Instead, I stare at the velvet tamarinds, and I remember the first time she came back with boxes of those creams. Esoterica, Movate, Skin Success, Ambi. It was around the time the television commercials started advertising them—the fade creams. And we'd go to the Everyday Emporium, and there'd be stacks of them at the entrance, neat pyramids of creams. It was around the time that the first set of girls in school started to grow lighter. Mama's friends, the darker ones, started to grow lighter, too. Mama did not at first grow light with them. She was cautious. She'd only grow light if she had the best quality of creams, not just the brands they sold at the Everyday Emporium. She wanted first-rate, the kinds she knew America would have. And so she made the trip and returned with boxes of creams.

Movate worked immediately for her. In just a few weeks, her skin had turned that shade of yellow. It worked for her knuckles, for her knees. Yellow all around, uniform yellow, almost as bright as Ekaite's pawpaw skin.

She insisted I use them too. With Movate, patches formed all over my skin, dark and light patches, like shadows on a wall. She insisted I stop. People would know, she said. Those dark knuckles and kneecaps and eyelids. People would surely know. We tried Esoterica next. A six-month regimen. Three times a day. No progress at all. Skin Success was no success. Same with Ambi. "Not to worry," Mama said. "They're always coming up with new products in America. Soon enough we'll find something that works."

We must have been on Ambi the day Ekaite walked in on us—into my bedroom, not thinking that I was there. I should have been at school. She was carrying a pile of my clothes, washed and dried and folded for me.

Ekaite looked at the containers of creams on my bed.

Mama chuckled uncomfortably. "*Oya ga-wa*," she said. Well, go ahead.

Ekaite walked to my dresser. The drawers slid open and closed. Empty-handed now, she walked back toward the door.

Mama chuckled again and said, "Uzoamaka here will soon be fair like you."

Ekaite nodded. "Yes, Ma." There was a confused look on her face, as if she were wondering at the statement.

Mama cleared her throat. "Fair like me, too."

Ekaite nodded again. Then she turned to Mama. "*Odi kwa mma otu odi.*" She's fine the way she is.

Mama shook her head. "*Oya ga-wa! Osiso, osiso.*"

The door clicked closed.

▒

I tell Mama that I'm not feeling well. An upset stomach. I excuse myself from the table before Mama has a chance to respond.

I carry my dishes into the kitchen, where Eno is waiting for me. Ekaite sits on a stool close to the floor. I feel her eyes on me and on Eno.

Inside the bathroom, the air is humid and smells clean, purified, a chemical kind of freshness. There is no lock on the door, but we make sure to close it behind us.

Eno holds the towel and stands back, but I call her to me, because I am again finding myself skeptical of the water and of the bleach. In my imagination, I see Clara's suspicious eyes, and I hear Boma's disbelieving laugh. Fear catches me, and I think perhaps we should not bother, perhaps we should just pour everything out. But then I hear Mama's voice, saying, "Foolish Eno. Dummy Eno." I take the towel from Eno. "You should go first," I say. It is a deceitful reason that I give, but it is also true: "Because you're not supposed to be here. That way you'll be already done by the time anyone comes to chase you out."

Eno nods. She concedes straight away.

She gets on her knees, bends her body over the wall of the bathtub so that her upper half hangs horizontally above the tub, so that her face is just above the bucket.

"We'll do only the face today," I say. "Dip it in until you feel something like a tingle." She dips her face into the water. She stays that way for some time, holding her breath. Even if I'm not the one with my face submerged, it is hard for me to breathe. So much anticipation.

Eno lifts up her face. "My back is starting to ache, and I don't feel anything."

"You have to do it for longer," I say. "Stand up, stretch your back. But you have to try to stay longer."

Eno stands up. She lifts her hands above her head in a stretch. She gets back down on her knees, places her face into the bucket again.

"Only get up when you feel the tingling," I say.

Time passes.

"Do you feel it yet?"

The back of Eno's head moves from side to side, a shake with her face still in the water.

More time passes.

"Not yet?"

The back of Eno's head moves again from side to side.

"Okay. Come up."

She lifts her face from the water first. She stands up. The color of her skin seems softer to the eyes, just a little lighter than before. I smile at her. "It's working," I say. "But we need to go full force."

"Okay," she says. "Good." She watches as I pour the liquid from the bucket into the tub. We both watch as the water drains; we listen as it gurgles down the pipe. I take the bucket out of the tub, place it in a corner of the bathroom by the sink. The bath bowl is sitting in the sink. I pick it up, hold it above the tub, pour the bleach straight into it. I get down on my knees, call Eno to my side, tell her to place her face into the bowl. She does.

Only a little time passes, and then she screams, and her scream billows in the bathroom, fills up every tiny bit of the room, and I am dizzy with claustrophobia. Then there is the thud and splash of the bowl in the tub, then there is the thud of the door slamming into the wall. Ekaite rushes toward us, sees that it is Eno who is in pain. She reaches her hands out to Eno, holds Eno's face in her palms. Eno screams, twists her face. Her cheeks contort as if she is sucking in air. She screams and screams. I feel the pain in my own face. Ekaite looks as if she feels it too, and for a moment I think I see tears forming in her eyes. Papa looms in the doorway, then enters the bathroom. He looks fiercely at me. He asks, "What did you do to her? What did you do?" In the doorway, I see Mama just watching, her eyes flicking this way and that.

"What did you do?" Papa asks again. I turn to him, pleading, wanting desperately to make my case, but I don't find the words. I turn to Mama. I beg her to explain. She looks blankly at me, a little confusion in her eyes. I stand in the middle of them, frozen with something like fear, something not quite guilt.

By then, even Emmanuel has made his way into the house, abandoning his post at the gate. He stands just behind Mama, and his peering eyes seem to ask me that same question: *What did you do?*

My legs feel weak. I turn to Eno, I smile at her. I think of Mama with her yellow skin, with her creams. "Don't worry," I say. "We'll find something that works." Eno screams.

They leave the bathroom quickly then, all of them, Ekaite and Papa leading Eno. The door crashes closed behind them, their voices becoming increasingly distant, still frenzied. I blink my eyes as if to blink myself awake.

■

Days later, when the scabs start to form, I imagine peeling them off like the hard shell of the velvet tamarind. Eno's flesh underneath the scabs is a pinkish-yellow like the tamarind pulp, only a little like a ripe pawpaw peel. And even if I know that this scabby fairness of hers is borne of injury, a temporary fairness of skinless flesh, patchy, and ugly in its patchiness, I think how close she has come to having skin like Onyechi's, and I feel something like envy in me, because what she has wound up with is fairness after all, fairness, if only for a while.

Pita Delicious

ZZ Packer

You know what I mean? I was nineteen and crazy back then. I'd met this guy with this really Jewish name: Gideon. He had hair like an Afro wig and a nervous smile that kept unfolding quickly, like someone making origami. He was one of those white guys who had a thing for black women, but he'd apparently been too afraid to ask out anyone, until he met me.

That one day, when it all began to unravel, Gideon was working on his dissertation, which meant he was in cutoffs in bed with me, the fan whirring over us while he was getting political about something or other. He was always getting political, even though his PhD had nothing to do with politics and was called something like "Temporal Modes of Discourse and Ekphrasis in Elizabethan Poetry." Even he didn't like his dissertation. He was always opening some musty book, reading it for a while, then closing it and saying, "You know what's wrong with these Fascist corporations?" No matter how you responded, you'd always be wrong because he'd say, "Exactly!" then go on to tell you his theory, which had nothing to do with anything you'd just said.

I don't know when I'd begun hearing when he went on that way as "*something something something something something*," but one day, he was philosophizing, per usual, getting all worked up with nervous energy while feeding our crickets. "And *you*," he said, unscrewing a cricket jar, looking at the cricket but speaking to me, "you think the neo-industrial complex doesn't pertain to you, but it does, because by tacitly participating in the *something something something something something* you're engaging in *something something something something something* and the commodification of workers who *something something*

something something something therefore allowing the neo-Reaganites *something something something something something* but you can't escape the dialectic."

His thing that summer was crickets, I don't know why. Maybe it was something about the way they formed an orchestra at night. All around our bed with the sky too hot and the torn screen windows, all you could hear were those damn crickets, moving their muscular little thighs and wings to make music. He would stick his nose out the window and smell the air. Sometimes he would go out barefoot with a flashlight and try to catch a cricket. If he was successful, he'd put it in one of those little jars—jars that once held gourmet items like tapenade and aioli. Before, I'd never heard of these things before, but with Gideon, I'd find myself eating tapenade on fancy stale bread one night, and the next night we'd rinse out the jar and voilà, a cricket would be living in it.

Whenever he'd come back to bed from gathering crickets, he'd try to wedge his cold, skinny body around my fetal position. "Come closer," he'd say. And I'd want to and then again I wouldn't want to. He always smelled different after being outside. Like a farm animal or watercress. Plus he had a ton of callouses.

Sometimes I'd stare in the mid-darkness at how white he was. If I pressed his skin, he'd bruise deep fuchsia and you'd be able to see it even in the dark. He was very white compared to me. He was so white it was freaky, sometimes. Other times it was kind of cool and beautiful, how his skin would glow against mine, how our bodies together looked like art.

Well that one day—after he'd railed against the Federal Reserve Board, NAFTA, the gun lobby, and the existence of decaf—we fed the crickets and went to bed. When I say went to bed, I mean we "made love." I used to call it sex, but Gideon said sex could be commodified. Making love—which if done right could be "tantric"—was all about the mind. One time, in a position that would have been beautiful art but he would have called "art for the masses," he said, "Look at me. Really look at me."

I didn't like looking at people when I did it, like those tribes afraid part of their soul will peel away if someone takes a picture of them. When Gideon and I did lock eyes, I must admit, it felt different. Like we were—for a moment—part of the same picture.

▒

That night, we did it again. I couldn't say for sure if the condom broke or not, but it all felt weird, and Gideon said, "The whole condom-breaking-thing is a myth." But we looked at it under the light, the condom looking all dead and slimy, and finally he threw the thing across the room, where it stuck to the wall like a slug, then fell. "Fucking *Lifestyles*! Who the hell buys fucking *Lifestyles*?"

"They're free at the clinic," I said. "What do you want, organic condoms?" We looked it over again but that didn't stop it from being broke. Then Gideon made a look that just about sent me over the edge.

I had to think. I went in the bathroom and sat on the toilet. I'd done everything right. I hadn't gotten pregnant or done drugs or hurt anybody. I had a little life, working at Pita Delicious, serving up burgers and falafel. Almost everything else there was Pine-Sol flavored, but the falafel was always amazing.

It was at Pita Delicious where I first met Gideon with his bobbing nose tip and Afro-Jewish hair. The Syrian guys who owned the place always made me go and talk to him, because they didn't like him. The first couple of times he came in he'd tried talking to them about the Middle East and the Palestinians and whatnot. Even though he was on their side, they still hated him. "Talk to the Jew," they said, whenever he came in. Soon we were eating falafels on my break with Gideon helping me plot out how I was going to go back to school, which was just a figure of speech because I hadn't entered school in the first place.

When I came back to bed, Gideon was splayed out on top of the blanket, slices of moonlight on his bony body. "All right," he said. "Let's get a pregnancy test."

"Don't you know anything?" I tried to sound as calm and as condescending as possible. "It's not going to work, like, *immediately*."

He made a weird face, and asked, "Is this the voice of experience talking?"

I glared at him. "Everyone knows that it's your first missed period."

He mouthed *Okay*, real slow. Like I was the crazy one.

▒

When my period went AWOL, I took the pregnancy test in the bathroom at Pita Delicious. I don't know why. I guess I didn't want Gideon hovering over me. I didn't even tell him when I was going to do it. One blue stripe. Negative. I should have been relieved, relieved to have my lame life back, but the surprising thing was that I wasn't. Then I did something I never thought I'd do, something unlike anything I've ever done before: it was really simple to get a blue marker, and take off the plastic cover and draw another little stripe across to form a blue "plus" sign. *A plus*, the test said, *means you're pregnant.*

▩

When I got back home, I'd told him the test was positive, and flicked it into his lap. I told him that I didn't know what I was going to do—what *we* were going to do. He paced in front of the crickets for a while. Then he tried to hide his shock and disappointment, then tried hiding his attempt to hide his shock and disappointment, then his attempt to hide his attempt to hide his shock and disappointment, and put his arm around me, hugged me with deep breaths, as if he'd finished a chapter in Stanislawski, and was method-acting condolences: how one musters up courage from deep within, how to enact compassion.

"What're we gonna *do*?" I asked. I don't know what I expected—whether I thought I'd catch him in a lie, or have him say something about not wanting the baby, or what—I forgot. All I knew was that something was pressing down on me, drowning me. If he'd said anything, anything at all, I would have been fine. If he'd started talking about the dialectic or about mesothelioma or aioli or how many types of cancer you could get from one little Newport menthol—I'd have been all right. Even if he'd cursed me out and blamed me and said he didn't want the baby—I'd have understood.

But he didn't say anything. I saw everything he was thinking, though. I saw him thinking about his parents—Sy and Rita—growing worried in their condo's sunny Sarasota kitchen; I saw him never finishing his thesis and going to work for some grubby nonprofit where everyone ate tofu and couldn't wear leather and almost had a PhD; I saw him hauling the kid around to parks, saying it was the best thing he'd ever done. *Really. The best.*

I walked out of that room, out of that house he rented with its really nice wood everywhere. I kept walking away, quickly at first, then so fast that the tears were the only thing to keep me from burning myself out like a comet. I wasn't running from Gideon anymore, but even if he was following me, it was too late. Even with no baby, I could see there'd be no day when I'd meet Sy and Rita, no day when I'd quit Pita Delicious before they quit me, no day when I'd hang around a table of students talking about post-postfeminism, no day when Gideon and I would lock hands in front of the house we'd just bought. Anyone could have told him it was too late for that, for us, but Gideon was Gideon, and I could hear him calling after me, hoping the way he always did that the words would do the chasing for him.

Candidate

Amina Gautier

She cannot know how it will all end, this weekend in Los Angeles for the annual convention. She cannot know that she will have talked herself out of a job and slept with a man with whom she will have no future (there is no connection between the job and the man). It is only the beginning of the conference—Thursday night—and she has just arrived in Los Angeles after changing planes in St. Louis to complete the trip. She has only just arrived and checked into a hotel within walking distance from both the convention headquarters and the Staples Center and she has just entered her spacious hotel room and deemed herself lucky that her department is willing to provide travel funds to grad students on the job market without requiring them to share accommodations.

Behind her are two full beds covered in white duvets. Just beyond the restroom to her left, two bottles of water too expensive to drink sit atop a cylinder table backed by a wide window and floor-sweeping draperies. To her right is a dresser with six drawers topped by a large flat-paneled television that she will not turn on—not even once—over the next three days.

In the spacious room she does not have to share, she unpacks her interview suit, a basic black number with subtle shoulder pads. It is a serious suit; when worn, it will show no hint of curves. It tells one and all to focus on her mind and not her physical assets. It tells folks to get their minds out of the gutter.

The suit is not her own, but a borrowed one from the graduate pool. She and four other women of similar height and weight pooled their resources to buy this Tahari from Burlington Coat Factory. She is a proud shareholder, owning one-fifth's interest in the suit. In the early autumn, the department's placement chair brought in two former graduate students to impart their wisdom. Just the year before, they had been preparing to go on the job market; now they were junior faculty members at important institutions who could look back and provide sage advice. They cautioned the group of job market hopefuls to provide themselves with every possible advantage. They told stories of brilliant job candidates who had flubbed their interviews because of inappropriate dress. "Clothes make the scholar," they said.

She has taken every possible precaution. She has come all the way to Los Angeles, all the way to the other side of the country, and she intends to shine. Like all of the other hopeful graduate students, she stepped out on faith, booking her hotel room and registering for the convention long before knowing if she'd have even one interview. She has been rewarded for her optimism and faith. She has one interview scheduled for tomorrow afternoon. She does not intend to blow it. She has done her homework, reviewing the university's mission statement, the department's website. She knows interesting facts about the two men interviewing her tomorrow and is conversant in their areas of interest. She is prepared to discuss possible courses she could teach. She has brought sample syllabi.

At a time when others have been working for at least five years, she is just now applying for her first full-time job. She is twenty-nine years old and she is ready to put behind the meager graduate stipend upon which she has subsisted for the past six years, ready to begin repaying undergraduate loans, ready to design her own courses, to have her own students, and to teach her own material. She is tired of grading papers for professors, teaching sections of composition and correcting comma splices. She is tired of being addressed as Ms. She cannot wait any longer. There is no indication that next year's job market will be any better and more reason to believe that it will be far worse. Originally, she'd had three interviews for the convention, but two have been canceled due to budgetary concerns. Universities were canceling searches and dropping new lines and hires without so much as a by-your-leave. She is in no position to be choosy.

▪

So easy to tell the candidates from the conference participants. The next day, she spots them at a glance, picking them out easily from among the other indistinguishable men and women in nondescript black suits. Candidates sit, lost in wide-backed armchairs the color of sand dunes, trying to pass the time before their interviews. They clutter the hotel lobby. They watch the elevator doors and the front desk. They time their calls upstairs to the minute.

She waits among them in the hotel's main lobby and calls up to get the room number five minutes before her scheduled interview, ignoring the twenty or so other conference interviewees dotting the lobby, conspicuous in their severe suits. She wears the same asexual uniform as the other female candidates. They are identical in their black, gray, navy, and brown pantsuits, their hair pulled away from their faces, their mouths devoid of lipstick. She has been trained not to call attention to herself during the interview process, not to give the search committee any opportunity to think of her as less than equal. She knows the drill. She will greet each search committee member with a firm handshake and sincere eye contact. She will not expect anyone to take her coat or pull out her chair. She will accept a cup of water if offered; if not, she will not ask.

Don't ask, don't drink.

Prior to her afternoon interview, she'd visited the book exhibit room and attempted to interest publishers in her fledgling book project. In the area just before the exhibit room, makeshift walls had been erected to list conference changes and candidates had clustered around them, young men and women in somber suits standing on tiptoe, scanning to see if a last-minute interview had come through. She eyed those candidates with pity, taking comfort in not being one of them. Like her, they had taken a chance on coming to the convention. In the crowded elevator, she pushes thoughts of the unlucky out of her head.

It is all a gamble, she tells herself.

The search committee consists of only two members. The two men greet her and usher her in. One shakes her hand and the other follows suit. They direct her to the hot seat, a chair placed at an angle that allows her to face them both across the coffee table. They offer her a choice of water or coffee; they ask about her flight and her overall trip.

The man seated to her right then says, "Tell us a little about your dissertation," the academic counterpart to the corporate "Tell us a little about yourself," signaling that—niceties over—the interview can begin.

She describes her dissertation succinctly, in under two minutes flat, delivering the rehearsed recitation she has been trained to memorize. She answers every follow-up question admirably. The two men take turns asking about her teaching, her courses, her research. It is all going very well.

In the middle of discussing the unique advising system implemented at their university, which has now become a model for many other research universities with a focus on undergraduate education, she is asked, "Do you have any questions about opportunities for partners?"

"I'm sorry, I don't understand," she says. When the placement chair brought in the former grads, they'd advised the hopefuls to be honest during interviews and not try to bluff one's way through any questions one failed to understand. Bluffing, they said, would only make it worse.

Silence fills the awkwardness and she sees the exchange of glances over her head. She has not read anything on the department's web page or in the university's mission statement mentioning a program called Opportunities for Partners. She suspects it is a program in which the university partners with the local community. Perhaps it is a new micro lending project. Opportunities for Partners. How has she missed reading about this? It is obviously important enough for them to change the direction of the interview and interject a question about it. Opportunities for . . . partners. Partners: their politically correct way of alluding to a significant other without making presumptions about one's sexual orientation. "Oh," she says. "You mean 'partners' with a little 'p.' I understand now."

"And do you have any questions?" she is asked.

"No, thank you."

As one, the two men stand and extend their hands. The one to her left says, "Thank you for coming. We intend to be in touch with all of our candidates early next semester to arrange campus visits." The one to her right says, "Enjoy the rest of the convention."

▩

At the conclusion of the interview, she returns to her room, which has yet to be cleaned by housekeeping. Stepping carelessly over strewn pajamas and balled nylons, she strides to the window and parts the draperies to look at the view that is no view. Though her window is as wide and high as the wall, it looks out only onto a pebbly area, beyond which is a well-loved city important to her only because it is hosting the convention. She steps out of her sensible shoes, losing two inches in height, and feels her smallness. In this city, she is nothing and in the hotel suites where the interviewers convene, she is even less, a number on a list of candidates, a dossier that has made it thus far but will go no further.

She slips the Privacy Please placard onto her room door's outer handle. She weighs her options and realizes she has none. Her graduate funding has run its course. The only way to secure more funding is to teach adjunct courses, which would only hinder her research agenda.

She undresses. Carefully, she folds her black suit and packs it in her suitcase, hoping it will serve someone else a better turn. She has no more need for it. The look between the two men had been subtle but definite. There will be no campus visit. She lies down on her unmade bed.

Just the other night, upon her arrival, she took comfort in the expensive and spacious room she had all to herself. Now she longs for a roommate, or any other person to explain it all to her, help her to understand just what went wrong. Now there is no comfort in the small cube refrigerator, discreetly hidden behind the faux mahogany door panel, nor the granite marble sink with the individual coffeemaker beside it, accompanied by two packets of coffee—one regular and one decaffeinated—and an inadequate supply of sugar packets. She takes no comfort in the waxy cups individually wrapped in plastic nor in luxury soaps and conditioners she will not use, preferring the familiarity of her own toiletries.

■

After two hours of lethargy and self-doubting, she heads downstairs for dinner, hoping to get there while everyone else is still at cash bars and receptions, hoping to beat the convention crowd.

The hotel boasts two restaurants—a bistro and a pub—on opposite sides of the lobby. She decides she will stuff herself on the department's dime. She will order dessert. Maybe she will have a drink. All she has to look forward to now is reimbursement.

Both eateries are full. She leaves the hotel and walks until she finds an eating establishment that looks a little less congested, only to turn in and find it as full as all of the others. She is too tired to keep walking, so she gives her name to the hostess and is told she'll have to wait for a table to become available. She is welcome to eat at the bar, but she doesn't feel like having her feet dangling from a too-high stool just now. She wants to sink into something; she wants her back supported by the cushiony leather of a booth.

Scholars and critics fill the small pub. All around her, people are eating or standing in line in collegial groups. She catches snatches of conversation on material culture, historicity, and the subaltern. She appears to be the only one intending to eat alone. When the hostess moves to lead a group of five to a back booth, she is nudged into the man in front of her.

"I'm sorry," she says. "We're packed as tight as sardines in this vestibule."

He looks out over her head and then back at her. "An apt metaphor," he says. "Although not the most original."

"I'm all out of originality," she says.

"Tough day?" he asks. His dark cheeks are dusted with short dark hairs, his lips lost beneath a mustache and goatee. His name hangs from a plastic sheath secured at either corner by a clip, dangling from a navy blue lanyard, but she cannot make out his institutional affiliation.

She smiles noncommittally.

"Did you give a paper?" he asks, glancing at his watch absently. Behind them, more people are filing into the restaurant, though none of the tables seem to be emptying.

"No," she says. "Were you on a panel?"

"I'm chairing a search," he volunteers. "It's pretty much the only kind of service the department can rope me into. I've already done everything else. You name it. Undergraduate studies committee. Graduate admissions. Placement chair. Honors College. Faculty Senate rep. Been there, done that. Now I get to pick and choose the ways in which I prefer to be a good university citizen. I've paid my dues."

The hostess returns and tells him his table is ready.

"Would you be averse to joining me?" he asks. "Otherwise, I think you're in for a good long wait."

Early on in her program, she learned to be wary of the seemingly sympathetic professor, especially the black faculty members in her department. (Actually, no one ever called themselves "black" in her department. In academia, they became "people of color." Whenever she identified herself as black rather than as a woman of color, they eyed her with the pity and contempt reserved for the unlearned.) She grew disillusioned with her female professors of color who promised her women of color gatherings, potlucks and writing groups, "community" as they called it, and then begged off, whining and complaining about being overburdened and underrepresented. They expected her to understand when they unapologetically returned her papers late or not at all, when they ushered her out of their office hours because they had not yet prepared their day's teaching and needed to encroach upon the time they'd set aside for students. They expected her to understand and view them as role models when all they showed her was ineffective time management. But she has very little experience with male professors of color, so she does not bother to be wary of this man inviting her to join him for dinner. Right now, crowded into the small waiting area at the front of the pub, jostled between the hostess's stand and the coat rack, surrounded by a camaraderie and conviviality from which she is excluded, it seems harmless enough to view his offer to join him as one of collegiality, harmless enough to accept.

He strides to the table with a long, loose-limbed gait, indifferently navigating the obstacles on the way to their booth, dodging chairs pushed too far back, bulky coats dragging from the backs of chairs, the wayward straps of laptop bags looping out across the tiled floor, ready to trip the passerby. He strikes her as one who perches on desks, leans against dry erase boards. She's had one professor like that before, an energetic man who could summon Madame Merle with one gesture of his hand and make Henry James, American Realism, and *Portrait of a Lady* come alive. This man whom she is joining for dinner makes her feel at ease. He seems as if he could be at home anywhere.

She cannot know that there will be more to it than dinner.

She cannot know that when he later identifies himself as a feminist scholar—albeit a new wave one—that his commitment to respecting women and championing their equality is limited only to his research and scholarship and will not actually be extended to her. She cannot know that one day from now, he will offer to visit her after they both return to their respective cities. Nor can she know that after she has slept with him, the offer will become vague and indefinite. Two days later, when she mentions spring break will be a good time for him to come, he will explain that he did not intend a visit so soon, but was thinking of sometime in the fall during the next academic year when he would already be in the area for a discussion panel at another university. The flattered sense of excitement that washed through her at his initial overture will slow to a trickle once she understands that his intention to see her is motivated more by convenience than desire. Once they have left the conference, and they have taken to talking over the phone, that muddied invitation will transform and reverse itself into a suggestion that she visit him instead because he is simply too burdened with academic commitments to travel to her. When she asks him about the glaring contradictions in his request—for surely, if he is too busy to take a weekend to see her, then surely he is equally too busy to spend time with her if she should come to him—he will shut down completely, awkwardly defensive, accuse her of interrogating him and refuse to answer her question or discuss the issue any further, forgetting all about his touted feminism as he preempts her right to speak.

She can know none of this as she slides into the booth beside him, believing that her day is certainly looking upward and that this offer of a friendly meal is a harbinger of good things to come.

▩

Once seated, they agree to ask for separate checks before they order. Their departments will reimburse them.

He says, "You look like you need a drink," and removes the drink menu from among three tall, waxy candles.

"I had an interview earlier this afternoon, and I'm sure I bombed it."

"Oh?"

"I'd really prepared for it. Perhaps even overprepared. Have you ever done that? Read every single thing about the university that you possibly could, just in the hopes that something might be useful? You know, trying to make yourself knowledgeable and unstumpable? Is that a word?"

"No," he says.

The server comes and takes their order. When he leaves, her dinner companion helps himself to the bread and says, "It might not have been as bad as that. Sometimes you've done better than you think, but you misread the cues because you're misled by your own nervous energy. I see it all of the time. You get so nervous during the interview that you block out or misinterpret signs of encouragement. You probably did as well as the next candidate. In any case, the interview is over and there's nothing you can do about it now. It will be up to the committee to determine who they'd like to invite to campus. It's all about chemistry from this point on. You want to believe that it's about your erudite writing sample and your glowing letters of recommendation. Maybe it was about all of that before the convention started. That's what got you in the door, but now it's all about chemistry. They want to know if they like you, if you and they click, if they can see themselves working in the same department with you for the next twenty or more years, whether they think the students will find you engaging and approachable."

Their meals and drinks are placed before them. They have both ordered gourmet sandwiches and thick-cut fries. He has ordered her his favorite beer.

"How can they surmise all of that from just thirty minutes?" she asks, feeling ever more hopeless.

"Something tells you whether or not the candidate will be a good fit. You're sitting there, listening, and then you see an image of him or her at the front of the classroom, interacting with students. It's just like that moment in dating where the initial chemistry between two people blossoms into a second date."

"So academia is like dating?"

"Very much so." He nods and removes the tomato from his sandwich. "Let me ask you this. Do you like men?"

"Excuse me?" Then, as if she is being interviewed, she answers, "I mean, yes. Yes, I like men."

"Can you, with any semblance of accuracy, pinpoint the exact moment wherein romantic interest is developed?" he asks. "Of course not. Something clicks, and you just know. It's instinctual."

She fidgets. "I don't think I can really measure something like that. Attraction takes time," she says, watching his throat work as he drinks his beer.

He eyes her appreciatively. "Believe me, it doesn't."

▩

She is twenty-nine years old, but in PhD years that is like being only twenty-three. So—despite her age and academic wisdom beyond her years—an unfeigned innocence induces her to accept his offer to walk her back to her hotel without reading anything into it. Unlike others her age, she has not enjoyed her twenties. She has not had six or seven years after graduation to discover herself, to burn out on parties, heartbreaks, and just getting by, or to come to the place where she feels ready to settle down. In the years immediately following college, when others were partying and spending, she was barely subsisting on a meager graduate income, going without health benefits, and eschewing relationships and the complications they could bring in favor of passing her comps, orals, and field exams.

She has no idea how they have ended up here. She has no desire to be the person who attends the convention merely to misbehave. The laxity and impropriety, the wickedness of being strait-laced and then letting loose, has no appeal for her. Yet here she is. Dinner is over and he has come back to her hotel room. It began as mere courtesy, a casual offer to walk her back to her hotel in the warm southern California air. They pass by the Staples Center and a large statue of Magic Johnson, past the Wolfgang Puck's and the large convention center. There are two Marriotts in use for the convention, but she is not in the nearby one, so he offers to walk her since she is too thrifty to take a cab. That offer brings him up to the door of her hotel room when they both know he could have said good-bye in the lobby. Then—at the door—he experiences an urge to use the restroom. May he come in? And now he is in and there is no polite way to ask him to leave.

He does nothing untoward, merely sweeps assessing glances over her room, over the bucket of melted ice, the three cans of diet soda lined up near the alarm clock, the Gideon Bible open and nestled on her pillow (she read in it earlier and offered a quick prayer that her interview would go well), the damp twisted towel she has deliberately left lying on the floor in defiance of the hotel's request at ecological preservation, the ear buds of her MP3 player dangling from her laptop, the folder of supplemental materials she has brought with her, the bra hanging off the back of the desk's chair, which she cannot remove without drawing undue attention to its presence.

"May I?" he asks, lifting the folder from the second bed.

He opens it and flips through extra copies of her dissertation abstract, three sample syllabi, a copy of the interviewing university's mission statement, a photocopy of its faculty handbook.

"Looks like you really did your homework," he says. "I wish some of our candidates today had been half as conscientious."

She wants to ask him everything, to pick his brain and know—for future reference—what she could have done better.

He lies beside her on the bed. She is fully covered by the sheet; he lies above it on his side, answering question after question. He tells her about his own department, and what it felt like years ago when he was a recent hire.

It begins as a murmur, a small negligible sound on the other side of the wall. Then the walls seem to purr and she understands that the couple in the room on the other side of hers is having loud and enthusiastic sex. It becomes harder and harder to talk over them. As he tells her of the hard time he is having acquiring all of the necessary permissions for his forthcoming book, she can only imagine the bodies in the next room over, slick with sweat, entangled in sheets.

"It must be good to have a book coming out," she says, unwilling to count the years it will take her to transform her dissertation into a monograph.

"It looks like getting a tenure-track job is the pot of gold at the end of the rainbow when you're in graduate school," he says. "But that's just the beginning. One book will never do. Each promotion requires a book. And then there's service and administration."

As he speaks, he rolls closer to her, until their hips are touching.

"You're like a tonic," he says. "I wish I could keep you around me all the time. You're a natural confidence booster."

"What do you mean?" she asks, unsure if he is mocking her.

Hands casually roaming, he says, "Seeing this world through your eyes is restorative. When you first become a faculty member, you spend all of your time comparing what life is like on the other side, but pretty soon that feeling of self-satisfaction kicks in and you realize that you've made it. Maybe you don't have tenure yet, but you're on the tenure track, which seems like the most amazing accomplishment when your friends and cohort have taken visiting instructor positions, become adjuncts, or left academe altogether. Soon you forget how lucky you are to be on the other side. Pretty soon you forget there ever was any other side and you forget all about grad school and its attendant worries. You forget that grateful feeling you had when the contract letter came, spelling out your salary and moving expenses. Talking to you reminds me of that old feeling I'd felt then and it feels like I'm waking up after a deep sleep and opening my eyes for the first time."

"Professor Van Winkle," she teases, preening under the compliment, momentarily confident enough for a rejoinder. She does not think to move when he eases the sheet from around her neck and lowers it to her waist. Nor when he lowers the strap from her shoulder and licks the now bare skin. It does not occur to her that perhaps he does this type of thing at conferences all of the time, namely because she does not think of what they have begun as this type of thing.

▩

She cannot know what awaits her the next afternoon, the next evening. None of this can she know as she checks into her hotel room and proudly hangs her borrowed suit. It is only the beginning of the conference—Thursday night—and she has just arrived in Los Angeles. She has tipped the bellhop. She has unpacked her things. She has an interview tomorrow afternoon and she intends to wake up bright and early in the morning. Despite what the clocks here say, her body tells her it is three hours later. She will not lollygag the night away. She needs her rest so that she can be ready, prepared for any possibility.

She calls her mother to say she has arrived safely. She spends an hour reviewing the information she has printed. She showers, taking an extra ten minutes to shave and sing, then completes her toilette and readies herself for bed. Her hotel room has two full beds and she flips a penny to see which one she will sleep upon tonight. Bright and shiny, the copper coin lifts into the air—she has heard these things now cost more to produce than they are actually worth and it requires little effort for her to draw comparisons between the production of pennies and humanities PhDs—soaring and then coming down easily. She catches it in her right hand and slaps it onto her left, eager to know her luck.

How to Leave the Midwest

Renee Simms

It must be, DeAnn thought, that her sister was not a sexy thirteen. Not like DeAnn had been the year before. She gathered this by the way the boys in gold chains paused to look up and down at Crystal then turned hugely away. DeAnn had warned Crystal about her little girl hairdos. That day, her sister wore her hair in an Afro puff, which sat like a geranium on the crown of her head. "Not cute," DeAnn had told her. Crystal said that DeAnn's straightened flip, which swept down over one of DeAnn's eyes, made her look, quote, extra cheap.

DeAnn was not insulted—was never insulted—by Crystal's assessment of her, especially when the boys in chains were turning to glance at DeAnn again. DeAnn was cute. Boys liked her because she was cute. Boys wanted to have sex with her. She liked sex. She'd had sex at least a dozen times, maybe two dozen times. These encounters happened in basements, swimming pools, in wooded fields, at the mall, or in cars if the boys could drive. She couldn't explain how incredible it felt to be with a boy in an unlikely place then return home to eat dinner with her mother and sister. It felt the way Christmas felt before you knew. It felt like someone out there thought you were special. Sometimes, before she did it, DeAnn thought she might explode into a cloud of atoms from anticipation. But afterward, as she'd pull on her jeans, she never felt special. She felt nothing. Mostly, she felt alone.

If she had to live here—in a city that offered her nothing and with parents who moved her toward new terrors—she would, at least, try for sexy.

The boys were still checking her out when DeAnn looked over at them. They stood near the school staircase, a huddle of backpacks, chains, sneakers. DeAnn and Crystal had not gone to public school in years, since Crystal was in second grade and DeAnn in third, so when they walked through the doors of Edward Bigley High School that morning, DeAnn was holding her breath trying to feel how her body was different from the jangle of sounds and rhythms she would join. It was her father's idea that the girls attend a regular high school.

"Where's your homeroom?" DeAnn asked.

Crystal unfolded her class schedule and examined it. "Mr. Glover. Third floor," she said.

They looked up at the same time. Bigley High was enormous, so big it had elevators. Her mom said that when she'd gone there, the post–World War II boom had swelled the graduating classes to close to a thousand teenagers. In the late sixties, a separate L-shaped wing had been attached to the original building to accommodate the sudden surge in students. Now, there were half that many kids in the whole school and the emptiness made the smallest sound echo throughout the eight floors. From the outside the school looked like a big warehouse, like everything else in Detroit.

"I'll meet you at this staircase at the end of the day," DeAnn told Crystal.

"We have the interview," Crystal said.

"I know."

She watched her younger sister navigate past a group of big-bodied girls. Crystal moved ungracefully: she did a duck-walk down the wide hall.

DeAnn started toward her first class. From her peripheral vision, she saw one of the boys break from the group and begin following her. She stopped to tie her shoe.

"What's up, you new?" the boy asked.

She stayed crouched on the floor and peered up at him with her one exposed eye.

There were no boys at her previous school, Our Lady of Mercy College Preparatory Academy. DeAnn chose her boyfriends back then from the sons of judges, doctors, and legislators with whom her parents socialized. These were preppy black boys who, like DeAnn, lived in neighborhoods of the city where grand homes overlooked tennis courts and a golf course. These boys bought her Coach purses in exchange for the blow jobs that she gave them.

"Who's your homeroom teacher?" the boy asked.
"The name sounds like icky?"
"Miss Nozicki."
"That's it," DeAnn said.
The boy had the whitest sneakers she'd ever seen, and a chipped tooth that was graying. Probably from a fight, De Ann thought.
"Miss Nozicki never takes attendance. You can ditch her class."
DeAnn looked to her left and then right. "Where would I go if I ditched? There isn't much around here."
"I drove. We could hang out at Belle Isle," he said. He ran his fingers over the leather face of her purse. "Nice," he said. "The new Coaches got dope design."
"Thanks," DeAnn said.
"So, you coming?"
"Maybe. Are you a senior?"
"Not exactly," the boy said.

▩

They left campus through a remote door in the B-wing. DeAnn felt the usual thrill; it rattled in her shins as she walked. She had high expectations for their day. Her father believed in high expectations, not for skipping school, but in professional life. That's why he was not content to be a judge and wanted to run for Congress. That's why her dad had formed a political action committee, and why their family would sit for an interview this afternoon with Channel Four News. At one time, DeAnn thought, her family at least pretended to be about academics. It was the reason she and Crystal had attended Our Lady of Mercy. In his conversations with other adults, her father had often mentioned the value of a good education, and the "fight that King waged for little black girls and boys." Now, DeAnn and Crystal were attending Bigley, which was a decent high school though nothing extraordinary. DeAnn's dad said they were going to Bigley to save money for college. DeAnn understood something different. Her father would have more in common with voters if his daughters attended a public school. But he couldn't say that, just like DeAnn couldn't say that she liked sex. True desires, DeAnn knew, were best kept folded inside your pocket.
She climbed into the boy's car, which was expensive and smelled of the vanilla air freshener they sell at the car wash. He lit a joint and they

smoked. Outside the window, the struggling businesses on Jefferson Avenue rolled past like a scene from a detective show. Soon she saw the glittering top of the river as the car drove onto the bridge that led to the municipal island. She was not supposed to be on the island; it was dangerous. In the late nineties, a woman had been beaten on the Belle Isle bridge until she jumped to her death into the river. But that was years ago and DeAnn believed she could protect herself.

The boy parked in the middle of the island next to the water. DeAnn noticed, on the other side of the river, the sad, boxed-shaped buildings of Windsor, Canada, and she thought of her mother. That morning before leaving for school, she saw the keloidal scar where her mothers' breasts used to be. DeAnn pulled off her T-shirt. "Your tits are big," the boy told her, "bigger than the rest of your body." DeAnn ignored this. She slid her tongue beneath the rough edge of his chipped tooth. She climbed on top of him and unzipped his jeans. She rocked back and forth and watched his head fall back on the leather headrest as he came. She liked watching him let go.

When they were done he rolled down the windows and wiped his sweaty forehead with the edge of his shirt. "I'm thirsty," he said. "You want to go to my place and get a bottle of water?"

"Will your parents be at home?" De Ann asked. Her mother did not work. Not before the surgery or after.

"I have my own place not far from here."

She looked at his leather car seats and gold necklace. "Are you a drug dealer?" she asked.

He laughed. "Bitch, stop asking me questions before I have to kill you."

DeAnn believed this was one of those jokes that could reveal if she were cool or a punk. She decided not to act unnerved.

He drove to Van Buren Avenue just on the outskirts of downtown. The buildings on Van Buren were more rundown than those on Jefferson had been. At least Jefferson Avenue had the mirrored General Motors building and a view of the river. Here, in the middle of the city where everything was concrete and gray, the storefronts had hand-painted signs and bars over the windows. There was no pretense of urban revitalization in this neighborhood.

They pulled up to a dark building that had a Mohawk Vodka ad painted onto its brick façade. Now it was DeAnn's turn to be sarcastic. "Oh nice," she said. "You live in an abandoned building?"

"It ain't abandoned. It just looks that way," he said.

He told her his name was Curtis and led her through a side door. DeAnn noticed that there wasn't a proper lobby and that the floor was concrete that had not been covered with carpeting or tiles. DeAnn saw a few doors but they lacked apartment numbers.

"We have to go up to the second floor," he told her. He approached an elevator shaft where a freight car should have been. There was no door over the shaft. Instead there was just a huge canyon that looked like it could swallow you whole. DeAnn was no longer amused.

"How old are you?"

"I'm twenty. I graduated from Bigley two years ago."

He pushed the button to call the elevator car. He turned to look at DeAnn. She'd stopped several feet away.

"The building's raw, I know," he said. "A handful of artists live here. You have to hear about the place from someone who knows." As he talked, the freight elevator appeared before them.

"We can take the stairs if you'd feel more comfortable."

"You're an artist?" DeAnn asked.

"Art student," he said. "I'm studying industrial design."

▩

Curtis unlocked the door to his loft, which was one long sweep of workman space. The unit was big enough to fit a table-saw, lathe, and other woodcutting equipment. A wooden wardrobe that he'd made sat in the middle of the room. There were no straight lines on the wardrobe, only wavy ones, its legs as curvy as a woman's. The furniture looked alive. It looked like something drawn by Dr. Seuss.

"That's different," DeAnn said.

"One of my professors wants to enter it into an exhibition in New York," Curtis said. He ran his hand along the left side of the wardrobe.

"How did you know you could do this?" she asked.

"Do what? Make furniture?"

"Yeah."

"I didn't."

Curtis walked over to a compact refrigerator and retrieved two bottles of water. "I better call the school," DeAnn remembered. She dialed the school office on her cell phone. "Hi, this is Judge Porter's wife," she began. "I'm calling to let you know that my daughter came home this morning. She wasn't feeling well. DeAnn Porter. Thank you."

Curtis looked at DeAnn. DeAnn looked at the loft. Clearly, it had not been renovated for residential use. Wires sprouted from some of the electrical sockets. The floors were unfinished. The room lacked insulation and was cold.

DeAnn decided that she could never live in this building, but being there made her believe that she could live somewhere else. Somewhere unexpected.

Curtis walked over to her with the water. When she'd taken a sip and had placed the bottle on the floor, he took her hand and placed it on his cock. She gently squeezed his testicles. She wondered if she'd ever get used to how male genitals felt and looked. Testicles reminded her of jellied sea creatures.

"What's so funny?" he asked.

"Nothing," she said. To stifle her laughter, she practiced a sultry look. She narrowed her eyes and slowly parted her lips.

▩

Curtis dropped her off at school before the end of seventh period. She entered the school through the same door through which she'd left. She passed the rows of empty classrooms in the B-Wing. Why were so many buildings empty in the city?

Soon the bell rang and DeAnn was in a section of the school where kids ran about the hallways talking smack. She made her way to the staircase. She saw Crystal's profile from among the crowd. From that angle, DeAnn saw how her sister's upswept hair complimented her long, slender neck. Two boys walked past Crystal and looked her over. "Erykah Badu," one of them said. "Erykah Ba-doo-doo," the other one cracked. DeAnn elbowed past them.

"Where have you been?" Crystal asked her.

"Come on," DeAnn said, "I saw mom's car out front."

Their mother sat in a Volvo at the curb. She looked relieved to see their faces. "How was your first day?" she asked as they climbed inside.

"Bigley's not bad, huh?" DeAnn saw that it had not been a good day for her mother. Her mom had dark circles beneath her eyes. DeAnn hated pretending that her mom's life was not collapsing around her knees. "It was perfect," DeAnn replied.

They arrived home as the Channel Four News truck drove up their tree-lined street and onto their circle driveway. DeAnn's mother pulled the car into the garage. Her father met them there in a pale blue shirt and red tie. He looked at his watch.

"That was a little close," he said to DeAnn's mother.

When DeAnn got out of the car, she saw her father's eyes move over her body with the proprietary look that she hated. "Precious, go comb your hair out of your eyes," he said.

DeAnn went to the bathroom off the foyer. She left the door open and watched as her sister and mother went to greet the news people, who were now coming through their front door with lights and cameras. DeAnn grabbed a comb from the drawer within the vanity. She pulled it through her thick roots. She knew that she stood inside her house although she felt anywhere but there. She was outside the bathroom window, above the Mohawk Vodka building. She was igniting far away: exploding, emerging, gone.

She decided her hair was fine and joined her family on the sofa. When the photographer began his urgent clicking, she stared down the camera's dark lens.

The Perfect Subject

Ramola D

When Dr. Sabina Kannan, the youngest gerontologist in America, was seventeen, she returned one morning from her daily run to find her parents' secluded Vienna home encircled by protesters. She paused a moment, then zigzagged through the crowd, fine misty rain of a Virginia spring cool on her sweaty skin, her jerky jog-jog *Excuse Me*s cutting a swath through young mothers pushing babies in strollers, little girls in light-up princess shoes, oily-haired teenagers with printed blue bandannas knotted at necks, older women and men in nondescript barn coats. The protesters held up handmade cardboard signs with grainy black-and-white photos pasted on top, of cats, dogs, monkeys, in restraining devices, with open wounds. Sabina wrenched her eyes away; she could not bear to look. She hurtled past the sodden magnolia, past the splitting-open of taut umber buds, past the dampened trunk. Stop Experimenting on Animals, the signs said silently. Let Animals Live Free. A thin blonde woman in narrow jeans was leading the group in a chant. Her intense blue eyes fixed on Sabina. *Stop hurting animals*, she shouted. *Shame Shame on you!* The crowd echoed, waved signs, and poured up the drive, stopped only by her father's black Cadillac and her mother's beige Camry from engulfing the lawn, the front steps.

Sabina entered the house. In the front parlor, partially hidden by the red brocade drapes, stooped, bespectacled, thin, in blue and white plaid pajamas, peering uneasily out the window, stood her father, Dr. Kannan Veera Mani, the noted animal researcher and obstetrician. Beside him, calmly seated on the mango-colored raw-silk couch and sipping her morning coffee, immaculate in her beige Neiman-Marcus suit, reclined her comfortably endowed mother, Dr. Usha Kannan,

Inova Fairfax's lead cardiologist. Call the police, her mother was saying, in her trademark firm, pragmatic way. They could be dangerous. The gold bangles on her arm glinted as she waved an arm at the window. Her father did not seem to hear. He did not have his glasses on. His hands pulled at the curtain tie convulsively. I don't recognize even one of them. His tone was worried, as if he feared this lack of recognition could be his undoing.

Sabina stood by the window and looked, too. A lilac haze of morning fog and wavery sun surrounded the protesters. Rain fell, the same pearl-on-thread rain she'd seen cling in translucent webs to leaf buds, tree bark as she ran on the bike path, past redbud, forsythia, decorative pear. People walked, up and down. People chanted, decrying the work her father did. Through the mist she saw many were young, almost her age. The peculiar delirium she often felt, being her father's daughter, washed over her. These people despised what her father did, day after day in his university lab. Little did they know, she thought. That they echoed her, expressed her own chaotic, often helpless sense of rage. She could be out there, picketing, yelling with them. Secretly still, after all these years—of learning, burning, striving to forget, she *was* one of them. She *hated* what her father did: he researched the effects of drugs on mothers and babies, or rather on maternal and fetal "subjects." He sliced up kidneys, cannulated arteries, laparoscoped uteruses. He injected drugs, induced disease, withheld drugs. He studied disease progression, compared rates of increase, applied stresses such as the excising of eyeballs, fracturing of bones, removal of bladders. He did these to various mammals—dogs and cats and rabbits and rats—but mostly to monkeys. He had become a specialist in the use of rhesus macaques in research in gynecology, obstetrics, and pharmacology. He wrote papers exclusively on them, on his use of them in his experiments.

Sabina was very young when she learned what her father did, was paid to do, was acclaimed for doing. She was eight at the time, a tender eight, sensitive and questing. She had come upon the knowledge quite innocently, unexpectedly. Her father had not gifted her this knowledge. It had come through an accident, on a visit to his office, a momentary separation. Then, she had felt the universe open a hole, burning, remorseless in her. Into this hole her home fell, her father fell, her mother fell. Into this hole she herself plunged, into the senseless, featureless abyss.

Over the years, as she learned more, the hole deepened and swung further into the void.

For a long, sweaty moment in the mist of the morning then, as she stood in their golden Madurai-marble-tiled doorway, watching her father nervously watch the protesters, she saw only the curtain's blood-red brocade framing the photo of a monkey on a sign—a tiny baby macaque clinging to his mother in a cage, as blue rubber-gloved hands bearing steel implements reached inexorably for him.

▒

It is this moment Sabina thinks of, now, as Lucy Kendall leans forward in her rocking chair, her frail blue-veined fingers smoothing, over and over, the scrap of ruffled white lace that looks like a Victorian child's bonnet, and the swirled, tiered ruffles of lace that make up the dress.

She loved to wear this, Lucy says, pulling apart the nubbed satin ribbon at the back and retying the bow. She was like a child; she loved to play dress-up all the time. Behind Lucy—displayed on the wall in their pastel satin hangers, pastille rose and powder blue, peach puff and blanched almond, in fluffs and falls of varying baby-dress fabrics, organdie, batiste, muslin, even sateen, arranged in an arch—hang other children's dresses, sweet with scalloped collars, French rosettes, smocking, and ribbons. Sabina looks from the dress in Lucy's lap to the display on the wall and slowly back again, to the intricacies of the lace. Outside this room in the Fairfax nursing home is a stretch of grass and a gnarled and twisted pear tree, its burgeoning blooms papery white, rustling stiffly in a breeze. Against that luminosity the hue of the dress is faded, antique.

It's beautiful, says Sabina, touching the lace, trying to shake from her mind that picture of the baby monkey in a cage she saw so long ago on a protester's sign. Was she a chimpanzee? She knows people keep chimpanzees for pets. She has seen them in movies, on television.

No oh no, says Lucy, putting a hand to her welling eyes, my beautiful Delilah—she was a rhesus macaque. From India, like you.

Oh. Assailed by this syntax, Sabina pauses in her listening to Lucy's breathing, lifting the stethoscope off for a moment. She does not say what she instantly thinks, which is, *I am not from India. My mother is, my father is, I'm from Virginia.* How long did you have her?

Lucy is weeping, her tears soundless. Not long enough, she whispers. They took her from me.

Sabina frowns. Took her? Who did?

The people who stole her. She was stolen, says Lucy, I know she was stolen. She rocks in her chair, eyes glazed over, as if remembering. The day she was gone the glass in the back door was cut out, removed. Nothing else was taken—no money, credit cards, nothing. They knew she lived there with me. They waited till I was gone to work, then they came for her. My baby my baby! In her agitation Lucy rocks forward and the chair tilts alarmingly. Sabina puts her stethoscope down and steadies her.

She is a little shaken, herself, at the image of that cut-open door, the sudden absence.

She always came flying at me when I came home, says Lucy, through the mist of tears oozing and falling in shiny drops on her lap. Monkeys are very affectionate; they cling. Not everyone could live with a monkey.

No, thinks Sabina, looking in fascination at the little old lady in her striped and flowered calico dress, the coral bursts of miniature dianthus scattered across the clotted cream of it. I would never have dreamed you could. (She does not, of course, say this.) They are very demanding. Lucy is wiping her eyes with the white dress that looks like a baby's christening frock. Sabina is undecided whether to stop her or not and so doesn't. They see you as their mother. They want you there all the time. Delilah would get very agitated every morning when I left. In the early days she tore the house up every day. I would come home; everything would be upside down. She tore up the newspapers, knocked dishes to the floor, pulled pictures off the walls. It took her a long time to calm down, to understand I would come home every night.

Inwardly, Sabina is marveling at the clarity of these memories. She has come to expect a fog of recollection from the patients of dementia, a slurring of moments, a blurred forgetfulness. She has come to expect not merely disorientation, but removal. Lucy is not removed from her memories. She is fixed in them, like a fly in sticky amber.

She was my child; I was her mother. Lucy's tears are streamed and quiet on her face. We were earth and stars to each other. House and home together, earth and stars. She folds the white frock in loosely geometric folds. I let them take her.

It wasn't your fault. Sabina is careful to be soft-toned, gentle. You cared for her.

I could have kept her safe, let no one see her. Lucy is twisting the frilled skirt of the dress and Sabina puts her hand on hers, to still it. Why, she wonders aloud, murmuring—who on earth would want someone's pet monkey?

Circuses take monkeys. Lucy stares dully at the white flowering pear. She was taken to a circus.

Sabina looks at the pear, then down at Lucy. She can remember monkeys in blue satin pants and striped sailor shirts driving a tricycle, a bicycle, a unicycle in a circus she went to once, as a child. Flickers of ultramarine blue in the chalk-white baseball cap on one monkey's head, the way he put up his paws and pulled the cap down when the glare of stage lights hit his eye. She can remember the clown on stilts in tall, yellow pantaloons slamming his decorated wooden stick on the rails and watching the monkeys jump, the cycles jump, while the audience laughed and clapped and the lights burned hotly down and she saw how the monkeys cringed when the stick came down again Whap! and cringed herself, and wondered why they laughed. The cerise and fuchsia satin streamers wound tight around the stick unwound and fluttered when it struck, bells on the cycles rang, and the monkeys jumped.

Why would a circus steal a monkey, she wonders. In India, when she has visited, monkeys are everywhere. She has seen them in the city of Chennai, in pockets of garden with trees, at parks, libraries, museums. Her mother has told her about monkeys at school, peering in at French class, or stealing bananas at lunch break from the children. Her grandmother has told her about monkeys at the hospital, at temples. These very kinds of monkeys, that ride bikes and trikes and was it unikes in American circuses. Rhesus Macaques. Big-eared, wild-haired, large-eyed, scrawny.

She wonders about Lucy. What kind of life was that, to live with a monkey? Where was her family, her children? Had they all grown up and gone away by then?

She hesitates, not certain how to voice this. From somewhere, words arrive. Did your family help you look for her?

Lucy wipes a hand across her eyes. Delilah was my family. For many years I looked after my mother. My mother lived with me then. I took care of her. After she died there was Delilah.

Sabina feels shocked but tries not to show it. It was good of you to take care of your mother, she says, to be soothing.

Lucy smiles slightly at Sabina. You are good to us old people. You are a good listener.

I learned from my grandparents. The response, the smile, are automatic. Since she graduated (seven months ago, at the tender age of twenty-three) and started work at her first nursing home, Sabina has learned she must talk calmly, freely with her patients. She is not always certain this is the best thing to do; they don't always seem to want to listen, or hear. They lived with us when I was growing up. I loved being with them.

She wants to say, *They taught me what I must do with my life. They taught me without saying anything.* When she thinks of her grandparents she feels she has swallowed an ocean. There is so much to say, no way to begin. Waves push out of her in every direction. She takes a deep breath. Without them, she says, I would not have known I could become a doctor without studying medicine.

▪

After all, it had become quite simple, in the end. After all the years, hearing the house refrain: *You must study medicine!* And: *We come from a medical family; we must continue the tradition!* And herself, running after psychology, philosophy, aging. Reading and reading, lost in libraries, in bookstores, by herself under trees in springtime, fall, alone at a table, late at night, at the George Washington University (GWU) cafeteria. Volunteering at a hospice, taking the neighbor's shaggy golden Lab mix in on weekends, to help cheer the inhabitants. Drawn without thought to the comfort of being with the quieter, calmer, gentler ones who were the old to her—her grandparents, always there in the house, when her parents worked late at their respective hospitals and labs—to make extravagant, delicious South Indian teatime snacks for her—coconut *barfis*, chewy peanut sweets, molasses-stuffed *bolis*, tiny carrot and pea *samosas*—then later dinner, and cups of tea when she was studying, and plates filled with crunchy-munchies, *muruku* and mixture and spicy peanuts "to keep her strength up."

Her Paati and Thatha—ambitious in their own way, who had pushed her father to become what he was, nationally known in a nation not theirs but surely the most famous nation now in the world, famous really in his field, his mind at work razor-edged, clinical—they were calm and soft and encouraging with her, listening and nurturing, all things angelic. When her Paati was sick on occasion, Sabina nursed her without thinking, heated milk for Horlicks, cut pills in two with her pill-cutter, made potato soup with garlic, buttered bread, served her in bed.

Now she was drawn without thought toward caregiving despite being turned, angrily, intentionally away from medicine. Not merely because the latter was what her parents wanted, but because of what she knew it entailed: cutting open cadavers in medical school, and later, probably, cutting into people, dealing with the simultaneously sticky and slippery matters of the body—muscle, fat, blood, veins, arteries—all those inside intimacies she had no desire to approach too closely.

Worse, vivisections, animal research. Some medical schools, she knew, were entrenched; in this day and age, they—faculty, students—still practiced surgeries on live animals; she could not conscience the thought of existing in such a space, of being importuned in this way, *required.*

■

Truly it was not far, that memory in her, when she was eight, visiting her father in his laboratory, when she took a wrong turn in the building, and looked for her father, and found instead she was surrounded by a high-pitched keening from beagles, a rustle and stir of eager eyes and limbs as she wandered past, *horrified.*

She was in a long, low corridor, stacks of metal cages on one side, three stacks high.

In each a beagle, brown and white with black patches, whimpered, or barked, or exhaled a crude, continuous whine. She stopped, stared.

Metal bowls of water, dry pellets of dog food. Scraps of blanket. Paws reaching through bars. Against the skin, shaved-in-places, electrode-implanted skin on some, matted fur on some, bloodied bandages on some, strange devices pressed against skulls, ears, eyes. Beagles prone, dragging themselves, beagles comatose, weirdly silent, watching her, brown, limpid eyes pleading and deep, reproachful.

Puppies, she thought. *Puppies.* Numbers in plates on cage doors: 432, 433, 434. Sabina felt the breath knot and pull tight inside her. Daddy, she breathed. *Da-dd-eee!* She was shouting, running.

What was it; what had she seen? She was in a shifting hole, a black hole; it was a tidal wave, it pulled at her, dragged her into those cages of living breathing creatures with eyes shrinking, shadowed; it swirled and spiraled her, memories crashing, into the tense, inexorable thrust of metal drilling down the tender cave of her four-year-old ear canal when the ENT specialist had had to drill down to remove that recalcitrant ear wax that had grown, encrusted, deep inside her skull, three nurses holding her down.

She heard them now, heard her own eight-year-old self screaming.

They held her down; she felt them, hands like iron bands on her, biting skin, thudding on bones, the packed, inescapable horror of it; she had only to look into one beagle's eyes to know, in painful immediacy, what it could feel like. The wave swallowed, drowned her. Her breath extruded in squeezed, unwieldy gasps.

By the time she reached the wide-open steel door, the pound of footsteps, keys, women and men in white lab coats, somewhere her father behind them, she was hyperventilating, in shock, asthmatic, wheezing; she stumbled over her own feet and fell; they caught her.

▩

These things you could not forget.

She was eight; it was the day she saw her father fall, into that abyss she would never comprehend.

What he said later that night in the house remaining forever incomprehensible. For mankind, he had said, the good of mankind, when she shouted, *Why, daddy, why!* Not even, she pondered, years later, *womankind.* Who were, after all, the subjects of his enquiry, his practice.

She was crying, and the tears fell between them. She gazed at him as if he were a stranger, parts of his face suddenly winking into disappearance, the trimmed yet uneven moustache, sprout of black on cheeks, hair curling out of one nostril, the restless, seeking eyes.

In a way, this is how he remained to her, all through the rest of her childhood. A little disappeared, a little remote, those parts of him she had once believed essential elided, forgotten, removed from reality. She could believe him monstrous. Perhaps she did. She would not question too closely what any of it meant. For a long time the hole was a vacuum of silence in her. She would not speak of it.

She would look at him instead, in stray moments, at dinner sometimes, or later at night, watching television, or on Sundays on the Mall, visiting museums, walking through gardens in spring—at Dumbarton Oaks, the Arboretum—gazing at varieties of his favorite blooming shrub, azalea. He would walk past scintillant bursts of coral, mauve, magenta, touching, marveling, murmuring. She would see her father, loved, beloved. The same father who swung her up in the air when she was a child, who helped her fly kites in the park, held her hand on hikes in camping spots in the dark. And she would see, walking in his shirt, his pants, his shoes, too, that disappearance in him, that excision from meaning that he walked around with for her, a body incomplete, whole cells of him stamped mysteriously into oblivion.

Such a father could not be relied on, nor, in an essential, visceral way, be turned to. Such a father belonged, in part, to a void.

I will never be a doctor, she screamed into his face that night, *Never like you—never!*

And later, years later, her grandmother smiling calmly at her, advising. A PhD is a doctor who is not a doctor. Get a PhD in whatever you want. *You don't have to study medicine.*

▒

Now, sitting across from him at dinner—balding, his thin, gray hair combed loosely across the dome of his scalp, concentrating on his rice and sambar—she darts the question at him almost unwillingly. Dad, would a circus steal a macaque?

A rhesus macaque? Her father's eyes gleam, as if he has uncovered a treasure.

From someone's house, I mean? A pet macaque.

Ah. Her father leans back, sips from his glass of ice water. I would not know about circuses. I do know that rhesus macaques are still in demand in labs.

Oddly, Sabina has not thought of a lab. As yet.

It was very easy, once, he says, to import them from India. You know they are plentiful in India. But after the Indian government put a ban on importing them in the late '70s—you see they were almost becoming extinct then in India, thousands were exported, over the years—one had to look for other means.

What do you mean?

After the ban, primate supply switched to breeding. Rhesus macaques today are bred here in the United States in large colonies, in captivity—they are bred purely for research. Sabina knows already she wants to stop this conversation. She shifts in her chair; her face stiffens into a mask. The image of the kind of monkeys Lucy talked about, loving, affectionate, clinging, brought up in families yet caged from birth, bred for the laboratory, for experimentation, is almost too much to bear. Such monkeys are more malleable. From the beginning they get used to the technicians. But the most malleable subject of all that I ever knew—he pauses and sips his water, smiling reflectively, oddly enough—was not captive-bred.

Sabina feels faint, as if she needs to sit down, although she is indeed sitting down. This lady I know, she says, faintly, her pet was stolen and taken to a circus.

Her father resumes eating. They are alone at the dinner table tonight as often enough, her father and herself. Her mother, an interventional cardiologist on call many nights, has been called away again and is in surgery. Possible, he says. Pets are stolen for labs also. Dogs, cats, rabbits, hamsters. Monkeys too, he offers, reaching for an *aplum*. In that interim period, after the ban, there was a dearth of monkeys—we were lucky to get them any way we could.

Through stealing? Sabina's voice is hitting an octave. *Stolen pets?* You *knew* they were stolen?

Her father does not answer immediately. He is eating with his fingers, meditatively. Jim, that is, James Netherton, he says finally. He was our best Class B supplier. Of course they got animals from everywhere. Flea markets, dog pounds, newspaper ads, country auctions—unwanted animals, you see. The Class As are the breeders, the class Bs are the random sources. Of course you knew there were bunchers involved.

Inside of her, Sabina is feeling a familiar feeling, gritty as sandpaper, raw as crude oil, tear upward and through her. *Bunchers?* What were *bunchers*? She doesn't know, but it doesn't sound good. *What is the "of course" about it*, she wants to shout.

But she has lived too long in this house, with her parents, all through high school and college—she was a day student at GWU, she just took the Orange Line in to Foggy Bottom—too long with removal sitting beside her, peeling an orange, wiping a face, straightening a collar, that she has forgotten what to say to it. In some ways she has forgotten she *can* say something to it. In this oblivion of acceptance, day after month after year, not intending to, she has lost that part of herself that could speak, that could shout, that spoke once, that shouted once, that has shriveled into a fetal ball and rolled deep away inside her.

Her cousins, her Indian friends, the ones she knows here in northern Virginia—they too live at home. Well, not all of them. Sonya is at Princeton, Tarik is at MIT. But the rest are at George Mason, George Washington, Georgetown—all close to home. It's not expected, to leave home, like the Americans do.

Sabina had thought about it for a while, dreamed of it—Berkeley, she had dreamed, or UC-Davis or Harvard or U of Michigan at Ann Arbor—then surrendered to her parents' wishes to study close by. They would be all alone if she left. She was an only child. She owed it to them. She had grown up with this knowing, that there was no one else to take care of them when they became old. It was an expectation she'd heard voiced often enough by relatives growing up that it began to grow inside her. Besides, she wanted to. Didn't she? Now, looking at her father crumpling *aplums* in his fingers and talking casually of *bunchers*, she is not so sure.

Bunchers were often employed by Class Bs, says her father. I know Jim had some.

They stole *pets*? Sabina has stopped eating. She can hardly speak.

They got them from pounds, auction sales. I told you. Too many unwanted animals on the streets, in the shelters. In this country, most shelters kill the animals. But this way they are saved from being euthanized. It is a good thing to rescue them for science. I just told you, those animals who were once pets make good subjects.

Sabina feels frozen to her chair. Her father is speaking calmly, ruminatively, as if he were pronouncing facts and not opinions, as if she weren't sitting there at all. The best subject I had, no, the perfect subject came to me from Jim. Let me think, what was its name? Jim insisted I use the name always, he says, it answered only to the name.

A *stolen pet*?

Her father shrugs. May have been. Who knows? It may have been from a pound, a private owner. Sometimes people give animals away, you know. When they get posted overseas or have children, sometimes—these animals are too much in a house full of children. He adjusted his glasses. Sometimes you see how dogs are left alone in a yard all day. Bunchers rescue them.

You mean, steal them!

These animals are docile, says her father firmly. Trusting, easy to handle. Not wild or fearful, they come to you willingly. Well, he pauses, at least at first. And for a long time. He looks at Sabina searchingly, as if seeing her for the first time. Did your mother tell you if she made anything for dessert?

Sabina jumps up. Her napkin falls to the floor. Her plate is still full with rice, dhal, vegetables. She has barely eaten. It is only habit that keeps her here, taking care of her father. There's *gulab jamun*. She pulls the box out of the fridge, puts some in a bright yellow dessert bowl. From Sarla Sweets.

Ah, says her father, good! He slides his spoon into the sweet rose syrup and conveys it to his tongue. He tests the *jamuns* slowly. Too hard, he says after a minute. Not cooked enough.

You want ice cream instead?

Her father is eating the hard *gulab jamuns*. He shakes his head. This is enough sugar. He pushes the bowl away. You finish it!

Sabina does not answer. She is half inside the fridge. She is staring, not at bowls of food, bottles of condiments, sweet relish, mango pickle, apricot jam, but at sunlit acres of yards with dogs and cats being invaded by men called the peculiar name of *bunchers*, at cages of animals being transported in vans to secret supply centers, moved from hand to hand at universities and research labs where her father has worked.

I kept the name tag Jim gave me with that animal, her father is saying. I cannot recall the name now. He frowns, gets up. I will show it to you.

Sabina closes the fridge and returns slowly to her plate. Once before in her life, when she had contracted a terrible stomach flu virus, the world went black before her; she actually fainted. Now she feels something as black and wave-like, tubular, steal across her vision.

She sits but feels the table is tilting. Ahead of her the long, forever dismal corridor snakes in a mist of remembered misery, insistent whining fills the air, and in cage upon cage she sees the desperate, golden eyes of beagles.

Her father holds out a round, metal object to her. It is flat, an aluminum name tag, the kind you might put on a dog or cat's collar. A name, an address, a phone number. These details are slight, worn thin. Hints of dirt fill the crevices. Her fingers rub automatically over the dented, engraved letters. She rubs, to glimpse the almost-faded name.

Funny name, her father muses, for a macaque.

Sabina's head jerks up. I did not know it was a macaque.

Oh yes, her father says absently, wiping his glasses with his napkin. One of the most-used animals in the lab. All of us used that one. It was ideal, almost human. A willing subject. Yes, for a long time it came to us without reserve. Like a child it was—excitable, it would rush at us.

Lucy Kendall's voice, frail and remembering: *She always came flying at me when I came home.* Sabina hears this. *Not everyone could live with a monkey.* Through the willowy mist clouding her eyes, the horrid metal sinking cold inside her, Sabina sees the cascading white lace of the dress, the ruffled skirt, the billowy collar, not in Lucy's papery hands, empty and longing. But in a cage in a lab, luminous and shimmering in a hidden-away basement, a monkey in it, the beautiful, hungry-for-love macaque that Lucy had loved like a child.

Yes, her father is reminiscing aloud, some macaques are better than others. Rubbing earnestly through the dirt, the fading, the almost-erasure, the cold blade of premonition knifing through her, she views the name she has already heard this morning, the name she wants desperately not to but wills herself to see, a fate stamped in tilted lurching capitals: D-E-L-I-L-A-H.

▪

Later, she thinks: of the worst things in the world, the thing you cannot believe when you hear about it, and then the thing you want with all the force of your being never to have happened, *these things too happen.*

Later she sits in the living room, a wash of sound and light engulfing, consuming, as her father watches television and she sits, in a fugue, unable, herself, to engage in the slightest act of conscious, external perception.

▪

It is a day and a week from that moment when she enters Lucy Kendall's room in the nursing home again. Lucy is sewing something, her needle glinting as she raises the thread and loops and pierces the pale peach batiste of the dress in her hands. A pattern of stars and moons on it, so delicate as to seem watermarked into the fabric.

This belonged to my mother, she says, so long ago. Do you see the years on it?

She holds it up. Sabina sees the sprawling tea-colored stain on the chest and reaching under one armpit.

Hot coffee, says Lucy. My mother always spilled food and drink on her clothes!

Sabina feels dizzy with exhaustion, as if she has not slept for days. It is true, for many nights, she has stayed awake, trying to take in what has happened. In her right hand, buried in her pocket, she rubs the cold metal tag with the name engraved on it. She has carried it here, feeling in some intricate way a need to return it to Lucy. She is not certain how this will transpire, what response might ensue. To have a pet for years, to have loved a creature so long, to not know whether she is still alive or has died—Sabina cannot bear to contemplate that kind of emptiness.

Tossing and turning on her bed that first night she kept seeing an image of that monkey in white rushing at Lucy, and Lucy, the eternal child, without a child of her own, caring selflessly for her mother, then her macaque. Her sleep when it came was split open by dreams that were explicit and troubling. The blackness of corridors, cringing animals in cages, the sound of her own soft-shoed footsteps, cold shine of steel in hands, and in the room her father. A shadowy, central figure in a white lab coat with a glittering mirror globe in his hands, multiple bar-like protrusions on it. In North America, Nepal, India. Where the monkeys are bred or taken from, she realizes, waking. But in the dream it felt like her father was everywhere in the world, the globe ominously turning. She could not escape him.

She woke with a singular want, the burning need to give Lucy something, to comfort her in some way, ease the desolation. It is what has brought her to this moment, clutching the tag like a talisman.

In a dusty part of her mind she senses the tag, so freighted with memory, might not be what Lucy would want after all, that seal of certainty it would put on her pet's departure—but she ignores it. The part that is still child in her is eager, hopeful. Surely it is something? A closure, an acknowledgment. Surely Lucy would want to keep it beside her forever?

The child part of her insists the tag belongs to Lucy, it has to be returned.

True, there is a problem—how to bring it up, tell the story? And how much to tell really?

Sabina lets the fingers of her right hand tease over the indented lettering of the name inside the shadow of her pocket. The molten sorrow she feels, touching the tag, erupts inside her. Each time she touches it, she finds herself inside that corridor, staring into the eyes of a caged beagle.

In her left hand she holds a pen and the chart. She should be thinking up a story, a way to approach the subject. But without wanting to, she returns inescapably to thoughts of her father. Underneath, in her longing, as she is used for years to doing, she is trying, mentally, to disassociate what she has learned from him. He is not the only one to blame, she thinks. Surely he is one in a long line of those behind him who used the animal model for research, who swore by it, who didn't care where their animals came from. She should have an awareness of that, she cautions herself.

But crowding her vision, swarming her breath, is an implacable desire to escape, to leave home, set up house on her own. For years she has resisted doing this. She has felt close and bound to her family for as long as she can remember. There was a moment, just before she got into college, when she could have struck out on her own, pursued her independence. But, just as the applications from out-of-state colleges fell away, unfilled, so did that moment. Perhaps it segued, seamlessly, into her growing awareness of her parents growing older, her need to take care of them. Always, underneath, her conscience, ticking.

Now, she thinks (blanketing that guilt), she could rent an apartment. She is an only child, close to her parents. She is a good Indian child, even if second generation; she *wants* to take care of them. The love one has for the mother and father who have raised you, from the beginning, can never be forgotten. But here she is, wanting to escape, to do something American. Live on her own for a while, even if it is only a short time. She could share with someone. She could dream up a plan for saving those baby macaques and other animals from their breeding places, their labs and dungeons.

▩

Talking, Lucy has slipped into a memory of her mother. She would take me out to Carlyn Springs for ice cream, Lucy is saying. In the summer the ice-cream parlor was always full. But she would wait till we got a booth.

Sabina sees how the days and wind have dislodged petals on the burgeoning white blooms of the pear tree outside the window; they lie in a drift on the pearled, dusted-with-mist grass. It is a cloudy silver-gray day. Mist swirls under trees, in the distance. Through it, a cardinal calls, sharp and sweet. A wetness drips from the leaves of the linden. Red cherry ice cream with chocolate bits in it, Lucy is saying, we ordered that a lot. It was my favorite. She pauses. Or was it my mother's? She fingers the delicate gold chain at her neck, touches the oval cameo of her pendant. Look, she says, Look, Dr. Kannan—and she snaps it open to the beautiful sepia hues of a woman in profile, smiling, hair pulled high and back, a high ruffled collar, a row of shiny buttons on her blouse. My mother, says Lucy, and touches the picture. A watery drop follows. Lucy is crying.

Sabina looks quickly away, to the dissolving contours of the misty scene outside the window.

She slides the pads of her fingertips gently over the metal tag in her pocket. She thinks, now is the moment.

My mother is the one who suggested having a monkey as a pet, Lucy is saying. When you are sick, you need an extra pair of hands, she would say. So I got one! And it is true, when I was sick, Delilah took care of me.

She did?

I remember once I woke up at night coughing. Delilah gave me the bottle of cough syrup from my night stand. She found a spoon. I was so sick, I could not get out of bed. Delilah took care of me. She had her own bed, but she would sleep with me. And when I was sick, especially, it was a comfort.

Sabina listens as Lucy speaks, lifts her hand, bare, from her pocket. Slowly, she does her work, recording breathing, heart sounds, pulse. I will tell her about the people who loved her first, she resolves, the lab technicians, even her father, the researcher. Then about the bunchers, the way it was with the dearth of macaques in the '70s. Then show her the tag, give it to her. I could start by saying, *Wouldn't you like to know . . .*

When it comes to it, words fail her, even her voice weakens.

You know, she begins.

But Lucy is still speaking and does not hear her. When she was sick, I took care of her too. She was healthy, mostly. But she had a stomach problem sometimes. I gave her apples then; I would make applesauce for her, and steam vegetables.

Sabina stares at her. Her heart feels like it is thudding very loudly in her chest. She had so prepared herself to tell this soft, bearable version of the story she is still trying to compose that she feels tense and untrue from head to toe.

It is what I thought of often, afterward, Lucy is saying. Her eyes are misting over. I wondered who took care of her, if they fed her the way I did, if they held her in their arms and comforted her when she was sick.

Sabina takes a breath. She stares at Lucy and sees only sad golden eyes, looking up at her.

That is my hope for her, Lucy is saying, that whoever took her, they cared for her, that she was loved.

Lucy is gazing at the pear tree, and tears are running down her face. Sabina finds the box of tissues and hands it to her. She stays a little longer, making consoling sounds, trying to change the subject. Inside of her she feels frozen, as if the lump in her own throat has become an unscaleable obstacle. She steals away.

▩

All through that day she carries it, like a secret, burning weight in her pocket. All through the day the mist lingers, streetlights beginning to glitter under the trees. When her shift is over, in the late evening she walks into the nursing home's garden toward the white pear tree that Lucy can see from her window; she lifts the already-burgeoning ground ivy with her hand, digs a small hole in the dirt with one end of the tag, buries it.

A small desolation sweeps through her. She looks up. Lucy has come to the window as if to see what she is doing. She waves.

She weaves her way back through flowerbeds, now in the slow descent of damp twigs and flowers grazing her cheek, eyes fixed on the new, thrusting leaves of feathery yarrow and salvia at her feet, keeping her tread firm, as if she can see, etched in front of her in the garden's private dusk, a path through all of it.

A Different Story

Ivelisse Rodriguez

Our war—our *love* war—bravely fought against our mothers for the past three years, the war that led my friends to unabashedly fall in love our first year in college and left me waiting for our summer break to start fighting again—that war—I know is going to come to a very resounding end a week or so after we come home from college, all because the boyfriends quickly start reneging on a thousand pledges made through the course of relationships started, at most, a mere eight months ago. Ruthie's man writes her from California saying he's dropping out of school and is moving to Alaska to work on a fishing boat and that maybe in another life they can continue where they left off. Alexa's man just stops calling her back. And Yahira. That's the worst one of all. He tells her that every utterance of love, memory created, caress given—stomp on grapes, suck the juice—all of it's a lie.

Yet the most important contract being broken because of the departure of these boyfriends is the one we girls made between each other when we started this war against our mothers: to believe in love. Just the summer before—fighting, yelling, believing—me, Yahira, Alexa, and Ruthie, and a host of other girls, would tell love stories. And our mothers would tell anti-love stories, and we did this every week in Springdale Park for three years until we went off to college.

This was our war.

And now, love is fighting all of us—it's kicking our asses.

"Maybe they were right," my friends say about our mothers.

"I don't know what to say. I mean, I'm sorry this happened to all of you, but I don't want to give in to what our mothers want," I say.

"Did you even date anyone?" Baby Ruthie counters.

"Yeah, Rosie, you spent this whole year doing what?" Angry Alexa asks.

"How can you know how we feel? We can't believe in this love shit anymore," Yahira, my best friend, says.

Their worlds may be falling apart, but my *worldview* is falling apart. Listening to them, I start to think I *do* know what it's like to be heartbroken. They don't even want to go out there and fight. They're sluggish when we go to our side of the park. Their declarations are muddied, half-hearted, broken-hearted. My friends sometimes seem to linger on our mothers' side of the park before they cross over to ours, and I imagine that if there were a fence between the two groups, my friends would leisurely hang on it, heads resting on their hands, and actually listen to our wacky mothers.

Decimated hearts. Blood everywhere. I'm looking at a battlefield full of wounded soldiers.

■

My mother, along with a long line of conspirators, told us always: Never trust a man. A man only wants one thing and as soon as he gets it, he'll be gone. The repercussions for falling in love were always the same—a broken heart and a bad girl rep, at best. At worst, a life of welfare checks and a baby every other year. Our mothers wanted something new for us. But it was really something old. Something borrowed. They wanted marriage. The divine notion of marriage. Our mothers didn't believe in love between men and women anymore, though. They just wanted our future husbands to stay. Marry, they said, but don't believe.

The neighborhood women always gathered at my house to preach on about how dirty men were. They'd begin by discussing a literary figure and note how she too had been scorned by men. And see, don't women come from a long line of rejected people? Then they'd move on to the neighborhood women and how times hadn't changed. Mr. Rivera, who left his wife for that no good Ms. Medina, was seen coming out of—you guessed it—Mrs. Torres's house and Mr. Torres was out of town visiting "*familia*," again. Men cannot be trusted. Amen. This was their weekly prayer.

It all started with my mother. The day my father left, all anybody could hear throughout the neighborhood was twenty-six years of marriage breaking. The dishes breaking. Her heart breaking. Everything they had ever been told about love, marriage—all broken. And the women started coming one after the other, bringing handkerchiefs, pastries, and their own stories of broken love. For that one night, their lives held no clear trajectory. No absolute truths. Only emotion, chaos, and open doors.

During the first year of their meetings, all my mother could do was talk about my father. Stories about him were bubbling from her mouth at every meeting. And it was like you could see inside of her—the tributaries of memories pumping into her heart and back out. But then one day in the Chicopee Public Library, she came across "Ethan Brand" by Hawthorne (she had taken to going to the library in order to find out why her husband had left her) and she realized that she didn't have to spend the rest of her years with her heart dangling from her blouse.

I imagine that she came home that night, lightly coated with snow, took off her winter coat, looked at herself in the mirror, and realized that nobody had *really* told her her husband could leave her. She looked around her bedroom and started to move the furniture around. Noticed the dust that had accrued over the years and thought it was easy to wipe away. And placing her bed in the center, she must have reached into a medicine man's suitcase, full of tubes, syringes, cotton, and marble. Laid down and allowed the blood to drain out of her, while the marble poured in. And much like my father the year before, she walked out of her bedroom, unencumbered by a heart.

▩

"Boys? At your age?" My mother looked at me, Yahira, Alexa, and then Ruthie. If I was guilty, so were they. As it turned out, the news for this week was that Yahira's mother had caught me getting felt up by Robby Rodriguez in her stairwell last week.

Three years ago, when we were fifteen, was the first and last time they let us, their daughters, into one of their meetings. We walked in looking sober, but deep down inside we were giddy. We had been listening to them since their first meeting, when we were twelve, envisioning their expressions as they talked, and I always imagined that the room looked different whenever they went into it, that like a dress it took on their shape.

"You're old enough to be running around with boys, huh?" My mother's voice was one notch below yelling. I knew she was mad, but she said this all in English, so I knew we, or I, hadn't reached her capacity for anger. "Don't tell me. Don't tell me that's what you really think?" The other mothers shook their heads in unison. "I know you girls live in a more liberal world, a more *American* world." (My mother liked to throw out the A-word whenever she really wanted to insult us.) "But *we* don't.

"Carmencita was the one we compared ourselves to," my mother continued. "If we did this would we be going too far? Is this something Carmencita would do? And if we thought the answer might be yes, no matter how fast the thought came and went, we didn't do it. We were not going to be like her. Clearly, Carmencita was a. . . ." I knew my mother wanted to use the word *puta*, but she was a coarse prude who wouldn't really utter such language. My mother's raspy voice grated on my nerves constantly, but today more so than usual.

Instead of telling us stories about people doing it, or pulling out a story from one of their books, they told us a ghost story. The story of boogie-woman Carmencita. We had all heard versions of the Carmencita story. Her name was the one whispered in back alleys, around campfires, and under the faithful light of slumber party-goers, way after the parents have gone to sleep. As if she's made a pact with our mothers, she comes howling in the middle of the night. Carmencita tells ghoulish bedtime stories of love gone awry. She comes to girls and women who believe in love, when they shouldn't. But our mothers offered something new. They said they knew her. When she was alive. So they knew the truth.

My mother pulled out a newspaper clipping, yellowed and in Spanish. She passed it around before she read it to us, even though she knew none of us girls could read Spanish very well.

Girl, 15. Still Missing.

May 13, 1955 (Arecibo, PR)—The search for Carmencita Vazquez has ended. The young girl, missing for several months, has not been found. The search has been called off, however, as pieces of her clothing and her shoes washed ashore several weeks ago on Los Negritos beach where she was last seen. Multiple theories abound, including that the girl met a terrible end. The young boys who were out with her the last

> time she was seen maintain their innocence. Some speculate the girl has just run away. But, again, none of these can be substantiated. In an interview the mayor of Arecibo, Guillermo Cardenas, stated, "I remind all citizens of Arecibo that all we can really be sure of is that this young girl has not returned home."

"We saw her at the beach and were probably the last ones to see her alive." My mother uses her lips to point to the other women in the room. "Carmencita came down the beach with her boyfriend Luis, his older brother who worked in the United States, and two of their cousins from Rio Piedras we had never seen before. Imagine, a girl unchaperoned with one, two, three, four men." My mother throws a look my way. "They stopped and talked to us for a few minutes. Then, we didn't see them the rest of the night. The next day there are the rumors that she's missing, can't be found, her mother's worried, thinks Carmencita ran off." My mother paused to inhale exhale from her cigarette. She did this constantly. Start. Stop. Smoke.

"All kinds of rumors. Screams heard. Nobody knew what where. Sand poured down her mouth. Raped by each boy. Two boys on top of her at once. Beat up like a man. On and on they went. There were so many. Then, the worst rumor: that Luis set her up."

My mother then stated that months after these stories, girls began to hear her screams by the beach. Carmencita started to come to women before weddings nights, before third dates, second dates, first dates, and before *quinces*. She told these women and girls her story and as the years went on, she had so many stories, so much hurt to pass on to other generations of girls.

My mother finished by crushing out her cigarette and looking each of us girls in the eye.

"Carmencita's going to get you," girls would say to each other in elementary school. It was a game to us. But as we got older, the less we heard this story, so we became more concerned that boys *wouldn't* be able to get us, not some boogey-woman.

"See, if she hadn't been out . . ." One mother started, and the rest continued.

"If she hadn't been out with those boys . . ."

"I'm sure they were guilty . . ."

"I had to walk by the boyfriend's house every day. He didn't even seem sorry . . ."

They all talked over each other, forgetting for several minutes, lost in the haze of their past constrictions that they were making sure to pass on to us, that we were there.

"You remember how fast he was after little Maria . . ."

"Didn't stop to mourn Carmencita . . ."

"Still lives in Arecibo today. Nothing ever happened to them . . ."

"*¡Ve como los hombres engañan a las mujeres!*"

My mother had the windows open, but we sat scrunched in between them, so all I felt was an intense heat. I looked at the six women in the room—most of them our mothers. They came out in their housedresses, stretch pants, oversized T-shirts, and hair dyed a "Boricua bronze," as we liked to call their particular hair color. Looking at them, spreading in their seats like melted ice cream . . . no wonder our fathers left. I mean at first I was on her side. I really was. But over the past few years, my mother had morphed into someone I could never know. Didn't want to know.

"But this is what our mothers taught us, and this is what we want you to learn: her boyfriend wasn't just some *cualquiera*. He was someone who we all thought was kind to her. So the person who betrayed her was someone she knew, not someone she would suspect would hurt her. Of all the rumors we heard, that was the worst one.

"Like you, we didn't listen to our mothers. We only paid attention to the first part of the Carmencita story, the sex part, but we didn't heed the love part. Don't ever be that stupid. Don't ever trust a man."

They told us that we must not live lives like Carmencita, that we should stay away from men (until an appropriate age, of course), or they would be the cause of our destruction. Didn't we want to marry in white? Be good girls? Make our mothers happy?

> Chorus (Mothers): Arrows from under your skirts.
> Chorus (Mothers): Polish your marble.
> Chorus (Mothers): Warriors scalping hearts.
> Rosie: This is what our mothers wanted.

▒

I saw the looks on my friends' faces after our mothers dismissed us from their meeting. "God, I can't believe them. Telling us that story. I mean, why don't they focus on how fucked up those boys were?" I said.

The girls were silent.

"Why would they blame her? Basically, it was like she was stupid for trusting those boys and then she gets raped and killed. That's not fair," I continued.

I looked at my friends again. They were still silent.

"I mean where's the proof that he set her up? She didn't do anything wrong by loving Luis. I mean that could have been any of us," I stated.

"I never believed that story, but I mean they had a newspaper article. What if Carmencita is for real? I mean none of us have really been in love, so what if she does come to people who are?" Baby Ruthie asked.

I sighed. "Come on. That's just a story. Do you believe in the tooth fairy too?"

"Okay, well even if that isn't true, it's true that this girl disappeared. And just look at how our fathers left. What if that's the way they all are? What if that's all we have to look forward to?" Alexa asked.

"Listen, our mothers weren't always like this." I tried to emulate my mother's booming voice as I dramatically walked around the room as we had all seen my mother do at the height of her fervor. "They were happy once. Things change. I assure you that if they had new boyfriends now, they would feel differently."

I knew their stories. Heard them. When I was younger, before the meetings, the newly single or unmarried women clamored around our house and said things like "I'll die without him—I'll die without his love." Because I never saw them die, I always assumed it was because their love had been maintained in some way. By the time I knew that people didn't literally die because of love, my father left my mother and I saw the way she died.

"Just think about how you've felt every time you've even just *liked* a boy. Remember how that feels, then imagine what *love* must be like," I said.

I saw their faces change—open up a bit to let my ideas in. I imagine that every love/like sensation they had ever felt came flooding back to them, soaking their resistance, drenching their fear, washing the boogie-woman away.

Seizing the moment, I asked, "What do our mothers want the most?"

Everyone looked around, but no one answered.

"I'm confused. I don't know what they want. Why do they even want us to get married?" Ruthie said.

My sister Betsy, who was a bored graduate student on break, popped in then and said leisurely, "You know, they're traditional, there are still some things they can't shake. I mean it would take a whole other revolution before they get to that point."

I nodded my head, but Betsy kept spitting these random comments at us, some that we understood and some that we didn't.

"Yeah, and they want us to keep our legs closed," Alexa finally ventured.

"Or they don't want us to get felt up by boys in my hallway," Yahira said, and the girls started laughing.

I gave her a dirty look and tried not to laugh. "They want us to get married. And today, we will swear we will never get married."

"Are you serious?" Yahira asked.

"Yeah," Ruthie said, but really asked.

"You're crazy," Alexa said.

Betsy smirked.

I looked around the room at the faces of the girls who have mothers who believe the same stuff as my mother. Did my mother have such a hard time with their mothers?

"Well, why don't you explain more, Rosie," Betsy said.

"Thank you," I said. "Well, what I mean is that above all they want us to get married, but I think instead we should focus on falling in love." The atmosphere dramatically changed after I said that. With more confidence, I continued, "They want us to marry and not believe, but I think we should believe and not marry."

"That makes sense," Yahira piped in, and the rest of the girls nodded in agreement.

■

We started a war. It was a communal effort. I, along with my friends, went down and wrote poetic verses. It was our offering; we did not want

Carmencita to be a hungry ghost for all eternity. Chased by the furies, whipped for eternity for being a whore. No, for being a woman. We took turns reciting our poem each night to all those who would listen. Hoping to recruit others who would not applaud her destruction but who would see the wrong in it. In the poem, we rewrote her story.

The kids gathered around me as I read and the news traveled quickly from porch to porch.

"That García girl is up to it again," they murmured from lip to ear down the four corners of our world.

But all the while that I stood fighting for human justice, my mother crept up to where I was. A great silence ensued and I was fooled into believing that I had gained the noble art of persuasion.

"*Niña*, what are you doing!" she bellowed in Spanish.

She stood there with her housedress on, hair pulled back into a tight Victorian bun, hands on her hips, looking absolutely ferocious. She snatched our poem and ripped it into 2, 4, 6, 80, 30, 40 million, zillion pieces and it spread into the wind like cremated ashes. She marched me home, but I kept my head up as we walked by the porches full of neighborhood women who awaited my appearance. I didn't even bother to look at these women perched on their porches even though they rumbled, rattled, and hoofed. The fact that they were out there let me know that I had become my mother's equal.

But when we got home, my mother thrashed out her words, letting them bounce off the walls. She would not have this, love is a farce, men do nothing but beat and trample on women and so help her God no daughter of hers was going to turn out to be low-life *basura de la calle*. So she beat me, telling me all the while that that was the way men would beat me. And for each stroke there was a story. She took me through history, through all the ages, telling me about the plight of *las mujeres*.

In ancient Greece, Penelope waited, weaving for a man who went out into the world and had a helluva time fighting the mighty Cyclopes and the Laestrygonians and shacking up with a different woman in every port. Then there was Julia, who lamented over Don Juan, gave up her life, her social standing, all the comforts of the aristocracy for mere sex. Even the Romantic poet couldn't make this romantic. After all, her only lot in life was to love again and be again undone.

“No more victims,” my mother finally whispered.

But the stories kept pouring forth, even through my delirium.

▩

The next day at school, though, I rose in esteem in the eyes of my friends. I could see the shift from hare-brained girl to leader. I took my place among them, and I knew I could lead them forward. From then on, it was possible to get them to do anything. And from there, our weekly battles ensued. We read about other revolutionaries. We read Sor Juana, Erica Jong, Julia de Burgos, Sandra Cisneros. We read about Che, Fidel, the Black Panthers, the Puerto Rican Young Lords. We got berets, puffed out our hair. Wore leather jackets. Got sunglasses. We even came up with a ten-point plan in order to keep us organized. We started a newspaper, passed out leaflets, had chants, gave speeches, had consciousness-raising sessions for the other girls in our neighborhood, in our schools. We were cohesive, we yelled, we marched, and every Saturday until we went to college, we rallied against our mothers.

In our height, we heard about other girls fighting against their mothers in other neighborhoods. Storms of girls, bursting into their mother's meetings, and pouring out into the streets. And even though it was rare for us to meet any of these other girls, we were filled with hope, awe, bravado that we had been able to accomplish these feats. By the end of it, we became heroes, and I think we surpassed our mothers in terms of our stature. Nonetheless, I think they looked forward to our fighting because we raised their profile. They were able to spread their word because we spread ours.

> Chorus (Friends): We leapt.
> Chorus (Friends): Crashed into the concrete.
> Chorus (Friends): Lovers were no different than liars.
> Rosie: I recognize those lines. Our poem. Changed.
> And now, our war is over.

▩

I wake up and I'm surrounded by my friends. I had fallen asleep in my mother's living room.

Yahira takes my place among the girls. "We want to talk to you," they might as well say in unison.

I'm too tired to fight, plus Alexa has blocked the doorway, so I feebly nod my head. "What's up?" I say in an overly chipper voice.

"We want to tell you our stories."

I want to dearly roll my eyes, but I feel like these furious girls might smack me down. "Fine, tell me your stories," I say instead.

"You know, when Hugo walked out on me, Rosie. For the first time, I felt what your mother felt."

Punch one. The last bit of sleep rolls off of me. "I doubt that. You would compare yourself to that woman?"

"Yeah, I would."

"How can you even say that?"

"Rosie . . . I wish I could explain what it feels like to have someone leave you. It's like someone ripped out your heart. Stomped on it, bruised it all up, and shoved it back into your chest."

"This happened one time, and all of a sudden what we believed in and fought for is disappeared?"

"Yeah, Rosie. Once is enough."

All the girls nod in agreement.

Yahira continues, "For almost a year he told me he loved me. One day, he just changes his story. You're watching marble crack, Rosie. Something you thought was so solid, isn't." Yahira sits down, exhausted.

Ruthie picks up, "Everything, including me, especially me, he drops. And he moves to Alaska. Moved me out of his life so easily." She shakes her head. "And that's probably how your mom felt when your father left."

I stare at Ruthie hard. But I don't say anything. I just listen.

Alexa finishes off, "It's pathetic. I stare at the phone and will him to call, but he doesn't. One day he loved me, the next day he won't speak to me, and there is just no way that I could ever make sense of that. I feel like I'm banging on this door. I can see him and he just refuses to open. So, I think I know what your mother felt when your father crossed her out of his life—confused, lonely, and like I am falling off a cliff."

Yahira then speaks. "We don't expect you to understand, but we wanted to tell you."

"You don't want to hear what I have to say?"

"No, we know what you'll say, and this is not about you anymore. Think about what we said instead."

"No, I'm going to state my piece too. Love, I never said it was easy, but I wanted us to believe in it because I thought it could be a balm on future hurt. I thought it would make us better people. To be so cold, to be so joyless, to be like our mothers . . . I didn't want us to be them. I mean, no, I wasn't in a relationship, and maybe that's what allowed me to keep believing in love. Maybe you won't always find the love you are looking for in a relationship, so I say, separate those two things. Are they really the same thing?"

"In the end, Rosie, they are the same things as that is where we get love. So until we find a different mode of loving, then love is going to continue to suck." They get up to go, but as they walk by my mother's bookcase, Yahira turns around and delivers her coup de grâce: "We didn't even need a boogie-woman to come."

■

"Betsy, can you believe this? Can you believe these traitors?" I had tried to talk to my friends again yesterday, but they refused to listen to me. Baby Ruthie called me quixotic. (Me? How did she think she got her name?) Angry Alexa said I didn't know shit about shit. And Yahira said I was *Jane Eyre*–delusional and didn't live in the world that she and the girls lived in. Then. Then, they said absolutely, under no conditions, would they come out to war and they stomped away.

"Rosie, they're hurt. What do you expect from them?"

"I expect them to get up and start fighting again."

"Like they have reason to. Rosie . . . please. The problem is that you don't know how they feel. Maybe you need to go find a boyfriend, have him break your heart, then come back and tell me how you feel."

"Ha. Very funny. How come no one sees my side?"

"Cause as far as everyone is concerned, you don't have a side. At least not a valid one."

"Okay, can you just be a big sister and tell me how I can fix this?"

"Yeah, I have the magic answer. See their side of it. Seriously."

■

My father. *El Malo*.

He looks thinner than I remembered, but I haven't seen him too often over the years. He has dishes in the sink and shuffles around the apartment in his house slippers. His black skin that used to be firm folds on his cheeks now. His short brown Afro has sporadic gray hairs and he has started to smoke again. Something that he had always joked he had given up for my mother and her love. When he sees me looking at his lit cigarette, he reminds me of the time I was eight, and I had pleaded with my uncle to give up smoking the day after someone had come to school and told us of the dangers of smoking. My father laughs now and tousles my hair like I am eight again.

He starts to reminisce about the old times, even though I am sure he knows why I am here. He tells me about when they first met, and for the first time I can imagine my parents as young people. My mother with long hair and long legs in a completely different world. How she snuck out to San Juan to hear El Gran Combo. And how those were the happiest days of their lives and they couldn't be reproduced for all the love in the world.

Then, he sits around and tells me jokes in Spanish that I figure only people who have lived in Puerto Rico all their lives can figure out. And he laughs to himself when he delivers his punch line and I in turn give him a strained smile.

I try to be as patient as I can be, but I finally interrupt him. "Pop, I wanted to talk to you about something. You know we've been having this love war, and now my friends don't want to fight anymore because their boyfriends left them. I figure if I can tell them why, then they'll fight again. And well . . ." I shift in my seat, not sure how to get the last words out.

"And you want to know from me how you stop loving someone?"

I nod my head.

Even though I'm sure he knew this was coming, he has an uncomfortable smile on his face. He's quiet for the first time today. He leans back in his chair and interlaces his fingers behind his head. He exhales and finally says, "That's a tough question. Really tough."

"I know. I didn't come to blame you or anything."

"Well, one thing I want you to know is that people think that because you're the one who leaves, it's easy for you, but it wasn't easy to leave your mother. I know it's harder for the one who's left, but it wasn't right to stay anymore."

I sit silent for a second waiting for him to continue. "Yeah, but how do you get to that point? You left a woman you were married to for twenty-six years."

"Sometimes, oftentimes, you just stop loving people. That's the truth. But when I loved your mother, I loved her."

Crash into the concrete. "What do you mean?" I try to scramble back up. "How do you just stop loving someone?"

"It happens over time. One day, one week, one month, one year, I didn't feel the same way."

"Did mom do something? I mean she must have done something to make you stop loving her."

"I'm sure your mother and her friends tore us apart, said we were this and that, but you're not *bad* because you don't love someone anymore. It'd be easy to blame her, like she blamed me, but loving someone or not loving someone doesn't really say anything about who you are as a person, or even if you did something wrong."

"But don't you think if you love someone you love them forever?" At this point, I feel like I am eight again.

"I bet you think love is all you need, huh?" He pauses and takes a deep breath, and is about to continue but I cut him off.

"Yeah, I mean, if you love someone, you make it work. Doesn't loving someone mean you do anything to stay together? That your love has some value other than just words." And all of a sudden I feel like I am channeling my mother and asking the questions she would ask. Asking for the things she must know. And I start to wonder what her side of the story is.

He laughs. "Love gets forgotten in daily living. When you are in the midst of a fight, trust me, the last thing on your mind is whether or not you love someone. You know, we all say we want love, and we get there, and then, one day it's like it doesn't matter, like it never mattered."

"Did you really love Mom?" I strangle out. I am aware that my chest is heaving like my mother's all those years ago.

"Of course I did. Of course. But, Rosie, I don't know if love can possibly last forever, and I don't know if it should have to, but I think you're right in thinking one should try." He pauses and scratches his head. "People make too much of love. People think it's all you need, but love is a starting point. There is so much that comes after love, so much that you can't even imagine."

He pauses then and looks at me to see if I understand.

I picture him and his buddies, sitting in their living rooms for the past six years, drinking Coronas or Bacardi Limón. They sit around a table and play dominoes and each time they throw a domino down—Smack!—it is as if they are scattering the past. "I still remember how she looked back in 1963, how I thought I could live off of her smile," my father may say. And he sweats through his *guayabera*, the one that my mother bought from the Dominican man who used to live down the street. Lamenting the loss of these women, maybe they look at each other and judge who has suffered a greater loss and who is stronger for suffering less. Or perhaps, they think too that they were told that marriage was forever and they never imagined themselves walking out doors.

■

Anna Karenina, *The Color Purple*, *Medea*, *The Joy Luck Club*, *The Odyssey*, *Madame Bovary*, *Native Son*, *The Scarlet Letter*. Boogie-woman Carmencita. My father, *El Malo*. My mother's library plaits together different cultures, different eras. No part of the world is left unscathed, unturned. How my mother has made her case.

I sit in my mother's living room—where her and so many of the neighborhood women spent so much time living, breathing, fighting. I remember how this room was normally closed off to us. How it was their gathering place and at one point we had superstitions of coming into this room. It was almost like catching the cooties if we even touched the door. Even after a year away, though, I can still feel all the ghosts of women suffocate me.

Looking at my mother's bookcase, I no longer even focus on the texts. I can only pinpoint what woman in that text has been abandoned, mistreated, rejected—all those adjectives for the way women are treated—none of them good. I almost want to eulogize over these women. Dearly departed, here lies Anna Karenina, here lies Bessie, here lies Hester Prynne. Women who loved. Women who were wronged. Women dead in books, mere words etched in cotton. How my mother has breathed life into them.

I think back to all those years we spent at war. How every night, to stave off her life, I lay in bed and listened to the beating of my heart. Sometimes I could not wait to get to bed, to be alone with my heart. I loved how it heaved and spread a tingling joy throughout my body. And it was in those few minutes with my hand on my heart that I felt the most absolute delight. And I always wondered how my mother could tell me not to believe, how she could have forgotten that this is how she once felt for my father.

But I didn't fall in love on purpose this year. I didn't fall in love because I wanted to love love for a little bit longer, hold onto it in ways that the broken-hearted cannot. I would visit Yahira at UMass on the weekends and every time I did, I was always reminded that boys existed in this world too. I met and met boys, sometimes I thought they would catch me, but I continued to cycle past them. All year. Because I worried that if I ended up broken-hearted, I couldn't be here to stand up for love. I almost knew that we would be here this summer. That this would be our new battle. And regardless of how the rest of this summer turns out, I know I am ready for love. But right now, to save my girls, I know what I must do. I climb the steps to go to my mother's room.

Last summer, the night before we went off to college, she came into my room to help me pack. As I had gotten older, our day-to-day interaction had become stiff. Two rivals in one house. But that night, we laid down our arms. It was a truce. She smoked in my room even though she knew I hated the smell of cigarettes and was superconcerned about secondhand smoke. And I chewed gum, even though she hated the noise and always said I sounded like a cow. She sat on my bed and watched me fold my clothes into my suitcase.

"I want you to be careful," she said.

"Be careful of what?"

"Life. Boys."

I smirked. "I think I can handle that," I said as I folded my clothes. "There won't even be any boys at my school." I was going to Smith College.

"There are always boys."

"I suppose so."

"Even if you are not going to be bothered with boys. Take care of your friends. Don't be surprised if you need to mend a few broken hearts this year."

"Ha! They'll be fine. We have fought long and hard."

"Yes, you have. You've fought very well." She smiled at me and for a second I thought she was proud of me.

"Anything else?" I asked.

My mother looked up at me and stayed quiet for a few minutes.

"*Hija*, I have told you everything about love. I have prepared you as best as I could, but you have not listened. So what do I tell a daughter who does not listen? What would make you believe? I could tell you about how I've been hurt, but I think that hasn't shaken your faith; in fact, I think it strengthens it."

I asked her about Carmencita. "Do you think she still comes to those who believe in love?"

My mother smiled. "I don't know. I know that was really our story, our story for our generation, but for you girls, in this world, I don't know. I don't know if she ever came to girls in Chicopee. But for us, me and my friends, it was a different story."

"Whose side do you think Carmencita would pick?"

"Side?"

"In our war."

My mother got up and put my remaining T-shirts into my suitcase, and she didn't look at me when she answered. "I don't think she would ever pick a side. I don't think we could ever choose one, even if we're sure we have. I think we move back and forth, always back and forth."

Part 2

Reinvention

Can we truly reinvent ourselves? Can we use history to propel us forward or do we unwittingly repeat our parents' mistakes even as we face new and different challenges? The idea of reinvention—and the process of establishing a new identity—can be found in the novels of Toni Morrison, Jhumpa Lahiri, and other noteworthy writers.

In this section, stories such as Princess Joy L. Perry's "A Penny, a Pound," Jennine Capó Crucet's "Just the Way She Does the Things," or Joshunda Sanders's "Sirens" examine history and the environment. We are born into certain histories and environments, and the stories in this section detail the enormous effect our past history has upon our present lives.

All these stories, then, return to one fundamental question: do our pasts and environments prevent us from reinvention or make it possible to locate new opportunities for escape?

American Child

Manjula Menon

Reshma married him in spite of his assertion that he was a modern man. She had been instantly suspicious when he had described himself in this way, of course—who wouldn't be—but had been charmed by his gentle smile and his dark, shining skin that appeared to be completely without blemish. She had lived in her small town in southern India all twenty-one years of her life, and the idea of moving with him to America, a place so far away from all that she knew, both frightened and attracted her. She sensed that her parents had mixed feelings about him. They knew and liked his family. But to send their only child to such a faraway and foreign place? When she had shyly said yes to the proposal, their hopes for her had outweighed the fear and they gave her their blessings.

"I work as a waiter at an Indian restaurant in Boston called Star of India," he had told her during their first meeting, "but don't think that being a waiter is all I want to do in life. I have a bachelor of arts in English literature. I have just been unlucky in finding another job so far, but maybe you," and here he had averted his eyes shyly, "will bring me good luck."

He had returned to India specifically to find a spouse, and when both parties agreed to the match, a wedding was quickly planned and carried out in the village temple. For the occasion, she wore a heavy cream sari that added weight to her otherwise small, frail frame and darkened her eyes with kohl to further contrast them against her copper skin. After the wedding there was an ultimately successful interview with a suspicious American visa officer in Chennai, a teary but proud farewell to her relatives, a long flight, and then she was in America. As the wheels of the 747 hit the black tarmac of the landing runway and sped toward the terminal, she felt a shiver of anticipation. A new husband, a new country, and all at once.

Her husband had told her that he currently lived in a two-bedroom apartment that he shared with two other men, also waiters at Star. At first she was anxious about living with two strange men but as she soon found out, they both worked other jobs in addition to their shifts at Star. Except for the snores that trumpeted from their room in the small of the night, she rarely noticed their presence.

Although Reshma missed her family terribly at first, she adjusted quickly to her new life. She came to intimately know the Chinatown neighborhood around their shabby brown five-story building—where the freshest vegetables could be had, which store could be relied upon to have the sweetest mangoes and the tenderest coconuts. She hung picture frames over the water stains on the walls in the apartment and fixed the windows so that they wouldn't rattle with every gust of wind. She made friends with Shaila, the Pakistani woman who lived down the hallway, and from her learned to make the most delicious-tasting tea: a rich and creamy brew, fragrant with cardamom, cinnamon, ginger, cloves, and a touch of black pepper. She had been taught English in school, and because her husband insisted, she also practiced her English, using language tapes and books with titles like "Speak English like a Pro in Twelve Easy Steps!" that he checked out of the library. He also bought her some modern clothes—two pairs of heavy cotton pants, four shirts, three long skirts, and the only thing she liked, a white cardigan.

"We are in these people's country so we should try and adopt their customs—if nothing else at least dress like them," he had said, in answer to her pout.

Her husband was in love with America, his adopted country. He extolled American virtues and was forever explaining to her why America was so great. One night as they lay in their bedroom, he spoke admiringly about the ability of his American customers to drink.

"Back home they drink too but it is not the same," he boasted. "In India if they drink like this, they would have to be carried home. But these Americans drink and they drink but they still walk straight and talk proper, maybe a little more loudly, but still."

But it was not just their ability to drink that her husband respected. He would nod approvingly at the American joggers who trotted by the apartment in the mornings and say, "See how the Americans run—not like at home where nobody breaks into a sweat unless they have to."

She accompanied him to airy museums and glossy galleries, where he jotted down copious notes in his small yellow notebook. He particularly liked to look at paintings with just lines and squiggles thrown around. When she first saw one of these, she giggled and said she had seen better pictures drawn by schoolchildren at home, and he had replied huffily that she didn't know anything, that these paintings were abstract art and please not to simply gas about things that she knew nothing about.

Although she loved to tease and make fun of certain of his mannerisms (his stooped walk or the way the hair on his head stuck straight out in the mornings), she was deeply in love with her husband. She loved everything about him, from the way his arms cradled her at night to his amazing inability to carry a tune—any tune—in the shower. As for his modern views, she regarded them with the affectionate indulgence reserved for the harmless eccentric. Till one day he went too far.

"You really should get a job," he said primly one summer evening when it was so hot that she had brought the blue and white fan to the counter in the kitchen. She almost burned her hand turning over the *chappati.*

"You mean another job in addition to cooking and cleaning this apartment with three men living in it?" she cried.

"American women have careers, just like American men," he replied, squaring his shoulders proudly. "But even in your village, the women worked in the fields with the men, did they not?"

The thought of spending her days with total strangers, so foreign to her, filled her with apprehension.

"Everybody knew everybody else in the village."

"We will have enough money to move. Just think, only you and me, without having to listen to Murugan and Shankar snoring like demon kings every night."

That gave her pause. It would be good, no—more than good. She would be able to walk around in her nightie all day if she felt like it or wash and dry certain of her garments in the bathroom without embarrassment. And of course, as her husband had said, a peaceful night's sleep would be wonderful.

"But what kind of job will I get? Even you, with your bachelor of arts in English literature, are working in a restaurant as a waiter."

He walked behind her and placed his chin on her shoulder. "Don't worry, I have an idea."

The next night he came home flushed with the good news that he had found her a job. The owner of the restaurant where he worked also owned a string of motels and needed an English-speaking receptionist to work the night shift at one of them, and he was willing to give Reshma a chance.

"I have to work through the night?"

Her husband replied that it would be just to start and that they paid more for the night shift.

"Try it, nah," he pleaded.

The following night, they took a long bus ride to get to the motel. Her husband left her there, saying that he'd be back in the morning when her shift ended.

The motel was a twenty-room single-story building; the rooms linked to each other by a gravel path and were painted a dusty blue on the outside. The small beige office that she would be working in had one heavily barred window, and all customers had to be buzzed in through the front door.

She was given a white cotton blouse with a small coffee stain on the front left pocket, a black skirt that was too big for her so she had to use a safety pin, and a small name badge that said Hello I'm Karen. The plump, butter-colored Indian man who was training her and who would be her coworker through the night said that of course he knew her name wasn't Karen but it was better to use American names.

"Make easy for them," he said, pointing at his own nametag that said Hello I'm Dan even though she knew his name was Avi.

She began her training by learning to work the motel telephone switchboard—how to answer the phones, how to transfer calls to rooms, and so on.

"You have good English," Avi said approvingly, after she had smoothly transferred several incoming calls to the right rooms with the right words.

"I practice with tapes," she replied modestly.

Then he showed her how to fill the reservation information into the big black book that they kept inside the front drawer by the register.

"Computer kaput," he said, "so we use book."

With their first customers, she learned to operate the credit card machine and with the next, count out change in cash. In this establishment, the customers paid up front.

At about midnight, two young men in plaid shirts rented a room, and soon other cars began to pull up into the parking lot. The sound of music, voices, and laughter punctured the night and soon they were fielding complaints from neighboring rooms.

"They are making too loud party," Avi said. He made a warning call, after which the noise subsided, but not for long. Avi called the room again.

"Sorry, but to please be quiet or leave this place." They did neither.

"Out of room, or I call poh-leece," threatened Avi, with his third call. Reshma felt her heartbeat quicken. Didn't the customers rent the room to sleep in? What was going on?

Then at about one thirty in the morning there was the sound of a fight outside that same room, and Avi, followed by a scared Reshma, ran outside to try and break it up. In the ensuing confusion of shouts and loud gestures, Reshma was pushed by a man in a banana-colored shirt and fell heavily down onto the dusty ground. Avi immediately helped her up and brought her inside the office but she could not stop sobbing. So he took her to the back room where a small cot had been set up, and she did not leave the cot or the room for the rest of the night but lay there listening to the police sirens come and go in the parking lot outside.

The next morning, she emerged from the room her mind made up. She gave the blouse and the skirt and the Karen badge back to Avi and said she was sorry but she was too scared to work here. When her husband came to pick her up, she feared that he would be disappointed that she had quit after not even one night of work. But back at home, after she told him what had happened, he put one arm around her shaking shoulders and said it was okay, of course; she had done the right thing.

And that he would find her somewhere else to work.

The new job was at a twenty-four-hour convenience store. One of the Indian waiters at the restaurant that her husband worked at, Kumar, doubled as the night-shift clerk there.

"Night shift again?" she asked, already worried.

"Very good money," he replied.

Again, the store wanted somebody immediately and so the next evening found them waiting at the bus stop. They had to change buses twice and it took such a long time to get there that Reshma fell asleep for part of the way.

Kumar, a tall young man with a neatly kept beard, was waiting for them outside the corner store. There was a long line of other stores, all shuttered for the night. Her husband wished her luck and said that he would return in the morning.

"New manager wants to see you," said Kumar, shrugging. They walked up a flight of dark stairs behind the store and into a small, dimly lit room, where a man with brown bushy hair sat behind an untidy desk and sorted through papers.

"You the new girl?" he asked and she nodded.

"Yeah. I need to see your ID to make sure you're legal an'all."

She looked at Kumar, who shrugged again. She reached into her bag and gave him her navy-blue Indian passport, the only form of ID she had, and thought that she was lucky to have brought it with her.

The bushy-haired man thumbed through the passport and soon tossed it back on the desk toward her.

"You call this ID? She-et."

Kumar spoke up.

"She can work the night shift. Starting right away."

The bushy-haired man's mouth relaxed. "Why didn't you say so to start off with?"

Kumar shrugged. "Training day today."

"She can fill the paperwork out tomorrow then." The man yawned. "Nice to have meet yah, hon, and see you guys tomorrow, okay?"

So dismissed, Kumar and Reshma returned downstairs. Kumar walked her down each of the six aisles in the small store and, as their shift hadn't started yet, pointed out what went where. Then he gave her a broad white apron and showed her how to restock fruit and cheese and milk from the big refrigerated storage room directly onto the shelves. When their shift began, they stood at the cash register, which she quickly learned to operate. Unlike the motel, there was a steady stream of customers here and soon it was already two in the morning.

"People from bars will be coming soon," said Kumar, and soon enough they were—mostly men with bloodshot eyes that squinted at the bright lights in the store and who bought packs of cigarettes and fistfuls of beef jerky.

Then at about three in the morning, when there was a lull and Reshma's eyes were beginning to get heavy, a young man with delicate features and straight blond hair that fell to his shoulders came in. He stared at Kumar and Reshma for several seconds before turning to his friend.

"We should nuke all them A-rabs, just fucking nuke 'em, dude."

His friend was short and wiry with dark hair cropped close to his head. He looked at Reshma and Kumar standing behind the counter.

"Ye-ah! Nuke 'em all to hell."

He added as an afterthought, "Ka-Boom!"

They both laughed loudly. Making "boom" noises, they stomped around the store. Reshma cupped both hands over her mouth in terror. What was going on? Why did these two men seem to want to hurt her? She slid slowly behind Kumar. Unfortunately, this show of fear only served to embolden the two boomers, and one of them promptly knocked down a display of paperback books in the center aisle. "Whoops," he said, and they both laughed.

She was amazed that instead of being afraid, Kumar raised his voice.

"Get out of here," he shouted. "Out! Out!"

He picked up the white phone on the wall and without dialing any numbers said, "Is this police station?" in a carrying voice, after which the two men stomped a hasty exit to the door.

"Police don't like no A-rabs either," one of them shouted.

"They'll deport your asses right back to where y'all came from," yelled the other.

Before they left, the dark-haired man paused and looked back for a moment. Then he turned away, pulled down his trousers, and exposed two bright white buttocks with a large pimple on one that glistened yellow under the store's florescent lights. Screeching with laughter, he pounded off behind his friend, into the warm Boston night.

After they left, Reshma's shaking knees needed a break, and she retired to the refrigerated room at the back of the store and sat there shivering for the rest of the night. Then she gave Kumar the big white apron back and asked him to tell the bushy-haired man that she was not coming back, ever.

Her husband soon came to pick her up, and when they were safely at home, she told him all that had happened. But to her astonishment, this time he was not as sympathetic.

"Just your bad luck," he said, shaking his head. "Once in a while something like this happens, but not every day."

"Once is enough!" she cried. "What if they had cut my throat? What if they are waiting for me tomorrow?"

"They were just talking," he grumbled. "You don't understand how people just talk."

But she was adamant.

"Why did they think we were Arabs? We don't even look like Arabs. I know Arab women are beautiful—much more beautiful than me."

This last sentence she uttered with a quick sideways glance at her husband.

"You are the most beautiful woman in all the three worlds," he replied quickly.

After a brief pause, he continued, with a look of shame spreading across his face, "Americans are not so used to Indians, so they get . . . confused. Sometimes they think I'm from Africa, other times they think I'm Mexican, but nowadays, well nowadays, mostly people think I'm Arab."

He shifted in his chair uncomfortably.

"But in New Jersey, where there are more Indians, there are gangs called the Dotbusters, who go around attacking them."

She had been listening to him with growing horror and was unable to contain herself at this.

"And knowing all this, you sent me out to face these kinds of people every day? Why don't you take a second job instead?" she cried.

He drew himself up. "You know I need time for my hobbies," he said, in a hurt tone.

"Your hobbies?" She was beside herself. "You scribble your so-called stories once in a while or sketch some flowers by the lake like some big-big painter, what possible good can come of all that? Ai! Instead of behaving like a normal man, you send me, a poor, simple woman, to face those crazy people."

He didn't reply to this but sat sad faced for a few seconds. Then he rose from his seat, shuffled into their bedroom, and lay stiffly down on the bed, face up. A few minutes later, she felt guilty, followed him into the bedroom, sat down next to him on the bed, and kissed him on his forehead.

"Never mind," she said. "I'm only tired. You need time for your hobbies. Go and find another job for me."

Almost exactly one week later, he returned from Star and produced from the pocket of the black trousers he wore to work a piece of paper that he had folded neatly into a square.

"It is a job with a family," he said, "to take care of their child."

She felt her face grow warm and heard him continue hastily, "Nice pay—enough for a deposit."

"Ay-yeh! What are you saying? You want me to work as a servant?"

She had grown up poor—her father had owned a small, barely profitable general store in town, but he had made sure that neither she nor her mother would ever need to work in somebody else's home cooking and cleaning for some sharp-voiced harpy. Now here was her husband, asking her to do just that.

But he was saying with a swell in his voice that this was America, not India, and that in America working in other people's homes was nothing to be ashamed about. He said they called the people who took care of their children a nanny and that she wouldn't be expected to cook or clean, just take care of the child.

"And the pay," he added, "is top-top."

She looked at him with such undisguised contempt then that the words withered on his lips and no more was said about it. But that night's sleep was punctured by snores from the next room that rolled over them like the darkest thunder.

The next morning, she raised her red-lined eyes from the cardamom-infused cup of tea in her hands and said, "No harm in telephoning—as you say, this is America, not India."

The small piece of paper was unfolded once more, and with her husband perched anxiously beside her, she dialed the number.

A soft-voiced woman answered the phone. Reshma said she was calling about the nanny job and the woman's voice perked up considerably. They agreed to meet the following evening.

Reshma's husband spread out a map on the floor and located the address. He jabbed excitedly.

"I knew it. The great American poet Emerson was born on Summer Street—very close. If you get this job, you are a lucky, lucky woman."

Her husband dropped her off by the bus stop the following evening at the appointed hour.

"Third floor, on your right," said the woman when Reshma rang, her voice sounding unnaturally loud and harsh through the buzzer.

Upstairs, the door to the apartment was ajar and immediately upon entering, she was somewhat disappointed by what she saw. From the great esteem with which her husband had spoken of Emerson, she had expected something altogether different from this couple who lived so close to where that great man had been born.

Clutter made the small apartment seem even smaller. Bulky pieces of furniture crowded each other on dark carpets that covered the blond wood floor. Heavy curtains draped the sides of the dusty windows and a crystal chandelier hung somewhat incongruously above it all. A small corridor led to what was presumably the bedroom door—now closed. Reshma's face must have betrayed her thoughts, for the young woman with the short yellow hair who had opened the door and who now stood towering over her said, "Sorry, it's a little untidy right now, but please do take a seat." The woman introduced herself as Frances and the small, bespectacled man who had been sitting quietly in the chair in the corner as her husband.

When they were both seated Frances asked a few cursory questions without paying much attention to the answers. It seemed that she had already made up her mind about Reshma.

"Well, the important thing now is that you meet my daughter, Trish," she said, and almost on cue, the bedroom door opened and a little girl not more than two years old emerged, pushing her golden locks sleepily away from blinking, wide green eyes.

"Hi, Honey," trilled her mother. "Meet Reshma, am I pronouncing that right?"

Reshma nodded. Such a pretty baby, she thought.

"Oh look, she seems to have taken a liking to you," said Frances, her lips stretching into a tired smile.

Frances explained that they needed a nanny to look after Trish while she and her husband were vacationing in Europe—they were leaving at the end of the week for ten days. Trish would be staying with her grandmother in Rhode Island during this time and Reshma, if she took the job, would be expected to remain with her there.

"Have you seen the movie *Reversal of Fortune*?" asked Frances.

Reshma shook her head no.

"Anyway, our house is only a few minutes from Sunny von Bülow's. I'll point it out to you when we're there."

Reshma arranged her features into an impressed look but she did not have any idea who this Sunny von Bülow was. Perhaps another famous American writer, like Emerson, she thought and made a mental note to ask her husband.

Meanwhile, Trish brought Reshma a small doll, shyly holding it up with one hand, and Reshma was instantly charmed. She decided at that moment that her husband had been right—this was America and things were different here. She was going to like being a nanny to this baby who was so sweet and pretty, almost like a little doll herself.

"I'll call you tomorrow to arrange," promised Reshma as she left.

Frances opened the door, the husband looked up from his magazine to wave, and little Trish smiled and gurgled nonsensically at her, and outside in the waning sunshine, she thought of them and felt pleased. What a delightful family they were.

At home she told her husband, "It will only be for ten days and then we will have money to move from this place."

He looked worried. "But we don't know anything about these people. They could be anyone—murderers even. And the job is not even in Boston."

He shook his head and looked at the floor. "With your luck, who knows what will happen?"

She was pleased by his concern for her but also mildly annoyed. It had been his idea in the first place and now here he was, doubting her good judgment. She remembered what Frances had told her.

"Their house is close to that of the famous Sunny von Bülow," she said, carefully pronouncing the name.

Her husband did not react well to this news. He began to pace.

She spoke in her authoritative voice. "They're a nice family; I could see that just by looking. So different from all the riff-raff people in those other two jobs you found me."

She also thought that perhaps she could continue being a nanny to Trish in Boston and bring home a steady stream of money. She did not voice aloud that ambition though—hoping to spring it as a pleasant surprise for her husband when she got back. Instead, she reassured him of her talent to judge people accurately. He continued to look worried.

"As long as I can talk to you every day," he said.

The next morning she called Frances to say that she was ready to take the job. "Terrific," said Frances and gave her a time to meet that Friday. Just before she hung up, Reshma asked her for the telephone number in Rhode Island for her husband.

"Of course," said Frances, "and you can call him anytime as well."

On Friday, the day she was leaving, her husband looked into one of his books and said that she was a lucky woman to be going to Rhode Island because the great American author Henry James had lived there for some time. After rifling through his stacks of worn books on the table in the bedroom, he triumphantly pulled one out titled *The American Novels and Stories of Henry James* and slipped it into the side pocket of her packed bag along with a dictionary.

It was a rainy afternoon. When she got to the apartment, the little family was ready to leave and they all got into the silver car that had been parked in front of the building, Reshma and Trish in the backseat, Frances and her husband in the front. Trish soon fell asleep and Reshma almost did the same herself, listening to the rhythmic swishing of the wipers, the steady drumming of the rain on the roof, and the low whine of the car maneuvering over the wet road. Frances and her husband talked in low voices to each other for a while. Soon Frances twisted around to face Reshma. Her face had lost the wilted look that Reshma had noticed the other day and instead glowed with a happy anticipation. She began to talk animatedly about how nice a time Reshma was going to have this coming week, almost as good a time as she and her husband were going to have in Europe.

"We have a beautiful house on the ocean," she said. "It has been in my father's family for a very long time. And my mother's very sweet. Everybody just adores her."

When they got to Newport, Frances pointed out the famous mansions as they drove by. Reshma recognized not a single name and usually could not even see the house—just a set of tall gates. After each name, Frances's husband said something like "Ugh, gaudy marble monstrosity" or "Ugh, ugly Louis fifteenth furniture."

After one such remark, Frances said in a testy voice that it was a shame that everybody did not have the impeccable taste of Staten Islanders like him.

The rest of the short drive to Frances's home was silent.

When they got to the house, they first had to stop the car and open a set of iron gates, and then there was a long road through some sparse woods. Finally in the distance a large, dark house came into view, the gray ocean merging with the slate sky behind it.

"We have a small, sandy patch along our shoreline that Trish loves to play in," Frances told her.

The house was so big that it reminded Reshma of pictures of European palaces she had seen in books, and when they came to a halt in front of the main doors, she fully expected a uniformed man or woman to come out and greet them with a bow. Instead a handsome, gray-haired woman in gray pants, a white blouse with broad lapels, and a gray cardigan came bustling out. She said her name was Gilda and she was the mother of Frances and the grandmother of Trish. She hugged her daughter and her son-in-law and insisted that she carry Trish inside the house herself.

Frances and her husband left soon thereafter to catch their plane. Reshma's first real job in America had officially begun.

Excited, she bustled along with Gilda to put the sleeping Trish on a sofa outside the kitchen. Gilda said she would make coffee, and while they were waiting for the water to boil, she asked Reshma if she was from India.

"Yes, I thought so," said Gilda. "You people have nice hair."

"Thank you," said Reshma, confused.

What could Gilda mean by "you people"? If she meant all Indians, she was certainly mistaken and Reshma could even point to the heads of several members of her own family as proof. Gilda continued to keep up a steady patter of conversation.

"My mother was from Argentina, you know Argentina?"

When Reshma replied in the negative, Gilda said that Argentina was just like Europe, all the people there were just like Europeans, and no family more so than Gilda's own.

"My father's family," continued Gilda, "have been in Rhode Island forever. They probably arrived on the Mayflower."

When the water boiled Gilda put one teaspoon of instant coffee in her cup.

"I take mine black, you?"

Reshma nodded but later had to ask for milk and sugar when she had been given her coffee and realized what taking coffee black meant.

They had not taken more than a few sips each when there was a small cry from the next room.

"Oh, Trish has woken up," said Gilda and they both hurried over. Trish was sitting up on the sofa and Gilda hugged and fussed over her.

Trish said, "Ma-ma, Da-da?" She looked around her with a questioning smile.

"Mama and Dada are not here now but NaNa and Nanny Reshma are here with Trish," said Gilda.

She pointed at Reshma and said again, "See? Nanny Reshma."

The little girl's smile slowly faded when she heard this, and she stared at Reshma as if it were the first time that she had seen her. The child's face then underwent a transformation. The eyes narrowed, the cheeks puffed, and the little nostrils flared. Perhaps Trish had just realized what Reshma's true place in the family was or maybe she felt that Reshma was somehow responsible for her parents not being there or perhaps the word "nanny" held unpleasant connotations for her. Whatever the reason, Trish then took a deep breath and let out a big bellow, so loud that Reshma thought her ears were going to burst.

"NonoNonoNono," screamed Trish, and it was only when Gilda took her in her arms that she calmed down a little.

"Oh poor baby, you have your Na-Na right here," said Gilda. She motioned for Reshma to follow her and then, cooing and clucking at the baby, led Reshma out of the kitchen. First they went through a large hallway with dark wood floors and heavy curtains covering the big windows. Doors on either side of the hallway led to other rooms that Reshma only got a brief glimpse of as they went past.

"We only use a small portion of the house these days," said Gilda, "and I have a cleaning crew come by once a week."

Then they passed through a burgundy-carpeted room with dark, heavy furniture and climbed up a broad staircase. Upstairs, paintings of old men, some of them with large white wigs on their heads, hung on the walls.

Finally, Gilda opened up a door and they walked into a blue room with very high ceilings and enormous windows through which Reshma could see the garden and the ocean.

"This is your room," said Gilda, waving one arm expansively around, "and this is your bathroom," she continued, opening up a door.

Past the green marble walls, the white-framed windows, and the claw-footed tub was another door, which Gilda opened. This room was cream, with light pink chairs and a painting depicting a lighthouse towering against a stormy ocean that almost took up one entire wall. There was a white daybed by one of the windows overlooking the ocean and a fluffy pink baby bed in the corner, which Gilda pointed to and said, "Trish's." Then Gilda said she was taking Trish downstairs and that Reshma should unpack and make herself comfortable in the blue room and come down when she was ready.

Reshma opened up her suitcase but instead of unpacking sat gingerly down on the side of the bed. She was worried. The big house, with its cordoned-off areas and dark wood hallways, frightened her a little. And why had Trish suddenly taken such a dislike to her? She hoped that Trish would come around soon. Otherwise, she would have to add this to the list of her other job failures in America.

Trish did not come around. The screaming began afresh the next morning when Reshma tried to pick the child up to give her a morning bath. She growled so ferociously and from so deep within her, "NnnnnOOOOO," that Reshma backed away.

"Oh God," she muttered, "what has that good-for-nothing husband of mine got me into this time?"

Luckily for both of them, Gilda bustled into the room just then. She bathed and dressed Trish and off they went in a big black car. Reshma was told that they were going "visiting" and that there was plenty of food in the fridge, and she should help herself.

As soon as they left, Reshma called her husband and told him that it was impossible to work here, so she was going to pack her bags and leave at once. But now he again changed his tune and insisted that she stay.

"You have promised the parents, nah?"

And then he whispered caressing things to her about the new apartment that they would move into when she got back, just the two of them, and when she finally put down the phone she felt somewhat better.

Gilda and Trish continued visiting the next few days and Reshma had the house to herself. She tried to be useful. She washed the kitchen dishes, tidied up Trish's room, and cleaned the bathroom till it shone. She quickly put aside *The American Novels and Stories of Henry James* in favor of a glossy magazine that she found in the bathroom. In the evenings, she turned on the television in her room but nothing interested her and she kept it on mainly for the company. She began to feel guilty.

"I am getting paid to sit here and look at the sky," she complained to her husband on the phone.

"You should feel lucky," he replied.

In the middle of the week, Gilda's son came to visit. He was a sullen man of about Reshma's age, with tufts of dark hair that he had gelled into a puff above his forehead. He nodded at Reshma, said hello to Trish, and then the mother and son disappeared into a room from which the sounds of raised voices could occasionally be heard. He left soon after but not before Reshma heard him tell Gilda that he got "scarred" every time he came home. That evening Reshma looked up the word "scar" in the dictionary her husband had put in her bag. She read: Scar—lasting mark left by damage etc. It was noted that the damage referred to could have been caused by physical or psychological trauma.

That evening there was a knock on Reshma's door. It was Gilda, dressed in a dark, blue velvet robe and with a glass of red wine in one hand.

"Making sure you're comfortable," she said.

Reshma nodded. "Yes, very comfortable, thank you."

Gilda walked to the window.

"You can hear the ocean from here, the waves hitting the shore. Do you hear?"

Reshma said carefully, "My house in India was by the sea. I like this sound very much."

Gilda turned back from the window and took a long sip from her glass.

"Did I tell you I've always wanted to visit India? No? Well, it's true.

We almost went one year when the children were small. Then one of them, Frances, I think, fell ill and we cancelled."

Reshma noticed that Gilda's hands were shaking.

"Please sit down, Gilda," she said, offering her a chair as if Gilda were a visitor to her own home.

Gilda seemed not to hear her. She emptied her glass in one gulp and spoke, almost as if to herself.

"Children. You love them, you take care of them, they become your whole life, then they leave and one day they return as strangers."

She waved one finger in the air. "Grandchildren, now, they are a completely different story. Grandchildren are, and always will be, perfect adorable angels."

Reshma smiled. "My grandfather thought like you. Why can't we just go directly to grandchildren, he used to say."

Gilda laughed. "Your grandfather sounds like a clever man."

She walked to the door. "And I should let you sleep."

The next afternoon, Gilda boiled a small plastic bag of rice, saying, "I know you people love rice." But there was nothing to eat with the rice and so when Gilda wasn't looking, Reshma threw it away in the garbage under the sink in the kitchen. Trish continued to scream if left alone with Reshma, no matter how hard Gilda or Reshma tried to soothe her.

Reshma found it hard to sleep at nights. What could she do differently that might lessen the baby's dislike of her? Perhaps if she dressed differently, more like Gilda maybe—but although she had brought only her American clothes on the trip, she knew that they were very different from those that Gilda wore. She remembered her small ambition of continuing to work with Trish in Boston. That, she knew now, would never be.

The next morning, Gilda introduced Reshma to a large man with thin white hair and red cheeks.

"My husband. Came in from New York late last night," she said.

He asked Reshma a few questions in a booming voice—what is your name, where do you live in Boston, and so forth. Then he swept Trish up and began to energetically throw her in the air. "Whoop-iddyy-day," he'd cry as he threw a delighted Trish up, and "Whoop-iddyy-doo" as he caught her on her way down.

They had visitors that afternoon, an old man well into his sixties and a much younger woman. They cooed at Trish and declared that she was the cutest child in all of Rhode Island.

Gilda's husband waved at Reshma and said to them, "Oh, and this here is my cousin, Reshma."

He began to laugh like he had made a tremendous joke, but Reshma couldn't understand why this was so funny. She looked at the guests to see if they were laughing too but she could tell by the way their eyes shifted about that they didn't think it very funny either.

"My cousin," repeated Gilda's husband, and, still laughing loudly, he led the visitors out into the garden.

That evening, Gilda and her husband left for a party. Gilda wore a long, shiny blue dress and her husband dressed in black. When Trish realized that they were leaving, she clung screaming to her grandfather's leg and was only extracted by the combined effort of all three adults. She calmed down almost immediately after they had left however, much to Reshma's joy. It was the first time that she was alone with the baby and already things were going better than she could have hoped. She brought out coloring books and crayons for Trish and sat next to her saying encouraging things.

All was going well till suddenly Reshma felt a sharp pain in her arm. It was Trish. She had bitten into Reshma's forearm and was about to chomp down for another mouthful.

Hard, hot tears welled up in Reshma's eyes. She was suddenly very angry. She leapt up to her feet and raised one hand as if she were going to strike Trish.

"Stop it!" she shouted.

Trish immediately started bawling and Reshma cried again, "Stop it! I will hit you!"

Her arm began to descend threateningly. Trish's eyes widened in fear. She cowered against the sofa and began to whimper. Reshma hissed at her.

"I've had enough! You understand me? Enough!"

An intense desire to pick up and shake the child overcame her but it passed without incident and with it, all her anger. She sank down onto the edge of the sofa, shaking with a sudden exhaustion. Trish sniveled at her feet. They remained like that till Gilda and her husband came home not much later.

Trish did not rush over to Gilda like she normally did. Instead she remained gibbering and crying by the sofa. She spoke volubly but it was in her baby talk and the only understandable words were the oft-repeated "Na-Na. Na-Na." Gilda picked her up and Trish clung tightly to her, resting her little head on her grandmother's shoulder. Gilda looked sharply at Reshma and asked her what had happened. Reshma shook her head.

"Baby is sleepy, that's all."

Pleading a headache, she went upstairs to her room, put some cold cream on the bite, took two aspirins from her purse, and then lay stiffly on the bed. She was awake for most of that night. The image of her raised hand and angry words haunted her and she shivered when she remembered the cowering child. At home in India there had been occasions when she had threatened her nieces and nephews with violence but it had always been as a joke.

"Do you want a hit?" she might ask.

But she would smile as she said this and the children more often than not would reply "yes" and pretend to run away, hoping that she would run after them. But never in her entire life had she raised her hand in anger and meant it. This was what shamed her the most, the knowledge that she had been prepared to hit Trish, had wanted to strike a two-year-old baby.

Although Reshma had resolved during the night to tell Gilda what had happened, the next morning, she found that she could not. She felt too ashamed. Trish whimpered when she saw Reshma now and Gilda, apparently suspecting that something had happened, had turned icy. With a hard glint in her eyes, she told Reshma that she herself had had "a what do you call them—an Ah-yah" from Argentina when she was growing up.

"The Ah-yah never brought us water at night, even though we children begged and cried for it," she said, and Reshma cringed guiltily as if it were she, and not the other long-ago Ah-yah, who had failed to bring the small and thirsty Gilda water in the middle of the night.

Gilda had been watching Reshma's reaction closely and now added that she had talked to her daughter and son-in-law the previous evening. Reshma's heart immediately began to race. What had Gilda said? That Reshma had willfully deprived their only child of drinking water? Would they shout at her when they got back? Would they refuse to pay her?

Her thoughts collapsed in turmoil but she tried to appear calm on the outside.

She spoke to her husband that evening but could not bear to tell him what had happened. Instead, she directed the shame she felt toward him.

"You don't know the things I have had to go through here," she whispered vehemently. "You should be ashamed, putting your wife through this."

He asked her to tell him what had happened but she just said that she was "scarred" for the rest of her life and that she would always blame him. Then she hung up the phone with satisfying violence.

Her last morning in Rhode Island dawned blue and clear. Frances and her husband returned in their silver car and claimed that they were in a hurry to get back to Boston. The bags were put in the car and it was time for Reshma to say her good-byes.

"Thank you," said Gilda stiffly.

"My cousin," said Gilda's husband with great merriment.

It was a quiet ride back to Boston. Trish fell instantly asleep and Frances's head bobbed up and down as she dozed. Frances's husband drove silently and swiftly, and Reshma stared out of the window and worried. What if they refused to pay her? Her poor husband. She imagined his disappointment when she told him. But did she really deserve the money? After all, Trish had disliked the very sight of her and there had been that horrible moment when Reshma had raised her hand in anger and meant it. She twisted in her seat in shame just thinking about it.

Reshma was prepared for the worst when they finally came to a stop in front of the apartment. Frances turned sleepily around.

"It was nice meeting you," she said.

Reshma began to open the car door. It had all ended in failure after all. She was to go home to her husband empty-handed.

"Don't forget this." Frances handed her an envelope. "And there's ten dollars extra inside."

Reshma hopped out of the car then and transferred her bag to her other shoulder. She stood and watched as the silver car snaked away down the road.

"Bye, baby Trish," she thought.

She discovered later that she had been pregnant with her own child all the time that she had been in Rhode Island. She told her husband what had happened there and he claimed that her pregnancy explained that burst of irrational anger.

"All the changes taking place in your body, nah?" he had said.

She had nodded, not wanting to argue, but knew that he was wrong.

Her husband began to read Emerson's *Nature* out loud to her. "Babies hear things even when they're in there and it's never too early to learn about Beauty."

He was, as ever, a modern man, but no longer insisted that she go outside to work, now that she was pregnant. He was, instead, on the hunt for a job that would better support the growing family and had begun to talk about New York City, where he said there were better opportunities for men like him. In the meantime, they continued to share the two-bedroom apartment and wake up to the sound of snoring that emanated from the other room.

■

Sometimes when Reshma is alone, she puts her hand on her belly and speaks to the person who is growing there. "Will I be able to be a good mother to you," she asks it silently, "my little American child?"

She waits.

Arcadia

Hope Wabuke

I am the only son.

One sister ahead, one sister after—still yet to become—and my ghost brother, dead before my forming in our mother's womb. Here we sit, bowing to our father's God. His cries press upward into heaven, but we are mute. In my thirteen years as Father's son, I have learned that this is one of the many languages we do not know. One of the many questions we must not ask to understand.

Older Sister's eyes are opening. She sits watching us from the corner; I know she is thinking of our mother. I do not want to think of Mother—or of Sister, thinking of Mother—so I close my eyes and listen to the sounding of Father's voice calling out to the thing he believes has saved him from the anger of the men with guns, their steel-plated black boots crushing green growth underfoot in the loud night marching to move through still darkness until, in the sudden silence of the arrival, the press of cold iron barrels sharp against weak wooden doors would have been the sounding of the cold stillness of the morning after when the village had become burnt ash, embering flame. When, in line with another and the next, the rest of his body family would have been disappeared.

He has never told us anything about them, at all.

▩

This is the little we know from Mother: It is 1976. It is the year of Amin and his purges. They sneak across the border to Kenya: Mother, Father, Sister.

They are free.

The soft sounding of Mother's voice as she would say this, and the words would become light, funny, cocktail entertainment. But beyond this, nothing. For, from the body family, he has been taught to understand that the seeing of the nakedness of the father—by the son, by the daughter—is anathema.

So we believed, my older sister and I, every time we heard this story as we would move between the groups of our parent's friends inside the prayer rooms of Father's church after his sermon up until the still white light of the finding: that cold morning when my sister walked into the kitchen and saw our mother—her mouth shallow, eyes closed, red blood becoming faded red lines marking the cold white tile.

How Older Sister had said only that this does not fit, with the story we know; how I had told her she was right, she should find out.

How Older Sister had only laughed, hearing my words. How she had said that I was the son, Father would only listen to me—and I was reminded yet again of what I am never allowed to forget by any of them: I am the only son, the chosen one, the fragment kept secret and safe to raise up the family in this place, strange and alien, and begin again.

■

It has been three months since then.

I see the tiredness with waiting growing darker in Older Sister's eyes, but I know that Older Sister will not speak of this again until I do. She waits. She watches. She does not understand that I am not the first-born son. She cannot understand how First Son, Ghost Brother, changes everything between Father and me, after all.

I know how the worlds blur and collide in my culture, never separate—spirits and earth one. How I can feel them and my ancestors pressing in, but I do not know enough of the home I have never been to, to understand. Are they the messages I hear? The understanding I receive in dreams when I wake, each night, clinging to ghostly blurs of disappearing memories I have never lived?

I want them to stay; unlike Father, I am not scared of the ancestors and essences because I am not scared of who I am, what I may be called upon to do by this world or the demands of others. I am American. I think I will have the chance to say no, to become my own individual person with my own choice, not a collective tribe knowing they have none but the weight of other's actions made right and permanent in history and culture, in ritual.

I think I am allowed to question—to be anything I can desire. I think I am allowed to speak.

■

I have waited until the morning, when Father is driving me to school—an old and favorite tactic of mine when wanting information or conversation. Here he is my captive audience. For the ten-minute ride to Foothills Middle School he cannot hide or evade; he cannot tell me he will answer my questions later and then later still, hoping that eventually I will forget and no longer need to know anything at all about the place that I am from and have never been.

There is too much to know, and not enough time to tell, he says. How well I know this stratagem; it has been practiced upon me before.

After the fumbling for something specific, I tell him, alright then, that he can start with the story of the names.

But still he escapes. He wants to listen to this bit of news about the crisis in the Middle East, he says, increasing the radio volume.

After it has ended, I ask again and he brings up the fact that the car is too cold, concentrating with utmost attention on the car heater.

Dad.

But now we are pulling up in front of the school. Time to go.

I do not move.

He sighs, putting the car in park. He does not look at me, and it is only one thing, but still, it is more than my sisters will ever hear, from him—this soft sounding of his voice as he tells me the ritual of the naming—in the understanding of our body family.

■

Tonight, Ghost Brother has come again to see me.

He is quiet. I know that he is angry because of how his ghost frame vibrates, shimmering in the white moon's light pressing through half-open window blinds. I have seen him angry before, but rarely. I ask what is wrong, and he says Grandfather has come with him to see me.

I have never seen Grandfather before. I had not known I could; I do not know his name. But now, understanding the story of how his name came to be found, I know who Grandfather is; I know to see him now.

He stands beside Ghost Brother, his smile shining arms spread wide, eyes bright, and I see my naming ritual: the sounding of words made into shapes—how Grandfather's ghost frame would have pressed closer to my mother dreaming of the lost village at lake edge under green trees, green mountains, his ghost lips sounding the name I was to be given into her ears.

Somehow, I do not stop to wonder how I can understand the sounding of his voice until I see Ghost Brother, shimmering even brighter in the anger of being the thing that must translate between us. For even here I am mute—in Father's denial of our language I cannot speak directly. And if I could, I would not know what to ask. There is so much, too much, and already Ghost Brother is telling Grandfather that they must leave. That Grandfather must have realized I am not of them. What is Grandfather playing at? He, Ghost Brother, is still the son—the first-born of the first-born of the first-born since the beginning of our village—not me, this remnant, this American shadow.

Come on now.

And so, even as Grandfather is leaning over me to whisper his name—my true name—before leaving, I understand that to Ghost Brother, maybe even to Grandfather, I am a different kind of fragment—not wanted but a shameful thing fragile and easily broken, pressed into the space between what once was and what has not yet been made manifest to be understood.

▩

Sometimes, I dream of how it must have been day.

They are stopped.

Here are the soldiers, insecure in their power, blocking the way with barely working guns and mismatched fatigues. In the fumbling of their fingers against their cold steel gun barrels, the white identification papers fall softly through hands onto ground, pressed underneath the heavy treads of black steel-toed boots as the soldiers' wide hands grasp Older Sister's tiny body to see what is being smuggled out inside her diapers.

But Older Sister is crying. She is leaking wet spit and wet shit, they mutter to each other, pushing Older Sister's tiny baby body back into my mother's hands.

The barricade is raised. They are let pass.

▩

I sit in school.

Here, we are all still becoming, we are all new to this place.

Here, too, we all have black hair. The strands move softly in the soft sounding of Spanish rising up into the spaces of soft notes descending downward; Chinese, Japanese, underneath teacher's clipped American English, his accent as cold and light as the people who, because of our coming, have fled this tiny Southern California town called Arcadia where we are all still becoming.

How I used to envy, so much, their knowing of the language to understand their body family—how, too, I used to envy that their light skin made their black hair not matter so much to the others in this place who had been here before us all, now absent because we have come.

But today, this morning, the coldness that fills the air around me after the sounding of teacher's voice is pushed away with the shimmering of Grandfather's ghost frame, dancing around me. In the press of white light through window fractured through his ghost body the sounding of his voice calling my name is spreading like summer love to warm everything inside me and I am become sunlit; I am become light.

▩

I am so happy I tell Father.

In the watching of his hearing the sound of my voice, I am nervous. I concentrate on his ink-smudged hands and speak, and, after my words have run and babbled over each other until I am dry, I wait, nervousness increasing, but he says nothing.

And when I chance looking up from the ground and back at him, he is standing up to open the door for me to leave and saying that we will speak no more of this; there will be no devil worship in his house.

▩

Outside Father's house, I pick up my nunchucks.

It is the end of spring; the hot wet heat drags me down. I practice the katas, fitting myself into centuries-old patterns of strength and grace. Grandfather has told me how he would practice with his own weapons, a warrior. I do not know how he can be a devil.

I think of China, of the Shaolin monks. How they do not speak but practice, silent and meditative, from sunrise to sundown. I think of the lineage of knowing they pass down, in line with another and the next. I think of the understanding of self, too, they must then possess: the presence and whole consciousness as single mind and body.

While I have been practicing, the light has begun to fade; night is rising. And with it is the faint sounding of Ghost Brother's laughter. But he does not appear; it is not yet his time—the sky has darkened from red to deep purple, but it is not yet night.

I take a breath and bow to the unseen boy body who has partnered me in mirrored movements of parts of body, steel, and wood. A match flares red in the darkness and there is the smell of cigarettes. Older Sister. Father must be gone then.

I walk over to her, sitting down on the damp grass. She is silent, as am I. How strange we have become to each other in this slow, long process toward separation begun with my birth.

I tell her I tried to ask him. I tell her I am sorry.

She doesn't answer me. Her fingers are pushing a tiny hole in the dirt. She drops her finished cigarette inside, covers it with earth.

The light has faded completely now; I know this is her favorite time of the day, this in-between time, neither one thing nor the other. It used to be mine, too, but since Ghost Brother has begun to come and see me, that is no longer the case.

I shiver, waiting for him to appear, as usual, with the rising night. To distract myself from thinking about Ghost Brother, I watch the tiny movements of Older Sister's hands, burying cigarettes. I tell her that Father will find them when he starts to garden in the spring anyway, but Older Sister says it doesn't matter. Then she says she has found out where Mother is. She is going to go see her and she wants me to come.

In remembering the cold light of the morning of the finding, I am scared, and, before I can stop, I have asked Older Sister why I have to come. Why can't she go without me?

Looking down at the ground as I wait for her to speak, I see that Older Sister's boots are digging more tiny holes in the earth, mounds of brown pushed into tiny valleys, tiny rivers: a whole world, complete.

She'll talk to you, Older Sister finally says. Because of who you are.

So we are here again, Older Sister and I—these familiar ending words from her that I can neither negate nor deny. I am never to be able to forget that I am the only son—our parent's desire, their hoarded secret. I am to be molded from unused potential and multiplied by Western advantages; I am to raise up the family, begin again.

Okay, I say. We'll go.

▩

Sometimes I think what happened was that my father has to kill a man.

They are hidden in the back of a truck. It is night. It is the time of the endless changing—the sudden bursting and disappearance of rainstorms, and through the wash of mud raised up by worn and patched wheels on dirt road they cannot see anything through the slats of the truck bed. They are covered in blankets soaked with kerosene to confuse the packs of wolf dogs—hunting cries rising loud outside, to sound—but Mother worries only that my older sister is being choked by the smell.

They come to a checkpoint. The truck stops.

They have bribed the driver. But perhaps, feeling the sudden jarring movement, Father is thinking that he should have given him more money, been somewhat more frightening and intimidating instead. Father will close his eyes and hold his wife's hand tightly within his own. Perhaps he is praying. In any case, he cannot see anything with his eyes open anyway.

Now the soldiers are approaching. Mother and Father can hear the steel-toed black boots pushing heavy through thick mud.

Then silence—it seems as if even the rain has stopped.

And then the sounding of my older sister, crying.

The back of the truck is opened. Here are the two soldiers—their shadows pressing sharp against Father's body in the brief pressing of sun flash through rain, breaking. For some reason, perhaps too cocky, perhaps too impatient, their guns are still strapped across their chests. And as hands move to pull out, unsafety . . . already Father has shot first one, and then the other with his father's old WWII-issue pistol. Mother is shaking and Older Sister is crying, her screams shattering the darkness.

They take each other's hands and run.

▩

I am called to the office right before lunch. The assistant nods at me in a concerned manner and says she is sorry about my grandmother. For a second, I think, illogically, that this is true—somehow news has been sent from the home we do not know. Then I see my older sister, slouched in one of the plastic chairs by the door.

The car she has borrowed from her friend is a rumbling 1960s mustang. She unlocks the door for me and we merge onto the freeway; it occurs to me that I don't even know if she has her driver's license. But I do not ask her this now; this is neither the time nor place for one of our uncomfortable and increasingly rare conversations.

So, we do not talk during the two-hour ride. Occasionally she lights a cigarette. Occasionally, I mess with the radio.

She does not look at the map.

▩

In front of the hospital, we sit in the car long after my older sister parks, each waiting for the other to move. Finally, she pulls the keys out of the ignition and presses her door open gently.

I follow.

▩

Inside this place, there is only silence, whiteness.

A nurse approaches, her pale blonde hair and pale skin blending so well into the white shirt and pants of her uniform I have trouble seeing where flesh and cloth meet. The nurse speaks quietly to my older sister but I cannot hear. The movement of the black clock hands against each black slash on white background is loud in my ears and the room is fading and shimmering slowly, as is usual when the movement of sound—and other forms of energy—begin to behave oddly, begin to shift into strange wave and light patterns to announce the appearance of Ghost Brother or others from his spirit world. He cannot be here; it is not his time, it is not yet night.

But still, afraid, I cannot move closer.

I watch the nurse leave and my older sister absently pull a cigarette from her new full pack, then put it back. She will sit down, then stand up and take a few steps before turning around, sitting back down. Then she will stand up, repeating the entire process yet again.

She is making me nervous, but I can't stop watching. So I stand and move to the window, my back toward her, and stare out at the tiny, dying patches of grass that stand for outdoor space instead.

This is no better. I am remembering how before this, my mother and my older sister would wake before the sun and go out to work in the garden, their brown fingers dropping round seeds into brown earth, their lips pushing out melodies in the language Older Sister and I do not know, to grow tiny fruit seed, tiny flower—all life—underground.

▩

Here she is, the nurse's perky voice is announcing. There is Older Sister's sharp intake of breath and I turn around.

Our mother sits in a wheelchair—head hung down unseeing, her already thin body become so tiny, too thin, and I wonder why her arms are still pressed down with restraints until with the movement of recycled air from machine her white hospital gown lifts slightly and I see, in line with another and the next, the tiny lines etched upward along arm from wrist, knee to thigh, knee to ankle, faded only a little from that day of red blood on white tile that marked the finding—how some do not appear to be faded at all, but rather recent and deep.

My older sister has begun crying; she lets her body fall to her knees to press arms around our unresponsive mother, holding tight to her body. But I am scared; I cannot move closer. I tell Older Sister that mother cannot hear us. We should go; it is late.

There will be anger now, from Father, when we return to his house.

Older Sister doesn't hear me, but our mother slowly turns her head toward the empty echo of my voice through air. She opens her mouth to speak, but, finding herself unable, closes it and tries again.

The first word she gets out that I can hear is *dead*. Then: *He said you were dead.*

She says nothing else, only these words over and over, her voice rising louder and louder until the nurse, alarmed, hurries over to sedate and tranquilize.

But in the moments before the medicine moves through body to calm, in the darkness of the becoming night, I hear the soft sounding of laughter and I know that if I look I will see—in between Mother's body, my body—the shimmering body of Ghost Brother, his laughter rising louder, then louder still.

Older Sister will be asking what is happening, what is wrong, the first beginnings of panic and alarm rising loud in her voice too. For she is a girl and not the only son; the ancestors do not visit her. She cannot see Ghost Brother; she cannot hear the echoing of Ghost Brother's laughter—cold and harsh throughout the room; she cannot feel the sounding that is pressing through Mother's body and my own—sharp and deep and shining as the razor lines etched into Mother's arms.

I realize, suddenly, that the reason I am having difficulty in seeing Ghost Brother is because he is shimmering harder than I have ever seen him, pulsing so quickly in the rise and fall of his angry light that my eyes cannot hold the brief flashings of his body to register the seeing as sight.

And still, in the echoing of his rising laughter, Ghost Brother is pulsing so quickly in the rise and fall of his angry light the space in between is becoming unrecognizable as well; he looks like he is almost becoming solid flesh. But in the shimmering—faster now, then faster still—the ghost body cannot hold the press of the force, the ghost frame is beginning its breaking apart. First one arm, falling softly to ground. Then the other. One leg, then the other. Then foot, separating from leg, toes from foot. Finger from hand from arm.

Head from neck. Tongue from mouth.

Eye from socket.

And still, the sounding of his laughter. And still the sounding of his voice, telling Mother he will not stop showing her what was done to him, no he won't, haha, won't stop showing Mother what was done to all of the body family before he was Ghost Brother and he was still first-born son of the first-born son left behind to guard the village, the many parts of the body family, as had been done by the first son of the first son in line with another and the next throughout memory while Father—no longer the first son but the first father—was sent with Mother and Older Sister overseas in this place as hope: the fragment of the body family kept secret and kept safe to begin again.

▪

In the car, on the way back, it is an hour before my older sister asks.

In hearing the sounding of my voice telling her what I saw—why she could not see—she says nothing.

But from time to time, in the mirror, I see her wipe her hand across her face.

■

And sometimes, of course, I wonder if it is just chance.

Father has been in the fields or at the school or at the market with Mother and Older Sister and, when they come back, the village has been disappeared.

In the soft fall of ash and graying smoke, I see Father's arms rise up to hold Mother. Perhaps they can still see the dust of the military transport. Perhaps, in the distance, they hear an echo they try to believe is not gunshots.

Here is Father holding Mother, reasoning with her not to run after them, holding up my older sister as everything that will become.

But if he had known what was to become, would he have released her body, let her run after them?

Would he have rushed after her, holding Older Sister, and let it end there instead?

Perhaps this is what he is already beginning to wonder as they walk for days—hiding, tired, hungry—until reaching the border and wondering if this, too, exists solely inside his head and will upon closer seeing be revealed as nothing more than a sun-crazed hallucination.

But it cannot be a hallucination, he is thinking. Here are Amin's soldiers—marching on the ground and from lookout towers or in trucks shooting at nothing, drunk with revolution, their sudden power and agency.

I see Mother crumple to the ground. I see Father lift her up. I see the three of them take a step.

And another.

And still, no one notices.

I see them cross the border into Kenya, but no one else, not even the soldiers, sees them.

And perhaps, as they walk, the guards looking straight at them and yet through them, my Father sees the towering genesis angels with swords of flame who sent away from the garden the first man, the first wife.

Only this time, the deep echo of winged thunder is the sounding of paradise.

Sirens

Joshunda Sanders

There wasn't enough music in the world to block out those sirens. I would hear 'em in the middle of the day, a few streets over, rushing past gypsy cabs and Maximas to save somebody else. With my french fry fingers looped in a braid, I wondered how I might get those sirens to come for me.

Maybe I didn't look like I needed help. I kept my braids tight, since Moms had hot dog fingers, short and formless like her waist. She was thick all over from all the eating she'd been doing all my life, trying to get full but only getting fat.

I had only ever known Moms to answer every pain with a bag of chips and all confusion with a fried pie. When she was tired, she ate. When Moms was stressed, in love, broken hearted, angry, happy—whatever. Food was the answer.

She would try to quit food for days and weeks at a time, which was never good for me. That's when her mean side came out. If she was on that Slimfast, she talked down to me like I was a homeless dog that followed her home, talking about how she wished she never had me. I would watch her with the Dexatrim pills, her face in a permanent frown.

I would just do my hair and stare at the street.

▩

Moms had tried putting extensions in a couple times, but the braids always fell out.

"Tasha, girl," she would say to me. "You have your daddy's hair."

Why she bothered to try and blame him, I don't know. Me and Moms had the same stubby coarse hair and I didn't wear the kind of slick black wigs she did, so the fake hair just slipped off. I was nine the year I started doing my own hair, planted on a toilet seat in the P.S. 26 bathroom, holding the dingy, tattered braid that had unraveled and dropped like a hanky full of snot. I fumbled with my hair for thirty minutes and my ass got numb. It wasn't a perfect braid, but at least when I got back to class, I didn't look like some ghetto unicorn with that one section of my hair shooting up from my forehead.

Moms only cared what I looked like when we went to Lego-looking New Jersey once a year. I was the quiet tomboy nerd wearing extra-large T-shirts and jeans that made me look closer to Moms's size. The rest of the Washington clan was pure Jersey suburbs by way of Alabama—country loud, beans cooked in turkey neck and pork.

I sat at the edge of everything, counting the hours until we could leave. While Moms cussed and drank, I parked myself on the plastic-covered couch in Uncle Larry's living room, partway between the kitchen, where a Spades game was already in full swing, and the back porch, where somebody had already lit a joint.

"She used to be a looker like you, Tasha," Uncle Larry said. He had these dimples so deep you could hide quarters in them, and he must've had that couch since he was born. Anytime you sat down on it, it sounded like ripping scotch tape from a wall.

"Boys ran after her so much," he said, shaking his head. "You don't remember this, you were a baby then, but she used to do all that she talked about—running the streets, hitchhiking and shit to get to the Lenox Lounge. You ain't heard that from me, though," he said, dimples tucked in from his secretive smile.

"I won't say nothing."

"Your daddy was one of those shady cats she liked—lots of game—but she barely finished high school when she got pregnant and he left. She blew up after that. She'd just be eating and carrying you around like a football under her arm. That Janet is something else."

"Yeah," was all I said back. The question was what else she was.

"Look after her, Tash," Uncle Larry would say, not knowing it was me who needed looking after. The first thing I noticed heading back into the city was how quiet it had been outside of Uncle Larry's house. The loud honks of cabs and fire trucks greeted us as soon as we walked out of the train, muffled by the roof of Penn Station.

■

Moms couldn't move around without pain from the weight, and her fat made her wheeze while she slept next to me. She only cared about everything above her neck and her feet. She kept a stack of razors in the bathroom cabinet, to peel off her corns and to shave off her eyebrows real neat so she could draw them back on straight.

I would be hearing Uncle Larry's voice in my head, *Take care of her*, when I would sneak some food off her plate in the kitchen. I got bolder as I got older, bored at home after school by myself with just the radio and TV for company. I never knew where she was going, when she was coming back. She was like a sneaky roommate.

She kept the fridge full of leftovers, and this moldy half-eaten ham and cheese sandwich from the corner store tumbled out from in front of two others. I tossed it out, found some leftover corned beef hash, and warmed it up. I fell asleep watching *Square One* on the couch and woke up with the tight pulling of her chubby hand on my ponytail.

"What did you do?" she yelled, snatching me up by my hair. It felt like the hair would rip right from my scalp. "Get up. Get up!"

I leaned into her hand as she yanked me toward the kitchen. She opened the trash lid, holding my ponytail toward the can, like I was a dog she wanted to see the poop it crapped out.

"Mom, let go."

"What the fuck happened that you throwing out food now?"

"It was old. I was just cleaning out the fridge."

I couldn't shake my head without a sharp pain shooting through my scalp. She let my hair go and started punching me hard, like open stinging sores on my skin, warning me not to touch her food again. Her fists on my skin sounded like the start of a storm: hard rain, thunder, lightning, then the slow, fading clap of water, but they felt like hail scraping against my thighs and my arms.

The city was bustling outside, music playing, sirens wailing far off in the distance. I needed them closer, I thought, while I was trying to slip out from underneath her. Maybe it was because I hadn't screamed, because I knew from seeing my cousins get beat that that was just how it was supposed to be—kids got hit, sometimes with switches or cords or curtain rods. While it was happening, I would rap a few lyrics in my head, imagining my body on the fire escape, where I sat when she was sleep. It wouldn't take too long before our bodies ended up rumpled like tossed clothes by the side of the bed where we slept, near the windows with the rusty safety bars.

The next day, the next hour, the next moment, it would be like nothing happened. I knew not to touch her things. From then on, I saved all my cleaning-shit-out for my hair, eating only when Moms came home and then, only a little bit.

▪

At school, it was like the world saw a sign on my back that said, "Kick me, I don't fight back." The year I turned twelve, it started getting me aggravated. When you're weak and don't know how to be strong, it helps to keep your hands busy braiding, but there was only so much keeping my hands busy with that.

Moms would come home and after dinner she'd be slicing at her corns with a razor, watching *Jeopardy*. She would put the old banana-colored skin on a perfectly folded piece of toilet paper before she threw them out. "My dogs are killing me," she would say, rubbing at her callouses. I would just look straight ahead. Wouldn't be so hard to walk if you wasn't so big, but that wasn't something I was brave enough to say.

Moms didn't move real fast but she had a smart mouth. I got that from her.

She got into it with a neighbor once because the lady from 4B said something stupid. Something like "fat man bitch" when we were all walking up the narrow staircase together and Moms was moving slow and breathing heavy. We were about to keep on going up the stairwell when Moms flew behind the couple, pounding her fist on the door like a slab of meat tossed against metal. "You said I look like a man, bitch?"

"Get off my door with that bullshit!" the lady said, her hands touching the hairnet that held her big pink rollers together.

"Say it to my face. Don't you ever talk that way in front of my child again, or it'll be me and you. Come on, Tasha," Moms said to me, waddling back to the steps. The Child Protective Services cat said Moms had mental problems. Bipolar something. She wouldn't take medicine, though. She said medicine was for pussies.

The good thing about Moms beating my ass was that I stopped caring for a while about getting beat up at school. It took a couple of fights before I finally went off. I'd been proud for keeping my temper under wraps, and then one day it just got the best of me.

I saw this one commercial about MedicAlert bracelets, how they could help you in an emergency, so people would know what was wrong with you. All that other shit they sell late at night, it ain't no good—shit to get the dirt from the soles of your feet or make white girl ponytails look fluffy.

But I needed something to tell people what was wrong with me, so they couldn't say they didn't know. Maybe that's why those sirens were always headed past me; they didn't know there was someone who needed them in 4B at Daly Avenue Projects.

The bracelet was $9.99—sterling silver.

The one time I saw a doctor, he did say I had an irregular heartbeat sometimes. He made it sound like my heart hiccupped in my chest. Even my fucking organs weren't reliable.

Anyway, I had the MedicAlert people inscribe that on the inside of my bracelet, so if anybody ever came to save my ass, they would know what happened to me.

I slipped out of bed that night, after Moms started snoring, and put the bracelet on my wrist. I ran my fingers over the top of it, like I was blind trying to read Braille. It was dull silver with a snake in the middle and MedicAlert in red. It felt cool against my wrist. It made me feel wild safe, almost powerful, like I was rocking a low-budget Wonder Woman cuff. I wondered if I could use it to make Moms's knuckles bleed. I made up this little story in my head about how I was a tough girl now, as ghetto and hard as all these other chicks. All I needed was the chance to show off my new superpowers.

▪

I needed the bracelet for more than just Moms, though. This dumb broad named Michelle liked to catch me after school and fuck with me. Michelle was big as hell, bigger than Moms. She probably had the heart of an elk in that big-ass barrel chest. She'd been in sixth grade for like four years, mad as fuck, staring at that same math workbook year after year.

Michelle was like the Puerto Rican version of Macho Man Randy Savage. Even the big kids got punked by Michelle. She wanted your tater tots? Gone. She wanted your wack-ass pizza with bad tomato sauce and too much crust? Housed.

The teacher sat me right next to her in the back of the dummy class. I never got a bad grade at any of the schools I went to, but I'd been to so many, the district said I had to be in the slowest class in the sixth grade.

Michelle sat right next to me, chomping on all the Bubble Yum in the world, spit at the sides of her mouth. Halfway through our spelling test, this gust of sugar wind interrupted me staring out the window.

"Yo, let me see," gum face whispered.

I covered my loose leaf with my arm.

She sat straight up in the cramped chair, taking her gum breeze back with her. "I'ma fuck you up after school," she said.

"Michelle!" Ms. Boswell said her name like it was a curse word.

Michelle sucked her teeth and pretended to write. I got 100. Michelle got a zero.

I should have been proud, but bullies don't fuck around. I should've given her the answers just so I could have some peace, but it was too late.

I thought I was slick, leaving out a side door when school was over, but Michelle spotted me in my worn-out denim jacket and my raggedy jeans with my regular-ass, no-name book bag before I saw her.

She grabbed the hook of the bag with one of her meaty fingers.

"Punk bitch," she said in that husky voice. She sounded just like Moms. She didn't say much else and I knew better than to say anything, either. I didn't fight her back, I just let the beat down happen. Last thing I knew, I was crawling out of the empty dumpster on the far side of the parking lot that doubled as our playground.

"Fuck you," I said to myself while I climbed out. An ambulance raced down Southern Boulevard on the far side of school. Somebody out there was getting rescued.

I went home with old banana smudges on my jeans. Moms didn't go to the Laundromat; it cost too much—all the quarters and the detergent. I washed those jeans in dishwashing liquid like we washed everything else and put them on the radiator to dry. The radiator left these rusty-looking bars on the few clothes we had, like the backs of our bodies were in prison.

"What happened?" Moms asked. She had a razor in her hand, her left foot crossed over her right thigh.

"I fell."

"Girl, be careful," she said. Then she went back to slicing off the rough skin on her heel with the razor.

That bracelet seemed to work, though. Maybe two weeks passed and Moms was calm and we didn't have a test every minute, so I'm thinking that the red snake on the bracelet had power, even if no one noticed me wearing it.

Michelle cornered me in a stairwell on the way out of school one day, anyway, just for fun. She was chewing the hell out of some gum. I pretended to scratch my eyebrow with my right hand to make sure she saw the bracelet. I was wearing a short-sleeved shirt, too, so it was easy to notice.

"I got a heart condition," I said.

"I need candy money," she said, towering over me. This time she smelled like bologna and tropical fruit and sugar.

"All I got is pennies and food stamps," I said.

"Oh, snap, you on welfare?" Her chubby face had a hint of pity in it for a second, then she busted out laughing. "Welfare kid!"

I wanted to call her retarded. Stupid bitch, you been left back since kindergarten. You gonna be a welfare queen when you grow up.

That's what I wanted to say. And then I heard this raspy voice say, "You probably on welfare, too."

We both looked up. It was this white girl, Jeanie. She got to C.S. 67 around the same time I did. She was in the smart class, 6A. She always had fly nails, though—acrylics—and heavy brown braids that weren't extensions braided perfectly even in two rows on either side of her head. She was the only white girl I ever saw in the Bronx, and the only one at school, which is how I knew her name.

"Yo, white girl, shut the fuck up," Michelle said, turning around. "This ain't your business."

I found a $1 food stamp. "You can have it," I said, showing off my MedicAlert bracelet again when I squeezed my arm up through the small alley she left between us.

"Nah, stop playing. I don't want no food stamps," she said, backing off, looking at me like I was a fly distracting her from Jeanie on the top step. "Jeanie, give me some candy money."

Jeanie looked bored. She was digging in her JanSport all calm, like a ninja. She plucked out this bright orange box cutter and flicked up the edge of it. It looked just like the razors Moms kept at home. She didn't say a word, just clicked the black button on the side, showing off the blade without looking at us.

"I got a heart problem," I said again, folding my food stamp and putting it back in my pocket. My bracelet was still dangling from my wrist. I wanted Michelle and Jeanie to know that they couldn't go too far with the box cutter in this dark stairwell without repercussions. "Doctor said if anybody startles me, my heart might give out."

Michelle was standing further away from me now. Jeanie was clicking the blade up and down. Michelle rolled her eyes at Jeanie. "Nah, no beef."

Jeanie stared at her, her mouth in a straight line with the box cutter in her hands.

Michelle turned back to me and said, "Bring real money next time or I'ma beat your ass."

▪

Maybe in rich neighborhoods, girls poison shampoo or put laxatives in your drinks, but in the Bronx, when girls hate girls, they dig their sharp nails into cloves of garlic so that if they pierce the skin on your face, they leave scars that don't heal right. Real hood chicks put razor blades in their braids so that if you pull them, you slice yourself.

At least that's what Jeanie told me at lunch. We started talking all the time at lunch, even though I didn't want to sit with nobody. I was fine solo. I didn't need no extra attention with the white girl on my squad.

I was never pretty, I told her, so I never had to worry about shit like that. Nobody wanted to scar my face or make my short nappy hair fall out. "It don't take much to get people mad 'round here, though," Jeanie said, using the spork to clean dirt out from under her nails. "You gotta do what you need to do."

"I don't want nobody to bleed, though."

"They don't care what happens to you, though, right?"

I just looked at her.

She had a drug dealer boyfriend who went to Clinton. She was wild smart, almost smarter than me, I thought. We would meet up at the library after school and giggle and shit until we got kicked out because they were closing. She slipped some money for food in my book bag a couple of times, too, and I every time I saw her after that, I wanted to give it back but it was already spent.

"Why do you care if Michelle beats me up? You don't know me like that," I said to her after a couple of months. It turned out that Jeanie lived with her uncle and she said she got the box cutter to keep him off her at night.

"I can't stand a bully."

"You mean for a white girl," I said back. And we both laughed.

Jeanie was the one who told me that I needed to get a couple of those razors and braid them into my hair, just in case.

"You crazy," I just said back. But I was thinking about it. It would serve Michelle right for me to cut her hands one day. She would never fuck with me again after that. Plus, I knew where to get some good, sharp razors.

"I take care of me," she answered. "You either fight for you or you ain't a fighter."

▩

Michelle flunked out of C.S. 67, so I never got to test out my bracelet any more on her. I would've been relieved, but bullies are like roaches—you get rid of one and there's always another one that pops up. This one was a chick named Aisha who said she was my friend, which I almost believed until she almost killed me.

Aisha was a beanpole like me with dark brown skin smooth like chocolate sponge cake and soupy eyes. She had a radio with a tape deck and I didn't, so I listened to a lot of music at her house. We would sing along with the radio, her with a brush and me with a comb, then giggle at ourselves for being so dumb. But she stopped being nice when we were in front of other people, like she didn't want people to know she knew me.

We got into it over a bag of Cheez Doodles I was bringing home for dinner. Me and Moms were between welfare checks and out of food stamps. Aisha snatched the bag while we were walking down Tiebout Avenue and said, "Thanks for the chips."

"Stop playing," I said, reaching over to get the bag, but she held it above her head, out of my reach. "Aisha, give it back."

She kept chewing like a cow. I tried to climb up her shirt and shoulder to get closer to the bag, and before I knew it, I fell right on my narrow ass on the sidewalk. Aisha plopped on my chest, to the laughter and cheers of the women around us, like this was the World Wrestling Federation.

I struggled under her weight. "I can't breathe," I gasped. My Medic-Alert bracelet was scraping the ground. I tried to hold it up so she could see. "Get the fuck off me! I can't breathe!"

She eased up, and when she did, I threw my weight around her neck and smacked her on her face. I don't know how long we were fighting, but she started to cry and one of the ladies split us up.

I ran upstairs, brushing off my clothes and catching my breath. I checked my legs and face with my shaking hands and noticed that my bracelet had popped. A lot of good it had done. I shoved it in my back pocket.

Inside the apartment, Moms was watching TV. I wanted to tell her I had finally stood up for myself, but she didn't even look over at me. Now, my damn bracelet was broke and so was I. In the bathroom, there was a fresh pack of razors. I took five.

▩

The more time I spent with Jeanie, the bolder I got. I started wearing my braids in a ponytail, like hers. Just a few weeks before I started at another new school, and Moms got wild again, sweating and pacing in the kitchen. She wanted to know if I was running the street with boys. "I was just with Jeanie," I said, and curled up in bed, watching wind move the sheets she'd nailed to the wall instead of curtains.

I had been braiding razors into my hair like Jeanie told me to, and I reached up into my ponytail to find a couple, flat and sharp against the back of my head.

Moms shuffled toward the bedroom. When she planted herself in the doorway, I was facing her in the fetal position, looking up without saying a word.

"What are you staring at?"

"Don't hit me," I said, my voice shaking.

"I brought you into this world . . . ," she said, getting loud, barreling at me like a cannon. I moved back and she was writhing around in the sheets like a dolphin in a net.

"I'm not gonna let you hit me no more."

Her eyes got wide. "I'll do what I want. I pay the bills, don't you talk back to me! I hate you!" she yelled. "I will fucking kill you in here!" She lifted her right hand to hit me and before I could stop myself, I opened my mouth and bit it.

Her blood was in my mouth. I was as stunned as she was, but my mouth moved into a smile, like I was drunk.

"Don't you ever in your life raise your hands to me," she said, muttering as she stumbled back to the kitchen. She used her left hand to call 911. She stopped wheezing long enough to tell the cops she was bleeding.

My heart was beating loud and uneven in my chest. Moms started to sob, and sunk down to the floor, holding a washcloth over the bite. The moon outside was gone. The streets were silent, no music and no cop cars. Quiet like it was never quiet in the Bronx.

There was a time when I would have gone over and told her it was going to be OK. But after she said that one little word—kill—something in me broke.

"You won't hit me again," I said slowly. I didn't look her in the face. I was looking at a spot between us on the fake linoleum.

"I made you," she whispered huskily, now heaving herself toward me. She looked beached, a tired whale lugging along the floor. She threw her weight on me again, grabbed me, and then began to drag me back along the floor by my hair. Her screams suddenly sliced the silence, as a warm spattering of her blood, like drizzle, fell on my arms. The only thing louder than her screams were the sirens, which had finally come to save me.

Just the Way She Does the Things

Jennine Capó Crucet

The day I got my Honda Civic del Sol—almost two months ago, for my seventeenth birthday—Osniel was over *that night*. And yeah, he talked to me, sang happy birthday and ate cake and pastelitos and whatever, but I caught him later, talking to my dad about what else but Hialeah's Finest. Papi's the reason Osniel ever even talked to me way back in the first grade, because Papi had insisted—*insisted*, Mami says—that they name me Mercedes (If God won't give me a son, the *least* he can do is give me a Mercedes!—he tells the story all the time and without fail on my birthday, like a present I can't return), not realizing that I'd get picked on by boys, the first one ever, after Papi of course, being Osniel.

The night of my birthday, my little brother, Carlos, had put himself in charge of the car hype—he smiled, opened the doors, and ran his hands over the frame like trying to sell it to my cousins and friends. I was letting him do all the talking so that he'd feel like a boy, even though it was my car; even Papi told him, when Carlos had asked when *he* could drive it, that first Carlos would have to ask him, then me. When my brother tried to get everyone to lie on their backs and look underneath the car at the suspension (all my girl cousins refused, but Lazaro from across the street was unbuttoning his shirt), Carla elbowed me and whispered that Osniel wasn't out in the driveway with us anymore, so I went inside.

I found him sitting across from Papi at our dinner table, a little less than half the cake still between them, Papi picking at it straight from the box with a fork. As he chewed, he stared at Mami, who was still at the sink rinsing plates. Her back was to us; her waist looked narrow compared to her butt, which was kind of huge, square-shaped, jutting toward us like a shelf. I could tell Papi only half-listened to Osniel as he watched Mami from his grin, betraying himself and showing a few crooked teeth. Papi didn't have a shirt on, just his blue shorts, and yellow crumbs sat in the wires of his chest hair. I brushed them off for him, onto the floor. He looked down at my hand, stared at his big stomach for a second, sucked his teeth, then just kept eating cake and running his tongue over the whole fork, licking off frosting while Osniel talked.

"Señor," he said, looking down all shy (and calling Papi "sir" *in Spanish* because Osniel's *such* a suck-up). "Señor, you know how it is—it's not just about cars—it's la comunidad, Señor."

My dad had been in a car club when he was our age—Osniel knew that, as did everyone in our neighborhood. A lot of other people's dads had been in some sort of car club or gang before we came along. Osniel had heard enough stories about it from Lazaro's and Danny Garcia's dads (who, between the two of them, made up almost one whole dad for Osniel, whose dad nobody—not even Osniel—had ever seen or met) to figure out he could get to *my* dad if he did it through cars. But Hialeah's Finest is as local as a car club can get, basically just this neighborhood—nobody from *East* Hialeah is even in it yet. The guys who founded it (Lazaro from across the street, two houses down, and Danny Garcia, my girl Carla's boyfriend of eleven whole months) have no aspirations to go countywide. I joke to Osniel that Hialeah's Finest is made up of guys whose cars aren't hot enough to get them into Miami E.L.I.T.E. or Xplicit ILLusionz (Osniel's right that they're tacky, but still, they're big, and picky, even if it's in a tacky way). But to be fair, Hialeah's Finest doesn't have those mad fees that the other ones do, so members can put that money into their cars instead. At least that's what Osniel says, but if you ask me, Osniel talks *too* much, especially to my dad.

"Forget it, Osniel," I said, smiling.

"Girl, you don't even know what we're talking about."

He leaned back in the chair and winked at me because Papi was focused on his frosting. Mami warned Papi three times a day that God would send him diabetes if he didn't watch himself. She'd said she would *not* cry when God sent him a heart attack; what else could God do with a heart full of fried platanos? Papi would just laugh and ask for more of whatever he was eating, and Mami would bring it. And if it was dessert, she'd bring two spoons.

I said, "What else do you talk about besides Hiale—"

Papi put his hand up flat in my face, stopped me from finishing, didn't even look at me. Then he leaned forward, his belly pressing onto the glass tabletop, and carved out another hunk of cake too big for the fork. He sat back in his chair.

"You think a Honda del Sol is car club material?" Papi said toward the surviving cake. "Ha, shit!"

"Come on, Mr. Reyes. Seriously, Hondas are hot right now. They're *sporty.*"

If I'd been allowed to talk, I would've agreed with him. The Civic del Sol is a '95, used but in good condition, black on black with red trim. My dad had spent weeks looking through Auto Traders to find one with decent miles on it. Papi finally picked out a hard-top convertible, super cute, and he told me it was fun to drive—he test drove it while I rode shotgun. The car definitely *looked* sporty. And according to 95 percent of Hialeah High, Osniel's car was supposedly the shit; he'd been bragging about his Civic since tenth grade, even before he got his learner's permit. When we were in Driver's Ed together, he'd talk up his new hi-gloss paint job, or those chrome spider rims, so much that he'd miss when the teacher called for his row of drivers to drive. He *never* paid attention and failed the weave twice.

"That's a four-cylinder engine, Osniel. What type of sporty is that?"

Papi laughed, and so did Osniel.

"It's all about looks now. And with that loud-ass muffler? Besides, Hialeah's Finest doesn't race."

They don't do much of anything, I wanted to say.

Papi laced his fingers behind his head. Little flakes of deodorant coated the ends of his armpit hairs. It looked like powdered sugar. Osniel raised his arms and did the same thing, but his sleeves didn't let me see if he even *had* armpit hair.

"A car club that *doesn't race*? Well, shit," Papi said. "At least it's safe then."

Yeah right, I wanted to say.

"I'm just putting it out there, Mr. Reyes. No fees or *nothing.*"

Osniel leaned forward and stuck his finger in the yellow icing at the corner of the cake and pushed a whole big chunk of it in his mouth, pulling his finger out real slow. Then he looked at me and said, "But I guess it's really up to Mercy, right?"

Papi kind of snorted and said, "Sure, sure. But I'm okay with it, mi'jo."

Papi pushed his chair back and stood, taking another forkful of cake to go, and said to me, "Is Carlos outside?"

"Yeah, showing off," I said.

"Sounds *sporty*," Papi said.

He put his hand on my shoulder and squeezed it as he passed behind my chair to go outside, leaving me there with Osniel. Papi's flat feet made little sucking sounds on the tile on his way to the front door, and he held his lower back like it hurt, or like he was pregnant. He yelled for my mom to come help him get rid of all the party people.

"Mami! Come help me get rid of all these people! Jesus Christ already!" he said.

She dried her hands with the bottom of her T-shirt as she walked over to him and said, "It's not even ten o'clock yet!" When she got close enough to him, she wiped her hands on his chest even though they were almost dry. He said, "Hey, C'mon!" and slapped her butt. She pretended to squirm away from him, saying in a fake squeaky voice, "What? What I do?"

Osniel came around to my side of the table, dragging his pointer finger right across the top of the cake this time—right through the word *Felicidades*—scooping another finger-full of frosting. He sat down next to me in Papi's chair and looked at the fluff of merengue balancing at the edge of his finger. Then he smiled at it.

I grabbed him by the wrist and said, "Don't you even *think* about it." He wrestled with me, and I screamed high like a stupid girl. Then he pulled the frosted finger away from me, getting his hand as far from me as he could.

"Okay, okay, you baby," he said.

I smoothed out my hair in case it had gotten messy just then, tucked it behind my ears. Osniel's shirt said *Polo Sport* in graffiti letters and I was trying to think of a joke to keep him paying attention to me. I had known Osniel since before I could talk, but now in high school we were in different levels of English class, so I had to be careful not to sound too nerdy.

Then he said, "Aight, I'm out, Mercy."

"Huh?" I looked up from his chest.

"I'm gonna take off, girl." He stood and leaned toward me, kissed me on the top of my head while I sat there. "Happy birthday," he said. Then quick, he slid away but moved his hand in close and smeared the frosting on my nose—almost *up* my nose—and he stuck the rest in his mouth as he ran toward my front door. And before I could even get up to try to catch him, he turned back around and cracked up, pulling at his belt with one hand to keep his baggy jeans from sliding down as he ran, the finger from his other hand still in his mouth.

■

Since then, Osniel messes with me every day at school about Hialeah's Finest. He makes this bad joke about me doing my *Civic duty* every morning in homeroom—he's not even *in* my homeroom, he just comes by to tell me before showing up late to his. The only class I have with him is Spanish. We're actually in Spanish II, which is where they put people who *already* speak Spanish but are stuck because the county requires you to take a language to graduate, but our school *only* offers Spanish. We sit next to each other and ignore Mrs. Gomez hardcore. She's super old and yells all the time about us speaking Spanglish and that everything's being lost. But she's got enough kids in there that are right off the boat to keep her happy—I swear most of them got here like last week, their Spanish is so perfect.

Today, during Mrs. Gomez's class, I super casually asked Osniel to grab food with me, just us two (though my del Sol only fits two people, so I don't know if he knows that I *want* it to be just us, or if that's just the way it is because it's not like there's *options*). But once we were in my car, he started up with the same noise about Hialeah's Finest. The car did look amazing—my dad had detailed it himself. He'd even cleaned parts of the display and the ridges on the stereo's volume knob with a toothbrush, all before I woke last Sunday.

"Damn, Mercy," Osniel said, running his hand across the black ArmorAlled dash. "When are you gonna hook up with us?"

I felt my hands get really sweaty on the steering wheel because he said *hook up* but I had a decent joke ready that time.

"Why do I have to hook up with anyone? Why can't I just be independent, like in politics?"

He blinked. Then he said, "*What*?"

"Like the parties—political ones—when you register? To vote? The Democrats and Republicans—because there's sides—not that there's sides with car clubs, but I mean, you gotta pick—you gotta register as something, but you can be independent, too—or, I mean, instead."

As I said this, *explained* this, I wanted him out of the car so I could whack my head against the steering wheel until I blacked out and forgot how to speak. He looked at me with his eyebrows scrunched up and his head tilted sideways, like either *I'm* the biggest idiot in the world, or *he's* the biggest idiot in the world. His mouth kind of opened a little and I'm thinking, Please just don't say anything please don't please.

"Oh. Kay," he said. He was trying not to laugh.

He turned completely in the seat, looked at me. He had the longest eyelashes. I was so close to his face I could see the dark brown dots of hair growing in thick all around his mouth and on his broad cheeks and I had to clutch the steering wheel *so* tight to keep my hands from rubbing up and down the hairless blank lines between the mustache and chin, like my fingers could make the connections grow somehow.

"Taco Bell? For lunch?" he said.

Whatever you want, I wanted to say. I love you, I wanted to say. I wanted to grab his face, kiss him so hard right there in my car, and then never get out of the driver's seat—sleep there, even, to keep him kissing me in my head.

I smiled—I think—shrugged, and backed out of the parking space.

▪

We hit the Taco Bell drive-thru.

"For $2.99 you eat like a king," he told me. I laughed even though he says this every time we get Taco Bell.

Power 96, the only hip-hop station that also plays Spanish hip-hop and some trance, plays my favorite Freestyle song, "Love in Love," every day in the Power Lunch Hour MegaMix, and it came on just as we pulled into a spot to eat our food. I convinced him the dining room was packed with people we don't want to deal with, but really I just wanted us to be alone. I covered it up by warning him he better watch my interior and handing him like fifty napkins. Then he did the kind of thing that keeps me watching his house from my bedroom window all the time, one of those moments that I replay in my head so many times that it makes me cry because I start to worry that I made it up, it's so perfect.

One of the things he does that makes me go, This *has* to be more than hanging out, more than just my car.

The song came on and Osniel, halfway through his first burrito, grabbed the second one still wrapped up and started *singing* into it like a microphone, doing this jerky side-to-side dance that looked like one guy doing the wave by himself.

"*Love in love, we are so on fire. Love in love, yeah I'm talkin' 'bout me and you.*"

He was really singing this to me, opening his mouth wide to show me his food and making gagging noises in between the verses. I had to pretend I was all grossed out by the ball of beans and cheese and sauce and spit he made dance on his tongue.

"*Cuz you're just the way I want the thing, because I know my girl is you.*"

These were not the right words (Osniel's got the words mixed up—the main guy in the group sings, *Cuz it's just the way she does the things, sometimes I worry love's untrue*), but I didn't care, because I liked Osniel's words better anyway. I didn't want to point out he sang the wrong thing because then he'd tell me, So what, he was just joking. He started scratching an imaginary turntable and shoved the wrapped burrito in my face for me to sing the back-up echo parts (*On fire, on fire, in love*).

The song ended (we both yelled, *Miami Freestyle in the house!*—the very last words) and we laughed big time—the kind that's so hard you don't even make a sound—and he smacked the dashboard a couple times, leaving a sweaty print of his whole hand on the Dad-cleaned dash. I grabbed a handful of napkins and tucked them under the bar of the emergency brake, so that I remembered to rub the hand off before my dad could notice.

I wiped under my eyes and said, "Thanks for the serenade—that was beautiful."

"All for you," he said. He winked and reached over toward my arm and at first I thought he was trying to put his arm around me, or maybe tickle my side. But instead he pinched me, hard. I swear he twisted the skin—it made my eyes water. He did this as he took another bite of burrito. Some red sauce dripped from the corner of his mouth.

I still have the dime-sized bruise on my arm because I saw it the day after, and I thought, That's what he's like on me. And when it starts to fade, I pinch myself in the same spot just as hard or harder. I don't stop twisting that soft spot on the back of my arm until I cry from how much it hurts because that's the only way I know I'm doing it hard enough to make it colorful again. Every day before getting in the shower, I stand in front of the mirror and lift my arm over my head and stare at it—a greenish yellow kiss. I press into it with my thumb to make it throb. I close my eyes and let my hand fall, tracing the rest of me, imagining my body covered with all these little spots, watching Osniel push them into me one by one.

▒

Once the song finished, once I'd parked and locked the doors, he said to me, "Mercy, for real, when you gonna come around to me?" and I swear I almost died right there until I realized he really meant joining the stupid-ass car club. But I was good—I threw my keys in the air and caught them (very smooth) and when I tucked them in my backpack, my hair tumbled down over my shoulder all dramatic like in some Spanish soap opera. He even reached over and tugged on it.

"Whatchu getting into this weekend?" he said.

"Whatever," I said. "No real plans—I have to call Carla."

My backpack started to slip off my shoulder, but he was looking at the ground right then and didn't notice how it pulled my tank top weird across my chest, shifting my boobs so that one looked higher than the other. I hoisted my bag up before he noticed.

"We should hang out," he said.

Like on a date? I wanted to say. But I just kind of nodded, the car between us.

"Aight, I'll call you then, to see wassup," he said.

He jingled his keys in his pocket.

"Yeah, okay," I said. But he had started walking away to his car.

He had parked a few spots down, but still in the part of the lot close enough to the school to be safe. Get too far into the public lot and your ride will be on blocks when you come out. Lazaro used to park out far to keep people from keying his Integra. I told him the best way to stop that was to quit pissing people off, but he just laughed and made fun of me for trying to be on everyone's good side all the time. (Carla didn't talk to him for two days for saying that to me.) And then one afternoon, we came out for lunch and the back two rims—I swear he had them on the car for like an hour, they were so new—were just *gone*, just two concrete blocks holding up the ass of the car. He wanted to beat the crap out of the school security people, but even *they* know better than to mess with people so set on getting some rims. Osniel told my dad about it, and ever since, Papi warns me every morning while I'm backing out of our driveway to park close to the school. The safest place for the car, Papi says, is in our driveway, locked behind the chain-link fence. Which is where it will sit all weekend, while I watch the phone.

▩

Mom jokes I'm praying to the cordless, I'm so all over it. I carry the receiver to the bathroom with me, resting it on a towel on the toilet while I shower.

"No one uses this phone," I announce to my family Friday night at dinner, pointing to the cordless sitting between the picadillo and the congrí on the table.

Papi has no idea what's with me and says, "What's with her?" to Mami. Mami shrugs and then winks at me when Papi looks back down at his food. Carlos ignores the wink and launches into his list of reasons why Ricky Alviar's bullying might force him to drop out of sixth grade. Through the glass table I see Mami's toes wiggling, tickling Papi's ankle. He smiles at his rice then stomps on her toes with his heel. She stomps right back. They keep playing this game until Carlos says, "Listen! He's trying to destroy me!" and moves around to their side of the table to show Mami what he claims is a pencil lead stuck in his palm.

▩

I tell myself that if by nine he hasn't called, he's not going to. So at nine-thirty, I really give up and go to my bedroom, to my window. I shut the door and turn off the lights, and at the window I close the blinds but leave them raised about two inches from the bottom. Then I crouch down on my knees to look, my fingers and nose pressed to the cold tile on the windowsill. This is where I watch him from.

If I push my face into the window and look hard to the right, I can see the back of his house. His is the corner one, three down and across the street, facing the opposite side of the road that intersects mine. I know which room is his, and I can see his window—it faces my house. I can see when the light goes on and off. It's off right now, so I stand up again and get the notebook with the red pen hooked into the spiral from under my mattress and write on the next line, *Friday, 9:30. NOT HOME (?).*

And then I wait. And I watch, and I don't move just in case he's looking back from the bottom of his own window (even though I *know* he's not).

This was how I got Osniel to drive me to school back before I had my del Sol: I'd get up early in the mornings—way earlier than him—and watch for when his light would turn on (because he was awake) and when it would go off (because he was leaving for school). I'd get up early enough so that I was all the way ready—dressed, eye-liner on and not smudged, hair smooth, books in my bag—so that all I had to do was watch and figure out when he'd be coming outside so I could walk by at that exact minute and he'd offer me a ride. Too early and I was on the bus. He made me work for it too, because he went through some stretches last year where he'd just skip all the time—two, three times a week—and I'd have to give up and go because I hadn't seen his light *at all* and I wouldn't make the bus if I waited any longer. But I took good notes and got down even his skipping patterns eventually.

Kneeling there in my room, my knees and calves start to burn, so I shift forward and lean on the sill. Osniel's got to be out with Danny Garcia, because Lazaro's car (a lot easier to see from the window than Osniel's place because he's basically across the street) is in the driveway, and the kitchen light is on, so they got to be eating dinner. His dad's work van is there, too, and that means Lazaro's *got* to be home. Carla had not called me, but I knew she was home; impossible as it sounds, her parents are stricter than mine, so on Fridays she can't go out with Danny Garcia unless I go as a chaperone. Which just leaves Danny Garcia—unless Osniel's out with someone I don't know, which can't be it because we've always rolled with the same people.

Whenever I watch and I start to get tired, or feel my chin go numb from pressing it in the sill, I think about just getting into bed. But I know better. I can't leave the window because the minute I leave, the next second, I know the light will go on in Osniel's room and I'll miss it.

▩

His Civic's engine works like an alarm for me, and I don't know what time it is, but he had finally passed by, home from wherever he was. I lift my head up from the windowsill in time to see him turn onto his street, and maybe two minutes later I see his bedroom light go on and then off again. So I cross out the question mark behind *NOT HOME* in my notebook and draw a dash and write, *Gets home LATE—in bed FAST.* I shove the pen in the spiral and stuff the notebook back under the mattress. I can hear Carlos watching TV in his room—something with a heavy-duty laugh track—and my dad snoring down the hall. My mom interrupts the steady, smooth rumble when she half-yells, "Papi, *please*! Roll over! Dear *God*!" Then I hear Papi grunting back, "I'm not snoring, that's you." Then Mami laughing, then the smacks and thumps of their pillows as they pummel each other with them to figure out who's right. The snores stop for only a few minutes, and when they come back, they're muffled.

Flopping on my stomach onto the bed, I think, If Osniel is drunk, he's falling asleep face down, just like this.

▩

He never calls that weekend, though I watch him from my window do something—can't tell what—to the engine of his car. It takes him a while, and he keeps having to knock on Lazaro's door to borrow tools from his dad.

In the afternoon, I go out to our driveway, where my dad's just changed the oil on the del Sol even though I've barely put any miles on it. He's put in some new windshield washer fluid that's supposedly better than whatever was in there. I can't see Osniel's house at all from our driveway.

I stand next to my dad and lean over the engine. He's cleaned it up, replaced the original hoses with braided lines—the kind that have steel reinforcements—and he's put in these chrome valve covers and header tubes. The whole thing shines. I think, Who's even going to *see* this other than him and me? Looking at all that chrome, hidden to everyone else when he closes the hood, I shift a little closer to him, but after a second he moves to keep the space between us the same.

"You like it," he says.

It isn't really a question—he takes the towel tucked in his back pocket and wipes around where the washer fluid goes.

"It's *sporty*," I say, but I laugh and so does he. And because he seems okay with my joke, I say, "Papi, I think it looks cool, but no one's gonna see it. I'm afraid to even open the hood cuz what if I don't close it right? What if I scratch up the paint?"

He wipes his hands with the towel and says, "Then don't open it. Even though I already showed you how to make sure it's closed, you just listen for it to click—but don't open it, if you're scared. You shouldn't need to open it anyways. And the less you open it, the less chance you have of scratching the paint. The paint people see."

He shuts the hood, letting it slam, so that any click it made I didn't hear. He rubs the towel over the edge of the hood, over scratches that will never be there.

"You just have to be careful," he says. "You won't scratch it if you don't play around—it's not a toy. I didn't buy it for you to play games."

He swirls the towel over the same places he's just wiped. He leans down close to the hood, squints, blows at some speck, squints again, then wipes at the spot with the towel wrapped around his pointer finger. He presses so hard it sounds like a squeegee. I fold my arms across my chest even though it's very hot and we're both sweating.

I say, "I'm careful. I'll be careful."

I worry he thinks I don't like the engine, so I add, "You want some water or something?"

He grabs my arm, so hard he might bruise me, his rough hands scratching my skin. He kisses me on the top of my head, a loud, smacking kiss. Then he pretends to bite my head, making fake growls, and I can feel his crooked top teeth digging into my scalp.

"Let go," I pretend cry.

He holds me out away from him, squeezing my arm even harder, grinning and growling at the same time.

When he finally frees me, I can make out every finger of his hand, glowing red on my upper arm.

"Yeah, water," he says, and he pushes me on the shoulder toward the house and I pretend to stumble.

"Tell Mami to make me café," he yells when I grab the doorknob. I look back at him, and he wipes his hands with the towel again and smiles.

As I pull the door closed behind me, there on my outstretched arm is Papi's handprint, still clear but starting to fade. The red parts had turned white; now it looked like all he'd left was an outline. I stare at it for a second and then decide not to shut the door all the way. I leave it a little open so I can hear him, even if he'll yell later that I let mosquitoes in the house.

Mom is already walking into the kitchen.

"People three blocks away can hear when your father wants café," she says.

She hugs me and gives me a kiss on the cheek as she walks past me to the sink. I grab a clean glass from the cabinet and stand next to her, waiting for the water to run colder so that I can be lazy and not have to refill the ice trays.

We watch my dad pace around the car from the kitchen window. He looks hard at all four tires, then opens the driver's side door and reaches in, and the hood of the car pops up a little. He comes back out, leaving the door open, and grabs the edge of the hood with his hand, which is draped in the towel to prevent finger prints.

"Is that one of my *kitchen* towels?" Mom says. "Dear God, give me strength."

I watch Papi open the hood, then close it, softly, bending down a little with his ear to the car. Then he goes back to the driver's seat and pops the hood again. He does the whole thing over again. As Mami keeps staring, I say, "Let me make the café, huh? I can do it." But even though the car's hood barely makes a sound, Mami doesn't hear me.

"What is he doing?" Mom says. "Your father and his games."

She packs the coffee into the cafetera, fills the bottom with water, and sets it on the stove. I fill the glass with water, and when I look up from the sink, Papi is on his fourth shutting of the hood. From outside, he gives me a thumbs-up. He even winks and says, "It clicks—you barely hear it, but I hear it—click!"

"Clickclickclick!" Mami says like a bratty kid. "I bet you that glass of water he loves that car more than us."

But she doesn't know what Papi is talking about, and he doesn't let her in on it, at least not then. Right then, me and him are the only ones who know what he means.

I yell through the crack I left in the door, "Hey, Papi, how much ice?"

▩

On Monday, Osniel talks to me in Spanish class like nothing happened, like it's not a big deal that he said he'd call but didn't. I went to bed the night before so pissed that I didn't even bother to wake up early to watch his light come on that morning.

"What's up your ass, Mercy?"

I don't even look at him.

"Nothing. Why?"

"You so quiet with me today, I dunno."

"Hmm." I shrug.

I curl my fingers around the edge of the desk, *into* the desk—my nails could cut the fake wood (if I *had* any nails). I grind my teeth and I almost listen to Mrs. Gomez. But I can't take my hands and teeth feeling so tight, and a minute later I turn toward him and ask him what I want to ask him.

"Osniel?"

"'Sup?" he says, pointing his chin at me and smiling.

"How come a guy says he's gonna call you but then doesn't?"

He sits up and looks around our classroom. He squints at Danny Garcia, on the other side at the back of the room, who is trying to get Carla to sit on his lap. He squints at Lazaro, who's asleep on his desk.

"*Who* said they were gonna call you?"

He sounds almost mad. He leans forward in the desk quick, like a reflex. He holds himself there, his eyes darting around my face, just *inches* from me. He's closer to my mouth than the day we went to Taco Bell together, closer than he's ever let himself be to me. I smile and look down so he can't see me trying not to smile.

"I'm just asking," I say.

He shakes his head no. "Mercedes Beatriz Reyes," he says. "Mercy. You know how we do. It's all part of the game, mama."

I say, like an echo, "The game."

He just has this big-toothed grin on his face. I let go of the desk. I look down at my hands—my nails chewed on and weak. They're so short, pushed so back into my fingers that I bet it would hurt to open the hood of my car. There isn't even any white part left to bite off. Something clicks for me, in my head—I can barely hear it. So I ask.

"Osniel," I say, "Hialeah's Finest? Is it really about the car? Or is it about me?"

He sits there quiet for one second too long, and then says, "Pshh," and forces a laugh. He leans back in the chair, yanking his face away from mine. He puts both arms out, his palms flat on the desk, raises his shoulders a little, and locks his elbows. He doesn't look at me, but looks straight ahead like Mrs. Gomez had just called on him. He wrinkles his eyebrows like he did that day we went to lunch and he sang to me.

Osniel finally looks at me straight in the face.

"Why would a car club be about anything other than cars?" he says.

I turn back toward the front of the class and I hadn't noticed until then that I'd been holding my breath. From across the room, Carla says, "Danny, stop it," and up at the board, Mrs. Gomez yells, "Por Favor! Atención, mis hijos." And I stare at her to keep from looking back at Osniel. When I start breathing again, I know I'm going to puke or cry, so I grab my bag and go up to Mrs. Gomez and ask for a pass to the bathroom. I don't even wait for her to fill it out all the way. I tear the yellow slip from her hands and rush out of the room, and Carla's screaming, "Osniel! What the fuck did you say to her? What the fuck is wrong with you?" The door shuts behind me, and down the hall I still hear Mrs. Gomez—"Asientos! Todos, take your seats!"

I run past the girls' bathroom, past the lockers and down the stairs, out past the portables where the freshmen have classes, out to the parking lot. I walk up to Osniel's car. It's so red and he has the perfect rims—complicated webs of chrome, almost impossible to keep clean, every right to brag—and he's got the official Honda seatbelt shoulder padding on both the driver *and* passenger sides.

In all the time I've known him and this Civic, I've never seen the engine close up—no clue what it looks like, what he's done to it. I wonder if there's any chrome under the hood, whether he'd show it off to me or not. I didn't need him to see it; I could break into his car, lift up the hood myself—my dad had taught me to pick locks when I was little, in case I ever lost my house key. When he was Osniel's age, my dad could hot-wire anything. Mami still tells stories about Papi siphoning gas from cars parked in front of house parties, about showing up at her school—ditching his own classes—so they could sit together in his Chevy Challenger during her lunch period. He'd refuse to unlock the door and made her late to fifth period so many times that the teacher had called her house. Once, in the middle of the night, Mami's neighbor caught Papi pouring sugar in his son's fuel tank, just because the guy'd sat next to her in the cafeteria three days in a row. Mami never admits how all this hurt—or helped—Papi's chances with her. She says she tells me these stories to warn me about guys like Papi, to stay away from them because they only do damage. And when I said, "Yeah, but you married that guy," she said, "Mercy, please, Papi is different. He's your father, he loves you." And from the way she avoids looking at me when she says this, I sometimes think she's bragging.

I reach into my bag and get closer to the car. I pull out my keys, hold them firm, out from my thigh, and walk past the car, down the length of it. The metal scraping metal sounds quieter than I'd thought it would. I scrunch my eyes at the screech anyways, a skinny ribbon of red paint peeling off, then turning to flakes as it falls away from the car, away from my keys. I don't look at the car as I do it—I can't—because I don't want to get caught like Papi did with the sugar. So I wait until I'm done keying Osniel's paint, and a few feet away, before I look back at the damage.

The line is a thin, crooked path from the front bumper straight to me. The rims and wheels looked wasted on his car now, like he knows his car is sad and he's trying too hard. A pinstripe done by a blind guy—that's what I bet my dad'll call it when he sees Osniel's car pass our house later. And maybe that's what I'll tell Osniel, if he ever asks what I was going for.

I can finally breathe right once I slide into my front seat, but my hands won't stop shaking. I hold them out in front of me; shiny red chips stick to the sweat on my palm. I don't brush them off on my jeans—I keep them on me, the stubborn flakes itching a little and sparkling. After curling my fingers over the specks to protect them, I stick the key in the ignition with my other hand. I throw my Civic in reverse and steer out of the spot, doing it all one-handed, riding out like a pimp or a gangster. And even though Papi has told me a million times this is *not* the safe way to drive—that God gave me two hands and won't think twice about taking one back if I don't keep both on the steering wheel *at all times*, Papi says—I do it anyways just to keep Osniel's fist shut. I drive home going way faster than I should because I need to beat Papi home—I don't want him to catch me acting stupid, with only one hand on the wheel after everything he's told me. Maybe—if I have enough time before Mami asks, "And school?" and Papi asks, "Any car problems?" like they do every day, talking over each other because they know they're asking the same thing—maybe I'll even wash my hand.

The Great Pretenders

Ashley Young

For my father and Trayvon Martin

11:00 a.m.

Dayne woke to the usual sound of racket and litigation. She never remembered to turn off the TV after the evening news, and every day since the start of her "vacation," she awoke to the sounds of the Trayvon Martin trial.

She rolled her brown, bald head into the comforter and faced the tiny bedroom window that overlooked her New York City neighborhood. The tambour of George Zimmerman's lawyer questioning a witness came in clear, though her ears were still adjusting to sound.

It was the day before closing arguments. Zimmerman's lawyers were pushing for an acquittal, dismissal of witness testimony, the entry of murder reenactments—anything the jury could view that could convince them he shot Martin in self-defense. The Florida state prosecutor—a handsome, blue-eyed, dark-haired lawyer predicted to woo the all-female jury—spent the last round of cross-examination theorizing about Zimmerman's motives.

Dayne had been watching the trial for days. It was hard to shake the shrill voices of news commentators speculating whether Zimmerman acted out of his own racist assumptions when he shot and killed a black, hoodie-clad teenager or if he was honestly defending himself against imminent danger.

It wasn't as if she hadn't experienced being followed herself. Slightly androgynous, Dayne sported hoodies over her long, curvy frame during her college days trolling the University of North Carolina's campus with her peers. But when she ventured into the surrounding neighborhoods in her solid-black hoodie, she suddenly warranted stares, and white women crossed the street to get away from what they assumed was a tall, menacing black man. And if she ever thought of entering a store, there was always a clerk following close behind, asking if she needed help while watching her every move.

In those days, she'd just chuckle at their ignorant behavior. But watching the trial, she considered herself lucky that her often mistaken gender but unmistaken race had never led to violence.

The constant streams of Trayvon's photo between trial breaks made Dayne's stomach turn. To calm her nerves, she rose from her bed to the kitchen to put on a pot of coffee, a workday habit she couldn't seem to break. Next to the coffeemaker, the answering machine flashed a bright red "2" in the messages-received box. Dayne knew she was the last woman in the city with an answering machine, but she kept it; it was her way of keeping in touch with her father.

He'd left his daily message, the one she listened to every morning as the coffee brewed. He'd been trying to say he missed her since she left for New York City a year ago, but instead, had only been able to rant about current events and the weather. Even so, the rattle of his husky voice reminded her of home.

"Hope you're watching the trial. Damn shame what that man did to that kid. Fifteen and armed with a soda and a pack of Skittles—and Zimmerman requests an acquittal? This coming from a lawyer who opened the trial with a joke? Dayne, honey, just 'cause we got a black president in the White House don't mean a black boy can't get shot down for fitting some idiot's profile . . . Well, I'm off to the site. Foreman's got me working six men on this job and your old man's gotta beat the sun . . . Okay, I'll be talking to ya."

Dayne smiled as she shook her head. She could see him tucking his shirt into work jeans with his shoulder supporting the rotary phone, watching the same TV set he'd had since she was a kid. But when her eyes looked back at the trial returning to session, her mouth turned flat. She knew her father was right.

Race politics keep this world crazy, she thought as she poured a cup of coffee.

The next message was from Sachin, the first friend Dayne had made in the city. Ever since he had declared himself her official New York tour guide, his messages were always friendly, slightly formal requests to meet. Dayne suspected it might by his coy way of trying to date her but he'd never made a move, which suited her just fine.

Dayne got back in bed with her coffee and returned to the trial. She couldn't decide if she would be up for being social after her three o'clock therapy appointment.

2:45 p.m.

Dayne missed her fifteen-minute window to try and hail a cab. Even though she could have taken the subway, she was running behind and assumed a cab would be faster—but she hadn't accounted for the number of cabs that would pass once they noticed her complexion.

She quickly slipped into jeans and a T-shirt, gathered her bag, and headed out onto Broadway. The thick, garbage-ridden heat hit her temples as she opened the front door, and Dayne fought back nausea as she walked to the street's corner.

She stood at the corner, shifting her weight in her boots and waving her hands to the passing cars. Every time she attempted to hail a cab, she couldn't help but feel like she was back in Ms. McGregor's first grade classroom, wildly waving her hand with all the answers but never being called on. She shook the memory as she noticed the time on her watch.

Yellow cabs whizzed by like an angry horde of bees. If the cab wasn't already full, the driver would slow, take a glance at Dayne, then speed away as if her very presence were offensive.

Dayne crossed the street in hopes of catching one at the opposite corner, only to see a white man in a collared shirt and khakis take the place where she'd once stood. Suddenly, horns honked as a cab buzzed through three lanes just to get to the corner's new occupant. Dayne watched, her hand still hanging in the air.

You have got to be kidding me.

The cab sped away while Dayne's arm twinged with pain. She shook it, adjusted her bag where sweat marks had collected under her shirt, then took a deep breath and began again.

Dayne was seconds away from sending a "Running late" text when she noticed an older white woman watching her. The woman had bright red hair and was awkwardly stork-like in her miniskirt, wobbly from stomping her pumps against asphalt. She was neither frumpy nor pretty, but determined-looking, with a frown that transmitted Dayne's own frustration.

"This is disgraceful," she said, gently moving Dayne aside and holding out her long, pale arm. "In this day and age, you can't catch a cab? It's disgusting. I can't believe it."

Dayne couldn't help but feel embarrassed and made little eye contact as her new cab-flagging ally cursed about "a fucked-up racist society." They stood for a few minutes before a cab pulled up.

The woman stepped back and opened the passenger door for Dayne.

"Where you going, sweetheart?" Her voice was still sharp from cursing.

"Broadway and 42nd."

"You heard the lady," the woman yelled to the driver in the open window. "Broadway and 42nd."

Dayne finally looked the woman in her bright blue eyes and offered her a quiet "thank you."

"You're welcome," the woman said as the cab drove away, "and I'm sorry."

3:00 p.m.

On the ride over, Dayne bit her lip to fight tearing up.

Shit. That was the most decent thing a white woman has done for me in a while.

Then she thought of her boss.

Dayne worked as the assistant of the media and marketing department for an independent gallery on the Lower East Side. It was curated by Vanessa Waters—daughter of art philanthropist Author Waters—a pale-skinned woman in her sixties who, after years of gilding on her father's coattails, decided to start a small business of her own.

Dayne found the part-time, hourly gig in the city paper and highlighted the fact that it could lead to "potential full-time employment." She could hear Vanessa's shrill voice the day she was hired, filled with promises of "income increases" based on Dayne's "progress and improvement over time." But now Dayne questioned whether Vanessa was blind to the efforts she'd made. Dayne worked three gallery events in one week and tolerated Vanessa's increasingly rigorous demands before she requested a "mental health week." Dayne hadn't told anyone she'd taken the days in hopes of never returning.

No one knew except for her therapist, Janice.

When the cab came to a stop at 42nd, she meagerly tipped the driver and crossed the street to Janice's building. Her office was in the penthouse, a small corner suite down a hall of reception desks.

She'd been seeing Janice since she moved to New York. When the daily drone of city life shocked her into insomnia, Dayne answered an ad for a private, affordable therapy practice. By doing so, Dayne had to shed an inherited shame: Dayne's father rarely showed emotions, and as an unabashed daddy's girl, she'd always followed suit. This wasn't helped by the fact that he'd always lamented in his slow southern drawl, "White people deal with their problems with therapy and medicine. Us black folks just learn to live with them." So she'd never told him she was becoming accustomed to the catharsis of her weekly confessions, convinced she could get much better advice from a woman she paid to listen to her talk. Some days, she felt like Janice was the closest thing to her.

Dayne approached the open door of Janice's office and headed to her place on the coach near the window. Janice was sitting at her desk when she came in.

"Welcome, Dayne," she said with a small smile. "Let me finish up these patients' notes, and I'll be right with you."

Dayne put her bag on the floor and watched as Janice finished her notes. Janice was a caramel brown with waist-length dreads that swung over her desk as she wrote. She looked light in her summer wear, white capri pants and a floral-patterned shirt.

"Thanks for waiting." Janice closed her notes and swiveled her chair closer to Dayne. "How's the vacation been?"

Dayne almost forgot she'd mentioned it last session; she looked down at her hands with guilt.

"It's not really a vacation. I took the week off to get away."

"Isn't that what a vacation is?" she asked.

Dayne didn't respond, so Janice tried to catch her gaze. "Tell me what you mean."

Dayne was quiet a moment longer. Then, she met the glow of Janice's hazel eyes.

"Janice, I'm never going to get promoted. Vanessa's been promising me a salaried position for months. But every month I watch her promote some pretty, white, and willing new college graduate. Meanwhile, I'm barely holding onto my hourly wages."

Janice sat back in her chair and listened.

"I'm just feeling exhausted, you know. Watching my coworkers take credit for events I promoted. Stepping in for Vanessa when her attitude flares up with the artists. Correcting stupid little mistakes for the head of the department—mistakes I wouldn't make if I had the position, a position that I was promised but never offered."

Dayne was out of breath when she finished. Janice leaned in.

"Are you willing to stay, knowing it may never be offered to you?" Janice asked, her cadence calm, inviting.

"That's the most fucked-up thing," Dayne said. "I keep sticking around, working with a dizzying amount of attention to detail, thinking that Vanessa will notice, pretending like I'm not sick of arriving to work to her empty promises. What kind of idiot does that day after day?"

"Don't go there. You're not an idiot. If I've learned anything from talking to people these last ten years, it's that we all do what we do for a reason, most likely because someone taught us to."

Dayne frowned, then chuckled.

"What?" Janice asked, smiling. "What did you just think of?"

"My father," Dayne said. "If anything, my father taught me how to work like a dog for so little."

"Talk more about that."

"My dad has worked for white men his whole life, building lavish pool decks and kitchen interiors for low, unpredictable pay. He's struggled. And I know he's struggled even harder because he's a black man."

"What kind of effect do you think that's had on your father?"

Dayne looked down at her lap until the answer came to her.

"He became the great pretender. He'd tell me it was the weather that bothered him when he came home—he dismissed his anger as some physical pain. But I knew even then he was never being paid well enough or treated fairly. After Mom left, he worked almost seven days a week, and he developed this smile. This smile I knew he'd put on, all big and fake for his employers—and he'd bring it home with him. He couldn't shake the need to pretend. Even with me."

"You were only a child, Dayne. I'm sure he wanted to protect you, especially after your mother left."

Dayne had never thought about it that way but when she thought of protecting children, she thought of Trayvon.

"You can't protect a black child in the South," Dayne said. "We barely know how to talk before we know something is wrong with the color of our skin." Dayne's eyes grew wet, though she'd never shed a tear before during sessions. Every time she tried, she remembered her mother's large, soft hands muffling her crying as a toddler—the only crisp memory she had of her. When she caught her father crying after her mother left, he'd pretended it was allergies.

Dayne wasn't sure she even knew how to cry.

"Are you afraid you may follow in his footsteps?" Janice asked.

"It won't be the worst thing." Dayne shrugged. "My father's always worked so hard because he is a dreamer, because he wanted more for us. I just don't want the same hurting heart that my father has from all the years of working. And pretending."

"What do you think you'll do?"

"I don't know yet. I guess I'll take the week to decide."

"Looks like we're out of time for today," Janice said. "I'll put you in the schedule for the same time next week?"

Dayne nodded and wrote Janice a check. As she handed it over, Dayne's palms were sweaty, shaking, and Janice held her gaze. She'd never hugged her clients; clinical training taught her not to get too close. But Janice had felt Dayne's trembling from where she stood. Before she could stop herself, Janice pulled her arms around Dayne's slender frame.

Dayne hadn't felt the close embrace of a woman in a long time. She held on as tight as she could, knowing it would only last a moment and unaware of when the comfort of touch would come again. When their arms unlocked, Dayne thanked her with a smile.

"See you next time," Janice called as Dayne gathered her bag and left.

5:30 p.m.

Dayne was usually exhausted after therapy. But now, with the sun to her back, she made the lengthy trek back to her apartment, thinking about what Joyce had asked.

Halfway home, when she couldn't bear the heat any longer, she found a shady bench in a park to catch her breath. She sat across from a scattered scene of park-goers, imagining she'd fallen into Seurat's pointillist *Sunday Afternoon*. By that hour the nannies, speaking firmly with thick Jamaican accents, were grabbing the blue-eyed and blonde-haired babies in their strollers before the sky darkened. City nannies were still a new concept for Dayne, who believed her father never taught her the word "babysitter" since he could never supply her with one.

I bet I can get full-time work doing that . . . taking care of someone else's children.

But it was too hot for Dayne to think seriously about her next career move. She turned away from the picturesque scene only to be confronted by her own disappointment. She wished a real promotion was as easy as a conversation, one where she would be heard beyond her color, beyond someone's perception of her ability as a black woman. She wished she didn't have to watch herself repeat a history her father told her she could never escape. She wished that she lived in a country where everything wasn't so heavily weighted by the politics of race.

Her eyes started to swell again when she felt her cell phone buzzing. It was a text from Sachin about going to see a concert, the morning invitation she'd almost forgotten.

Dayne held the phone close to her chest, trying to decide whether to go. Then she rationalized it was best not to be left alone with her thoughts, so she sent Sachin a reply asking where to meet.

Unarmed with a white ally for cab-catching, Dayne hopped on the A train and got off at West 4th. She liked showing up to Sachin's invites, if only to learn how to better navigate the city. Each adventure reminded her of the way her father used to take her on drives but would never tell her where they were going. Wherever they ended up, she always felt safe. She was starting to feel safe with Sachin too.

When Dayne arrived at the club, Sachin was outside smoking a cigarette. He was in striped linen pants and a button-down shirt, his dark copper complexion accenting the contrast of bright orange and blue stretching. He was always well and wildly dressed, recalling the origins of his Indian upbringing in every outfit. His face was chiseled to perfection—deep dark eyes, thin cheeks, and a strong jawline with a smile to match. Staring into the sky and taking the last few drags of his cigarette, he looked as if he were posing for a photo shoot.

He noticed Dayne halfway down the block and let out his bright, tooth-filled smile. Dayne couldn't help but notice how handsome he was.

"Hey—you made it!" he said, throwing up his hands. "I thought for sure you wouldn't want to go out and deal with this heat. I'm glad you came!"

"So, what's this? Who's performing?" Dayne asked.

"Funny you should ask. I kind of don't know. One of my coworkers has a friend who gave her two free tickets if she promoted the show. She passed them along to me and I thought of you. Apparently, the singer is incredible, a black woman named Robin Real. You heard of her?"

"No, I haven't. What's her stuff like?"

Sachin laughed, a hearty, rumbling sound emitting from his gut.

"That's the 'I don't know' part. I just thought you might like to join me."

"What? 'Cause I'm black?" Dayne was half-joking but she wanted to gauge his reaction.

"You're black?" Sachin said, in a sarcastic tone. "I could have sworn I never noticed because I am so 'color blind.'"

They laughed at their ability to make light of it all.

"I'm telling you, I never even heard the phrase 'color blind' until I came to this country," Sachin continued through laughter. "When a co-worker said it my first day at my job, I thought America was so accommodating to help the disabled. Seriously. And still, I'm the only one who looks stupid."

Dayne laughed even louder, imagining the scene.

"Well, you know us black women. It doesn't matter who can and can't see us. We all look and sound alike anyway." Dayne's sarcasm faded to irritation, which Sachin noticed.

"A little entertainment might do us some good." Sachin opened the door to the Duplex and pulled Dayne inside.

Dayne and Sachin made their way to the performance space, up a flight of stairs to the bar, then down another to a small seating area in front of an even smaller stage. Sachin brought them drinks, and Dayne sipped white wine as the rest of the crowd settled. They chatted for a bit, exchanging pleasantries until the lights dimmed.

When the room went black, a voice backstage announced a round of applause for the "lovely and talented" Robin Real. Dayne and Sachin clapped as they glanced at each other, unaware of what to expect.

The spotlight hit center stage and out came Robin, a Venus-shaped brown woman in a long, red wig and a slinking black dress. Dayne and Sachin had been expecting her to burst into song, but Robin stood silently at the mic, shifting her hips and smiling out at the audience. Then, Robin's music started, and she sang Billie Holiday's "Strange Fruit" as Dayne had never heard it.

A tear rolled down Dayne's check. The new sensation felt like a cool wind against the heat that still permeated her skin. She was concentrating on crying silently, so she didn't notice Sachin holding her hand until the baritone of Robin Real's voice had settled. She never looked him in the eye but didn't let go for the rest of the set.

A Penny, a Pound

Princess Joy L. Perry

I

Bayles & Son Crossroads Store was filled with bounty that had nothing to do with the heavy-laden shelves. It was a rare afternoon. There were no white customers, so the field hands spoke of more than white people allowed. Yes, one of the women—straw hat thrown off and plaits bouncing with laughter—told the story of Mr. Colbert, "Come home drunk and dropped a sack of turtle feet in Miz Jennie stew! She run him 'round the garden with a ladle!" But Stanford, the store clerk, also read aloud from the *Norfolk Journal and Guide*. A colored boy hung to a telegraph pole in Montana, a Goldsboro café closed for serving coloreds, while down in Georgia, two hundred whites signed a letter denouncing the KKK. President Harding said territory conceded by the Germans ought to be used to resettle Negroes. But who would go? The sharecroppers argued with unguarded words. They revealed their true faces the way boys bare their chests to the sun.

The signifying bell was lost in their commotion. When they noticed him, the young man already stood among them. In vest and creased trousers, he walked through the dirt-spattered Negroes as if he did not see them snatching back their feet so that he would not tread on them.

"I'm looking for Mr. Atlas Bayles. You know where to find him?"

"Yes, sir," Stanford said. "Keep up this road through town. Go on 'bout 'nother six miles. Turn off 'bout 'nother quarter mile to your left."

The young man left the way he came, a curt nod of thanks, hardly a glance left or right. Still, one woman shined dust-covered brown Oxfords against her clay-splattered calves and replaced her straw hat, a shield against disinterest.

Stanford coughed to expel the eager, boyish voice that had not come naturally to him for fifty years. He folded the paper as the field hands scratched at the prickle and bite of their overalls. Their RCs and Moon-Pies were suddenly too sweet, too syrupy, to swallow. They left half-drunk colas on the window ledge and tossed last bites of marshmallow and chocolate into the trash barrel.

With murmurs of "Take it easy, Stanford," they left for Atlas Bayles's fields, to bend and stoop for the length of the day.

II

Atlas Bayles's house had as much claim on the land as an oak or an elm. It was a placeholder in local memory, a landmark like the lightning-struck pine that marked the road to Windsor. Standing in one form or another since 1720, the house and the buildings that made it grand had once been a self-sufficient world: a blacksmith's shop, a grist mill and a saw mill, a dairy and a meat house, a half-acre kitchen garden to provide what the hands of seventy slaves could not create. For two hundred years, Bayles Plantation had passed from father to son, men who proudly traced their bloodlines back to Cheshire, England, but recognized no difference in selling a calf or a pickaninny.

Atlas Bayles appeared from the back of the house. He froze like a man apoplectic, then covered the distance quickly.

Deep lines grooved the patriarch's gray eyes; his lower lids bulged then buckled into the flesh beneath. His blond hair was salt-mixed. Weight hung from Bayles's farm-built frame; cheeks were jowls, belly overhung belt. His shoulders stooped. Pressed against the screen, he squinted against the penetrating sunlight. His face blazed hope.

"*Son,*" he croaked. "*Justin?*"

Journey long, the young man had felt, with each mile and minute, the tightening of a cord stretched from gut to heart. Plucked by that simple wish, the binding snapped. "Daniel," he answered, his own name a razor across the palate.

The old man blinked, a long rest behind closed lids. "Harold's Daniel?"

"Yes, sir."

Atlas withdrew a trembling hand from the door latch. "Go 'round back."

▩

Atlas Bayles set one glass of whiskey on the smooth-worn table and drained the other. He refilled the empty glass. "Sit," he said to Daniel, who stood stiffly just inside the back door.

"How is Harold?" Atlas asked as Daniel sat across from him.

"Fine, sir."

"Your Aunt Ida?"

"Well. They send their condolences."

Atlas dismissed the sympathies. "He died bravely. Fought five days. Six hundred boys went into Argonne forest. Less than two hundred made it out."

"Yes, sir. I read about it. I'm sorry."

"You didn't go to war?"

"No, sir."

"Not too many colored did."

"Many went, sir."

"Not you."

"Uncle Harold said I could do more here."

"You're gon' be a lawyer."

"Yes, sir."

Atlas' gaze was sharp. "Who you gon' sue?"

"There are many unjust laws, sir."

Atlas considered him for a moment. "There are." He drank. "I wanted Justin to remain in school."

"He was headstrong?"

"Indeed, he was," Atlas said with pride. "Harold says you're very bright."

"He's taught me many things."

Atlas leaned back in his chair. "He didn't teach you to come to the back door."

"No, sir. He did not."

"Why are you here, Daniel?"

Daniel shifted in his chair. He straightened his long legs and rearranged his arms on the table. "To see about you."

Atlas swallowed the rest of his drink. "You drove through downtown?" he asked.

"Yes, sir."

Atlas nodded. "You passed the place I like to have a ice-cream soda. I used to take Justin—do you think we can sit there and have a ice-cream soda?"

Daniel chose the more pressing fact. "You have no one left."

"You'll come to my back door?"

Daniel touched the whiskey. His fingers trembled against the glass.

"Windsor is my home, Daniel. I abide by the rules. My family made the rules. You'll come to my back door?"

Daniel looked Atlas Bayles in the eye. Atlas shook his head. "You won't do it again. You already made up your mind." Atlas pushed away his empty glass. "You ought to go," he said as he began to stand.

"Who is my mother?" It was a brick through the fragile pane between them. It was the declaration of a vengeful and particular war.

Bayles paused. The skin paled about his lips.

"She's colored," Daniel charged. He watched, somewhat satisfied, as the pall spread over the old man's face.

"Yes."

"Is she still alive?"

"Yes."

"Is she here? In this town?"

"She's not like Harold and Ida."

"What does that mean?"

"She's not somebody it would serve you to know."

"I should trust you to know that?"

Atlas gave Daniel a cutting look. "Harold raised you to talk to me like that?"

"No, sir," Daniel said, but bluntly added, "You don't want to know me. She might."

"She's never been more than thirty miles off the farm. Didn't make it past grade school. You're gon' to be a lawyer."

"Her name—please."

"You don't know this kind of people."

"How did you know her? Who was she to you?"

Atlas drew himself straighter in his seat.

Bayles Plantation had once been a world unto itself. That was Atlas's sole defense. Elise and Justin, his wife and son, were out visiting. At home, reviewing the plantation's books, Atlas passed the kitchen window and saw the young girl bent over the wash tub. She was growing out of her dress; it rode tight across her breasts and ass.

His wife's chemises and slips soaked in bluing solution ten feet from where he had the girl, behind the garden shed with the sun hot on his back and splinters knifing into the palm he used to brace himself. She smelled of wood smoke and lye soap, so different from Elise. He was not careful or kind. When he was done, he zipped his pants and tucked his shirt, but she stood like a shed plank, eyes squeezed shut, fists balled, legs stiffly gaping, drawers bunched around her left ankle.

"Fix yourself," he'd said.

She did not move. Elise and Justin might be coming down the path. He squatted to yank up the girl's underpants. He had to lift her foot. Her trembling shook the wall of the shed. Sensing a loosening scream, Atlas moved with care. He drew the rough, unbleached cotton up over the thin legs. Her waist was yet straight, like a boy's. Her limbs were lithe, muscle and bone—a body built for tree climbing. He threaded her hands into the sleeves. It felt like dressing a child.

He said, "She was the girl who did the laundry. She happened to be in the yard—"

Daniel scraped back his chair. The force scarred the floor.

"Some good might come of it," Atlas said, calmly. "You were raised by good people. I made sure of that. Educated. You might do great things for colored people. I would be glad about that."

Daniel looked down on Atlas Bayles. "The good I do will buy your pardon?"

Atlas's hand barely trembled as he reached across the table for Daniel's full glass of liquor. "Yes."

Daniel strode from the kitchen out into the white walls and varnished floors of the hall. Without pause, he swept past an ornate silver frame draped in black crepe. It sat squarely on a polished table in the wide and light-filled hallway.

From behind, in a strangled voice, Atlas said, "You bear him quite a resemblance."

"That is a shame," Daniel said. He left through the front door.

▩

Coloreds claim they can tell by the tops of the ears, the skin around the fingernails, the hue of knees and elbows. Whites claim to know from the walk, the jut of the jaw, bumps in the skull. Stanford could not have said how he knew. He stood across from the young man, separated by the width of the counter, surreptitiously watching as he counted money into the register, and it came to him. He saw something and recognized it, without surprise, the way he knew his own face in any mirror.

"Who your people?" Stanford asked.

Daniel lowered the whiskey bottle. Through clenched teeth, he drew in hot, humid air, but his voice was frigid. "You don't know my people."

"You don't care for colored folk much, do you?" Stanford asked.

Daniel studied the store clerk from the close-packed silver hair to the scarred toes of his boots. His face was bronzed, the cheeks speckled like the tough skin of a muscadine. His tea-colored eyes were shrewd.

"I wasn't raised to," Daniel said.

"Fair 'nough," Stanford said. "Why?"

Daniel snorted. He glanced quickly around the room before he set his whiskey on the counter. He walked toward the shelves and snatched up a box labeled "California Fig Bitters."

On the box was a broad black woman, her hair in stubby plaits, her thick legs in striped stockings. Her dress bunched above her waist as she bent over, exposing dark, naked buttocks. "Oh my!" she exclaimed as she expelled a cloud of gas. "Guess this will fix me!"

Daniel set the box on the counter.

"You b'lieve that's real colored folk?" Stanford asked.

Daniel scoffed. On any shelf in the store—lard, soap, flour, or candy—he could find a beribboned pickaninny, a banjo strumming "Coon," or a goose-stepping "Darkie" with goggling eyes and red, watermelon-slice lips, grinning and exclaiming, "Dis sho am good!" He could stand at Atlas Bayles's kitchen door and feel like one.

"Yes," Daniel answered. Groping for his pocket, he said, "Give me another."

▪

Daniel woke in a windowless room among shelves of canned meat and motor oil, between barbed-wire stretchers and cotton scales. The room was sweltering. He crashed into boxes and bags and knocked his shins against unyielding tools until he found the door.

The warm night air carried late the last sweetness of honeysuckle and privet and the clarity of stars. Daniel slid down the doorjamb and let his head rest against the frame. The numbing effects of the whiskey were almost gone. The sickness would come later. He did not know where he was; he didn't care enough to worry. Daniel's only sensation was unsatisfied want. Wider, deeper, hungrier than when he drove into town, it was the want of his childhood, adolescence, and adulthood. It would be the want of old age.

It wasn't that Harold and Ida had not been good to him. They were as good as circumstances allowed, but Daniel was a reminder of dark blood in a small, color-conscious community. Beneath the discriminating eye, the curl of his hair intimated kink. Summer sun exposed latent sable in his skin. Though he was near in age to her children and raised alongside them, Ida, his quadroon aunt, did not allow Daniel to call her "Mother." When new visitors came, she introduced him as "Daniel—my husband's family."

Uncle Harold was quadroon as well. His grandmother had been a slave in the Bayles family. Quietly and only once, it was explained to Daniel that Harold and Atlas shared a grandfather. But while Atlas Bayles lived and worked on the family's acreage, Harold made his way in the world as a boot maker and cobbler. He catered mostly to whites and white-skinned Negroes. He kept his clientele exclusive through excellent craftsmanship and extravagant prices. Harold relieved his conscience by giving liberally to causes for the "betterment" of the Negro—octoroon- and quadroon-run charities dedicated to the "uplift" of their black brethren—but Daniel, with barely enough yellow in his skin to betray him, was the darkest person to enter at their front door. Harold explained the delicate matter: "A better class of Negro we may be, but in *their* eyes we are still Negro. To associate with blacks is to become one of them."

One-half. One-forth. One-eighth. One-sixteenth. One drop.

In for a penny, Daniel reckoned, *in for a pound.*

▩

"Brung you something to eat," Stanford called as he stowed the whip and dismounted his horse, ol'Amy. "Bread and lard soak up the whiskey in your belly. Won't be so sick."

Daniel rose from his seat on the doorsill. Behind him, over the fields and low-slung store, morning approached like an eavesdropper.

Stanford thrust a cotton towel filled with warm pork sausage and biscuits at Daniel, who took the offering and held it, staring down at the breakfast so long that Stanford bristled.

"Ain't nothing wrong wit' that food. You don't want it, gi' here. Some at the house do." He reached for it, but Daniel drew back. Looking up, he asked, "How long have you lived here?"

"Sixty-five years. Never been nowhere else."

"You know all the people?"

"Them in the houses an' them in the graveyard too."

Daniel nodded. He looked over the fallow field that edged the store. The mist had not yet lifted.

"Where do you live?" Daniel asked.

"You got right many questions this mornin'."

"You had plenty for me last evening."

"What was you doing up at Bayles's?"

A lie can be a protective reflex, no different than throwing out the hands to save one's self from a fall. Daniel's lie was not self-serving but self-saving. Salvage something or be lost.

"Searching for my mother," he said.

If Daniel expected shock, he was disappointed. The old man looked off in the direction of Atlas Bayles's house, then studied the boy. "Wondered," he said.

"Do you know her?"

Stanford nodded. "You do too," he said, unable to keep the edge of punishment out of his voice. "Walked right past her in the store."

Daniel remembered that the women wore short-sleeved dresses, the men bibbed overalls and undershirts. They all wore faded head scarves or straw hats. He failed to recall faces. He saw, in his mind's eye, "field niggers" loafing around when there was work to be done.

He passed the food from one hand to the other. He did not ask, "Which one was she?" There was no point. Instead, in a tone quiet enough to be humble, he said, "Tell me about her."

"Lou Ella," Stanford said, "got a husband name'a Jack Pearson. He alright. Go off on a drunk sometime, but he don't bother nobody."

Stanford sat on a crate from the storeroom. Daniel sat on the sill of the doorway, biscuits and sausage occupying his lap and hands. He ate as he listened. "Six other younguns since you. Youngest 'round four, I reckon."

Daniel chewed slowly. He had not thought of other children. Brothers and sisters.

"She work the fields like everybody else. Pick more cotton than some men. A member down to Ashland, where I belong. Support missions." Stanford shrugged. "She a good woman, far as I can see. Way I heared it, won't her idea to let go'un you. Bayles give her a choice. You go or they all go. Times was changed. Couldn't have no chile look like you growing up under Miz 'Lise nose.

"Well, it was winter. Owners got all the families they was gon' take. Nowhere to go, and there was a lot'un'em. This 'fore her gandpappy and grandma died, so there was them. Her mama and papa. Five other children. Lou was fourteen, the oldest. Bayles said he'd put you with people who'd give you a life better'n she could. She put you in his hands, the Lord's I mean, and let go'un you. What else you wanna know?"

Daniel opened his mouth to speak but instead doubled over. He heaved globby chunks of biscuit and sausage into the dirt between his feet.

Stanford looked down on the mess and the red-faced boy with streaming eyes. He grunted. "Sometime it ease you," he said. "Sometime it don't."

Pressing his hands to his knees, he stood. "Guess I better get 'round here an' open this store."

Daniel cleaned up at the pump out back then passed through a doorway that separated the storeroom from the main store. Stanford was on his knees, restocking a low shelf with cans of cling peaches in heavy syrup.

"If you can spare the cot," Daniel said, "I'd like to stay a few days."

Stanford did not rise or even look over his shoulder. "You gon' see her?"

"I don't know."

Stanford shrugged. "Ain't my business."

Daniel stood awkwardly, still trembling from too much liquor and the violence of being sick. He wished the old man would turn around. "I don't know your name," Daniel said.

"Stanford."

"Daniel."

"Well, Daniel," Stanford said, finally looking the boy in the face, "you gon' stay, you gon' work." He nodded toward the battered straw broom propped behind the register. Daniel stepped toward it, but first he stopped to shelve the box of California Fig Bitters.

III

Daniel spent those first days in the background. He stocked, scooped, filled, and listened. Blacks became less strange. They talked of what everyone else talked of: weather, crops, and children—things that grew and changed; God and politics—things that stayed the same. They were quick-witted, possessed of simple good sense. "You see one a them Morris' in a fight with a bear, help the bear!" one vociferous hand advised about a notorious local family, "'Least you 'spect that bear to turn 'round and maul you!"

It was clear to Daniel, though, that in his presence they were not as raucous as that first day. He saw the looks they arched at Stanford. "That's Daniel," was all the old man would say, but his unuttered approval proved enough. They began to say "Mornin'" and "Afternoon" to Daniel before they cranked up the banter.

Each day brought a different set of hands, depending on who had already picked their "weight" and had pocket change. Stanford never signaled that Lou Ella was among them. Daniel was impatient but glad. He swept corners, kept out of their way, grew less afraid.

On Saturday afternoon, the buzz of gossip began to rise like the noise of cicadas. The hands propped their feet on crates and leaned against the soda chest. They pried the tops off their RC Colas and passed around a tin of saltines.

"Gimme a pig foot when you done," Sam said gruffly to Stanford, who wrapped cheddar chunks in little squares of white butcher's paper and lined them up on the counter.

"Daniel! Get Sam a pig foot!"

The store fell quiet enough to hear a metal cola lid plink against the concrete floor. Sam looked ready to recant, ready to deny his desire for vinegar and red-pepper soaked pig-flesh, but Daniel set aside the broom.

Dressed in a shirt and pants loaned by one of Stanford's sons, and wearing a clean but stained butcher's apron, Daniel did not look so out of place. He grasped the jar and twisted off the lid and frowned just a little at the smell. With a long-handled fork, Daniel speared a pickled pig's foot, then drew it up through pink brine and lacy fat. He stuffed it into a small paper bag, the size Stanford taught him to use for sour pickles or three cents' worth of roasted peanuts.

"In the hand," Stanford said without looking up from the cheese.

Daniel paused in the motion of setting the pig foot on the counter where Sam had already placed his dime. White folk and colored did not touch. But Stanford had just declared to everyone—Daniel and customers alike—that the boy was not white. In the eyes of Atlas Bayles and the people who made the staples—corn meal, flour—Sam and Daniel were the same.

Conditioned to obey, Sam scraped up the dime. Gazing at the coin or the counter or the floor, he held it out to Daniel. Hesitantly, he raised his other palm. Dirt moistened by sweat filled the lifelines. Hard years of farm work were banded in Sam's hand, embedded in gray layers of skin, his calluses as permanent as fingerprints.

The problem was not that Sam's hand was unclean or rough. The man Daniel was expected to touch was an unmitigated black. There was nothing about his color or wooly hair or full lips to indicate a hereditary encounter with white blood. Sam was pure black, the kind Daniel had been taught to shun most of all.

But if not Aunt Ida's, at least Uncle Harold's aversion to blacks had been tempered with the understanding that he stood only one or two rungs above them on a shaky, splintered ladder. On the days when suit-clad white men were inclined to pick up their own boots, Uncle Harold stood with their merchandise outstretched—the leather worked soft as infants' skin—free hand twitching at his side as he tried to anticipate: Would the money be handed to him or tossed on the counter to avoid the touch of his hand? Like Sam, Uncle Harold had to divine without reading the face.

Daniel's fingertips brushed Sam's as he took the dime. He placed the vinegar-stained bag on the trembling, upturned palm. He made change, drawer and coins clattering in the cranky old register. He held out the coins and, this time, Sam was quicker to raise his hand.

"Ha' a good day." Sam rushed the words.

Their gazes connected firmly, like palms meeting in handshake. "You do the same," Daniel said.

The hum of back and forth began again. Stanford grunted approval.

IV

From the swayback of ol'Amy, Stanford looked down at Daniel. "No work tomorrow," Stanford said. "Preacher down Willow Branch, so no church neither. I'll take you to her."

"Wh—where will she be?"

"Sunday? Oughta be home. You can meet all'un'em. Sisters, brothers too."

Daniel nodded. He began to step away from the horse, but then stopped and stepped closer. He tried to see Stanford's face clearly from the awkward angle, through the dusky light.

"If I'd asked you to take me before?"

"You won't ready before," Stanford answered. He tapped Amy with the horse whip.

Daniel watched Stanford and Amy until horse and rider flattened into the line between field and trees. When the sky began to darken, Daniel wandered to the back of the store. He opened the door of the storeroom, hoping to cool it enough for a comfortable sleep.

As he waited in the yard, a blue moon, the second full moon of the month, took the horizon, fading as it rose, from amber to pearl. Daniel marveled at the effortless transition, for he knew nothing was more impossible than the slip into another color, the shedding of a skin, the changing of a desire.

Atlas Bayles planted Daniel in Lou Ella's body by force, but he'd had to take the boy in the same manner. Perhaps it was not until she saw the child that she began to want him. But she *had* come to a mother's want. And if the boy returned to her, Lou Ella would throw the front door wide. Lou Ella would kill the fatted calf and set the welcome table.

To associate with blacks is to become one of them. But a child's yearning crushed Daniel like the weight of that singular, chameleon moon. He went inside to sleep. He wanted to be ready when Stanford returned.

▩

The regular sky had peeled away like old paint. Daniel and Stanford traveled beneath some kind of just-made, original-blue beauty. Stanford walked ol' Amy and mapped the land and past for Daniel.

"Now, through there, you'll find the sweetest stand'a blackberry bushes in the county. An' further on is good fishin' year round if you can stand the mosquitoes or the cold. That stream dangerous, though. One good freshet, it 'come a river. That meadow is where the men an' boys plays baseball every Sunday after church in summer. Pearson an' two'a your brothers plays, Rob and Tom, I think."

They moved further along the wide clay and rock road; the grass turned to sapling pine. Around a bend the meadow disappeared, but Daniel craned his neck in the direction they had come. He imagined himself barefoot, running the bases, slapping the hands of two boys with his face and eyes, exulting over the day's best plays in the quiet dark of a shared room.

▩

The sharecroppers' dwellings lay just beyond another line of trees. They were the same shack over and over again: zinc roofs, boards weathered gray, black where the paint had peeled and mold had set in. Where a shack rested on cinder blocks, a bedraggled dog or chicken flopped in the dust beneath. The yards revealed the lack inside of the leaning walls. There were privies of various size, in varying states of repair, some white-washed, some with doors hanging by a hinge. Women washed babies and clothes in pans and tubs set near spitting pumps or heaved buckets from wells. The breeze mingled the smell of greens and corn meal boiled outdoors with the stink of penned hogs. Daniel felt the bottom of his stomach weaken. His gaze skated over the vegetable gardens bright with squash, the pink bushes of crepe-myrtle. He winced to see a child run barefoot through shimmering chicken shit.

People paused in their washing, tinkering, or idling as the two men passed. At more than one house, a man or boy occupied only with chewing a toothpick stood to watch them pass. A woman who walked down the road with coarse string wound into her hair stopped to stare.

Everyone greeted Stanford. They eyed his companion suspiciously. Daniel stared back, equally wary.

In front of Lou Ella's house, a drawn, bearded man looked up from his fence repair. He moved a crooked, wet cigarette from one corner of his mouth to the other as the visitors approached. "There Pearson," Stanford said, "an' here some'a the younguns."

Caught in a game of hide-and-seek, Lou Ella's children appeared from behind a battered pecan tree, the rain barrel, from beneath the porch and from around the corners of the house.

Stanford drew the horse up to the swaying gate. With the agility of a much younger man, he swung a leg over the pommel and slid easily to the ground. Stanford looped the reins and shoved the whip between the leather straps.

"Daniel?" he said when the young man remained rigidly on Amy's back.

"What's goin' on, Stanford?" Pearson called.

Stanford turned in greeting. "Whatcha know, Pearson?"

"Nothin' good!" Pearson set down the nails and hammer. His gaze stayed on the man on the horse.

"Lou here?" Stanford asked as he stepped inside the gate.

"Yeah," Pearson answered. "What y'all want wit'er?"

"This here's Daniel. He been working at the store," Stanford said.

Pearson nodded to Daniel, an uneasy greeting likewise returned. "What he want wit' Lou?"

Stanford explained again, "This here's *Daniel.*"

Working tobacco-darkened lips, Pearson rolled the cigarette to the opposite corner of his mouth. He looked long at the boy.

"Hadn't heard his name," he said, shaking his head. "Even if I'da heard it, I never woulda 'magined—he *that* Daniel?"

Stanford nodded. "Come to meet'er."

"Jus' come?"

"Come when he could."

Across the yard, the children paused in their running and chasing. They bunched together. Men who looked like Daniel came where they lived only to collect insurance or when there was trouble. Never had one come riding on the back of a colored horse. The older children grasped the hands of the younger. Protective—the way their mother insisted. In all things concerning the children, Lou gave the last word. Pearson understood why it had to be that way.

"She be mighty glad," he said, his solemn gaze moving from his own children to Daniel. "I'll get'er."

As Pearson crossed the yard, Stanford beckoned to Daniel. "You heard what he said? Come on."

But reality overwhelmed Daniel's every sense. The house was not a whit different from any other in the neighborhood. Somehow, he had imagined it would be. But the cinder block steps were cracked. The porch planks gaped. Pieces of a broken chair—spindles, legs, a backless seat—littered the yard. A rusted headboard leaned against the pecan tree like a ladder. The front door stood open to flies and strays and the many children who stared at him like hungry pickaninnies he'd seen on city streets. They were tall and short, slim and stocky; all were barefoot, the boys and youngest ones bare-chested, in too short, tattered dungarees. Daniel's younger brothers and sisters stood with dusty feet, frayed cuffs, gaping mouths, and *to associate—*

Daniel lifted himself from Amy's rump into the saddle. With sweat-damp hands, he grasped the whip and reins.

Stanford shoved open the gate. "Daniel," he cautioned, just as Lou Ella appeared, frantically wiping her hands on a dishrag. Pearson stood behind her, his hands moving soothingly up and down her arms.

Lou Ella Slade Pearson was black, a color that seemed to well from within her. Her face shone with oil and sweat from cooking beneath a galvanized roof. Bare of straw hat or scarf, her hair was divided neatly into plaits. Her arms were large, the skin dimpling over her elbows. She wore a housedress, its pattern scrubbed down to blurred color and thin cotton that stuck in the folds of her waist and belly. Her stout legs and feet were bare.

Lou Ella's gaze skimmed the familiar faces of her children, dismissed Stanford, and darted past Daniel until Pearson nodded, "That's him, there."

"My son?"

Pearson nodded.

Lou Ella shoved the rag at him.

From the height of the horse, Daniel watched Lou Ella approach.

With each step, she transformed: A stranger-mother, broad-smiled, marveling at his presence; the kerchiefed, grinning woman on a box of pancake mix; the big-bodied, red-turbaned woman on a box of Fun to Wash; the Fig Bitters woman, like the girl who "happened to be in the yard," bent over, naked buttocks in the air.

Stanford stepped aside as Lou Ella pushed past and opened the gate, still uttering softly, disbelievingly, "My son? My son?"

She reached up to touch Daniel.

Daniel raised the whip.

Part 3
Borderlands

The final section of this anthology pays tribute to Lauro Flores's landmark anthology *The Floating Borderlands* (1998) and the idea that many contemporary writers live on the border. Several of the writers in this section can claim duel identities; they may "belong" to one or more countries, or one or more ethnic groups, and their writing may reflect an allegiance to one or more literary genres or styles. Whether it is Emily Raboteau's "The Rapture," a moving and surreal story about a baby born under most unusual circumstances, or Mecca Jamilah Sullivan's "A Strange People," a poignant story about a black carnival freak show, the stories in this section delightfully teeter between realism and fantasy, between truth and fiction, between the bizarre and the mundane. Our title story, Xu Xi's "All about Skin," appears in this section, and we thought there was an irresistible irony here: in an anthology written and edited by women of color, we are "all about skin" and, at the same, about so much more.

The Accidents of a Veronica

Toni Margarita Plummer

She has wedged herself in the doorway again, her hands gripping the small ledge at the top, her feet planted along one side.

"They told me to be like this for ten minutes," she says.

"Who did?" I ask from the couch, my highlighter hovering over a used copy of Aristotle's *The Nicomachean Ethics*. I want to get a heads-up on reading before the new semester begins.

"The little one." She reaches down to indicate a height below her butt, starts slipping, and reaches back for the top of the frame.

She must mean Eddie. She recently returned from my mother's cousin's house. He is the youngest and most rebellious of the kids, so I'm guessing he's the one who gave her this so-called advice on earthquakes.

"It's good to go to the doorway, but you shouldn't climb up in it."

She leaps down with a great thump and arches her back like a cat. "That is enough for today," she says, as though I've not spoken.

That's the thing about the Veronica. She has a knack for forgetting I'm around. She'll jump when I come around a corner. "You scared me!" she exclaims, her hand on her chest, as though it's shocking I'd be walking through the house. What am I supposed to do? Announce myself? Should I be banging pots together like I'm in the wilderness?

I turn back to my book, though it's hard to concentrate with her accented chattering and stomping around all day.

Veronica Sandoval is the daughter of Mom's second cousin Mari in Veracruz. She is fifteen years old, has lightish brown hair dyed ultrared, blue eyes, a tattoo of a shell on her ankle, and a piercing in her navel. She wears baggy pants, thong underwear, and an amulet around her neck that she claims wards off bad spirits.

She is visiting us American relatives for the summer to improve her English, so that she can test well on returning and get into a good school. We've been passing her around like a 120-pound Mexican fruitcake, from family to family, from Pico Rivera to Sylmar to Santa Ana, essentially to the most Spanish-speaking neighborhoods throughout these various counties of Los Angeles. But Mom and I get the pleasure of her company most of the time.

We spoke Spanish to her the first day she arrived, she and Mom conversing easily, me only getting every third word despite having tested into Intermediate Spanish. But after that it's been only English, so she can learn. This rule doesn't apply to the television or stereo, however, and the Veronica takes this to her full advantage. She's got the Spanish station on now, and I don't ask her to change it. Besides, Mom will not give up her telenovelas for the sake of her immersion, so what's the point?

The Veronica herself obeys the English-only rule well enough, although she lapses into Spanish phrases now and then. When she does, she gasps and covers her mouth, as if she has inadvertently cursed. For all I know, she has.

She came from Mexico bearing crosses and a note. The crosses were gifts from Taxco, a little town outside of Mexico City whose winding cobblestone streets hold stores filled with silver.

Tía Mari no longer practices and the Veronica herself has self-identified as atheist, although I don't know where the bad spirits figure in. I think Tía Mari must have known how Catholic Mom was and sent the gifts in a show of goodwill, as if to say her daughter was living under our Catholic rule now and should be judged accordingly.

The Veronica stood before Mom as she read the note, her eyes downcast, her hands behind her back, a smile playing on her lips. It offered salutations, many thanks, and concluded, "If she misbehaves, send her back." Mom looked up from the note to give me a troubled look. These words begged the question, what could the Veronica possibly do that would merit familial deportation?

We had yet to find out.

I have my guesses as to what vices she's into, though. For one, I'm pretty sure she's had sex. She admitted as much when I asked if she had a boyfriend.

"I used to. He wanted to do it all the time."

"Do what?" I asked.

She started to answer and then remembered herself. "Uh, he wanted to hug all the time. Yes."

Right.

The phone rings and we let the answering machine get it. I've finally managed to convey to her the beauty of screening calls.

"Hi, Olivia, this is José. I heard that I'm scheduled to give the 'Renouncing Satan and His Works' talk. But I'd like to exchange it for the 'Accept Jesus as Your Savior' talk, if that's possible. Anyway, call me back."

This merits lifting our eyebrows at each other.

The Veronica saunters to the kitchen. "Mmm, chocolate! No!" and there's a slapping sound, which I recognize as the Veronica slapping her own hand. She appears in the doorway, gathers up her belly in her hands, and pleads, "Look at me! I am fat!"

She does this, a lot. Usually after a grand meal of pizza and hot sauce, or that hazelnut spread she loves. She pulls her shirt up in ritualistic manner and slaps on her belly like it's a drum. When she hits her belly, a little shockwave travels through it and the rhinestone in her navel winks from the pudginess like a buried gem.

We'd like to tell the Veronica not to exaggerate. But the truth is when she lets her *pansa* hang out like that, it looks very round and big indeed. It's an impressive *pansa*, and we should give credit where credit is due.

My cell phone rings this time and it's Mom calling to ask what we're up to. She will be late tonight, going to visit her aunt, just returned home from the hospital. I tell her I have plans to go to a party down the street. Sonia Mendoza invited me at church last week. "And La Veronica?" Mom asks.

"What about her?"

"You could take your cousin with you."

"It's not for high school kids, Mom. She can't go."

"Why not? Will there be drinking?"

I'm not twenty-one yet. "No."

"Then you can take your cousin."

The party is only a few blocks away, across from the park, so we walk. I want to tell the Veronica, for God's sake, don't take your *pansa* out in front of anyone. And if you could rub off some of that blue eye shadow, I'd appreciate it. But of course I don't. I'm a little nervous because there will probably be people I know from grade school there. Sonia still keeps in touch with them. I don't even talk to anyone from high school anymore.

Louisa Campos is standing outside the house smoking. The Veronica makes like she's going to ask for a cigarette but I shake my head no.

"How you been?" she asks me, but her eyes drop before she finishes the question.

"OK. This is my cousin Veronica. She's visiting from Mexico." I feel a little relieved actually that the Veronica gives me something to say.

"Hi," Louisa says and blows smoke.

"I am the daughter of her mother's cousin," Veronica says, a little too enthusiastically.

I look at her. "That's what I said."

"It's kind of lame in there," Louisa says, nodding toward the house. "But there's beer in the kitchen. And Greg Ríos is here, I can't believe it." Her lethargy actually lifts and her eyes light up when she says his name.

"Greg Ríos is here?"

Greg Ríos was my first crush, the boy I saw nearly every day for eight years and who starred in my middle-grade fantasies as assuredly as any Hollywood actor since. In third grade he tugged on my cowgirl braid in the Halloween parade. In fourth grade he laughed when I called a dog a chichihuahua. And there are countless other such encounters fraught with potential romance. I want to see him alone, without my depraved blue-lidded Mexican cousin as sidekick. Surely a long-awaited reunion is worth the Veronica blackening her lungs a little.

"Louisa, would you mind if Veronica hangs out with you for a while?"

She shrugs, which I take to be acceptance.

"I'll be back," I tell the Veronica. "Just wait here for me."

She nods and winks at me. I'm not sure why. But I know she'll be fine. She's not shy, at all.

I walk into the house and it's crowded and dark and loud. There's someone playing DJ in the corner. I search for a good spot to stand and get trapped between two girls discussing a third girl's pregnancy and a fourth girl's indecision on a major. I scan the room, but I don't see anyone I know. Too much time is passing and I'm thinking of leaving. I've had my fill of disbelieving parents and shattered dreams. Oh, and the pregnancy too. And then I see him. Greg Ríos.

Back in grade school he carried around some baby fat. Now he's tall and brawny. And he still has those gorgeous brown eyes.

He's making his way to the kitchen, where I realize I'm strategically standing by the beer cooler. He stops to talk to a few people. He was always popular. When he's near enough, I say, "Hi, Greg."

"Hi." His smile is genuine.

When he doesn't say more, I say, "It's me, Monique. From Cantwell."

"Monique, is that you?" He grabs a beer from the cooler and straightens. "How are you?" He wraps his arms around me for a hug and for a moment I'm smothered.

"I'm good," I say when I'm released. "I'm going to USC now. It's so good to see you. I mean, really really good. I remember you from school. I mean, wow."

He's gazing at me now. He licks his lips and moves closer.

"Monique, you wanna go somewhere?"

"Go somewhere?"

He puts his hand on my waist and whispers in my ear. "We could go upstairs, catch up."

This is happening too fast. Go upstairs with Greg Ríos? Catch up? I fumble to stall. "That's an idea. Hey, have you seen my cousin? The girl from Mexico?"

He frowns like he used to when taking one of Mrs. Larchmont's math tests. Then he appears to have a thought and smiles. "Is she the girl doing tequila shots with Grumpy?"

"Tequila shots?" My heart stops. Grumpy?

He leads me to the backyard and there's the Veronica at a picnic table, all glassy-eyed and smiling, swaying even though she's sitting down. She picks up a shot glass and throws it back, wipes her mouth with her forearm.

Shit.

"Your turn!" she yells at the guy sitting across from her. He must be Grumpy and he's massive, straining the buttons on his plaid T-shirt, his keychain dragging on the floor, sweat glistening on his face. Grumpy is not smiling. He looks decidedly uncomfortable. I've arrived just in time to see him gag and stagger from the table to rush out of the yard.

The Veronica shoots up to applause. "I win! Monique!" She makes it out of the table easily enough, only to begin retching all over Sonia Mendoza's shoes.

"Gross!" Sonia shrieks and grabs onto Greg, who is laughing so hard he's caught off-balance and they fall to the grass.

I'd like to tell Sonia to let go of Greg, but I also don't relish the thought of her tearing into me over her shoes. And I have the Veronica to deal with. I haul her out of there, pulling her through the yard and away from the house.

Louisa is still standing out front alone. She blows smoke after us. "Told you it was lame."

We arrive home to find Mom watering the lawn. She turns off the hose when she sees me practically dragging a near-unconscious Veronica up the driveway.

"What happened?" she demands.

For one shining moment I think I could be rid of the Veronica, of her screaming making me feel like a ghost in my own house and having to entertain her and all the Nutella gone after one day. And I have never lied to Mom.

But it comes so easily I surprise myself. "I gave her a drink, to try. I'm sorry."

"You did?"

"Yes."

"That must have been one big drink."

I look away. She is examining me and I'm not sure what to do. I'm not usually in trouble like this. Finally she lets out a breath. "You put her to bed and make sure she drinks lots of water."

The next morning, I am groggy. Veronica yawns like crazy and is a little more subdued than usual. But otherwise she's no worse for wear.

I'm doodling. I find it calms me.

"You draw me," the Veronica says.

"What?"

"I want my picture done." She collapses on the couch with a laugh and throws her arms back over her head in a dramatic stretch.

"I'm not very good."

"Please, please, Monique!"

I cave, and after a few minutes, she gets up to look at the page.

"I am bald!"

"I haven't finished yet. Besides the hair is an accident."

"You don't like my hair?"

"No, it's an Aristotelian accident."

"Is that really bad?" The Veronica takes her head in both hands and runs to the bathroom.

"That just means that your hair isn't what makes you who you are," I call after her. "You could be a human being without hair. You could be Veronica Sandoval, without hair."

"I don't think I'd want to," she says, looking through the doorway, her hands tangled up in the dyed red strands. "Bald? Without any hair!"

"Never mind."

The next time I look up she is crunched inside the doorway again. "I'm not moving till you give my hair back!"

I move the pencil to the page, then lift it. "Well, I don't know—"

"Monique, please!"

I scratch my head with the pencil, look at my nails, whistle. The Veronica starts shaking from all her giggling, and I start laughing, both of us waiting for her to shake the earth.

The Rapture

Emily Raboteau

Now that the days shuffle into each other like a deck of cards I can't remember which of the eight classes was the one where we learned about the Rapture. But I can remember the name of the woman who first told us about it—Beatrice—because it was on our short list of girl names. As it turned out I gave birth to a boy and we named him Clay.

Beatrice was a willowy white woman with long hair, a long face, and a long torso. She was a modern dance teacher and spoke about being thrown off the dance by her new center of balance. I envied her ankles, which remained slender as pilsner glasses, deep into the third trimester. Even though her due date fell a week before mine, she looked a lot less pregnant. Her posture was perfect. She wore her new belly like an accessory. I, on the other hand, was not a graceful pregnant woman. I was as big as America. You name it, I had it: varicose veins, edema, zits, nausea, heartburn, hemorrhoids, gas, bovine brain . . . The load was almost too much to bear.

My legs felt like they'd been torn off and then rejoined the wrong way in the sockets of my child-bearing hips. My swollen feet no longer fit into my shoes. Plus, I was afflicted by something called "round ligament pain," which was far too anodyne a description for the stabbing sensation it produced in my groin when I walked. I had new sympathy for the little mermaid in the fairy tale, who, having traded her fish tail for love, felt on her brand new legs that she was stepping on knives. I'd never felt so uncomfortable in my thirty-five years. I'd never felt so powerful.

"So when are you due?" Beatrice asked. An ice-breaking question, so it was probably the first or second birthing class. It was probably the break and we were probably standing with our husbands by the snack table, munching on rice crackers, wasabi peanuts, or carrot sticks dipped in hummus. And we were probably smiling.

"May 21," answered my husband, Anthony. He patted my navel, possessively. He was always doing that then, as if to assure himself the pregnancy was real. I stopped myself from patting his middle in return, something I liked to do in bed at night to reassure myself that he was real too, that we were indeed a family. Over those nine months we gained the exact same amount of weight at the exact same rate. There was a term for that too—Couvade syndrome—though to my husband it was just an embarrassing spare tire he masked by leaving his shirt untucked. Secretly, I preferred him this way, a little bit fat. That's who Anthony was—substantial and solid but soft. He was fat when I first met him. Then he got successful, married me, and went on a diet, though not necessarily in that order. Before he knocked me up and started growing back alongside me he was a big man masquerading in a thin man's body.

▩

"May 21?" Beatrice's husband gave Beatrice a meaningful look. It was half-pointed and half-playful and he had to raise his eyes to deliver it because she was taller by half a head. I can't remember his name. Dave or Nick or something equally forgettable. He was a sad-sack, a balding tax accountant who favored plaid and clearly adored her. His face was perpetually anxious, except for the time he got overexcited while watching the orgasmic birth video and Beatrice had to smack his shoulder to get rid of his grin. They'd met on an online dating site. So had everyone else in the class aside from the couple with matching haircuts who met in a college a capella group, the lesbians who worked together at the botanical garden in the Bronx, and Anthony and me. We liked to think we had the most romantic story of all.

▩

By national, if not New York City, standards we were most of us old to be having our first children. Middle age was around the corner. Some of us were recovering from the desperation and fear that we couldn't conceive by choosing to birth naturally, to be present for every sensation.

How else, apart from her ticking clock, could Beatrice's husband have pulled her off?

"Don't tell them," she warned him.

"Don't tell us what?" Anthony asked.

"Nothing," said Beatrice.

"But now you have to tell us," I said.

"It's stupid," said Beatrice.

"What's stupid?" Anthony pushed, taking my hand. "Let us be the judge."

Beatrice was annoyed. "You tell them," she ordered Nick or Dave.

"I'm sorry," he said, looking at his shoes. "I shouldn't have brought it up."

"But you did. You did bring it up," Beatrice spat.

"Okay," he said.

There came an awkward silence, which Beatrice finally broke. "Your due date—May 21, 2011? It's supposed to be the second coming," she said.

"According to those evangelical yoyos," her husband apologized, adjusting his glasses.

"That's awesome," said Anthony, somewhat defensively. He refused to entertain bad omens as far as the baby was concerned. But also, because he loved comic books and horror movies and all characters with special powers, it appealed to his particular blend of optimism and drama to imagine our kid might be the savior.

"If you think the end of the world is awesome," said Beatrice with a weird hostility. She was probably just angry with her husband for bringing up the Rapture in the first place, but Anthony and I automatically stiffened at her tone. As usual when we were the only brown people in the room, we were quick to guard ourselves against subtle and not-so-subtle slights. Who was she to tell us there was something wrong with our kid's birthday when he wasn't even born yet? Hadn't the guy who predicted May 21 as the end of days already gotten it wrong twice before? And didn't we already learn in the birthing class that our due dates were relatively arbitrary? Our baby was just as likely to arrive some other day.

The birth instructor would have clapped her hands to signal the end of the break right about then. She was an earth-mother type who'd failed to make it in musical theater but still pulled out her bright stage voice to discuss labor. I loved her for her naked enthusiasm. It was getting harder and harder to find people who weren't sarcastic. "When your contractions bring you to the transition stage, do a dance. Don't lose faith, people! Your baby's on the way. Remind yourself you're about to meet the love of your life."

Maybe she showed us a homebirth video at that point, or had us look at a cervical diagram in the workbook, the stages of dilation configured in a bull's eye of concentric circles, or maybe she coached us to breathe through a contraction while holding ice cubes in our palms. She might also have demonstrated with her model pelvis and plastic doll where the baby's head would sit right before it was time to push. Anthony may have taken notes while I felt the baby quickening or hiccupping inside me. I'm thinking this couldn't have been the class where she told us how to deliver on our own in the unlikely event of an emergency. That probably came later.

■

Anthony and I first met at JFK when I flew in from my long sojourn in Brazil, finally exhausted from the effort of trying to find myself. There he was, as planned, standing in the arrivals hall with the cluster of chauffeurs, wearing a cheap dark suit from Big and Tall and holding a placard with a question mark on it. At that time I was a drug mule and he was living in Queens a mile away from the airport in his mother's basement. She charged him a little rent, which he earned from time to time by running errands, like this pickup, for an unsavory childhood friend.

I was a much bigger loser than Anthony. He just couldn't see it. I'd had my share of addictions, lovers, heartache, and STDs, and I was broke. I was smuggling five kilos of cocaine to solve this last problem but the fact remained that I was alone and unformed. I must have looked a soggy, frightened wreck when I got off that plane, but Anthony received me like I was the very answer to his unasked question.

"Here I am," I said.

"Here you are," he beamed.

I went home with him that night, partly because I didn't have anywhere else to go, partly because we were pawns in a crime that drew us together, and partly because he was so eager for me to read his latest screenplay, "The Devil's Razor Strap." It turned out this was only one out of fifty or sixty unproduced screenplays Anthony had written. He'd neatly stacked his work in various draft form around the basement. The only other thing down there aside from those towers of paper was a twin mattress on the floor. This bed was very neatly made. His room reminded me of a monk's cell, a picture of devotion.

Gently, gently, he helped me cut away the packs of coke duct taped around my midsection, thighs, and calves. He pointed his scissors at my wrist and asked about the ratty red ribbon. I explained that a beggar woman had tied it there on the steps of Igreja do Bomfim, knotting it three times with a warning that if I ever removed it my wishes would not come true, whereas if I let it unravel on its own, they might. Years had passed and the ribbon was still intact. I was so sick of wearing it, I told Anthony, but I believed in magic just enough not to cut it off.

"What did you wish for?" Anthony asked.

"I can't tell you specifically," I said. "But I can tell you generally. The first wish was for success. The second was for family. And the third was for love."

Anthony surprised me then by taking a great risk. In every way, it was greater than the risk I'd just taken as a narcotics courier. He grabbed my hand and snipped off the ribbon.

"That was a bold move," I huffed, unsure at first if I wanted to stab him or hug him.

Later on he built me a hexagonal terrarium, bought a star in my name, and hired a mariachi band to serenade me. But really, he won me with this initial gesture.

"I promise you," he bluffed, still holding my hand, "that all your wishes will come true."

▩

Anthony held my hand on the day before the baby was due while the midwife swept my membranes. May 20, a Friday. The anticipation was killing us. Neither one of us could quite believe our good fortune. We'd made a little money by this point, enough to buy a small apartment at the top of Manhattan in the shadow of the George Washington Bridge. The windows looked out on an alleyway rather than the Hudson River, but still. It was ours. We didn't buy it with dirty money, either. We bought it with the money Anthony made for *Amsterdamned!*, the screenplay he wrote in the Netherlands on our honeymoon. The movie went straight to video but that was okay. We were too excited about what was going down in my uterus to be disappointed by anything else.

So the midwife had two fingers deep in my vagina. I looked up at the mobile strung from the curtain rod in the bay window behind the couch. It was my favorite gift from the baby shower because it was homemade—a pinecone, a spool, a prism, a shell. The other gifts and baby things were carefully arranged and folded on a tall shelf in the hallway. The ruffled bassinet waited next to our bed. The maxi pads doused in witch hazel to soothe my ravaged postpartum crotch were cooling in the freezer next to the Tupperware containers full of frozen soups and stews to sustain us through the first exhausting weeks. The cabbage whose leaves would relieve my engorged breasts waited in the fridge. The pink plastic sitz bath ring sat next to the toilet. The inflatable birthing pool was boxed with its electric pump in Anthony's office. The basket of clean rags and towels was tucked beneath his writing desk. And on top of his desk lay several envelopes stuffed with letters to slip under our neighbors' doors. He didn't want anyone thinking he was beating on his wife if I screamed, or worry that I was in danger. *Greetings! I am writing to share the good news that Emma is in labor with our first child. We are doing a home birth. If you hear strange noises coming from our apartment, please don't be alarmed.*

Most people *were* alarmed we'd opted to give birth at home. Namely, our mothers, which was why they weren't invited. We didn't need their nervous energy upsetting the scene. My mom had delivered my brother and me in the hospital and believed, of course, that I should do the same with my child. "Dad was born at home," I reminded her, to get her off my back. He was caught by a woman called Nan Ophelia, the midwife who delivered all the black babies in that part of the Mississippi Delta. "Not by choice," my mother reminded me. "It was Jim Crow. The white hospitals refused them. That was then. This is now. What are you thinking, honey? Your pain threshold is so low. You used to cry over paper cuts and when you bit your tongue. This will be ten million times worse. God forbid, what if something goes wrong?"

"Why should anything go wrong?" I countered.

Anthony's mother was even more mystified. She came from Uganda, had run from the backward hospital in the capital with its crowds of women writhing on the floor, its placenta pit, its bribes and its flies, among other wretched things, and never looked back. She couldn't comprehend how we could refuse the comforts of the first world. "This is how the Dutch do it," I reasoned. "And the other mammals. The whales and the lions. Why not me?" But my mother-in-law only shook her head. "You know that it's going to hurt, don't you? My dear, it's going to hurt you like nothing you could imagine. My grandchild's sweet head will tear you from your hoo-hoo to your bumhole."

The old Dominican women around the way were no better. "*Sin drogas, mi hija, por qué?*" they asked me on the street or in line at the Quisqueyana Deli. Was it that my husband couldn't afford the doctor? Labor was a curse best slept through and forgotten. The drugs were a triumph over suffering, they said. Why be a martyr?

To prove to myself I am brave, I told them. That was the main thing. To feel the most ordinary of miracles. To have something that wasn't bullshit to boast about. To be able to carry the knowledge of my own strength with me for the rest of my life.

But those women took a perverse pleasure in telling me my life, as I knew it, was about to be over. That after the baby came I would never be free from worry again. They told me to get to the hospital right then, that very second, that I looked ready to go, I looked like I was carrying twins, I was as big as the earth itself, I was carrying low, I was carrying a boy. I would recognize his face and never remember not knowing it. They offered me blessings. They offered me unsolicited advice. They lay their hands on my belly and told me I could kiss my sex life good-bye.

Inside my vagina I felt a vague tugging. "I am circling the crown of baby's head," smiled the midwife, who was well-regarded, fifty, Chinese, and no-nonsense. "Your cervix is softer than butter. I can feel the tops of your baby's ears."

"What does that mean?" Anthony asked. "Is that normal?" He squeezed my hand in his. One of our hands was sweaty, I couldn't tell whose.

"Emma is fully effaced," the midwife explained.

"A face?" asked Anthony.

I hoped the baby would have his hair, my eyesight, his cheekbones, my ears.

"It's fine," I said, interlacing my fingers with his. We'd learned in class that birth was 90 percent mind. After so much waiting, we were finally going to see our baby's face and that was nothing but wonderful. It was time for "positive affirmation," for "refusing fear," for "mind over matter," for the powerful sincerity of clichés. I said, "The baby will come when it's ready to come."

I knew the baby was low, had been feeling the pressure of his head behind my pubic bone for days. I felt he was molding himself, preparing to make his grand entrance. But I also knew that most mothers delivered their first babies sometime beyond their due dates. And maybe, in spite of all our preparation, a part of me was counting on that extra time to ponder what possessed me. I was incubating a real live person. I couldn't really comprehend it.

"Everything's progressing normally," the midwife confirmed. She had a midwifery conference to attend in Texas on the twenty-fourth. She'd promised that if I gestated long, she would cancel the trip, but here she was with her agenda, intervening to make the baby come as scheduled. When she pulled out her fingers there was blood on her rubber glove. That too was normal, she said, before deciding to send me to somebody called Kang to help move things along.

Suddenly I was nervous. She was rushing me. I realized I was going to have a baby imminently. And, if we were blessed, the baby would always be there, would never not be. Sweet Jesus, we would no longer be without a baby. "Who's Kang?" I asked. "And why do we need to move things along if everything's normal?"

"My acupuncturist," the midwife answered. She pressed my knee, firmly. "It's time. He'll see you tonight at five o'clock." She scribbled his address in Chinatown on her pad, tore off the page, checked my blood pressure, told me to call her if I felt anything, and was gone.

■

Anthony held my hand on the A train down to Chinatown. He held my hand at 42nd Street, where the conductor barked we had to switch trains due to track work. My husband held my hand in Times Square, where we moved through the rush hour crush of tourists, pickpockets, panhandlers, buskers, hustlers, street preachers, theater-goers, pigeons, drunks, and crazies holding homemade signs: THE END IS NIGH. I enjoyed my volume, the real estate I took up on the ridiculously crowded sidewalk, the way my husband protected me with his arm, the way New York City parted for us like the Red Sea.

"This is the last walk I will take as a childless woman," I thought. "Every walk I will take from now on, I will be somebody's mother." I was so much more overwhelmed by this thought than the out-of-towners were by the blaring, blinking billboard lights. But something in the posture of their upturned heads was in sync with my feeling of awe, my awful feeling. My senses were overloaded, scrambled. I could taste the tourists' perfume. I could hear the shutters clacking on their Japanese cameras. I could feel my baby revolving his head. I could see my husband's jumpy nerves. A cartoonist beckoned us to sit and have our caricatures drawn. A comedian pleaded with us to take an electric blue flier advertising his stand-up show. A hot dog vendor barked at a man with a tambourine standing in his customers' way. A footless diabetic banged out his story on an upside-down bucket.

"Heaven will be better than this world!" cried a woman under the giant pointing hand outside the wax museum. She held a white bullhorn to her mouth and appeared, for lack of a better term, Midwestern. "Repent! The flames of the apocalypse are licking at your ankles and you do not know it."

"Shut up, lady," a businessman yelled.

"Repent, sinner!" she screamed. "The world ends tomorrow. The earth will crack and storms will sweep the seas. Only those born again in his name will be redeemed. So it is written and so it shall pass. I am trying to save you from the fire and the flood! Repent and be saved! You!" she spotted me. "Yes, you with the unborn child. Do you hear me? Your world is about to be over and done."

Anthony looked ready to pop her in the mouth. Instead he tugged at my hand and led me back underground to catch another train. It was sweltering down there. It was the first circle of hell. There were too many people yapping, shoving, piping loud music into their ears to block each other out.

"You okay?" Anthony asked, his eyebrows knitted in concern. I nodded, but it was getting even harder, if that was possible, to walk. I had a bowling ball in my pelvic girdle; I could barely lift my leaden legs. I was dense enough to sink into the subway platform, then the seat somebody relinquished on the Q train, then the massage table at the acupuncturist's.

Anthony kept hold of my hand while Kang, in a tight room in a tenement next to a seafood store on Mott Street, officiously read my tongue, pressed his thumbs against the dark circles under my eyes, stretched me out on a table, pummeled my back, stuck needles in my head, hands, legs, and feet to direct the energy of my blood, and covered me like a marathon runner with a silver foil blanket. I fell into a deep sleep and dreamed about fish. When I woke up at seven Anthony was still holding my hand. I could feel the overhead light buzzing in my teeth. "Let's get you home, darling," he said.

▪

Again, the train. What percent of our lives in this city do we spend underground in its bowels? The longest uninterrupted stretch of subway track in New York runs on the A line between 59th Street, Columbus Circle, and 125th Street in Harlem. Since the A train makes no stops between those two points, it attains its full speed on that ride. Twenty-five miles an hour may not be very fast but the A, compared with all the other trains, flies like a rocket. The wheels shriek on the tracks as the cars plunge forward. Children like to plant themselves in the grimy front window of the first car to watch the dark tunnel unfurling in the train's headlights. They press their foreheads against the glass and pretend they're conducting the voyage. I've done it myself. It's exhilarating. But on that night, the train's wild swaying made me feel the opposite. The faster it barreled, the more drained I became.

I was moving, I was being moved, and within me was motion. The train was a drunken cradle. I felt every bump, every shudder, and every blasted curve. My back was so sore. My sacrum, in particular, felt manhandled by the seat of hard gray plastic. The commotion of my bones and blood had me stunned. I felt a throbbing in my core. The clatter of the train rearranged my atoms until I was no longer myself. Dizzy, I was the train. I lay my head on my husband's shoulder and silently began to cry.

After a small eternity we arrived at our stop and somehow ascended to the level of the street. The sun slid down gorgeously, like a postcard of a sunset. I have to remember this, I thought, but I was already forgetting. Behind the bridge, the sky streaked pinkward to the Jersey horizon. Around us the apartment buildings glowed in the saturated golden light. Their bricks looked softer than usual. My edges also were blurring. I had to stop moving or I would seep into my elongated shadow on the gum-freckled sidewalk. I had to pin my shadow's feet with my shoes and close my eyes to keep myself together.

"Are you having a contraction?" Anthony asked. His hand was an anchor. If it wasn't for his hand I might have turned into a puddle.

"I don't know," I groaned. I thought the contractions would feel menstrual, a vise-like clamping isolated to my uterus, but what I felt, I felt with my entire body. Everyone told me labor would hurt, but what I felt was unlike any pain I'd experienced before. It was ignited from within rather than inflicted from without. Not like heat but what makes heat hot. That burning entropy belonged to me. I knew how to run away from pain by clenching my teeth, tightening my abdomen, shrugging my shoulders, fisting my fingers, or holding my breath. But this, I had to step toward. It was happening. I couldn't protect myself from it and I didn't want to. Rather than curling inward like a snail into its shell, I would have to unfurl myself like a wave spreading onto the shore. I steadied myself to turn inside out by loosening my limbs.

"I can't wait to meet you," I exhaled. I opened my eyes and looked at my husband.

"You beautiful superhero." He smiled.

And then I was ready to walk again.

Once inside the apartment I slipped out of my shapeless maternity dress, turned off the bathroom light, drew myself a bath, and stretched into the warm water. The island of my belly contorted, convulsed. I watched my *linea negra* bend like a bow. Time passed. This was the first stage, Anthony reminded me. It would probably last a while—hours, maybe even days. He hovered big and helpless above me. "What should I do?" he asked. "Should I time it?"

I nodded and began to moan. It was eight thirty. Then it was nine and dark outside. The contractions seemed to be five minutes apart. Then three minutes. I could talk. And then I couldn't.

"I don't know if I'm doing it right," Anthony said, fumbling with his watch. "It's happening too fast."

"Call the midwife," I told him.

What happened next is a blur. I can only remember it in uncontained bursts, out of sequence and, except for a jumble of inadequate metaphors, beyond description. But I will try.

I remember Anthony holding his cell phone to my head so that the midwife could hear the sounds I made. She'd been watching a movie in a theater downtown when he called. She doubted I was as far along as he suggested, even when she heard my voice. I think I lowed like a cow. I believe I tried every vowel and settled on O. She told him to call her again in an hour. By that point I was on my hands and knees in the water, tilting my pelvis forward and back. I remember Anthony disappearing in the back room to blow up the birthing pool, coming back to announce there was a part missing, disappearing again to put on the mix of songs he'd compiled for the occasion. The majority of the songs were by Metallica. I think I asked him to turn the music down before yelling at him to turn it off. I remember him reporting, with great relief, that the midwife was now in a taxi heading home to fetch her supplies and that she expected to arrive in Washington Heights, if traffic allowed, sometime after 11:00.

I remember radiating heat. I remember how good it felt when Anthony placed a cold washcloth on my forehead and another around the back of my neck. I remember how bad it felt when he coaxed me out of the tub to the toilet to empty my bladder, and that I wanted only to get right back into the water for the weightlessness it offered me. Fuck, I said. I kept saying it, *fuck, fuck*, like a thumb flicking a lighter. It was the best word because it was hard, it was what I had done and what I had gotten into by doing it, and because what I was doing now was so very hard. I remember my belly pointing like a football. I remember sipping coconut water through a straw in a blue cup.

Around midnight Anthony called the midwife again. She didn't pick up. I could hear his fear when he left her a message. Then I vomited over the side of the tub and the room tilted like a ship. The nausea came at me in waves that surged with greater and greater strength until the moments of relief between surges thinned to nothing and I could no longer hear the current of traffic on the bridge or the corner boys playing reggaeton outside and I could no longer speak. I knew this was the transition stage, the shortest and hardest part, the point of no return, the void. It was May 21. The end of the world. Soon I would have to push, whether the midwife came or not.

"Breathe," Anthony reminded me, "breathe."

We breathed.

Then again, the nausea. The nausea was the worst part. It carried me toward a black hole wherein my mind revolved and collapsed without room for thought. But to be unthinking was strangely freeing. I became sloppy. Loud. My throat was so hoarse from groaning. I used the ragged sound to bring my baby down. I visualized the vibration of my voice pulling him like a string as I steadied myself to push. I tucked my chin to my chest, planted my feet, held on to my knees, lifted my hips, and opened my thighs like a book. I felt the intense pressure of my baby's head nearly rending me apart, the tectonic plates of my pelvis shifting to allow for his passage. I pictured him moving like a train, rounding the curve of carus, sliding through the ring of fire.

"I have to push," I told Anthony.

"Are you sure?" he asked, but I was already doing it. With each surge, I pushed again.

"Do you see the head yet?" I asked between surges.

"Not yet," my husband said. He stood on his knees next to the bathtub in a half inch of water that sloshed over onto the tiles, his pants sopping, his face a picture of concentration.

"Is he coming?" I panted.

"I think so," Anthony said.

"You think so?"

"He's coming," he said more decisively. "You're doing great."

I pushed again. I felt I was taking the biggest shit of all time.

"Don't you see the head now?" I begged.

"Not yet," Anthony apologized.

"You've got to be kidding me," I shouted.

I pushed again, but really the baby was pushing himself. I hollered to bring him down. I remember the water bag finally bursting right before he crowned, a satisfyingly warm volcanic gush. Later Anthony told me the baby's head behind the bag of waters looked like a dark ostrich egg, the tiny hairs waving like cilia on clay. Clay's head was out, underwater. We didn't yet know he was a he. He turned his head to make way for his shoulders. Then with a roaring terrible cleavage that was the multiplication of my self, I pushed out the rest of him.

Anthony lifted our son out of the bathwater like a trophy. He laughed, a little maniacally, placed him on my chest, and kissed me.

The baby bleated like a lamb and opened his dark eyes. I marveled at his head, the way his hair whorled like Van Gogh's starry night. I gave a great sigh of relief and gratitude. He rooted into me, grabbing at my breast as if to make sure I was real. Amazed, Anthony said, "You did it."

▩

In the days that followed we lost all track of time. What with the sleep deprivation, the isolation, the mess of diapers, piles of dirty laundry and dishes, the bloody nipples, the lapses into panic, the stab of love, the incontinence, the incoherence, the endless nursing and the baby's reversal of night and day, it was hard to say exactly how many days had passed. I couldn't say whether, when we finally ventured out of the apartment with Anthony holding Clay in his arms like a fragile lamp, and me taking tiny mincing geisha steps along 181st Street toward the river for our first walk as a family, only to discover at the lookout point over the Westside Highway that the bridge had collapsed into the water, I was dreaming or not. All I know is that those women were right.

Everything had changed.

But they were also wrong. I didn't recognize my son's face at all when my husband first handed him to me. He looked like a turtle, purplish and gray and totally alien. And I wasn't gobsmacked by love when I first met him. Not instantly. In that moment, still steeping in the water, I was just relieved to be done birthing him. I remember the surprisingly rubbery texture of the umbilical cord and that when the placenta bloomed out of me chased by a silk parachute of blood, it was time to separate him. Anthony clamped the cord close to the baby's belly with one of my barrettes and prepared to cut it. His hand shook with the scissors as if with delirium tremens. Adrenaline and terror mixed. Clay's color was changing like a mood ring from gray to pink. Me, I was riding the good raft of oxytocin, feeling the child squirm against me. Pain was the wrong word. I was just so motherfucking proud.

"Maybe we should wait for the midwife." Anthony paused.

I knew by then she wasn't coming. "I promise you," I bluffed, "everything's gonna be alright."

And then my husband cut the cord.

The Lost Ones

Aracelis González Asendorf

Efraín hadn't been out all day. He didn't really need anything from la bodeguita, but the house smelled like dirty, wet socks, and it would for the next couple of hours, until the dust burned off the coils. It happened every year the first time the central heat was turned on for the winter. Now the sour, musty smell combined with Emelina's cigarette smoke, and Efraín had to leave.

"Emelina, I'm driving to la bodeguita," he said to his wife, who sat in a flannel robe watching television, her once-blue slippers propped on the coffee table. "Did you hear me, Eme?" Emelina didn't look away from the set. She tilted her chin up to exhale, and the details of her face were lost in a haze of gray. He knew he was wasting his words on the woman he'd met smoking behind a stand of palmettos forty-five years ago, but he added, "You shouldn't smoke inside the house. You shouldn't smoke at all."

Emelina looked at him and blew two perfect smoke rings his way.

Efraín shook his head and shifted his weight from his weak foot to his strong one. Housebound after the roofing accident, he now knew Eme's afternoon routine. This was one of the four Newport cigarettes his wife allowed herself each day. After coming home from St. Anthony's Elementary School, where she worked as a kindergarten aide, she changed out of her work clothes and sat in front of the TV, placing her cigarettes single file, yellow filter tips uniformly aligned, on the coffee table. She smoked two while she watched *Ellen*, and two during that idiot *Dr. Phil.* Then, she showered and made dinner. That's when he would arrive from work before his accident, when Eme had dinner ready. He hadn't known that she even had a routine until three months ago, when he'd fallen and shattered his ankle. He was inspecting work completed by the crew of the small company he owned when the edge of his foot caught an upraised shingle, sending him, shocked and spiraling, down the length of the steep-pitched roof.

Fell off a goddamn roof after spending the better part of my life roofing.

That's what he said to people who asked, more curious than concerned, at la bodeguita. Of course, it wasn't really a bodeguita at all, not like the little stores in West Tampa stocked with Cuban products, smelling of root vegetables, cumin, and dry-salted cod. This one, barely a mile from his house, was just a regular mini-mart: gas pumps, beer, bad coffee, prefab sandwiches, and lottery tickets. Still, it offered a break from the house and Eme's smoking.

Efraín had always disliked Emelina's cigarettes, but her smoke, blended with the smell from the air system, made the house even more unbearable that afternoon than it had been during the last three months. Emelina tended to him dutifully following the accident, just as he had cared for her years ago during her pérdidas. That's what they came to call her repeated miscarriages over the years. Her pérdidas. But while he had given his attention generously during her losses, he felt Emelina was miserly with hers. She was impatient as she helped him out of bed and to the bathroom. She was brusque in manner as she settled him on the couch in front of the television or helped him bathe, the ordinary necessities of the day. It humiliated him to need help.

"You can leave," he said to her a week after the accident, more out of disappointment and weariness than anger. "Go back to work. I don't need you to stay."

Emelina was visibly relieved to return to her job and the children, and he made do alone. Efraín had to admit he envied her the distraction of work. Without it he felt lost. Without it he felt the way he did as a boy standing on the tarmac of the Miami airport with nothing but a small suitcase and a name tag.

Outside, the chilly dampness of the afternoon startled his body as if he'd been dunked in icy water, and it wasn't even all that cold yet. Not really. Not Nebraska cold. It was the first day the Florida temperatures had significantly dropped for the season, and they'd continue to fall as day turned into night. Efraín hated winter. He hated the way the cold seemed to find him once it started, creeping up his sleeves and down his collar, pinching his ears and smarting his eyes no matter what he did to guard himself against it. And this winter brought with it a previously unknown discomfort, a constant ache from the pins that now held his ankle together.

Efraín started his truck and waited for the engine to heat up. He waited for warm air to blow from the vents, and when it did he rubbed his hands in front of them as if in front of a fire. He figured he'd go get his weekly Lotto, and get away from Emelina and her afternoon cigarettes as the house warmed up.

Emelina had been smoking the first time Efraín met her, back in 1966. It had been at a get-together at his friend Rafaelito's house, and he'd only been in Tampa a few weeks. He'd gone to the backyard, away from the noisy chatter of the house, to the end of the property where a stand of palmettos grew. He found Emelina behind them. She wore a short navy-blue dress with a white sailor collar, and stood there in white high-heeled sandals with perfectly polished coral toenails, holding a cigarette with the tips of her outstretched fingers.

"You caught me," she said, adding quickly, "Papi doesn't approve."

He mumbled something apologetic, and turned to leave, but she stopped him.

"When did you get here?"

He knew by the way she said "here" that she didn't mean here as in the backyard, or even here as in Tampa, but here as in the United States.

"Over three years ago," he said. "Pedro Pan. You?"

"Just this past year. Camarioca Boat Lift. ¿Directo a Tampa?"

He shook his head. "Nebraska."

"Nebraska? Where is that?" Emelina asked.

▩

The truck warmed up during the brief drive to the mini-mart, but the steering wheel felt thick and cold in Efraín's hands, and the chill of the vinyl seats made its way through his clothes. As he pulled into the mini-mart, feeling his pockets for his cell phone, his attention was drawn to an ordinary woman by the notice of two unremarkable things. She'd gotten out of a taxi, an unusual sight in this suburban part of town where everyone drove themselves; and, even though he couldn't hear her, he knew by her body language that she was speaking Spanish. She touched her heart with one palm, and held up the other flat, patting the air before her, shaking her head and scrunching her shoulders all in one simultaneous motion.

Efraín parked, and rummaged in the glove compartment for his penciled Lotto play slip. He finally found it beneath some paper napkins he'd carelessly tossed in a few days before. The slip was worn and dog-eared; he needed to fill out a new one.

"Why don't you buy Advance Play?" Emelina asked him once. "You play the same numbers every week; just buy the same ticket weeks ahead without the bother."

"Because," Efraín said, "it would be like spitting in the face of fate."

"Do you believe in fate?" Eme asked.

Efraín wasn't sure. If he hadn't met Rafaelito he wouldn't have come to Tampa, and he wouldn't have met Eme. He wouldn't have started roofing, and broken his ankle. Was that fate?

In the parking lot of the mini-mart, Efraín kept the truck motor running, and enjoyed the blast of warm air. He used the center of the steering wheel as a table top, carefully penciling in his numbers on a crisp play slip. The knock on his door window startled him. It was the woman from the taxi.

He rolled down the glass, and cold air invaded his truck.

"¿Habla español?" the woman asked him.

Efraín nodded.

"Mire," the woman started. She said el chofer, el taxista, had brought her here from the bus terminal, but she didn't think this was the address, and she didn't understand anything he'd said. He'd driven her back and forth, she said, pointing to the road that fronted the mini-mart, and then made her get out of the cab.

Efraín looked at the woman, trying hard to follow what she said. He had no trouble with Spanish, even though his conversations with Emelina usually fell into English, and he'd stopped thinking in his native language God knew how many years ago. He still spoke rapidly his Cuban Spanish with swallowed final syllables and nonexistent plural *s*'s. He spoke effortlessly with Puerto Ricans who couldn't roll *r*'s, and emphasized everything with bendito this, and bendito that. But this woman's Spanish was clipped, yet lilting, rising and falling in a cadence that left him wondering if she was asking a question or making a statement.

She stood there, pushing stray strands of hair away from her weathered face, clutching a piece of paper, telling him she was lost.

"Tell me what your paper says," Efraín said.

"No puedo," she responded.

"Why can't you?"

"Because I can't."

Efraín looked at the woman, realizing she didn't know how to read, and said softly, "Por favor, Señora, let me see."

He looked at the scribbled address on the wrinkled paper, a Fletcher Avenue address, the road behind him. He glanced over his shoulder, the east-west artery already filling with rush-hour traffic, and saw the taxi pull away. He looked down from the truck at the woman. She was squat and round, wearing gray sweatpants and an oversized men's jacket. Efraín sighed, half in pity, half in resignation, and asked her to get in the truck.

She climbed in with a knapsack and a small brown duffle. He began to say she could put them in the flatbed, but she put them on the floor in front of her and placed her feet carefully on top of them. Efraín noticed the side of her black sneaker was taped with a silver strip of frayed duct tape. A doughy smell of corn tamales emanated from her knapsack.

Efraín studied the address as she explained she was trying to find her brother.

"Where are you coming from?" Efraín asked.

"Carolina del Norte," she said. "I came for the strawberries." The strawberries were ripening and picking season would begin soon on the east side of the county. Harvesting work would be plentiful.

"It is very early for them," she sang, "but, well, usted sabe, la Migra."

Efraín stuck his play slip over the visor, and backed toward Fletcher Avenue. He believed from the numbers on the address that it shouldn't be far, just slightly west of the mini-mart. He waited for a break in traffic, as the afternoon crawl began.

"Gracias, Señor," she said.

Efraín shrugged a de nada as they waited for a red light to change.

She rubbed her hands in front of the air vent as he had done earlier, and asked politely, "What is your country?"

"Cuba," he said.

"How long have you been here?" she asked. "¿Hace mucho tiempo?"

"Sí," Efraín said, "it has been a very long time."

"¿Desde cuándo, Señor?"

"Since 1962."

Efraín was fourteen. Fidel had closed private schools and formed youth patrols; young teenagers were being sent into the interior to work on agricultural farms and teach illiterate campesinos to read. They can't get their hands on him, he heard his mother tell his father one night.

Efraín inched his truck along with traffic, west toward the sinking sun. The woman rearranged her feet around her belongings. She lowered the top of her jacket zipper just slightly where it had been pressing against her chin. He realized it made it more comfortable for her to breathe and speak as she repeated his words back to him.

"It has been a very long time," she said. "You came with your family, no?"

Efraín darted his eyes back and forth repeatedly from the wrinkled paper in his hand to the red brake lights of the car in front of him as if that would wipe away the images of the day he left Havana and his family.

"Señora, I believe the address is not far from here," he said, his voice tight and strained, although there was no zipper pressing against his chin.

■

Pedro Pan. Efraín remembered standing on the tarmac of the Miami airport, wearing a name tag and feeling lost. Many children, some so young they clutched a stuffed animal or doll, were met by relatives. Others, like him, were placed on a bus and driven to Camp Matecumbe, a processing center.

That's where he first met Rafaelito; he too, was alone. Two weeks later, with no word from his parents, he boarded another bus, together with Rafaelito. This time they were escorted by a young nun from Catholic Family Services, who rode with them to a boys' home in Nebraska.

The longer Efraín rode on the bus, the colder the weather became. The monjita spoke to him cheerfully. He knew it was cheerfully because she smiled and patted his hand, but he couldn't understand a word she said. She even said his name wrong, Efren, as if it had no *a* or *i*.

▩

Efraín felt a sudden chill as he drove cautiously in the stop-and-go traffic looking for the address on the worn sheet of paper. Suddenly the numbers were too low, and he cursed silently, assuming he'd missed it and doubling back. It happened again: a ten-number jump. There was an entrance to a condo complex where the number he searched for should be, and Efraín knew it wasn't the place, but he turned in anyway. It was a gated complex that didn't allow passage past the main driveway without an entry code. He turned the truck around, pulling along the length of a white-painted curb.

Did she have a phone number, he asked. Was she certain of the address; was her brother waiting? Bueno, she said and explained. Her brother expected her for the strawberries; he'd given the address over a pay phone to someone she knew. When word spread through North Carolina that la Migra was tightening down, she decided to leave early. She presented the address at the bus terminal and bought a ticket. She couldn't read, she said apologetically. But, she added proudly, she could count.

Efraín leaned toward the steering wheel and back again, shifting around in his seat; God, he hated buses.

▩

At the boys' home in Nebraska he bunked with Rafaelito. They were the same age. After lights out they traded stories about their families and homes as they boasted of baseball feats, carefully avoiding with false bravado how scared and lonely they were. They started to crunch English words out of their mouths as they awaited letters from home.

They hoped to be reunited soon, the letters said, although the ones from Efraín's mother contained no specifics. Ten months later, as if a present for his fifteenth birthday, Rafaelito received a telegram saying his family was in Florida. Efraín began writing home every day. When are you coming? he asked in every letter.

Things were uncertain, his mother wrote back. His father wasn't sure when they could leave. The letters became repetitious as Efraín turned sixteen, seventeen, and then could see eighteen. The sprawling house of his boyhood, in the elegant Vedado neighborhood of Havana, had been in his father's family for three generations. His father was reluctant to leave; Castro would certainly fall. Efraín wrote one last letter before he turned eighteen.

Understand, niño, we cannot leave what is ours.

Now, decades later, he remembers the veranda that wrapped around his house in Havana. He has hazy memories of Soledad, the maid who prepared his noonday lunches while his mother played canasta with her manicured friends. And while he can no longer conjure his mother's face, he remembers her voice in that letter.

When he turned eighteen the orphanage provided a one-way bus ticket to any place he wanted to go. He'd received letters from Rafaelito, frequently at first when he left to join his family in Florida, more sporadically as the years went on. Rafaelito wrote that he and his family lived in Tampa, much farther north than Miami, but warm nevertheless. He told Efraín that Tampa had a boulevard called Bayshore, which hugged the bay the way the Malecón did in Havana, and although waves didn't come crashing over the seawall as they did on the Malecón, it was still quite a sight to see.

▩

Efraín now wondered if the address was missing a number or had an extra one. It couldn't be any farther west. The avenue changed names shortly past the condo complex as it crossed a large intersection and became a curving tree-lined road leading into well-established neighborhoods.

He decided to turn around and head east.

Traffic moved slowly as they passed the mini-mart from where they'd started, continuing east, under the interstate overpass. The area changed abruptly on the other side of the interstate. He drove through Suitcase City, a low-rent area of town where worn hookers, homeless people pushing shopping carts, and scab-skinned meth-heads roamed the streets.

Efraín drove on diligently on the lookout for an address he was now starting to believe didn't exist. The dimming winter sun cast a yellow shadow, and he felt his ankle begin to throb. He asked the woman about her family, making conversation to keep the pain in his foot at bay.

"Tengo cinco hijos," the woman said, telling Efraín of the five children she'd left in Mexico with her mother, and how she sent money every month to keep them fed. She'd followed the crops alone for almost two years, and now her brother was here. It would be easier, verdad, with someone?

"It must be so hard," Efraín said mindlessly, and the obviousness of his statement actually shamed him.

"I do whatever destiny asks," she said. She smoothed her gray sweatpants, and delicately placed her crossed palms on top of one knee. "¿Y usted, Señor? What is your work?"

"Techos."

▩

He'd come from Nebraska to the house of Rafaelito's parents, where for a short time he was allowed to stay. Construction work was readily available, and even though he had no skills, he could hit a nail with a hammer. A friend of Rafaelito's family found him work—framing roofs. Efraín swung himself across the trusses under a hot Florida sky, vengefully pounding nails. He peeled off his shirt and let the sun blister his skin. Sweat poured out his body. He finished each day with aching muscles, and a profound exhaustion that gratefully brought him sleep.

Two weeks after meeting Emelina behind the palmettos, he saw her again at a birthday party for one of Rafaelito's cousins. From a distance, he watched Emelina dance in the living room, then watched as she headed for the back door and followed her to the corner of the yard where rose bushes surrounded a thigh-high, plaster San Lazaro.

"Caught me again," she said.

"What?" he asked, "no cigarettes?"

Emelina giggled. "No cigarettes, but too much cidra. Do you dance?"

Efraín shook his head.

Before he realized what was happening, Emelina leaned his way and kissed him, softly and fully. At eighteen, he had never been kissed before.

"Seems there are two things I'm going to have to teach you," Emelina said.

Efraín stood there breathing hard, his face burning, and said nothing.

"I had a boyfriend," she motioned with her head, "back there. An official boyfriend. Comprometida. My father said we could get married when I turned twenty."

"What," Efraín started and cleared his throat, finding his voice, "happened?"

"He didn't want to come with us when we had the chance to leave," she said. "There was room in the boat, but I guess he loved the Revolution more than me. He sent a picture a few months ago. He's standing by a truck, holding a large transistor radio. He wrote he'd won it cutting sugar cane—he was the first to meet the required quota. I sent him back a picture of me with a radio. I told him I'd won mine by eating ham." Emelina turned around quickly and went back into the house, leaving Efraín alone in the yard.

▩

In her sing-song voice the woman recounted the names and ages of her children, adding some detail about each, telling him Roberto, her eldest, ate whole tomatoes the way americano children ate apples, and Luisita, her youngest, was afraid of thunder. Then she told him her husband was gone. Se nos fue, she said, and Efraín chose not to ask if she meant he'd died or had abandoned them. And when he said nothing, because he didn't know what to say, she asked if he was married.

"Sí," Efraín nodded, "sí, Señora, sí."

▩

In the same way Efraín found roofing work, knowing someone, or someone who knew someone, he found a small room to rent. Two years later as they both turned twenty, to his happy surprise, he married lovely Emelina.

One night in bed, while on their brief honeymoon, Emelina held her arm toward him, her wrist pulse side up. "Bite me," she said.

Efraín let out a snicker, shook his head puzzled, and pushed her arm away.

"Do it," she said. "Bite me!"

When he said no, Emelina grabbed his arm and sunk her teeth into his flesh. Efraín yelped and yanked his arm away.

Emelina looked directly into his eyes. "Remember this," she said. "You couldn't, but I could." She took his arm again and gently licked the red crescents her teeth had left, then she trailed her tongue up his arm, across his chest, and down his body.

■

"¿Y usted y su esposa?" the woman asked. "Do you have children?"

Efraín shook his head. They were stopped. The truck idled as they waited for traffic to move, but Efraín did not look her way.

"¡Qué lástima!" the woman said, and having expressed her pity, fell silent.

Emelina had lost six. The first one they conceived and lost before their first anniversary. Ten years later, the last one, the one she carried the longest, bled out of her before she'd reached the third trimester, even though she'd diligently stayed in bed for weeks.

"You can leave too," Emelina had said to him. "I don't need you to stay."

■

They continued along, leaving behind Suitcase City and entering the part of Fletcher Avenue that housed medical offices and backed the research area of the university.

"It is not here, is it?" the woman asked.

It was time to turn around. Efraín looked at her. "Do you know anyone else?"

"No."

They drove in silence, through the early dusk, back the way they came. Efraín felt a weight deep within him, as he considered options. He could drive her to a shelter, rent her a motel room, take her home; what would Emelina say?

They were now reentering Suitcase City again, when she said loudly, "There. Stop there."

"Where?" He looked where she pointed.

In a strip mall, housed between an Amscot and an Asian nail parlor, was a small storefront; the sign above it was a replica of the Mexican flag labeled Productos Mexicanos. The storefront window read: Tomatillos, Masa Harina, Envíos Directos.

"That's not the address," Efraín said.

"It does not matter."

Efraín parked in front. He grimaced as he stepped down from the truck, and walked to the passenger side. He intended to help her with her bags, but she was already out of the truck, possessions in hand, holding tightly to what was hers.

"Señora, are you sure?" Efraín asked uncomfortably.

She nodded, reached in her pocket, and pulled out a crumpled five-dollar bill. Before she could offer it to him, Efraín held up his hands, palms flat, firmly saying no, hoping it wouldn't be an insult if he offered her some money.

She draped her knapsack over her shoulder, touched his arm, and said in her melodic Spanish, "God will pay you in his glory."

Efraín sat in the truck and watched her enter the market. The heat from the vents suddenly felt stifling and he turned it off, noticing that the floury corn scent lingered even though she'd gone. Finally, with an oppressive sense of loss, he drove away.

■

When Efraín entered his house it was filled with the pungent smell of sofrito. He closed the door quickly against the cold.

"Efraín!" Emelina said loudly. She walked toward him, wiping her hands on a dish towel. "You left your cell here."

Efraín opened his mouth to speak, but Emelina didn't give him a chance. "Where have you been?" she asked and he saw genuine worry in her eyes. "You're gone forever, it's dark, and you're out there with that damn foot of yours, all descojona'o. You hear all the time about people having strokes, forgetting where they live."

Emelina reached out and took his hands in hers. "What happened, viejo? Did you get lost?"

Noelia and Amparo

Glendaliz Camacho

Amparo met him on a Friday night when the brothel was resurrected by the women's laughter—too high pitched to be sincere—tobacco smoke, and dimmed lights winking off chipped glasses of rum. She strode into the bedroom, where he was sitting with the posture of a war hero's statue in the plaza.

Amparo introduced herself by offering her back so he could unzip her dress. His hands were smooth and weighty like rocks worn flat by constant water, unlike the calloused sugar cane cutters who sometimes held her by the throat, as if she were a goddamn reed herself. Amparo removed his fedora, somber gray suit, tie, shirt, shoes, socks, and underwear, hanging up and folding as necessary. She was as thorough the rest of the night, so that the scar on her right index finger, the faded burns on her left forearm, or her pendulous breasts that hung like a wet nurse's did not matter. He finished not with a grunt but with an anguished pant in her ear as if he had bitten into food that was too hot. Amparo poured him a glass of water from a jug on the nightstand.

"When can I see you again?"

She lit a cigarette, inhaled, and passed it to him, while he gulped down the water.

"Ask yourself." She pointed her chin toward his wallet, which she had placed conveniently within his reach on the nightstand. She would not remember his name until his fifth visit, when she wiped the sweat from his forehead with someone else's forgotten handkerchief and Fede told her he loved her.

■

Noelia had spent every year since her twenty-third tightening the habit of spinsterhood around herself so that now at thirty-three, men were wholly obscured from her sight. Men were something to be sifted through like the pots of uncooked pigeon peas that as a child she would watch the cook inspect for pebbles. Noelia had no shortage of suitors, but sooner or later—thankfully always sooner rather than later—they revealed themselves as pebbles. Noelia saw no good reason to risk what was certain to be a cracked tooth.

Noelia's brother introduced her to Federico on a Sunday after Mass. He spoke to her for too long, too animatedly, about his work at the sugar refinery, the book of Pedro Mir poems he was reading, how the music young people listened to like that merengue sounded as if it barreled straight out of a bayou, his sonorous voice drawing curious glances. Noelia found him silly, especially for a man of forty-three, but there was something about his enthusiasm that made her smile as he spoke.

It was not until she was at the dining table, later that same Sunday, surrounded by her parents, brother, sister-in-law, sisters, brothers-in-law, nieces, and nephews that Noelia allowed herself a moment to indulge in wondering what it would feel like to have a man seated next to her that she could look upon with tenderness, as he brought a forkful of food to his lips. To her surprise, she pictured the somewhat endearing laugh lines around Federico's mouth.

Noelia declined Federico's first invitation for coffee after Mass—since visiting London, she preferred tea—and a subsequent one for lunch—she ate with her family. His dinner invitation was far too intimate, but she finally acquiesced to a walk in the plaza. He was shorter than she would've preferred and his spicy cologne was so overpowering, she was grateful their proper walking positions—he on the outside, closest to the curb, and she on the inside, closest to the houses and shops—did not place her downwind. Yet she found herself wondering if his kiss would taste of his last meal, the mints that clattered against their tin prison in his suit jacket pocket, or nothing at all.

Their courtship was much like that first stroll—pleasant, unhurried, respectful. Saturday afternoons they enjoyed films at the local cinema—*The Bridge on the River Kwai*, *An Affair to Remember*, *Tizoc*. They attended dances at the San Juan Social Club, established by the burgeoning community of Puerto Rican émigrés, thanks to the refinery. Noelia waited for him to lie, make a disparaging remark, or cross the line of propriety between a man and a woman, but the moment never arrived.

One evening, after the customary light dinner with Noelia's family—fish soup, white rice, toasted bread, and marble cake that night—Federico smoked his cigarette on the porch. Noelia sat beside him on the swinging bench that cupped them in the breeze. The full moon hung low and heavy like an expectant mother.

"How beautiful." Federico's exhaled smoke drifted up to the moon like an offering.

"If you like old rocks," Noelia teased.

"That old rock has been illuminating the darkness for millennia."

"Don't we have the sun for that?"

"The sun is a tyrant. The Earth is forced to revolve around it or die, but the moon orbits around us."

"That makes the moon nothing more than our slave."

"Not at all. Because as much as we pull the moon toward us, she also pulls back and rules a part of us. The ocean." Federico clasped Noelia's hand in his. She was no longer looking at the moon. Six months later, they were married.

▒

Amparo had not seen Fede in a couple of months, but she only realized it when he reappeared seated at the foot of her rickety bed with a box in his hands. From the way Fede's eyes grew large behind his glasses and he cleared his throat, Amparo could tell he was not expecting to see her hand holding another's. I bet this will put out his fire, she thought. Her son peered at Fede from behind her thigh. She leaned down, whispered in his ear, and the boy slipped away.

"I noticed you have pierced ears, but never wear earrings." Fede handed her a red box tied with white ribbon. Inside was a pair of diamond earrings mounted on white gold. Amparo resisted the urge to bite them, but considered their utility in an emergency with a visit to the pawn shop.

"You have new jewelry too." She eyed his wedding band. Even in the caliginosity of her room, Amparo saw Fede's cheeks flush. She began to unzip her skirt, but he grasped her wrist and patted a threadbare patch of sheet next to him on the bed.

"I've been promoted. To civil engineer."

"Congratulations."

"I want you to stop working."

Amparo nodded as if she were indulging a child. "You don't say." She marched to her door and swung it open, fist planted on her hip. "You don't want me to stop working. You want me to work for you instead." A panic rose inside her like a wave and crashed in her head. It was that same feeling that made her believe in a man once. Back then, she needed to believe in just one man's word. Because all the girls in her barrio did before getting married. Yet she was the only one in a whorehouse. She misstepped in her choice of man or how much of herself she gave. Her mother always said if two people are in a relationship, make sure you're not the one in love. Her heart still limped at the memory of her son's father, like an animal that manages to survive a trap, but not without broken limbs and missing patches of fur. Amparo wondered if it wasn't too late though to get back to where she was supposed to be in her life.

"Get out," she whispered hoarsely, barely louder than the din in her head.

Fede extracted bills from his clip and placed them on the nightstand. "You owe me time then. Or change."

Amparo cut her eyes from Fede to the money. She closed the door, but hovered in front of it, fingers wrapped around the broken doorknob. The door trembled against its ill-fitting frame every time the girl and customer in the neighboring room exerted themselves.

"What did you dream about when you were a girl?"

"If you're going to ask me stupid questions, I'd rather give you your change." Amparo lunged at the money.

"Wait. Just answer me. What kind of life did you want to have when you grew up?"

"The same shit all the girls wanted." Amparo stopped riffling through the bills. A blanket of dust had long settled over her wants and she was afraid she would regret this moment, disturbing it. "I wanted more than what I had. A clean house. A handsome husband. Children.

A dog. My mother said it would be cruel to make a dog go hungry with us."

Fede guided Amparo to sit next to him. "When I was a boy, I had a piglet. León. I fed him with one of my sister's old baby bottles. He slept with me every night until he grew too big.

"Oh, don't look at me that way. Pigs are intelligent animals. We've just limited them to being food. Anyway, one day, a hurricane ripped everything away. The only cow we had, the chickens, the two other pigs, the mango tree, the roof, and two of the walls. León was the only animal left. Until my father told me to fetch León.

"Look, there are things we want and things that ensure our survival. When they're one and the same, that's a blessing, but when they're not . . . Well, we are animals too so we'll always guarantee our own survival above anything."

Amparo brushed invisible crumbs off her skirt and tested the truth of what Fede said against the misery of her twenty-five years. Survival was wrapped around her life like a plantain leaf around a pastel.

"Now . . . I may not be exactly what you dreamed of," Fede said as he lifted his fedora and ran his palm over his receding hairline, "but I can give you a better place to live. Your son can go to a private school. And I do love you. You and I are like two different fruits, but grown in the same *conuco*."

Amparo narrowed her eyes. "What about you? What do you get out of this?"

"I've already secured my survival. Now I'd like to have what I want."

Amparo did not receive another client—after Fede made arrangements with the madam, of course. Two weeks later Amparo had chosen the row house Fede would rent for them.

▒

Fridays and Saturdays, Amparo and Fede expressed what they didn't have time for during the week. He, his ardor, through roses, Neruda poems whispered in the dark and love letters left on the nightstand before Sunday dawns. Amparo, her cautious gratitude, with stuffed peppers, meatballs, and stewed codfish.

Amparo was very clear on her place and wasn't in love with Fede anyway. That didn't mean she was indifferent to his well-being or happiness; in fact she cared so much she was willing to be the reason for his. That was some kind of love, not the one he wished he would see in her eyes when he was on top of her, she was sure, and not the love that made her blood dance like her son's father did, but it was something and it dug into her a little deeper each day.

▩

Federico's absences did not go unnoticed by Noelia. She came close to asking him several times, fortifying herself through the night with the belief that truth was preferable to illusion and questioning what good principles of character were if they crumbled at the slightest pressure. Hadn't she considered herself a woman *hecha y derecha*? Well, here was an opportunity to distinguish herself as a woman who is, rather than a woman who thinks she is, but when Federico arrived Sunday mornings there was only enough time to get themselves ready for Mass. Then Sundays did not seem appropriate for anything but devotion to God. The rest of the week settled into a rhythm she was averse to disrupting on the distant hope it would continue through the weekend.

Noelia was certain, however, and she took that certainty and busied herself in the kitchen for fear the turmoil would devour her—which gave the cook heart palpitations about losing her job, but Noelia assured her this was just a whim and she would be needing her for the real work. Noelia's fingers found peace in the repetitive chopping and stirring that quieted her mind so that only the dish mattered—not her charred ego or slices of jealousy. Cooking filled any holes that had eaten through her soul like moths, made them not quite whole but aromatic and vibrant. Noelia remembered how much she enjoyed the smell of onions and garlic sautéing, heralds of the good meal to come, before it became improper for her to spend her days as if she were the help. When her sisters were pregnant, they craved her *rellenos*, bursting with pork seasoned with salt, pepper, garlic, oregano, and only her hen soup would do when her father came down with a cold.

At first it was random things—*ñoquis*, bread pudding, goat marinated in bitter orange and rum—until the first time Federico did not come home on a Thursday. She escaped the mocking of her empty bed before dawn and began a purposeful banquet, by the light of an oil lamp, so that her shadow on the wall resembled a witch hunched over a cauldron.

▩

There was a knock at Amparo's door precisely as she was adding *auyama* and carrots to the simmering pot of *arvejas* for Fede's lunch. When she opened the door, a young black woman in a servant's uniform stood on the porch. Avoiding Amparo's eyes, she thrust a large basket in her arms. "*De parte de Doña Noelia.*" The girl scampered away before Amparo could say or do anything.

From Federico's car, Noelia thought Amparo looked more like a cook than a whore. She was a sturdy mulatta with coarse hair held away from her face by a red headband. She'd actually come to the door in a faded housecoat! Noelia couldn't decide whether to be relieved or offended. When her maid climbed back into the sky-blue Ford, Noelia asked the driver to take them home.

▩

When Fede arrived at noon, he showered as he usually did. As he dried his glasses and sat at the head of the table—which Amparo liked to point out was square so for all they knew the empty seats were the heads—Fede asked, with a pinch to Amparo's bottom, if they were having an indoor picnic.

Amparo unpacked the *ensalada de vainitas y repollo cocido*, *higado*, *pan*, *aguacate*, even *dulce de naranjas en almibar* for dessert. The lettuce, string bean, and cabbage salad glistened with olive oil and vinegar, reminding Amparo of the schoolgirls with shiny long hair who always chose to stand next to her and shake their tresses in her face. That bitch, Amparo thought as she served the liver. The one thing that Amparo couldn't stand to eat—there was just not enough garlic and oregano in the world to make liver taste better than sucking on a handful of coins—and here it was reminding her of the things life would serve her whether she liked it or not. You don't know who you're fucking with, she fumed as she bit into a piece of crusty bread. She had never swallowed anything life threw at her—not her father's nighttime visits, not her son's father leaving soon after her menstruation stopped, and not this now.

"How is everything?" Amparo asked Fede as he chewed a mouthful of liver.

"Very good. As always."

When she told him the meal was courtesy of his own house, his wife, he turned a shade of yellow to match the center of the avocado slice on his plate and choked on that mouthful of liver as his food went cold. As did he.

■

Noelia arrived at her parents' house with two suitcases. Her parents looked at them as if they were stuffed with tapeworms instead of clothes. When Noelia confided to her mother that she had followed Federico, her mother shook her head. "Who told you to go snooping?"

Her father, the voice of reason, merely suggested finding a solution because while allowing Noelia to stay unmarried for so long had only inspired a few whispers—which they tolerated out of love—this was more serious. Besides, they were getting older. Where would she run to when they were no longer there? Perhaps a child would keep Federico at home more, after all the man had no family, no roots in the Dominican Republic.

Noelia did not bother to stay for dinner. As her father's driver took her home, she thought of Adam and Eve being expelled from Eden except she could no longer agree that their sin was egregious enough to merit exile.

A child. Apparently, she was herself only a child whose life decisions were really only indulgences her parents had granted her. Her life was like the tea parties she had with her dolls as a girl—she controlled the proceedings, but only until she was called for dinner by the real adults. She was not a moon, a sun, the earth, or an ocean; she was a woman. Just a woman.

Back home again, Noelia's unpacking was interrupted by a knock at the door. She told the maid she would answer, relieved for the distraction and yes, despite everything, hoping it was Federico, but it was a boy. About five years old, with beautiful brown eyes that swept about nervously, he handed her a bag he could barely carry and ran off the steps, down the street.

She unpacked the bag on the mahogany dining room table and almost said "Touché" out loud. The smell of *sancocho de mondongo* made her insides lurch. It was accompanied by steaming white rice, avocado, and *dulce de coco con batata*. She hated when *mondongo* was cooked in her parents' house. Everyone was insane to even think of eating beef tripe. That was only a few degrees from eating entrails and they might as well be savages if they ate that way. She didn't back down and she expects me to. Noelia forced a spoonful of *sancocho* into her mouth. She's got nerve, but that doesn't only grow in barrios and campos. Noelia continued to plunge her spoon into the food until it was all gone. There was another knock on the door, but Noelia could remember nothing but the sound of her own retching and the acrid taste of bile after the policemen gave her their condolences.

When her throat still burned the next morning and her stomach would not stop convulsing, her mother and sisters insisted it was the impact of such a terrible tragedy, but it occurred to Noelia that Amparo could have poisoned her. A visit from Dr. Linares proved them all wrong though. Noelia was pregnant.

▒

Amparo watched Noelia from the gate of the cemetery as mourners filed past her. Noelia's face was hidden behind large sunglasses and a hat with a veil, but the hair that peeked out against the nape of her long, ivory neck was fine and blond. Despite the balmy weather, her black dress, and gloves, she seemed encased in a block of ice, apart from all those people around her. She moved only to dab her cheeks with a white, silk handkerchief.

At the end of the service, Noelia motioned to her family to walk ahead, that she needed a moment. She walked over to Amparo, lifted her veil, and removed her sunglasses. Neither woman spoke; they stood side by side, watching workers shovel dirt onto his coffin.

"I'm pregnant." Noelia's hand rested on her stomach.

"You'll have to eat better." Amparo turned to face her.

Noelia was the first to pucker her lips to dam the laugh in her mouth, but it was no use. Both women burst into laughter behind their palms, until tears spilled over and all that was left at the end was a deep, simultaneous sigh. They drew more than a few stares and whispers from mourners walking to their waiting drivers. Both women regarded each other for a moment, curious but too spent to ask.

"Take care." Amparo turned and walked away, remembering her cravings for freshly baked French bread with butter when she was pregnant. She stopped at the bakery for a loaf. As she bit into the handfuls she broke off, her tears mixing into the butter, she wondered if Noelia's growing belly would eclipse the memory of them all and she whispered a blessing for that baby.

A Strange People

Mecca Jamilah Sullivan

We-Chrissie will let the white men see and touch our difference. She will smile for doctors and handlers like Mrs. Susan's old china trinket dolls, tilt her head just so and laugh, her hand grabbing at our hemline. In the next town, we'll see banners and broadsides proclaiming our "charm." We-Millie will not understand why they would write us that way. She will taste the word like coffee grounds in her mouth and wonder how they can print it so small and neat below the headlines: "Double-Headed Darkey," "United Negress Freaks," "Two-Headed African Beast." We-Chrissie will not have these questions. She will know that the nice words are for her. She is the one who has always hated us.

When we were young, decades ago, We-Chrissie wrote her version of our story, and everyone who knew us was surprised. She got most of the facts straight, told about our slave birth and the scandal we caused on our first master's farm, how we were sold from Master John and Mrs. Susan, then slipped like a wet hunk of soap from hand to hand, master to master, growing up and filling out the carnival circuit, seeing things most North Carolina nigger girls wouldn't even think to dream of—the darting English steam cars, the white-choked winter at the Cirque des Champs-Elysées. We-Chrissie spent a few words on the best time in We-Millie's part of the life, when we ended up back in Mrs. Susan's arms. She said a couple of things about our life on the midway, the place between the circus gates and the big top, where freak acts wander about and ballyhoo, preening and fanning their freakhood, squeezing awe like from the norms' eyes like milk from a fat cow's udders.

We-Chrissie is an all-star bally, has always been. She preened and flaunted in her story too, playing our difference up and down like a yo-yo tossed to thrill a child. First it was a "malformation," then it was a "joy." Our join was a curse we were proud of, she said, painting on our minds the paradox of our body. And she refused to let them think for a second that the slightest drip of difference ran between we-two. "We are, indeed, a strange people," she began her story, and it continued on like that—"a people," two, but one. She refused to tell anyone it was she alone who had written the story, without letting We-Millie so much as touch the pen or smell the ink when the manuscript was done. We-Chrissie wrote then, and will tell anyone who asks now, that there is only one heart in the body. We-Millie sits silent when she says this, and lets her go ahead with her show. We-Millie knows, though, that our hearts are separate. Our wombs, our backs, our hot puddles and buttons come in and out of each other like corset laces; We-Chrissie feels We-Millie's itches and We-Millie rubs on We-Chrissie's aches, but for We-Millie, our hearts are separate things, different as the sun and the moon pinning down the ends of a long day's sky.

It is obvious to everyone that We-Chrissie is the charming one. She is the one the newspapers talk about when they say we are beautiful, alluring, delightful. We-Millie is the one that scares people, we think. She is quiet and unsure, and if we were not us, if we were norms, or nigger girls at least, We-Millie would never find herself within a stone's throw of a stage. We-Millie speaks German and Spanish better than We-Chrissie, better than Mrs. Susan, who taught us. But she stays quiet, the small, silent half. We-Chrissie is stronger; We-Millie is frail. We-Chrissie is pretty; We-Millie is darker and with a gnarling nose. While We-Chrissie smiles at the doctors and invites them to probe the body, We-Millie plays along and feels her heart burn in its cage. It is her feebler puddle, her crookeder pit in which they will splash and plunge to their hearts' content.

While We-Chrissie talks to reporters, doctors, midway norms, We-Millie moves her mouth and smiles along, but sends her mind inside. Both of we-two make up stories. We-Chrissie likes to say hers, shout them out from the stage, read them in the papers, write them down in books. We-Millie keeps her stories to herself.

When Mrs. Susan heard about We-Chrissie's story, she smiled, her soft pink cheeks glowing like the virgin's as she chuckled. "I know I tried with you-all, but you couldn't have convinced me that that one ever learned to read. Least not by my hand. Don't know what you-all picked up on the road, I suppose." We-Chrissie has never been bothered by Mrs. Susan's comments. We-Millie gulps down Mrs. Susan's words like iced tea. We-Chrissie always took Mrs. Susan in sips, swishing her around in slow judgment whenever the woman was around, sometimes spitting her out when it was just we-two alone.

The biggest fight we-two ever had happened the morning of Master John's funeral. We-Chrissie wanted to wear our star-spangled taffeta costume to the service. She said we'd be the blow-off, the grand finale of Master John's long-lived show. To her, he was a freak on his own, and a gaff at that. She said he passed for a kind master, an innocent roped into managing us like a child lured to the midway with candy and fairy tales, but that he was really a mastermind who had plotted our course from the time of our birth, calculating our lifetime's revenue by the time we were two months old. We-Millie liked her skepticism, but got hot at the thought of disrespecting Mrs. Susan by wearing the dress. We-Millie has loved Mrs. Susan forever, in the way that norm women, she thinks, love the people who take care of them, make them feel like the secret of life lives between their two limbs.

We-Chrissie loved our midway life, and We-Millie liked it well enough too. Although it was clotted with people and noise, We-Millie enjoyed the camaraderie that came with a traveling pack of freaks. Zip Johnson, the What-Is-It?, adopted us as his niece, visiting our tent in costume after his "missing link" show, spinning us around in pirouettes and sharing some of the bananas he was paid to hurl at his audiences. Bearded and fat ladies of all heights and temperaments mothered us, pressing our hair and teaching us how to send our minds away from the body when norm men came to us with their pointing parts and probing smiles. For We-Millie, Miss Ella Ewing, the Missouri Giantess, was heaven itself, and the nook between her chest and her yardstick arm was a personal paradise. Miss Ella had traveled with Buffalo Bill's show, and it had filled her with stories we-two drank like raindrops. We-Chrissie loved to hear about the high, steady pay she received, and the handsome Indian men she performed with. We-Millie simply liked the sad, deep moan of the giantess's voice. She dragged the body to her every chance she got, just to curl her into that nook and hear her thunderstorm breath and earthquake heartbeat.

We-Chrissie has always insisted that we have no real family, though she didn't write that in her book. We-Millie sees it differently. For her, the midway freaks and the circus staff, the managers' wives and children, and sometimes men like Barnum himself make a collage of a family portrait we can hang proudly enough on the wall of our life. We-Chrissie's face sours when We-Millie says these kinds of things, and she spits. "You also insist on thinking that the man who sold us to the stage loves you." We-Millie thinks Yes, I have to think that, and I have to think he loves you too. But she doesn't need to say it, of course, because We-Chrissie knows.

Mrs. Susan and Master John hold our story together like bookends—we both agree on that. They were there just as life set us whirling about like a spinning top, and here they are again—the lady, the ghost—now that things are starting to slow down. Master John was still living when he and Mrs. Susan came to England to get us from Lars Rachman, the most recent man to have crept into a tent and taken us in the middle of the night. Master John was brusque as usual, but kind enough, returning We-Chrissie's buttermilk smile as he ushered us out of the Liverpool courtroom. Mrs. Susan was slower, warmer, as was her way. She rose at us like a pan of biscuits, pulling the body toward her with her scent and her feel and her promise of home.

We were too young to know then that home doesn't exist unless it's far from you, that either it or you must disappear the moment you return. North Carolina after the Civil War was like a rabbit shank after a wolf attack, and Master John's house was no more a home than a floor tile was a blacktop. We-Millie will swear it was the shock of our return, and the swelling presence of Mrs. Susan's misery, that first brought the fever and the cough to her side of the body. We-Chrissie has always laughed those claims off, not so much to dismiss her as to keep her focused on the tasks at hand. Master John died of gout before We-Millie had a chance to feel all of her pain, and our status as breadwinners for his family and for ourselves became official.

We-Chrissie became our manager, making contacts with the North Carolina showmen we'd known before we left, dazzling them all with her smile and laugh, running her bally to keep them interested. Her act was tight and she always got her ding, as circus folks say, the clink of whatever capital she sought against whatever pot she passed around. We needed money, of course, but We-Chrissie was smart. She knew that a few dollars weekly from a traveling sideshow gig was alright for a pair of young nigger-girl freaks without the need or right to do for themselves, but we were grown, almost old, and as free as we would ever be. We needed money, We-Chrissie knew, but it was information that would make us. She enlisted the help of Ron Samuel, Master John's old stableman, and set the body flitting about the marshlands of Columbus County with her ear to the tracks of the circus world, dropping Master John's good name like maple sugar candies whenever we needed white norm protection.

It was in a saloon near Soule's Swamp that we heard the news We-Chrissie thought would change our life. The barmaid was a woman who had ballyhooed for P.T. Barnum's show years before, when we were being billed as the "Two-Headed Cherub Monstrosity." She was a kind woman with a ruddy face and a mess of wheat-colored hair piled up on her head. She always liked Master John and Mrs. Susan, and We-Millie thought she was nice enough to us, though We-Chrissie insisted she was simply trying to get on Master John's good side, which for her meant the inside of his pants. Still, she smiled when we shuffled sideways through the door, and offered us a glass of lemonade, which We-Millie decided we would drink.

"You girls know 'bout the nigger show?" she asked, watching We-Chrissie's face for evidence that she felt or tasted the lemonade. We-two shook our heads.

"Man behind Buffalo Bill—not Cody, but the money man, a Yankee. He's doing a big show about niggers. You-all'd be perfect for it."

We-Millie could feel We-Chrissie's smile spread on the skin. We-Chrissie thanked the woman and yanked the body toward the door so quickly We-Millie had to pinch the spine to slow us down so she could pay. The woman smiled, and We-Millie felt her eyes on the body as we ambled out the door, We-Millie glad to be heading home as always, We-Chrissie dreaming of New York City, plotting the course of our life anew.

▩

The first thing Nate Salsbury saw as he stepped toward his office door, a hot mug of coffee in his hand, was the shadow of what looked like a lightning-struck bonsai tree hovering on his wall. The dark shape startled him, then drew him in. He paused at the doorway and gripped his mug, hoping to keep from dropping it or spilling the coffee, as he'd felt scattered and off-kilter since his morning meeting. But as the shadow begin to twirl along the wall, he decided to sip for a moment and watch it move. A perfect bonsai, he decided: mangled even in its symmetry, purely exotic, fine and lovely, but no less than grotesque. As the shadow rose and began to twist, he moved with it, slowly catching its rhythm, hurriedly catching his breath.

"I heard you were a dancer," he said, setting the mug beside his leather blotter. "But I could never have dreamed a figure of such brilliant grace."

The creature smiled with its slightly prettier head and halted, one half dipping into a curtsy that the other half mirrored perfectly.

"How can we respond to a compliment from a man so discerning and worldly as yourself?" the fairer head said. "We can only invite you to examine us as long and as fully as your least whim would have."

Salsbury smiled, taken aback by the pointedness of the creature's charm. This head was clearly the showman, he concluded, and the businessman as well. The other head was engaged, nodding and smiling throughout, but it seemed to maintain a certain distance, watching the scene as though through a cloud.

He had heard about this creature, touted as a Negress version of the two-headed Oriental that had made such a splash on the circuit some years ago. The comparison was logical, of course, but seeing this creature before him, he saw that that description missed much. The fairer head in particular had a clawing spunk that even the more animated half of the Oriental could never have aspired to. Some things about her he had seen in Negro women, performers and not, before. She had the bite of a Negro woman made tough and mannish by years of work, yet too smart to relinquish the last dregs of her girlish charm. Other things, though, he had never seen in a Negro, or an Indian, or talent of any kind before. This creature seemed to see itself just as a showman would see it, locating the lair of its dark allure and subduing its other parts to keep all eyes on the money spot. The creature bent its hind legs leisurely and fanned a smile, awaiting his response.

"Well, Miss McKoy, I am obviously honored by your offer," he said, settling in behind his desk. "But of course you'd want to know your talents were fully appreciated before having them committed to the whim, as you say, of a stranger. I hear that among your many gifts is a literary talent. Is that right?"

The creature nodded its heads, and the sullen face seemed to brighten up.

"Oh yes," the fair head said eagerly. "We know the best parts of Spenser, and many of the sonnets, as well as the major works of Molinet, and du Mans, as well as all of the Lay of Hildebrand, each in the original language, and in translation, of course."

"And," the plain head interrupted dryly, "we compose our own poetry as well."

"Yes," he sighed, leaning back. "I'd be delighted to hear an original composition from the very four lips of the poetess."

The creature opened its mouths, offering for the first time a taste of their vocal harmony. Salsbury had expected, at first, some tonal dissonances, as one often heard in the first few seconds of group auditions. The creature made no false starts, though. It launched flawlessly into a compelling rhyming bit about its life, its two voices perfectly pitched and ringing clearly as a single bell.

As the creature spoke, Salsbury felt his mind skip like a phonograph back on its track to the morning's meeting. He had had in this same office what initially impressed as an unremarkable group, also auditioning for his new Negro show. He had put word out weeks before among colleagues and busybodies that he was putting together history's largest Negro performance, to match dollar for dollar and ticket for ticket his success with Buffalo Bill, and to exceed that show in quality as well as moral heft. This exhibition, he had told them all, would showcase the finer qualities of the Negro. It would bring to the fore the darker race's evolution from African jungle savagery to New York civilization, and would recall all the delights of his character at each stage. The advertisements would mention the Negro's darker days, but would also herald his resurrection. Audiences the world over would be thrilled by all parts of the spectacle. They would cull joy from the Negro's triumph, and be relieved from their own pains by the utterly black drama unfolding on stage.

He had to acknowledge that it was a brilliant idea each time he thought about it. It was going swimmingly, and after only two months of planning, the first performance was nearly cast. The best minstrel actors had been recruited from the length of the eastern seaboard, and New York's highest-grossing stage writers were at work on scripts that would bring the high drama of the Negro's history to the stage. He was now in the more relaxed stage of booking specialty acts. As well as things had gone up to this point, the moment in which he found himself now was strange. Here he was, requiring himself to choose between this Negress freak, an embodiment of error, and the ostensibly unremarkable group he had seen this morning. And even as the cloven creature sparkled eerily before him, reading what was turning out to be a shockingly competent poem, he found himself pulled toward this morning's less-than-spectacle, a group called "That So Different Four."

He had expected the group to shuffle into his office at least five minutes late, as was the Negro way. His first surprise, then, was to find them dressed to the nines and reading newspapers casually beside his secretary's desk when he walked in to the office, twenty minutes before the meeting time they'd arranged. The surprise did not end there, but rather grew into shock as he heard the group speak and watched them perform. The two men and two women moved as a unit, and spoke as clearly and articulately as the creature before him, which, from the free-standing Negroes, was even more of a shock. The two-headed creature was made, sent even, to thrill and bewilder. But a pack of well-dressed, well-spoken darkies, mannered and reading, and operating together with an almost mechanical precision—this was the kind of spectacle no audience member could forget. The two-headed old Negro girl would alarm audiences, for sure. She would scare them and smile at them as they left the theater and returned to their lives. But the dandies—no, not dandies, one couldn't really even call them that—the "Different" negroes, with their finery just on the slight side of decadence, would bring the audiences to their edge, where jealousy gave its last agonized shout before dribbling into the childish mockery that proliferated on the minstrel stage. They would not let men and women tumble form theaters contentedly into their days. They would haunt them as they haunted him, their dark eyes flashing from wall placards, campaign posters, family portraits on parlor walls, or worse—and chillingly better—from the looking glass itself. The thought scared and thrilled him, and he found himself eager to see them at a distance, behind the fourth wall of the stage. They were performers, darkies on stage like so many, for so many years before; and yet unlike those darkies, or the black lump of oddity that sat before him, the "So Different Four" were not so different at all. They were black, of course, but otherwise, they were nearly . . . almost . . .

When the creature's poem concluded, the prettier head gave a confident, expectant smile, pushing the upper portion of her side of its body toward him.

"Well, you certainly are talented." Salsbury stood and walked toward her. "I imagine no one could be disappointed by such a treat. Thank you for your time, young lad—" he stammered, then put his hand on the creature's back, making sure to get a grab of the fleshy wishbone spine as he ushered it out the door.

▩

We stayed on in New York for three weeks after our meeting with Salsbury, in a property of Mrs. Amanda Bunting, a friend of Mrs. Susan's. Mrs. Bunting owned a boarding house on the southeast tip of the city, in the middle of a cluster of settlement houses, slaughterhouses, and Jewish bakeries. The house was empty, as Mrs. Bunting and her husband had just bought the property and had yet to carve it up into single rooms. Mrs. Bunting lived far across the city—a chess knight's move away, she said—and so there was no sense in feeding the coal stove daily just to keep our one body warm. Still, she promised us privacy and discretion at the boarding house, and, for the most part, delivered both. We lived off of money Mrs. Susan loaned us, though We-Chrissie refused to call it a loan—all of Mrs. Susan's money, she said, came from us at the end of the day.

We spent our time in New York City gazing out of Mrs. Bunting's garden-parlor window at the feet of norms, watching their heels pass lightly over the cobblestones. We-Millie felt a quick tug from We-Chrissie's side of the body when one of the new electrified streetcars passed by; We-Chrissie was as excited by the cars' speed and smoothness. She imagined the body perched in one of those cars, darting sleekly from one place to another. We-Millie shuddered under Mrs. Bunting's blankets when she felt We-Chrissie's tugs. We-Millie's side of the body seemed to grow heavier and heavier with each new day, each passing gust of wind.

When we didn't hear from Salsbury after a week, We-Chrissie asked Mrs. Bunting to load us in her carriage and carry us back to his office, a mile away up on Tin Pan Alley, where we waited with his secretary for two hours before being told he wouldn't be able to see us that day. It was a cool, rainy afternoon, the kind we have only experienced in the American North, where the wind feels mean and lazy at once, and the rain seems to pinch at the skin, as though to get its attention. We-Millie had been feeling lower and lower, her fevers coming stronger and more frequently since we'd left home. The coolness and the wetness made things worse on her side of the body, and, feeling it too, We-Chrissie promised that we would return to Columbus County as soon as we signed a contract for the Negro show. Once signed, she said, we would insist on staying home with Mrs. Susan until just before the opening performance.

Leaving Salsbury's building, we stopped near the entranceway to fumble with our umbrellas, each of we-two working to find an angle at which to hold our separate shields while making sure to cover the join. We-Millie had turned to protect her hair from a particularly fierce spattering of droplets when the finest group of niggers we had ever seen waltzed toward the threshold. A man and two women trailed behind, and at the head of the pack was a tall, slim brown man with eyes like pools of sweetmilk trimmed with lashes as long as a fox tail's fur. We-Chrissie's sent a rush of blood through the body and lurched so quickly toward him that We-Millie feared, for a second, that the join would tear.

The man's name, it turned out, was Carlo. He was the lead performer of a new musical group being courted to join Salsbury's show. We-Chrissie gave Carlo a smile We-Millie had never felt before, one that buzzed over the entire surface of the body's skin and burrowed down in the knots of its flesh. Both of we-two eyed the women, though We-Millie kept her gaze up only long enough to see that neither of them looked kind. Both were dressed finely, in smart streetcoats with silver buckles. One in particular looked to We-Millie like one of Mrs. Susan's blown-glass vases, her body curving in and out, her shoulders reaching up into the sky as though they were asking for something. We-two felt instantly ashamed, though we were wearing the best costume we had—a black and blue suede number with beadwork and embroidery that cinched at the body's waist. We felt the women's eyes fall on the body, felt the familiar mix of nausea and awe. We-Millie, of course, wanted to leave the scene, to find dryness and warmth and wrap the body in it. After a few minutes of conversation, though, We-Chrissie determined that the two women were Carlo's colleagues and nothing more, and, in some way that We-Millie could not understand, this meant something important to We-Chrissie.

Carlo said that he had heard about our act as a child, and had kept us in mind as icons as he dreamed about an entertainment career. This news fell on We-Chrissie like a marriage vow, and she began to gush compliments over him, being sure to work in details of our life that would indicate—in case he was too simple to know, We-Millie thought—that we were single and available. We-Millie gave him Mrs. Bunting's address, and suggested that he call on us to chat about our experience in the business, or anything else. He thanked her with a deep bow and proceeded with his company out of the rain, leaving us to continue the business of keeping ourselves dry, and giving us another call to wait for.

The following morning, We-Millie's fever broke like a cloud into sweat showers, and the coughs from her side of the body began to produce a pinkish phlegm. Still, We-Chrissie added days to our stay in the North, promising that Salsbury, or Carlo, or somebody, would call at any minute.

We-Millie finds it needless to say that neither call ever came. We-Chrissie resents this feeling from the body's other half.

What is remarkable, for We-Millie, at least, is the course our story was taking, even as we dallied in New York, holding ourself up for sale like the last rotting piece of fruit at the produce market. What is remarkable, even We-Chrissie won't deny, is the shock, still with us, of returning to Columbus on a Saturday morning, to be met with Ron Samuel's stricken face and shattered voice, announcing in an auctioneer's bewildered monotone how Mrs. Susan had passed, alone, late Friday night.

We did not know something like that could happen. We-Chrissie did not know how painful it can be to get one's way. We-Millie did not know how one's own will discarded to the wind can fly back to hurt the ones one loves.

But we knew Salsbury like we have known all the masters and handlers and doctors, all the white norm men all our lives, including

Master John. And somehow, Carlo now seems like one of them, no more sincere than Salsbury, no kinder than Master John. We should not have been surprised by Salsbury. We-Chrissie had felt his ambivalence as he eyed the body, even while we spun around his office, doing our most difficult dance. We-Millie felt him stare at us as though he expected gold coins to pour from between our legs, smelled his disappointment when they did not. We knew these shocks and the feelings they brought, but we needed money as badly as Salsbury wanted it. So We-Millie stayed quiet while We-Chrissie brightened her face and stuck out her bosom, waving the body in the white man's face like a flag before a firing squad.

We-Millie tries to be understanding as she reviews this scene. She tries not to think of Mrs. Susan, just as she feels We-Chrissie trying not to think of Carlo, the nigger show, and all the other things she feels we've lost.

"We were stupid to think it could work forever," We-Chrissie sighs, her head falling onto We-Millie's shoulder. "We were stupid to think they would always want us. A dumb thought, that we could be just the right blend of bile and sugar always, that tastes and people and times would not change and leave us here in this torture box, alone. How stupid we were . . ."

You were stupid. The thought slices like a knife into the body.

You were dumb to think they wanted you in the first place. You are the stupid one.

The shoulders twist. The heads roll apart. We are sharing a brutal wish.

It may have been one or the other who tempted the barrage, but we feel the shrapnel in all quarters of the body. The back hands reach for each other and stroke themselves. A hot sweat slicks up on the spine, a chill rushes down from the tender crevice of the join. We have never shared this wish before.

We-Chrissie's heart is slowing. We-Millie feels hers quicken.

Lillian Is an Ordinary Child

Metta Sáma

Lillian is an ordinary child, as ordinary as any freshly turned eleven-year-old who, by third grade, has been overstimulated with compare-contrast analysis teachings and exercises and who, by second grade, had creativity pretty much shattered by Mrs. Mason, whose underzealous teaching of cause-effect made Lillian, and her eight-year-old classmates, look at pancakes falling out of the sky and wonder if they were fluffier than pancakes made on a stove or not, and if the pancakes that fell from the skies were made in the skies, thus at a much higher elevation, would these high-elevation pancakes be fluffier than the pancakes they ate at home or in the local diner. Not to mention the complete silliness of pancakes, of all things, falling from the sky.

Lillian and her friends once sat in her room discussing the pure ridiculousness of her parents and their friends, who sat in the living room discussing the miracle of frogs falling out of the sky. They'd seen such in a movie and were convinced it was possible. Lillian and her educated nine-year-old friends scoffed, simply scoffed, and composed a group letter to the group of parents to explain to them how frogs settle in tress and that because of the monsoon-type conditions, which produced heavy rains and strong winds, the frogs could not stick to the trees, so they fell out of the trees, not the sky.

By the time Lillian was in the fourth grade (two years before this story begins), she was known to scowl at her parents and pointedly correct them: No, that is NOT a fox in the sky, that is a cumulonimbus cloud, a portmanteau of cumulus and nimbus, Latin for "heap" and "storm," so you may want to stop pointing ridiculously in the sky and take cover, because a storm was surely on its way. And on and on Lillian would go. At their homes, her friends went on and on in this way, too, thanks, by then, to Mr. Kelvin, who taught them the distinct differences between thought and idea, between the real and the imagined.

The fifth grade geology teacher, in week three, during an outing on a poorly planned spring day, sternly told her group: You all are nearly adults! A little rain is not going to kill you! For heaven's sake! Dig! In Charles Dickens's England—ask Ms. Collins about this—in Charles Dickens's England, you all would be working in a factory or you would be chimney sweepers, for goodness sake!

For Lillian's eleventh birthday (the day this story begins), she announces to her mother, as soon as her poor mother has put the sweet little swirl beneath the "y" in "Lily": I'm no longer Lily; Lily is a child's name; I'm Lillian, and I need a bralette.

Her poor mother has to carefully scrape the entire name away, make new icing for the pineapple-mango cake, and very very smartly write Lillian, neatly, because Lily, correction, Lillian, hates, more than poor grammar, sloppy handwriting. Lillian's mother wonders when her daughter's imagination slipped out of her spirit, when it began to dodge her mind, when her body stopped bumping into the impossible, when her heart turned into a cold, green chalkboard. But this is not her mother's story. This is the story of Lillian, the once exceptional, as exceptional as any up-to-the-age-of-ten-child, who is now just ordinary.

This birthday is not a big one. Eleven is eleven for any child. Even for Lillian, whose untimely training bra announcement has her father in his truck, rushing to Regina's, the local bra shop, to pick out seven training bras, as Lillian hates repeating clothes through the week, and prefers to have seven of every item of clothing: seven pairs of socks (no ducks chasing beach balls, no frogs singing to lions, and absolutely no pencils with eyes and a mouth! Plain socks (white, preferably), seven pairs of underwear (see the sock rule), seven school shirts (ironed), seven school slacks (ironed, too), seven playtime T-shirts (see the sock rule), seven playtime shorts (ironed), seven crisp white nightgowns, with just a little lace along the sleeves. The lace, a frilly adornment, leads her parents to believe that Lillian's imagination is not completely lost.

What does Lillian wish for, when the pineapple-mango cake is presented to her? For one, she wishes it were not called an upside-down cake; she'd helped her mother make enough cakes to know that there is nothing "upside-down" about this cake or any other: All cakes, Lillian, age six, said to her mother, have to be turned upside down, to get it out of the pan. She also wishes for, well, I can't tell you that, little Lillian has blown out her eleven candles, made two wishes, one for herself and one for her mother, who she knows is somehow connected to her very thoughts, after all, it is her mother who made her pineapple-mango, although Lillian only asked for a pineapple cake, but secretly wished for a pineapple-mango cake, and stared longingly at the ripening mangoes in the market, days before her birthday, and called the pineapple cake a pineapple cake and not a pineapple upside-down cake, and her mother, when she presented the cake this very afternoon, didn't call it a pineapple-mango upside-down cake, but Lillian's pineapple-mango cake for her eleventh birthday. Lillian's first wish, to be clear, is that through her mother, all other mothers, and eventually everyone else, would refrain from incorrectly attributing upside-down-ness to any one kind of cake. So far, then, Lillian's birthday is a smash.

To jumpstart Lillian's imagination, prior to her beginning life as a sixth grade student in middle school, where mediocrity reigns supreme, Lillian's parents take her and twelve other eleven-year-olds, Lillian's friends, to the local sculpture park, where there are exactly seventy-five sculptures. By Lillian's calculations, and her parents are sure she will have calculations, that is exactly five sculptures for each of the fifteen visitors to the site (Lillian, her twelve friends, and Lillian's parents) to claim as their own personal favorites. Lillian's parents bring along fifteen "goodie bags." Inside of each there is one disposable camera, one mechanical pencil, one grid-lined 3.5 x 5.5 inch moleskin notebook (each the dullest cardboard-brown), one set of binoculars, one birding book for the Eastern states, one whistle, one PB&J sandwich, carefully wrapped in wax paper, one baggie of her mother's famous homemade sea-salt and thyme-sprinkled potato chips, and one canister of water. The sculpture park, situated on eighty-four acres of personal property, includes a few trails with sculptures hidden in unexpected places.

As with every new visitor to the park, Lillian's eyes are immediately drawn to the largest sculpture in the park: the head of a man who wears a very long earring and reminds Lillian of photographs she'd seen of Blackfoot men in *National Geographic*. Goodie bag in hand, she runs to the sculpture, situated at the topmost part of the farm, and thinks: "My favorite!" She walks slowly around the sculpture, slightly disappointed by the large air-vent-type opening in the back of its skull, noting that it is likely needed to keep the plaster sculpture from being blown off in a heavy storm. On the opposite side of the sculpture, the ear facing away from the parking area, Lillian stops short. The man's ear is an open doorway. She peeps inside the head, and sees a staircase. She backs away from the ear and slowly walks around the head again, smartly guessing at the height of the head, thus deciding on the number of stairs, and thus, the number of floors in the head. She's looking for various windows, to decide if the walk up the stairs in the man's head will be worth it, just for a view of, she guesses, the Taconic Parkway. She returns to the open ear and remains standing there, unsure of her next move.

Lillian's second wish. It's here, on the tip of my tongue, but who am I to reveal Lillian's wish to you? Let us, then, redirect our mind. Here's a question to ponder: what will Lillian do? Will she let her curiosity get the best of her? Will she move, against her will, inside the man's head? Will she shrug, as she is wont to do, and decide the sculpture is slightly flawed, hang her shoulders at her uncommonly impulsive decision to claim the statue as hers, without first carefully examining it, weighing it against others in the park, using her sharpened compare-contrast skills so deliberately and systematically taught to her just three years ago? Will she walk away from the sculpture, head held low, knowing that her parents' ever watchful eyes are on her, that one of them, loving her deeply, will say, "Oh, Lillian! I wanted that one!" to bear the brunt of her shame, for being so uncharacteristically impulsive, as they are wont to do?

On one nonparallel plane, Lillian, the child who is rapidly losing her imagination, and increasingly believing in the synthesis of the cause-effect and compare-contrast schools of thought, thus increasingly adopting a model of responsible behavior, simply takes it—the great disappointment of disappointment—and climbs the stairs. The effect of her greed, mixed with a sudden impulsive act, will be a view of the Taconic Parkway that no one else in her party will have access to; had she strolled through the park, contrasting one sculpture with the next, one vantage point with the next, she would not have had to suffer the potential great disappointment of disappointment. (Yes, for a moment, Lillian imagines she might not be disappointed at all, that perhaps there is a, oh, she doesn't know, her mind is having a hard time collapsing and expanding, but oh, something something, a room, a nook, something, perhaps tucked into the cerebral cortex of the man's head, or sitting behind his other ear, maybe a book or pamphlet, or, oh something some *thing* that will make the climb worth it!) Lillian lives, in this parallel plane, in the great unknown, the very site of creativity, of imagination. Lillian will not, for example, shake her head, shrug her shoulders, and tromp off to another sculpture, or find a friend to chat with, or try to identify some trees. No, if Lillian fails to climb the stairs, she will live with this decision the entire day, twisting her hair around around around her fingers, biting her lower lip, chewing the inside of her jaw, digging the point of her shoes into the grass, shifting from one jutted hip to another, tugging at her white shirt, trying very hard, indeed, to not wonder: what would I have seen? And here is where Lillian's imagination, that much-abused, much-neglected organ, will begin to pump life into itself, into Lillian, recover from years of atrophy, and press Lillian into worlds that take shape in her eyes, worlds unlike the one she's currently standing in. Lillian will attempt to fight it, but since she's let her imagination suffer so, it will not splinter into many imaginations, thus leaving room for her to imagine a tug-of-war between herself and her imagination, or a boxing match, an arm wrestling session, none of that. Lillian's imagination will stay whole, and she will have no choice but to admit defeat; no matter how unconsciously it all happens, it happens.

In another nonparallel plane, Lillian has a temper tantrum. Her friends and parents, alarmed at such bad behavior, such outrageous, public fits, run to her aid, and discover that the giant head has utterly utterly presented a false face to Lillian. They each rush to remind her that she actually never said the word "mine!" aloud. Problem solved. Lillian gathers her senses about her, wonders, for just a brief moment, what came over her, what child possessed her, no, that's too imaginative, even for Lillian, whose dulling by the minute. No, Lillian chides herself: Grow up! And all is passed.

In yet another nonparallel plane, Lillian stomps off, away from all the sculptures, bottom lip thrust out, top lip mashed in, arms folded sourly across her chest. Her parents see this, and rush over to fix the problem. Lillian tells them, and one of them says, "But, you never said it's yours! I, personally, want it for myself! Shall we fight to the death for it?" (Clearly, this is her father.) Lillian looks sternly at him and says, "Don't be ridiculous, Father. We would never, either of us, kill the other!" She half-skips down the hill, triumphant, awesomely unaware of two things: (1) that she imagined the scenario playing out precisely as it had, only minutes before, as she stood at the base of the head, at its neck, trying to figure out the best course of action; and (2) that her mother, the most curious of them all, had already turned her back on her suddenly dramatic child, and wandered into the head. Lillian's parents were born in the eighties, when the country was busy cleaning up messes it had made overseas by fixing the economic system in order to make the country think it was experiencing an economic boom. The eighties were a time of money, pure and simple. There was no staggering president who wanted, more than anything, to reclaim the non-swagger of his youth, thus the nonswagger of his adulthood, who, in attempting to outdo his father, and to, subliminally, castigate his father by subtly blaming him for his poor reasoning skills, said, forget money, I want my childhood back! And the nostalgic moody crab that he was decided childhood was education, and thus instituted that horrible policy of No Child Left Behind, which Lillian and her cohort suffered through, whose imaginations, once free-roaming things that her parents still held on to dearly, were left behind.

And this is where the story gets thick with bird song and great winds ushered in on broad branches of low-hanging trees. Remember Lillian's second wish? Oh how convoluted it was. Lillian both wished to have different parents, ones who lived in the real world, one in which mothers called cakes "cakes," and she wished, simultaneously, for something different, yes, she wished to be surprised. By what? Life itself? By her parents? By an act or behavior or thought of her own? It's true, even Lillian was tiring of herself, of her caustic nature. One day, the very day she stared longingly at the mangoes, enraptured by their smell, there she stood in the middle of the aisle, her mind gone, her senses taking over, wavering, there, her body, wavering, in the market, Lillian had an image of herself, age older, half human, half machine, no, one-eighth human, the rest of her machine, analytical, mathematical, scientific; she and all of her friends, who would one day assume their expected positions and run the world would do so with efficiency, stamped: STEM-approved. Lily? Her mother. Lily, honey? Lily was transported back into her brain, she stopped wavering, and a thought a feeling a sense a memory of the future, synthesized and planted itself in her mind, waiting waiting waiting for her to one day retrieve it. And thus she did, on her eleventh birthday.

Here we are on this alternate plane. Lillian's mother has entered the head. Lillian will never see her mother again, but she doesn't know that, yet. Or maybe, if she allows her imagination to fatten up, to gain a pounding heart rhythm, to flex its spirit muscles, to have body, she will see her mother again, because, not out of grief or terror of never seeing her mother again, but out of terrorgriefcuriosity out of a deepening realization that there are many realities, that Mr. Kelvin didn't have all of the answers, out of wanting to see the thing that takes her mother away, Lillian will enter the head, will climb the stairs, will witness what her mother witnessed, will slip into another dimension, that of the imagination of the giant, bodiless head. And it will be so easy for her there, for she will not have to admit that her imagination is now just as alive as that of the giant, bodiless head's imagination; no, she can believe that everything she sees in that head, every floating, disembodied laugh, every pair of bent legs, hopping on invisible trampolines, every miniature guitar-strumming squirrel, every half-eaten sandwich conversing with the closest half-eaten banana, is all the imagination of the giant, bodiless head, and she can scoff at these images, as she surrenders to them, as she had, eventually, surrendered to STEM, forever in search of her mother, whose curiosity outweighed her own, and got them both trapped in this lovely, strange, terrible, beautiful world.

Entropy 20:12

Learkana Chong

This is the story of Tamara, daughter of Chea and Neary Rim, and Jude, son of Mary and Saul Barlow, and how they came to know each other only to remain fruitless and divided. And so on the seventh day of the spring semester, on the campus of California State University, Altanero, in the city of Altanero, Tamara tried to quench her thirst at a water fountain outside the science building. Tamara lifted her dark hair from her face, and bent low to drink, but the water did not spew forth. And she pushed the button harder, and still nothing came of it. And someone cleared his throat behind her and she turned around, and it was a comely young man with fair skin and a mop of light brown hair. And he smiled at Tamara, and offered her a drink from his water bottle. He said to her, "Fountain's broken. Want a drink from my bottle?"

And Tamara said to him, "I don't know, that depends. Do you have cooties?" But she smiled in jest, and the young man laughed in return, saying, "No, but you can waterfall it."

And Tamara said to him, "I suck at waterfalling, so I'll pass. But thanks for offering."

And the young man said, "I can't let you walk away dehydrated."

And Tamara said to him, "I'll just go to the library and drink from the fountain there."

And the young man replied, "Okay, but do you think you can give me your contact info, so I can make sure that your H_2O quota has been sufficiently filled?"

And Tamara laughed again and gave him her number, and asked him for his name. And the young man answered Jude, and asked Tamara for her name, which she gave to him. And they parted ways from the fountain, smiling.

Thus Tamara's striking dark hair and striking dark face found favor in the eyes of Jude, and Jude's fair skin and mop of light brown hair found favor in the eyes of Tamara. And Jude coveted the curves of Tamara, and saw her as wilderness, and Tamara coveted the ideal that was Jude, and saw him as sublime. And both thought the other good and kind, as early lovers are wont to do. And for seven days and seven nights they talked to each other by way of mobile device and became acquainted, and were together for those seven days and seven nights, and it was on the seventh night that they came to know each other. They came to know each other in the basement that Jude called his bedroom and in the glow of the television playing over their intertwining bodies, and they were not ashamed. And the parents of Jude were sleeping upstairs, and all was quiet. And Jude said to Tamara, "Is this your first time?" And Tamara said to him, "Yes." And Jude parted her waters and knew her, and Tamara thought as they laid with each other, no, he is not entering me; I am encasing him.

And so they continued on for forty days and forty nights, until Tamara missed her woman's flow and there was an unsettling in her body, and Tamara grew afraid. But to bring forth her fear would turn it into a truth, and so she kept her silence. Jude said to her, "My parents want to meet you." And Tamara said to Jude, "Okay." And she dressed in a more conservative manner than usual for the evening, knowing that Mary, mother of Jude, and Saul, father of Jude, were very religious. And she was received with a handshake from Saul and a hug from Mary, who welcomed her into their abode, not knowing Tamara had slipped inside many times before. When Tamara saw the cross on the door and the painting of Jesus hanging above the mantelpiece, Mary saw her looking and said to her, "That's Jesus. Do you know about Jesus?"

And Jude said to his mother, Mary, "Mom, stop."

And Mary laughed at her son and said to him, "I'm just kidding! Everyone knows about Jesus. He died for our sins." And Tamara smiled uncertainly, and said nothing. Soon they were all gathered around the dining table, where they bowed their heads in prayer and Tamara mimicked them. And then they ate and talked and laughed, and Tamara felt out of place and mostly fake-laughed. And then Mary said to Tamara, "I knew a very nice African American woman back when I was teaching grade school; her name was Melinda and she was as sweet as could be."

And Jude said to his mother, "Tamara is Cambodian. The prettiest Cambodian girl I've ever seen." He smiled at Tamara, who fake-smiled back.

And his mother said to Tamara, "Oh, what is that?"

And Tamara said, "It's Southeast Asian."

And Saul said to her, "Were you born over there?"

And Tamara said, "No, but my parents were."

And Saul said, "Can you say something for us? Say, 'This meal is delicious.'"

And Tamara looked at Jude, who changed the subject. And suddenly Mary was talking about wanting grandchildren once Jude was married and Jude kept looking at the ground and Tamara felt ill and asked to be excused. And later that night she went to the pharmacy alone and bought three tests that told her what she already knew.

Tamara sat on the seat of the toilet and thought, I am not the kind of girl this is supposed to happen to. And then she realized, she was exactly the kind of girl this would happen to. Sex had been a faraway country to her once. She accidentally had her mother sign her out of sex education in middle school, and ended up stuck in the receptionist's office for a week reading about talking mice while her classmates diagrammed penises. She hadn't even known there was a separate hole for urinating until she started college. Her last encounter with sex before Jude was the Harlequin Romance books she would sneak out of the top cupboard of her home when she was younger, the ones her pervy male cousin had dropped off before he moved down to Long Beach, the ones her parents had assumed were dictionaries or textbooks of some kind, affectionately calling her "smart child" when they saw her reading them.

Tamara was pregnant and there was no one to tell except the boy she dreaded telling. In the three years she had been at college, she had not met anyone she would call a friend. She kept to herself, focused on her studies. There was her high school friend Kendra, but she could not keep secrets, and if she were told, then everyone in the Cambodian community would know.

You're showing cleavage
Why don't you just show your pussy
and let any man have at it
Go out on the streets and sell yourself

Americans these days
Cambodia was never like this
Look at those sucking lips
Look at them having each other
Disgusting
Filth
Go ahead, be a whore
That's what you want to do, isn't it

She pushed down her mother's words from adolescence and called Jude through the bathroom door. And Tamara told him through the bathroom door that she was with child, and Jude cried to her, "Let me in. Let me in." And Tamara said no.

Jude said to her, "You could move in with me, and we could get—"

And Tamara said no.

Jude said to her, "We could make this work. My parents—"

And Tamara said no.

Jude said to her, "I'll quit school, get a job, and—"

And Tamara said to him, "I don't want this."

And Jude said, "What about the baby?" And his voice seeped through the door in a flood that drowned out the whisper that said, *But what about me?*

And she told him not to tell his parents and he said he wouldn't and she wanted to trust him but wasn't sure and she said again I don't want this thing and he said you mean baby and she said it's just a fucking clump of cells and he said baby don't say that and she thought it was funny, baby with a baby, and suddenly she was sick and he was pounding on the door and she shouted at him to stop, her suitemates would hear, and finally she let him in and he held her and said I love you and she said don't say it because of this don't say it at all and he said no I mean it and she said I want it out and he said don't think that don't say that at least keep the baby for now c'mon Juno did it and she said yeah, cuz when a white hipster gets knocked up she's quirky and cute and cool but if I do it I'm a dirty slut and he said you're being ridiculous and then she realized she didn't even know the month and day he had been born.

After seven hours of fighting, Tamara said to Jude, "I'll keep it."

Therefore it grew inside her, and she no longer felt at home in her body. And for forty more days and forty more nights Jude kept reassuring her and holding her hand and saying babe, baby, babe, this is going to work, this is going to be all right, but she stopped listening and withdrew inside herself where she imagined seeing the knot of cells grow little stubby arms and legs that she would snip off with nail clippers. Maybe she was a monster. Then how could she be a mother? Tamara tried to see into the future, to use her fabricated powers of divinity, but it was difficult and all she could picture was a life she did not want: trapped in the house of Mary and Saul, parents of Jude, and held hostage by a mistake no one wanted her to take back. She wanted to graduate college, she wanted to move out of Altanero, she wanted the time and space to fuck up her life without baggage. She wanted an empty uterus. Thus her grades suffered and she suffered and the relationship suffered. But Jude kept saying, baby, baby, baby, and he was going to quit studying engineering and get a job someplace and care for her, but Tamara's love for him was not as steadfast. Nor did she think it was love. And she was not ready to raise up anyone into this world but herself.

And so Tamara said to herself, "Enough." And she called the clinic to set her life on track again. And after Tamara did this she waited for Jude in her dorm, and he crawled into her bed and pulled up her shirt and traced circles around her navel though she did not show. And Tamara said to Jude, "I made the appointment."

And he said nothing.

Tamara said to him, "I can't do this anymore."

And he said nothing.

Tamara said, "I'm sorry."

And he said nothing.

And finally Jude said to Tamara, "So, you're gonna kill our baby, just like that?"

And she said nothing.

And Jude said, "I guess this is it then."

And she said nothing.

And Jude stood up and left and the door slammed shut behind him, and Tamara felt both empty and whole.

On the day of the appointment, Tamara still needed someone to go in with her and drive her back to her dorm afterward. And her parents were out of the question, for if they ever found out, they would kill her and pray for her and she was not sure how to say what she wanted anyway. And her sister and two brothers had their own lives to wrestle with. And she was contemplating this dilemma in her human evolution class instead of paying attention to the lecture of her professor, staring at her classmates and hoping one of them would reveal to her their spirit of understanding. And someone looked up and smiled back at her, and it was a girl named Miriam, and Miriam had been in five of her classes not counting this one and worked with her on a project once, and so Tamara felt relief and smiled back.

After class, Tamara approached Miriam as she was gathering up her things, and said to her, "Hi, Miriam. I don't know if you know me, but . . ."

And Tamara was startled by the bright eyes of Miriam, so unsettling were they, and stopped. Miriam smiled, saying, "Oh, I know you. We've had a lot of classes together. What's up?"

And Tamara said to her, "Can we talk someplace more private?"

And Miriam grew concerned and said, "Sure."

Thus they went somewhere private, and Tamara told her what was inside her and what she needed to do, and that she had no one else to turn to and was sorry for burdening Miriam, but Miriam touched the hand of Tamara and said to Tamara, "Okay."

And when Tamara was but seven years old, she went to her mother and tried to ask where babies came from. For her classmate Veronica said to her, "Babies get born either by your mom having sex with your dad, or your mom kisses your dad, but she has to do it every day." And Tamara wanted to know if this was true. But her broken tongue could not form those words in Khmer, and so instead she asked her mother, "Where was I born?"

And her mother said to her, "You were born here."

And Tamara said to her, "No, where was I born?" And she emphasized the words uselessly to get her mother to understand her nuanced meaning.

But her mother said to her, "You were born here. What, are you deaf?"

And Tamara said to her, "Where am I from? Where am I from?"

And her mother grew angry and shouted, "You were born here, stupid!" And looking back, Tamara pondered whether or not her mother had truly misunderstood. Nevertheless, Tamara grew up and learned where babies came from, and learned this through a health pamphlet given to her by a nice white lady.

Now Tamara and Miriam journeyed forth to the clinic, and it was a hazardous journey, for there were many protesters outside and they were screaming and waving signs that read CHOOSE LIFE and ABORTION KILLS and END THE SLAUGHTER. And Tamara held her head high and she met their hate-filled stares and thought, will you deliver this baby and provide for it? And she knew either way she was a whore in their eyes, and that it was just a matter of being a welfare queen or devil queen, and she had been told the road to hell is paved with good intentions. And as Tamara journeyed to the doors, she saw a familiar face among many faces, the face of Mary, mother of Jude, and Mary saw her and spat into her face and the gobbet of spit ran down the cheek of Tamara, and Miriam grabbed Tamara and said, "Fuck off," before guiding Tamara away, saying to her, "Ugh, she goes to my church. Ethnocentric bitch."

Now Tamara was inside the clinic, and as they waited and she filled out paperwork, she saw that the skin of Miriam was like coffee with creamer and the skin of Tamara was like coffee, and that Tamara was blacker than the black girl, and she laughed on the inside at this. Then her name was called, and Miriam squeezed her hand, and the lady who met her at the door was so kind and good that Tamara wanted to weep. The lady had Tamara remove her clothes and put on a backless gown and then she waited in another room, shivering and alone, until she was called into one more room, where they poked and prodded her and told her things she nodded to and laid her down and put her feet in stirrups.

And Tamara looked up into the glaring light fixture as they jostled and jabbed her and she ached and thought, whoever is up there, what are your thoughts on this?

But there was no answer. And Tamara quelled her thoughts as they plucked the seed out of her, and she saw that it was good.

Beautiful Things

Jacqueline Bishop

As if by magic it appeared there: the small wooden house with shuttered jalousie windows rising out against the dark green bushes. Emanuel was sure it hadn't been there Friday evening as he made his way home from the fields for the weekend and he was confused as to how an entire house could have been built in a matter of days. Even more confusing was the garden with its purple Joseph's coats and giant red ginger lilies. In the back, a huge Julie mango tree spread its gnarled branches over the roof.

Pale curtains blew at the windows and Emanuel was able to make out the sounds of someone moving things about inside the house, re-arranging furniture and carefully setting things in order. There was a happy feeling to the place and it seemed as if the sun shone directly down on the house, casting a soft yellow glow over the yard. Emanuel was still looking at the house in astonishment when the back door opened and someone stepped outside.

Without knowing why he quickly hid behind a large breadfruit tree, peering out every now and again to see who was coming out of the house.

Immediately he felt foolish for hiding. Hadn't he walked the foot-path of these bushes on the way to his fields for the past however many years? Hadn't he bragged to the other men in the district that this was the best land around for miles, the reason why his bananas were always so full and handsome? His cocoa and coffee beans so rich and fragrant? In some ways he felt he owned the land, for there would be weeks at a time when he'd be the only person to come this far into the bushes.

A woman stepped out of the house balancing something emerald-green on her shoulder. Emanuel passed his hands quickly over his eyes to make sure he was not seeing things and looked again at what was on the woman's shoulder. It was a parrot! A yellow-billed parrot! He could not remember the last time he'd seen one in the district!

The woman carried the bird as if it were the most natural thing in the world for it to be resting there on her shoulder, nudging her, playing in her long, dark hair.

Emanuel studied the woman carefully, how the long, loose, cotton dress she wore did not do much to hide her splendid figure. His eyes moved from her tiny waist, to the full round bottom, down to the curve of her legs and the ankles and feet resting solidly on the ground. Her hair was one long, thick plait down her back. She had the most beautiful complexion he'd ever seen, something that was a cross between honey and wild ginger. She was like a jewel, he thought, staring at her, something rich and dark, something you could spend the rest of your life looking at.

The woman slipped back inside the house and came out again, this time dragging a large white pail like the ones the women in the district washed their clothes in by the river.

He kept watching her. Why would she live so far away from everyone else, he asked himself? Most of the other homes in the district were set back from the one badly paved road over which hardly any cars ran anymore. When had she moved into the district and onto "his" land? How come no one told him about, or talked about, this woman?

The woman began pinning clothes on the line all the while humming to herself. Something about her appealed to him, something he couldn't quite put his fingers on. Perhaps it was her quick, lithe movements. Or perhaps it was the thick black hair like a rope down her back. Indian hair. Hair like his wife had when they first got together. That was many years ago and Urmilla did not have hair like that anymore. Now her hair had thinned out and she no longer took time with it and just rolled it into a coil on the top of her head. Urmilla had changed so much, Emanuel thought miserably. Now she'd gained too much weight and her disappointments in life, chief among them her inability to conceive a child, hung off her like its own weight.

Friday night after returning home from the field he watched as she squatted over the wood fire, blowing it back to a blaze, to warm his dinner. How big her backside had gotten, he thought to himself, and how heavily veined her legs. When she looked over at him he immediately noticed the creases around her eyes and how bloodshot and tired they looked. No, she was no longer the woman he married so many years before.

Emanuel refocused his attentions on the woman in the yard. She was obviously alone in the house. She kept humming to herself, reaching into the pail, pulling out clothes, and hanging them on the line. Her back all the time was turned to him.

He decided to come from behind the tree and talk to her.

Removing his worn, brown felt hat and holding it in his hands, Emanuel approached the fence.

"Good morning, Ma'am," he said to her and the woman stiffened. She did not answer him and she did not turn around.

"I hope I didn't frighten you much, Miss," he continued, "but I sure was surprised to see a house in these parts. To see you in these parts."

Still there was no answer.

"I works abouts here," Emanuel said to the trembling back of the woman, "have worked abouts here all my life and I've never seen your place before." He stopped, waiting for her to answer, or at least to turn around and acknowledge him in some way, but she still did not move.

"Well, most folks around here known me as Manuel, Mani for short. I live over there," he said, pointing in the direction where he was just coming from. "But I have my fields over there." He pointed deeper into the bushes. He stopped talking, waiting for her to say something, but still there was nothing. "It sure is a nice little place you have here, even though I'm not sure how you got it all up so fast. How *did* you get it up so fast?"

Emanuel began to shift uncomfortably when the woman still did not answer him and when she still did not turn around. He was close enough to see she was trembling slightly, to smell the bleach on the pail of white clothes she was washing, to see the tiny blue spots in the white shorts she'd hung on the line. Beads of sweat started collecting at the roots of her hair then running down her neck and shoulders and making small rivulets into her back.

He made to get closer to her, but the parrot began squawking loudly in protest, rapidly flapping its wings, doing everything, it seemed to Emanuel, to stave off the unwelcome visitor.

Emanuel took a few rapid steps backward, looking around for his machete. Were his eyes deceiving him? The bird actually seemed to be threatening him, even getting bigger and bigger!

"I wish you would say something, Miss," he said, a touch of anxiety creeping into his voice. "Perhaps you don't know this, for you look to me to be a stranger to these parts, but around here everyone speaks to everyone else. The very least you can do is respond to a greeting!"

Still there was no answer.

The sun started climbing overhead and Emanuel decided he should be on his way to the field if he wanted to get any work done for the day. He turned around, collected his machete, reached for the lunch Urmilla had carefully prepared for him, and walked away from the house. He shook his head in disbelief at the bad manners of some people.

All day long as he worked the woman was all he could think about. As he dug into the soft, moist earth planting new banana suckers, and later, as he reached up, fingering his coffee beans to see how ripe they were, he wrestled with the image of the house, the bird, and the woman. There had been no talk of another person moving into the district and this was a place where everyone knew everyone else. The entire district was enclosed by dark-blue mountains and so shielded it seemed the outside world had forgotten about the place. Even the district's name, Nonsuch, added to its obscurity.

"You know how we come by that name?" his friend Robinson asked him one Friday night as they sat playing dominoes. They were both slightly drunk, although Robinson was more far-gone than he was.

"We were really None-such you know. None-such place on the map of the island." Robinson started laughing hard at his own joke. "None-such, None-such, Nonsuch place."

This actually made sense to Emanuel, especially since the district was never more isolated than it was these days. Tourists no longer passed in vans on Mondays and Wednesdays throwing coins at the children who waved hibiscus flowers at them. The big, blue bus no longer carried passengers to the bay, where the stores were. (The roads were too bad and the bus driver got tired of having to repair his bus.) Of the two vans that still made the journey through the district one of them always ended up with a busted pipe or tire because of the road. So how indeed had the woman moved there? The question obsessed him.

As he settled under the cocoa tree where he ate his lunch and took out the food his wife had prepared for him, Emanuel continued trying to piece together how it all happened. Sometime between Friday evening and early Monday morning the house was erected. It wasn't a fancy structure, so perhaps . . . but more puzzling were the flowers and the mango tree because those you could not grow overnight. Probably she had just stuck the plants in the ground.

He took down the blanket for his afternoon nap out of the branch of a cocoa tree, shook it out, and laid it out under the tree. Before long he felt drowsy and though he wasn't quite awake, he wasn't asleep either when he began to see the parrot with the fantastic green plumage. It was a yellow-billed parrot, a species found only in Jamaica. A few months before, some government officials came and talked to the people in the district, explaining to them that the bird was threatened with extinction and it was now illegal to hunt the bird. Periodic checks would be carried out and anyone found hunting the birds, even if they were tourists, would face stiff penalties.

If tourists couldn't hunt the bird and everyone knew how the government bent over backward to please the tourists then this was serious.

After they left, he and Robinson laughed at it all. Imagine being told not to hunt the birds in one's own backyard! What were the government people going to tell them not to do next? Why didn't they come and fix the roads instead of worrying themselves over some measly birds?

But Emanuel was very fond of that bird in particular. He took great pleasure in the fantastic green plumage of the bird's lower body and the royal-blue feathers under its wings. In his mind's eye he carried a picture of the bird's hooked, yellow bill, paler at the tips, its hazel eyes, the rose-pink edged in gray of the bird's throat and neck. Such a beautiful, beautiful bird, he thought.

He always loved beautiful things and when he was younger kept a yellow-billed parrot in a cage on his verandah. He liked having the bird, rare even then, to show off to his friends. He taught the parrot all sorts of new and wonderful tricks: how to talk to him and only him; what embarrassing things to say about his friends when they came to visit;

how to scream his name and *only* his name if someone troubled it. He kept the bird like that for years, letting it out every now and again to "stretch its wings." He had in fact clipped the bird's wings so it could not fly too far out of his reach. One day, however, after letting the bird out, it did fly out of his reach. The bird circled the house twice before heading to the hills from which it had been taken. For three days he saw nothing of the bird but many others did. Some said they saw the bird looking for its lost flock; others reported its lonesome cry; some even talked about the sadness surrounding the bird like a dark-blue cloak. On the third day after again searching the woods frantically for the bird he eventually found it, tired and worn out and fluttering on the ground. He took the parrot home and tended to it assiduously, but to no use. The parrot never recovered and died shortly after being returned to its cage.

▩

Urmilla's body seemed heavier than usual to Emanuel that night and eventually he gave up the idea of lifting her legs over his. Instead, he kept thinking of the woman in the bushes. How young and slender she was. When he first met Urmilla she'd been that slender. A shy, slender school girl he would watch as she made her way home from school in the afternoons. He liked the fact that she did not have too many friends, that she was so shy and soft-spoken, that she always walked home alone.

But what he especially liked about Urmilla were the times she dressed up in the colorful, silky cloth she wrapped tightly around her body. Saris—that was what these clothes were called, he found out. Emanuel remembered the times he would steal onto her father's property at night just to get a glimpse of Urmilla in her saris. He especially liked to watch as she got ready for one of the Indian ceremonies she and her father went to once a month in Kingston. After putting a pasty yellow base on her face she would paint a dark-red spot between her eyes, gold bangles adorned her ankles and her arms, earrings in her ears and nose, and she would slip intricately embroidered slippers on her feet.

She lived with her father in the largest house in the district. Rumor had it her mother had died on her way to Jamaica from India when Urmilla was still a baby. The father never remarried, never had any other children, and Urmilla was forced to grow up alone. The father, it was further rumored, forbade Urmilla to be friends with anyone in the district, insisting they would be going back to India soon. "India" to the minds of most people in the district was some far-off place covered in a curry-yellow haze.

From the first time he'd seen her as a young woman in one of her saris, Emanuel was intrigued and he made up his mind that somehow and by some means he would get her. She would become the replacement for the bird he'd lost. His opportunity came faster than even he himself could have imagined, for, one Saturday, on one of their visits to Kingston, Urmilla's father complained of a tightness in his chest and was just able to pull to the side of the road before he slumped over in his car and died of a heart attack.

By then Emanuel was in his midtwenties and he sprang into action immediately. He dropped the woman he'd been seeing for a few years, Mavis, and, with the entire district looking on in astonishment, arranged a proper church wedding for himself and the grief-stricken Urmilla. And no sooner were they married than Emanuel started imaging what their children would look like. Their mixed-race children. They would have Urmilla's hair of course and a pale-brown complexion, for he wasn't that dark. His children with Urmilla would make up for all the years people called him black and ugly to his face and behind his back. He would show them, by his children, who was black and ugly. He would show all the people of Nonsuch district!

▩

The next morning, on his way to the fields, Emanuel had great difficulty finding the house. He was sure it wasn't too far from the breadfruit tree, yet he could not find it. He kept pacing back and forth from the breadfruit tree to where he was certain the house was yesterday, close to the flamboyant tree; still it was not there. For the longest time he wandered around in a circle, trying to locate the house. Perhaps he'd imagined it all, he said to himself after a while. Perhaps there had been no house, no woman, no yellow-billed parrot. He was just beginning to believe this when he saw it, the house, further along the path, tangled and almost hidden in the bushes. He noticed immediately that the vines had thickened into the fence, as if trying to keep prying eyes out. That the bushes were greener, denser. Some part of him knew that the vines should not have fattened and thickened like that overnight, that he should stay away from the house and its occupant, but he could not help himself. He had to see her again, the beautiful young woman with the yellow-billed parrot about her.

He started struggling with the vines until he forced an opening. The dark-haired woman was squatting in the yard, tending to the flowers in her garden. Her back was to him as before. He watched as she worked slowly, assiduously, humming a song he knew but the words of which he could not remember. The bird was there too, hovering around, flying low and coming close to the woman, before flying away again. It seemed to Emanuel as he watched the woman and the parrot that they were one and the same thing. That the bird was not a parrot at all but some wild, untamed aspect of the woman, both of them so spectacularly beautiful.

For a moment, as if she knew someone was watching her, the woman turned slightly in the direction where Emanuel was kneeling. While he could not make out her entire face he saw the profile of her eyes, her nose, her full, dark lips. She was perfect, just perfect, Emanuel said to himself, struggling to his feet. He would keep that picture in his mind all day as he worked in the field.

▒

From the beginning Urmilla was a quiet, hardworking woman who never asked much of Emanuel. In the evenings when he came home from the field his meals would be warm and waiting for him. He complimented himself on how wise he had been to get rid of Mavis, that Jezebel of a woman, always demanding that he help with chores around the yard when he stayed over at her house. *Do something!* that Mavis was forever saying. Urmilla, thank God, made no such demands and understood that when he came home from the field he was worn out and tired. Urmilla fetched the wood for herself, cooked the meals, planted all the thyme, escellion, and tomatoes she needed to season the meat with. The first two years of his marriage he remembered as bliss, and the only time he ever left the yard was reluctantly to go to the field. It got so bad that Robinson started teasing him that he never saw him anymore.

"Can't you give that poor woman a break?" Robinson would say whenever they ran into each other in the district. "Do you think you could find a little time to come play dominoes one Friday night like you used to do? Even I give Daisy a little break now and again!"

"You just don't understand," Emanuel would say, smiling that knowing smile, "you just don't understand."

"Oh, I understand alright!" Robinson would reply, laughing. "I understand only too well. I guess we should be expecting two little feet any day now?"

"Yes, any day now!" Emanuel would brag.

He could hardly wait for Urmilla to have a child. To have his child. Already he could see this child who would not look like any other child in the district, Urmilla's Indian blood running through its body. That child would be different, special; everyone would want to hold it. That child too would finally make him a big man in the district for then he would be a man who could make babies. Every month he watched for "signs" that Urmilla was carrying his baby.

But month after month no such sign came and after a while he became a little anxious.

"Milla" he said, coming close to her one night in the bed and calling her by the name he'd given her, trying his best to keep the anxiety out of his voice. "How long we been married now?"

Urmilla smiled without answering. They both knew the answer to that question. In a few weeks they would have been married a year and a half.

"Yes," Emanuel said, laying his head on her lap, "a year and a half we've been married to each other."

She was wearing the sheer-pink nightgown he'd bought her, the one that allowed him to see the brown nipples of her breasts. He reached up and started tugging at one of her nipples through the material before he again got serious. "Don't you think it should have happened already?" he asked, using his chin to point to her stomach. "Don't you think by now we should have had a baby?"

A sadness came over Urmilla and her body sagged. Doubt and confusion clouded her eyes. She looked at him but said nothing.

"Well, let's try again," he said, pulling her down on top of him, trying to lighten the mood, trying to stave off both their worries. "If not this month, then next month surely!"

But it did not happen that month. Or the month after that. Or the month after that. In fact, it would never happen; and none of the doctors, bush doctors, or herbalists they consulted could ever tell them why this was happening, for both he and Urmilla were healthy young people. It was the bush doctor, confounded because the bushes he gave them weren't working, who told Emanuel that perhaps having children was not his calling in life. Perhaps he and his wife were just supposed to live together without the headache of children, the bush doctor said, for once you had them you realize what a lot of problem children could be. Or, said the bush doctor when he saw the look on Emanuel's face, perhaps there is a little one without mother or father or being ill-treated by somebody you two could take and raise as your own. So many children on the island needed parents to love them. Had Emanuel thought about that? Emanuel had stalked out of the man's little thatched-roof place behind his big main house. He was not going to take up somebody else's responsibility. He wanted his own children to give him his own problems.

When, after several years, it became clear it would never happen, that he and Urmilla would never have children, Emanuel pulled away from Urmilla and every year became more resentful.

That woman had made him the laughing stock of the entire district. That woman had caused even children to question his masculinity. He could barely hold his head up in the district anymore because of Urmilla. Not when Mavis had a whole brood of children and now even grandchildren running all over her yard and Robinson had what he took to telling everyone was his own "cricket team." With each passing year Emanuel found more and more reasons to blame Urmilla for why she'd never gotten pregnant. Perhaps, he would wonder aloud, those spices Urmilla kept pounding in a mortar had something to do with why she hadn't conceived. He was sure the problem was with her and not with him. Perhaps she was doing "something" to herself, he would say aloud for her to hear him, perhaps she was putting "something" into herself, all those "leaves" some of the women in the district used to bring on their monthly "menses."

But the truth of the matter was that Emanuel knew that what he was saying was at the very least doubtful. He knew Urmilla would never do anything to harm anybody. Alright, he chuckled to himself one night, maybe she might harm him because once or twice when what he was saying got to her, she did make after him with a dutch pot. But she would never harm a baby. There were all the times he watched as her eyes traveled feverishly over a swollen woman's body, or how eagerly she would reach for a newborn baby. The woman he knew, had lived with for years, would never do anything to harm an unborn child. No, Urmilla would never do that.

▩

That evening, on his way home from the field Emanuel stopped by his friend Robinson to feel him out and see if he knew anything about the woman who now had her house in the bushes.

"Round Robin?" Robinson asked, after they settled down to a game of dominoes.

"Naw, naw," Emanuel said, waving away the idea. "I don't want to play dominoes tonight."

Robinson lit a cigarette and looked at his friend, who seemed to be thinking hard about something.

"Urmilla all right?" Robinson broached the subject tentatively. He knew how testy Emanuel got when anyone brought up his or Urmilla's health.

"Yes, yes." Emanuel again waved him off impatiently. "Nothing at all wrong with her, she only there getting fatter and fatter every day."

"She must be one contented woman," Robinson remarked, blowing white circles into the air from his cigarette. "It take a level of contentment for a woman to get fat, you know."

"She too big though!" Emanuel mumbled under his breath.

"There you go again giving that woman grief! I want you to know that you the only man round these parts that feels that way. You the only man I know complain about having a woman with some flesh on her bones. What you want? A meager gal pickney? You know us Portland man, us Jamaican man, we like our women heavy."

"I the only man *round-these-parts* who know anything good! I don't like anything too big and heavy unless it is money!" Emanuel replied, still impatient and miserable. He was thinking hard about the slender young woman he'd seen in the bushes. God, the last time he'd seen her, her skin had taken on the radiance of a big, yellow sunflower.

"In your mind, Mani!" Robinson was saying, "it's all in your mind. Urmilla is a good woman, a honest and decent woman. A churchgoing woman, for I stay here on my verandah and see her go to church every Sunday morning rain or shine. Nothing at all wrong with that woman!"

"Yeah, yeah." Emanuel again waved his friend away.

"Yeah nothing." Robinson looked closely at his friend. "What bothering you, Mani? What on your mind so tonight?"

Emanuel leaned back in his chair, unsure how to begin. He looked at his friend, trying to gauge exactly what he should tell him. "You hear any talk of anybody new moving into the district?" He could not meet his friend's eyes.

"Well," Robinson said as he leaned over and put out his cigarette, "one of Mavis's granddaughters is home with her a bit . . ."

Emanuel shook his head, impatient. "No, no, not like that, somebody totally new . . . a woman."

He knew Robinson was probably looking at him with questions in his eyes, but Emanuel kept his face averted, playing with something at his feet.

"No, I don't hear of any such thing. Why you asking?"

"Oh nothing, nothing." Emanuel was still staring at whatever was at his feet.

"Oh nothing, my backside! You and I, we have known each other forever, so don't come telling me this 'oh nothing!' foolishness!"

"There *is* a woman, Robinson, living near my field . . ."

"Living near your field, Mani? All the way over in *those* bushes?"

"Yes, all the way over in *those* bushes!" Emanuel snapped. He knew some of the men made fun of how far in the bushes he had his field. Said he'd bought his land so far out because he was too cheap to buy land nearer the road. It was like people were always talking about him behind his back, always questioning his manhood.

"Well then, no," Robinson answered, "I hear no talk about some woman living near your place over in the bushes! Mind is not duppy you seeing you know, mind is not bubby susan or rivermuma. You know enough to know to be careful of strange young women you see in the bushes, especially if they very pretty!"

If Robinson had just seen her, Emanuel kept saying to himself as he walked home that night, if he had just seen her then he would know why she was filling up his mind so. And he knew she was a real live woman because of the sweat that ran down her back and how she would tremble. She was no bubby susan or rivermuma, she was a real live woman. Of that he was certain.

▩

After a week of spying Emanuel decided he just couldn't take it anymore, he was going to talk to the woman whether she liked it or not. He was going to take her by the shoulder and turn her around to face him because it was just plain bad manners for her not to talk to him when she was the one who had moved onto "his" land. Plus he had to pass her house going to his field every day after all, and it was high time they got to know each other. Suppose she should need his help one day, he told himself to bolster what he was planning to do, suppose she should have some kind of emergency? Her talking to him was for her benefit. He did not care if she set the yellow-billed parrot on him, for he was prepared to fight the parrot off with his two bare hands.

Of course by the time he got to the breadfruit tree he could not find the house, but by now he was familiar with the games of the woman, the games of all women who loved to have men searching down the place for them. Yes, he said to himself, standing in the clearing and looking around, the house had to be around here somewhere. He took a deep breath, squinted his eyes the better to see, and began searching. If the thought occurred to him, somewhere in the far recesses of his mind, that this was not right, that the woman, the bird, and the house should not be able to appear and disappear at will, he just brushed the thought aside as one of the many games of women.

Emanuel searched and searched for hours on end, retracing his steps from the road to the breadfruit tree. Measuring the distance between the breadfruit tree and the flamboyant tree. The woman's small wooden house with shuttered jalousie windows had to be here somewhere. But no matter what he did, however many times he measured and remeasured his steps back and forth, he did could not find the house. Eventually, late in the afternoon, he found a path he believed led to the house and eagerly followed it. The path led him to a spot where there were only feathers: emerald-green and royal-blue feathers. Nothing else was to be found there—not the tiny wooden house with the shuttered jalousie windows, not the purple Joseph's coat flowers and bright-red ginger lilies. Not even the big Julie mango tree was to be found. As easily as the house, the woman, and the bird sprang up, they had all disappeared.

Emanuel sat down heavily on the ground. He felt defeated. For a long time he was thinking. He thought about Urmilla and all she'd done for him, all she'd put up with over the years. He thought about how every day she carefully prepared his meals, took care of his clothes, did everything she could to make him comfortable. Mornings she rose early just to make his breakfast, leaving her warm indentation in the bed to keep him company. She made the hot chocolate just the way he liked it, with fresh cow's milk and brown sugar. She always made his lunch. Sometimes, in the middle of the day, she would even dare the bushes by herself to bring him something she knew he liked, roast breadfruit and fried salt fish that she'd prepared for her own lunch, for example, because she knew how he loved salt fish especially if it was cooked with susumber. Those days she would sit and keep him company as he worked and then they would walk back to their house together. She had been a good woman to him. Emanuel had no choice but to admit that. Small as it was the house was always clean, and keeping a small house clean, his mother used to always say to him, was harder than keeping a large house clean, because so many things could get into all the tiny crevices and corners of a small house. He wasn't trying to say she was a saint, that Urmilla, for once or twice he had felt the full force of her anger. But she had stayed with him, stuck it out with him, and he knew, deep down, that he could always count on her.

And so what if they never had any children? Did that mean that they did not love each other? Did that mean they hadn't built a solid and stable life together? He knew the people of Nonsuch thought so—wondered aloud what would happen to him and Urmilla when they got old because children were one's old-age pension. This even from people whose children were driving them crazy. People who had to pay out their little life savings to get children out of prison in Kingston. People who hadn't even seen their children in God knows how many years, since someone else was raising them. Or, worst, people who mistreated their children who lived with them. Emanuel sighed a deep sigh. The old bush doctor he'd gone to see years before was right. If it was a question of just wanting children, he could have gone to the orphanage and gotten as many as he wanted. For years Urmilla had begged him to do this. But he had been stubborn. Foolish. He saw that now.

Getting up off the floor where he was sitting because he was so tired, Emanuel decided he would show Urmilla just how much she meant to him. Just how much she'd always meant to him. He could not believe the silly things that had bothered him about her over the years. He was glad he still had some life left in his body to thank her for being there; and if she still agreed to it, tomorrow, early in the morning, they would get dressed and go on down to the orphanage. Done what they should have done a long time ago. Yes, that is what they would do, if Urmilla was still up to it.

And somewhere in the distance, toward the mountains, toward the bushes he had just left behind as he walked home slowly to his wife, he heard the high-pitched "ah-ah-eeeeek" rising on the last note, and the "whip-whip-waaaark" of a bird in flight, and he knew that just like he was, a yellow-billed parrot was heading home again.

Lady Chatterley's Mansion

Unoma Azuah

Medua was not expecting to be admitted into the writing program at Brooks University of Virginia. Most of her professors at Heights University had told her not to hope for much. Brooks University was for the elite. She went ahead and applied anyway. When she had heard nothing by late August, she gave up hope and then sent in her letter of acceptance to Lantern University. That same day, when she got to the mailroom, she found a letter from Brooks University of Virginia. They had offered her admission. She was ecstatic and made copies of the admission letter and slipped one under the doors of all the professors who had told her she would never be admitted. She was not an elite but she had never underestimated her capabilities.

Before she set out for Brooks, she made sure she wore the bone pendant her grandmother gave her. She also wrapped her rosary around her wrist. To her, they were totems of good luck.

When she got to Brooks University, most of the housing was filled. Her tour guide suggested Lady Chatterley's mansion: there was always a room to spare though her rent was pretty costly. Lady Chatterley's building was indeed a mansion: four floors with porches and an orchard in the backyard.

Even the one self-contained room she got had its own back porch. Lady Chatterley, tall and elegant-looking, carried herself arrogantly. It was obvious she was a snob. Although she was probably in her seventies, she still wore high-heeled shoes that jabbed hard on the concrete floor of her building and makeup that concealed the many wrinkles on her face. She barely responded to Medua when she said to her, "Hello, Ma'am." Then she gave Medua instructions on how to pay her rent directly into her account.

Medua fell in love with her room as soon as she saw it: it was spacious and the largest window in the room faced the east. (One of her hobbies was to watch the sun rise.) The room was also cozy enough for loads of writing. And the other students in the rooms close to hers were quiet, studious types. They said few words to her whenever she met them in the common room. But she was grateful, for such housemates were nothing like the party revelers she had had as housemates at Heights University.

Her neighborhood was full of brick houses and massive statues of Virginian heroes. The caretaker of her building once told her that the brick mansions were built by her people: African slaves. Medua didn't know what to make of the information, which she absorbed with a mixture of pride and anger. (And besides, that word—slaves—made her shudder.)

Medua settled into the normal school rhythm until one day, she was running late to Mass and decided to sprint. A few feet away from the church, she noticed that her keys were hanging out of her jacket. She stopped, tried to grab them, and bumped into a lady. She stretched out her hands in apology, but the lady ignored her and swept past.

After a few days, Medua observed that every morning, at about 6:30 a.m., on her way to Mass at Saint Anthony Catholic Church, she'd run into the hooded lady. The lady wore a black shawl wrapped tightly around her head and her shoulders.

Medua decided to follow her one morning and discovered that she always went to the basement of her building and then to work in the orchard.

Medua wondered why the woman turned up so early; it was still dark. Surely, she could barely see the shrubs she pruned. And why spend so much time in the basement when her work tools were in a shack close to the orchard?

Curiosity got the better of Medua, and she began to trail the woman even more closely. Still, always she would stop short of entering the basement. One day, however, Medua gathered enough courage to walk into the basement after the woman. It was too dark in there for Medua to see anything but the blazing red eyes of a cat and its bared white teeth coming toward her. She turned on her heels and screamed her way out of the basement.

She chided herself later for being scared of a cat and wondered how the woman could have disappeared so quickly into the orchard. But when she looked in the orchard, the lady was not there. Medua ran through a gamut of emotions: Surprise. Worry. Then fear. She had encountered situations at home in Nigeria where humans transform to animals, but this was America. In America you were laughed at for even telling such a story.

The next day Medua waited for the woman, determined this time to confront her. The woman did not show. Nor did she turn up the day after. Days ran into weeks and weeks ran into months. The orchard became overgrown with weeds, but neither the woman nor the black cat was anywhere to be found. Then one fall morning, after five months, when the air was a bit chilly, the lady appeared and shuffled past Medua. She looked down; her hooded face was not visible. Medua followed, and she didn't care if the woman knew she was being followed or not. She headed to the basement close behind her.

The lady sat on the floor, on the same spot where the cat sat months ago.

"Who are you, and why do you come here?" Medua asked. She could see the lady's shadow in the dark. There was no response. Medua asked again. This time, the woman cleared her throat but still said nothing.

Medua ran up to her room to get a flashlight. She needed to see the lady's face. When she returned to the basement, for some reason it seemed darker. She directed her flashlight at the spot where the lady sat. She was not there. Medua stepped deeper into the basement. As she moved her flashlight around the basement, she heard heavy breathing behind her. She almost keeled over, afraid, and she felt a stab of a sharp blade on her shoulder. She grabbed her shoulder with both hands. The flashlight fell. She yelled with all the energy she could summon, ran into her room, dialed 911, then ran out and started banging on her neighbors' doors. Nobody answered.

■

At the hospital, she was taken to the emergency room. And before she was discharged, some of her classmates visited. When she told them the story behind her attack most didn't believe her. Still, some who didn't like Lady Chatterley did. They suggested she sue Lady Chatterley. She thought about it, but couldn't make up her mind. She blamed herself for stalking the strange lady.

Word got around to Lady Chatterley that she was contemplating suing her for the attack in her basement. The next day Lady Chatterley invited her to her ranch. The ranch was another white mansion surrounded by thick woods. There were many horses wandering around the open space. Some Mexican men were supplying hay and cleaning out the stables. Lady Chatterley asked her to sit. They were on the porch of the mansion; it overlooked a lake and more woods. The soft cushion of the matted chair was cozy, but Medua perched at the edge of the chair.

"How do you say your name again?" Lady Chatterley asked, puffing away at her cigar. She flung her long, scrawny legs on a small stool in front of her.

"Medua."

"Media?"

"No, May-DU-a."

"I see," she said and coughed lightly. A young Mexican woman came into the porch with a large tray filled with assorted drinks, including wine and beer. She smiled at Medua and asked her what she wanted to drink.

"Orange juice will be just fine."

The maid poured the orange juice in a long glass, gave it to Medua, and kept the rest of the juice-filled jar on a stool next to Medua's chair. She smiled again, nodded at Medua, and left. Lady Chatterley gazed ahead at the sparkling lake, and gnashed her teeth. A twirl of her cigarette smoke hung between her and Medua.

"What happened in the basement?" she asked without looking at Medua.

"I was attacked."

"Who attacked you?"

"How do I know? I heard it had happened before to one of your tenants."

"I do sympathize with you. That's why I'll be taking care of your medical bills."

"Why?"

"It would save us both quite some stress. And you don't pay rent for the next couple of months."

"Okay."

"I need to tell you something, though. I know that your people believe in spirits and the unusual."

Medua sat back on the chair. For the first time, Lady Chatterley looked into her eyes without blinking. And she told her a story that haunted her.

Lady Chatterley's grandfather was a slave master. Among his numerous slaves was one called Lucia. Lucia was one of his best plantation hands until she had her seventh baby. Lord Chatterley felt that Lucia's baby was distracting her from performing efficiently at the plantation. He threatened to sell the baby, but nobody would buy a baby that young. So he locked him up in the basement. The child crawled into the well in the basement and drowned. And Lucia jumped in and ended her own life.

It is said that Lucia's ghost never left the house. She keeps searching for her child. Lady Chatterley had invited many ghost-busters to lead Lucia to her final rest; none worked.

Part of what Medua's grandmother did as the keeper of her village shrine in Nigeria was guide restless ghosts who were trapped on earth into the beyond. Medua remembered watching her grandmother perform the rituals. But where was she going to get the tooth of a black cat, cola nuts, white chalks, and palm fronds? She was surprised that Lady Chatterley provided every piece of item she asked for. When she asked Lady Chatterley why she provided some teeth instead of one, her response was that she had asked her gardener to get rid of her oldest cat; she needed its whole teeth. The ranch mansion was also haunted.

On the night of the ritual, it was full moon. Medua faced the east. The sacrificial bowl was beside her and she shivered. She pulled the massive white cloth around her shoulder closer, knotted the ends tighter, and lifted the bowl into the night. She was not sure about how high her grandmother lifted it, so she raised it as high as she thought was right. A thunderous howling of foxes startled her and the water-filled sacrificial bowl almost fell from her hands. She held the bowl firmer; it tilted and some water splashed on her face. She spat out the water and the foxes shrieked even louder. She was chanting words, words that only her grandmother could have understood, and she heard the deafening sounds of a million human steps scuttling into the night, tearing into the woods. Then the wailings foxes were silent. She looked back at Lady Chatterley's mansion, and saw her peering through the red curtain of the smallest window in her mansion. A candle flickered behind her.

All about Skin

Xu Xi

For my muse Jenny Wai

I went to **Derma** the week before Christmas to buy an *american* skin. I was apprehensive because **Derma**'s expensive and doesn't allow trade-ins. But their salesman gave me credit on pretty generous terms, and let me take it away the same day, which made me feel good.

This was not an impulse purchase, you understand. I've been pricing *americans* for donkeys' years. My last topskin, which I got fourteen years ago at **Epiderm International**, was an *immigranta*. It was OK, but only really fit if teamed with the right accessories. That got to be a pain. Going *american*, though, is a big step. After **Derma**, there's no place else to go but down, at least, not as long as they're number one.

You see, my history with skins is spotty. I stay with one a long time, sometimes too long, because change makes me itch. The thing about an old skin is that even if it's worn or stained, it hangs comfortably because you know where it needs a bit of a stretch or a quick fold and tuck. Before *immagranta*, I wore *cosmopol* for seven years. The latter was always a wee bit shiny between the legs, although I knew enough to deflect glare with *corpus ceiling-glass*, my preferred underskin, from **SubCutis**.

But I'm getting ahead of myself. A chronology of my history with skins will keep names and dates straight. It's sort of like skinning a lion. First, you have to shoot the beast.

Like most folks on our globe, I got my first topskin from my parents on my eighth birthday. Now I know there are some who start off at six or even as young as five, like the wearers of *nipponicas* and *americans*. We were a conservative family though, and when I slipped into *china cutis*, the only product line **People's PiFu** sold back then, I was the proudest little creature strutting around Hong Kong. This was in the 1960s. My idea of skin began and ended with *china cutis*, basic model.

Mind you, there's nothing wrong with basics. This one gave me room to breathe and plenty of growing space. During the teenage diet thing, it adapted nicely enough, although Ma worried about premature tummy sags. You know what mothers are like. If there isn't a real problem to worry about they'll find one.

For years, I simply didn't think about skin. Passing exams was all that mattered so that I too could be a face-valued citizen. I practiced tending to wounds and cuts, bruises and scars, sores and boils. What fascinated me were bites—a plethora of bug nibbles bursting out on the back of my thighs; fang prints snakes sank into my ankles; crab kisses slashing my fingers; teeth marks dogs lodged in my shoulder. Papa was pallid the day I came home from the beach, my back and arms covered with huge, red splotches. They looked awful but didn't itch, which was merciful, and disappeared the next day. Sand crabs, Ma said. Durable, my old *china cutis*. There are days I miss it.

My problem began round about age nineteen. Being ambitious types, my parents packed me off to schools abroad. I salivated at **Derma**'s store windows in New York, desperate for an *american*. They were all the rage, and outrageously expensive. "You can buy that yourself when you're earning your own money," Papa declared. "I can't afford it." I stormed and pouted, scratching my face and legs till they bled, giving Ma something to really cry about. He wouldn't relent. It wasn't just the money. He and Ma had worn their *china cutises* since they were eight and couldn't see why I wouldn't do likewise.

From their perspective, I was acting like a spoiled brat. They were right, I suppose, but you find me a nineteen-year-old who isn't stuffed full of the fashion of her times.

So I passed the exams, got my face-valued citizen parchment, and, by my midtwenties, had this great job in advertising. Paris three times a year! Imagine. It was a pretty exciting life, I must say, despite my skin.

In the spring of '79, I dared to visit **Integume** of Paris.

If you think **Derma**'s hot, you've never shopped at **Integume**. From the moment you enter their store—no, "store" is too pedestrian—their boutique, you're engulfed by the unimaginable possibilities of skin. Moisturizer wafts through the atmosphere. Never, never, it whispers, will even the tiniest blemish dare to mar this surface. *Jamais!* You wander around this cutaneous paradise where an array of products tempts you with seductive promise: *euro trash tannis, decadence glorious, romance du monde ancien, french chic* . . . Skins! Meters upon meters of skins, both natural and quality synthetic, draped fetchingly, lovingly, placed with the kind of care that plunges skin deep.

The saleslady offered to take my old *china cutis* in trade, saying it was in big demand and commanded good resale value. Secondhands were rare, because few wearers upgraded abroad back then. I really didn't care one way or another because I was sick to death of *china cutis.* I mean, it couldn't tan or wrinkle, and even a little makeup made me feel all Suzie Wong. The only reason I stuck it out so long was, well, family is family after all. But enough is enough. It was time to go *cosmopol.*

The beauty of *cosmopol* is its flexibility. I could slip in and out of it into something more comfortable whenever I wanted. *China cutis* stuck to me like a fragile layer of dried rice glue. It flaked periodically—showers of scarf skin—and had to be treated with such respect. That was the worst part, the respect. Four thousand years of R&D had gone into its design. Personally, I thought the design had already run its course, but then, I've always been "one step too many beyond," as Ma says. When Mao, the primo *china cutis* wearer of the last century, created a big to-do by jumping into the Yellow River, thus proving its durability, it was downright asinine.

But the truth of the matter is my *china cutis* had gotten loose and sloppy. Fashion-wise, the look was making a comeback by then, but not in any real way. Mine sagged. I wallowed in free space. Ma had suggested I return it for a newer model, but those weren't a marked improvement. **People's PiFu** hadn't modernized their product line for global consumption yet. It was just an ill-destined style.

So I traded it in. My father would've killed me had he known. He didn't though, thanks to *cosmopol.*

I owe a lot to that **Integume** saleslady. She showed me how to enhance my *cosmopol* skin with separates and coordinates. Stuck with *china cutis,* I didn't know about all the accessory lines. I confess I was pretty extravagant for a while there. From **Integume**, I went to **Sub-Cutis**, where I bought three underskins—a *sub-four seas, lady don juan,* and *corporate rung.* They were expensive, but worth it. Like the saleslady said, you make the big one-time investment and add extras as you go.

Besides, **Integume** allowed layaway, and **SubCutis** was running a special promotion for customers of **Integume**. A year later, I added *underwired g-strung* and *corpus-ceiling glass* to my skinrobe. All in all, I made out OK.

Being able to slip any one of these over or under *cosmopol* was such a *liberation.* If I were feeling particularly daring, I could combine accessories by themselves. None of them worked that well solo, probably because they were all synthetic. *Underwired g-strung* slid off at the slightest provocation. *Corporate rung* was generally a tight fit, although the crotch was absurdly loose. The designer hadn't quite gotten the hang of that one, especially in female petite.

The real test, though, was passing muster with Papa. By wearing *cosmopol* with *sub-four seas* underneath, I could fool him into thinking I had on my *china cutis.* Things were looking good. But none of this explains why, after a good seven years, I decided to give up *cosmopol* for an *immigranta.*

To tell you properly, I have to go back to **Derma** and their *american* line. You have to understand that I never lost my yen for *american.* I'm a sucker for advertising, and **Derma** could really launch a marketing campaign. Even though they'd only been around a couple of centuries, everyone thought they were the real thing. It was a question of focus. Their entire strategy depended on narrowing everything down to one product. **Derma** equaled *american.* The same idea worked for **People's PiFu** a few centuries earlier. Their problem was different—times had changed and they hadn't. Renaming their company and sticking on a new logo back in the late 1940s were not, by themselves, sufficient to create the fundamental transformation they desperately needed.

But during the years I ran around in *cosmopol,* **Derma** had been steadily losing market share to **All Nippon Cutis**.

Let me digress a moment. **All Nippon Cutis** were smart. They invested in R&D for some ten years to produce a top-quality *american*-like skin. I read about them in Forbes. Their chairman sent fifty of their top designers and executives to Paris for two years to check out **Integume**'s styles. After that, those same folks went to New York for another two years to study **Derma**'s market leadership. By the time they actually started designing in Tokyo, they had the marketplace all figured out.

The world, they decided, wanted **Derma**'s strength with **Integume**'s flair. Somehow, the frivolous fun inherent in **SubCutis** needed to be integrated. The smartest thing **All Nippon Cutis** did was to compete in **Derma**'s primary marketplace, which was an easier target than **Integume**'s international market dominance.

You know the rest. At the beginning, the very rich would fly to Tokyo to buy an *america dreama*. By the mideighties, **All Nippon Cutis** had opened branches all over the United States. You remember their commercials—Lincoln's head superimposed on the Statue of Liberty crying, "Cutify!" Market forces being what they are, within a year, you could get an *america dreama* out in Jersey for half the price of **Derma**'s *american*.

Their *america dreama* impressed me. They couldn't call it *american*, of course, because of trademark infringement. I had moved to New York by then, but Ma told me that the product was a big hit even in Hong Kong. In Tokyo, it became very fashionable as a second skin to *nipponica*.

At that time, I wouldn't have dreamed of buying from **Derma**. Not only was my *cosmopol* still serviceable, but **Derma**'s prices were quite unjustified. Oh I know they were all natural, while **All Nippon Cutis** used blends, but big deal, my old *china cutis* was all natural too. Even when the hoopla about *america dreama* turning yellow after repeated sun exposure made the news, no one cared, not really, because, first of all, the scientists who claimed that were working for **Derma**, and most people had begun to believe that skins should be replaced after even as little as three to five years. I find that a little wasteful myself, but **All Nippon Cutis** made a good point by offering to recycle old skins.

As impressive as it was, I wasn't quite sold on what amounted to only a make-believe *american*. Which meant my alternative was **Epiderm International**, makers of *immigranta*, *asia personals*, and *ec*, among others.

My problem was that *cosmopol* wasn't fitting quite right.

Life in New York was expensive enough without keeping up my *cosmopol* skin. It was flexible, but only if pampered a lot. You needed the best face creams and lotions, and could only be seen in the most fashionable places. Worst of all, it radiated this worldly air, while hinting at a sexual undertow, but avoiding any engagements that would ravage its surface charms. Debt did not aid its sustenance, as I was still paying off my balance at **Integume**.

At least *cosmopol* could be cashed in. Unlike *china cutis*, which had great trade-in value but generated no cash, New Yorkers would kill for secondhand *cosmopols*. I actually made a profit, because naturally, with the original trade-in, I hadn't paid full price, although the interest alone was staggering.

For almost six months, I went around without a main skin. Luckily, I had all those secondary ones. Depending on my mood, I usually wore either *corporate rung* or *corpus-ceiling glass*, with *sub-four seas* underneath. It was an uncomfortable time. I was sometimes tempted to slip on *lady don juan* with *underwired g-strung* to get back that *cosmopol* feeling, but was just too embarrassed. I hated admitting I didn't have a main skin, but I needed to pay down debt, even if not completely, before my next investment.

The day I purchased my *immigranta*, I dreamed about flying back to Hong Kong to see my parents. This was the real reason to lose *cosmopol*. Lying to them was fine when I was younger, but now, it made me feel like a hypocrite. It wasn't their fault I didn't like *china cutis*. They couldn't have foreseen my life.

Even then, it was another six years before I finally made it home. I had retired *lady don juan* and *underwired g-strung* to my back closet, because the market for those secondary styles had pretty much gone bust. You remember the beginning of the dual-skin craze. Anyone who was anyone wouldn't dream of being without a second skin. **SubCutis** hung on, but just barely. Word flew on the street that they were going to file Chapter 11. I won that bet when they succumbed to a buyout by **All Nippon Cutis**. You have to figure there's a niche market somewhere for their questionable lines. Besides, the rest of their products did have mainstream appeal.

It was a big bet, which was good, because the money paid for my trip home. I had left advertising and was working on the fringes of Wall Street, a bad place to be after Black Monday. With my debt on *immigranta*, I lived paycheck to paycheck. Maybe I was sticking my neck out unnecessarily with that bet. But the great thing about my *immigranta* skin was that it absorbed immunity to risk.

I suppose that's why I kept it so long. I didn't have to lie to my parents because it was the one other acceptable skin in their eyes. Call them old-fashioned, but they like the chameleon complexion of *immigranta*, especially because on me, it looked enough like *china cutis*. What they didn't know was that I had slipped *golden peril* on underneath. I'd picked that one up cheap at a **SubCutis** fire sale before going to see them. I'm awfully thankful for fickle fashion trends; products in a downturn sometimes prove extremely attractive, given the right circumstances.

So why *american* now? You might say I got caught up in the wave of market forces, because I'm past much of that fashion stuff. **Derma** went through some pretty shaky years, losing considerable market share to **All Nippon Cutis**, who took their range way out there with *ho-ho hollywoodo*. Tacky, I think, but who could predict its huge appeal, from Los Angeles to Beijing? Even **Epiderm International** horned in on Derma's territory with their **Epiderm US** subsidiary, whose *emigrant* and *global villager* became ludicrously popular. **All Nippon Cutis** retaliated quickly enough with *worldo warrior*. For a while there, I almost shed *immigranta* for one of these newer models.

Derma had it all wrong. Their feeble attempt to launch *heritage hides* was laughable. Imagine thinking Mr. Ed singing "got to know about history" would make any impact? I think it was voted the worst commercial of 1988. Price was another factor. Some say they priced themselves out of their own marketplace.

Derma refused to entertain the idea of growth even though revenues were down 30 percent and profits almost nonexistent. In the meantime, **All Nippon Cutis** merged with the largest hairbank in Frankfurt, while **Epiderm** was borrowing heavily both in London and New York to finance their expansion. The *Wall Street Journal* suggested that **Epiderm**'s reliance on junk bonds would be their undoing, but you couldn't be too critical of junk in those days. Even **Integume** dived right in, expanding and grabbing share in markets like Moscow, Shanghai, and Prague, as well as in places like Cincinnati, Seattle, and Minneapolis, where *cosmopol* became more popular than *american*. By now, **Derma** was a distant number four behind those three global leaders, at least in sales and profits. If you count market size, **People's PiFu** is right up there, but of course, prices aren't comparable, given their rock-bottom manufacturing costs.

In the end, everything turned on principle, plus a little Chinese intrigue.

You've heard the conspiracy theories, about how the CIA negotiated with **Soong & Dong** to flood the global market with synthetic epidermatis. There are even whispers that it had to do with WTO membership for the motherland. I don't believe those rumors myself, but you must admit the sudden availability of top-quality synthetic raw material, at a third of the prevailing price per kilo, was unprecedented. Ever since the worldwide skin crisis of the seventies, the industry's been wary of shortages. Survival has depended on reducing costs, which meant going synthetic.

Price wars raged. Folks started buying five, ten, even as many as twenty topskins, never mind the multiples in underskins. Even my parents each bought a second, although Ma complained that synthetic just didn't feel as good. Suddenly, skin took on a whole new dimension. The markets for other body parts went into shock, unable to compete against this surge in demand for skin and only skin. Meanwhile, futures in natural epidermatis were priced 25 percent up even in the nearest months, which battered **Derma**. Rumor had it they were buying supplies from **People's PiFu**, who of course didn't suffer an iota, given their government-regulated market.

And then, in the middle of 1997, the worldwide skin market crashed.

It was bound to happen. Folks were carrying debt over their heads in skins. Even with cheaper prices, an average one still comprises a hefty percentage of most incomes. Besides, as Papa declared, how many skins can a person wear anyway? Used, recycled, and even slightly defective new skins flooded the stores. Now, everyone's fancy skins were worth less than a mound of toenails.

Things looked bleak.

■

Folks are funny. They self correct pretty quickly in the face of disaster. Everyone laid low on skins for a while. Television pundits compare the past few years to the Great Eyelash Famine as well as the New Deal in Teeth. I don't pay much attention to pundits myself. They invent connections where there are none.

Derma's comeback was quite the media circus. Among the larger companies, they had the upper hand now because they hadn't invested in growth, and consequently, weren't sitting on useless inventory or excessive debt. There's nothing quite like cash, is there? But I have to admire their new CEO for some pretty-quick moves. First, there was the hostile takeover of **Epiderm International**, instantly transforming **Derma** into the largest in the industry. That caught **Integume** and **All Nippon Cutis** completely off guard. By the time they proposed buying **SubCutis**, that company's parent, **All Nippon Cutis**, was too broke not to capitulate.

Ultimately, however, it was brilliant marketing that invigorated them. "Why pretend? Slide into a genuine *american*. One is all you'll ever need." Sales picked up, thanks to their clever offer of low-interest, long-term loans. If you bought a top-of-the-line skin, they threw in an **Epiderm** topskin or **SubCutis** accessory on layaway at a discount. They didn't have to lower prices or redesign their main line. Timing was all. Folks were sick to death of hype.

Well, I wasn't going to be left behind over something as important as skin. Skin buying is something you do once in a purple sun, or at least, that's the way it used to be in my father's day, as he loves to remind me. **Derma** refinanced my debt with **SubCutis** and **Epiderm**. It made my millennium celebration.

I'd like to stay with *american* for a while. You know, give myself time to get used to it. It fits well, neither too tight nor too loose. I still have faith in this classic model.

But the skin industry's so unpredictable these days.

Epiderm US launched two niche lines in time for Christmas, *indigo jazz* and *latin hues*, and sales were bigger than anyone predicted. Maybe they're not so niche. And how about that rash of IPOs of small companies in the middle of last year? Who would have thought the stock prices of *Kimchee Kasings*, *Hide-the-Curry*, and *TagalogitPelts* could triple by year end? Some analysts think these upstarts could give **Derma** a run for their money. Nothing's what it seems anymore.

Also, **People's PiFu** has been making noises recently about going public here, saying they'll list on the New York Stock Exchange. Now that's earth-shattering news in my books. They hired this youngish CEO a few years back—quite a change for them—and just launched a brand-new product line, *sinokapitalist.* I like it. It's got a kind of post-modern pizzaz, something I can't quite define, that seems right for this century. Papa thinks it's ridiculous, although he grudgingly admits now that *china cutis* has run its course.

Let's just say I've learned from my fashion mistakes. Besides, for all we know, the next trend will be in chins or something else equally as unexpected. I'll wait a bit, to see how this new model fares, before I even think about exchanging my *american* skin.

Contributors

Aracelis González Asendorf was born in Cuba and raised in Florida. Her short stories have appeared in *Kweli Journal, Puerto del Sol, Sunscripts,* the *Weekly Planet,* and the anthology *100% Pure Florida Fiction.* Her story "The Lost Ones" was nominated for a Pushcart Prize. She has been a contributor at the Bread Loaf Writers' Conference and a recipient of a New York State Summer Writers Institute scholarship. A former English and Spanish teacher, she is currently working on an MFA at the University of South Florida.

Unoma Azuah is a Nigerian-born writer, teacher, and activist. She has earned acclaim through her novels, poetry, and research on sexuality and LGBTI issues in Nigeria. Her debut novel *Sky-high Flames* (2005) received the Urban Spectrum Award and the Association of Nigerian Authors/NDDC/Flora Nwapa Award. Her other accolades include the prestigious Hellman/Hammett grant and the Leonard Trawick Creative Writing Award. Her latest novel, *Edible Bones* (2012), won the Aidoo-Snyder Book Prize. Currently, she is a college professor in Tennessee and is working on her second collection of poems, tentatively titled "Home Is Where the Hurt Hurts."

Jacqueline Bishop, award-winning poet, novelist, essayist, painter, and photographer, was born in Kingston, Jamaica, and now lives in New York

City. She has held several Fulbright Fellowships, and exhibited her work widely in North America, Europe, and North Africa. She is also a master teacher in liberal studies at New York University. For more information, visit www.jacqueline-bishop.com.

Glendaliz Camacho was raised in the Washington Heights neighborhood of New York City. She studied at Fordham University and labored in several editorial departments in publishing. Her writing has appeared in *Southern Pacific Review*, *Infective Ink*, and the *Acentos Review*, among others. She is a 2013 Pushcart Prize nominee. She is currently at work on a short-story collection.

Learkana Chong is a fangirl, critic, and writer interested in the subversion of mainstream narratives and the self-articulation of her own truths (which often run counter to mainstream narratives). She received her BA in English–creative writing at Mills College in 2013 and is still debating whether or not to go the MFA route. She currently resides in Oakland and is working on a screenplay.

Jennine Capó Crucet is the author of the novel *Magic City Relic* (2015) and the story collection *How to Leave Hialeah* (2009), which won the Iowa Short Fiction Award, the John Gardner Prize, and the Devil's Kitchen Award in Prose. The collection was also named a Best Book of the Year by the *Miami Herald*, the *Miami New Times*, and the Latinidad List. A winner of an O. Henry Prize and a Bread Loaf Fellow, she served as the 2013/14 Picador Guest Professor of American Literature and Creative Writing at the University of Leipzig in Germany. After several years working in South Central Los Angeles as a counselor to first-generation college students, she currently lives and teaches in Florida.

Ramola D's *Temporary Lives* (2009) was awarded the AWP's 2008 Grace Paley Prize for Short Fiction and was a finalist for the 2010 Library of Virginia Fiction Literary Award. *Invisible Season* (1998), her first poetry collection, co-won the Washington Writers' Publishing House award. Her second collection, *Against the Conspiracy of Things*, was a finalist in the 2013 Benjamin Saltman Prize from Red Hen Press. Her work has appeared in various journals, including *Quiddity International*, *Kartika Review*, *Kweli Quarterly*, *Urban Confustions*,

Los Angeles Review, *Short Review*, *Blackbird*, *Prairie Schooner*, *Agni*, *Literal Latte*, *Beltway Quarterly*, *Green Mountains Review*, *Indiana Review*, *Writer's Chronicle*, and *Indian Express*, and has been reprinted in *Best American Poetry 1994*, *Best American Fantasy 2007*, *Full Moon on K Street: Poems about Washington, DC*, and *Literal Latte*'s *The Anthology: Highlights from Fifteen Years of a Unique "Mind Stimulating" Literary Magazine*. Her fiction was shortlisted under 100 Other Distinguished Stories in *Best American Stories 2007* and included in *Enhanced Gravity: More Fiction by Washington Area Women*. A Discovery/*The Nation* finalist and five-time Pushcart Prize nominee, she is the recipient of a 2005 National Endowment for the Arts fellowship in poetry. She holds an MFA from George Mason University and a BS in physics and an MBA from the University of Madras. She has most recently taught creative writing at George Washington University and at the Writer's Center, Bethesda. She is the founder and coeditor of *Delphi Quarterly*, an online journal for writer, poet, and filmmaker interviews. She currently lives in the Boston area with her husband and daughter, and runs art and creative writing workshops for children while working on fiction and poetry.

Patricia Engel is the author of *It's Not Love, It's Just Paris* (2013) and *Vida* (2010), which was a *New York Times* Notable Book of the Year, a finalist for the PEN/Hemingway Foundation Award and the New York Public Library Young Lions Fiction Award, and a Best Book of the Year chosen by NPR, Barnes & Noble, *Latina*, and *LA Weekly*. She was a 2014 National Endowment for the Arts fellow in fiction, and her award-winning fiction has appeared in the *Atlantic*, *A Public Space*, *Boston Review*, *Harvard Review*, *Guernica*, and numerous other publications. Born to Colombian parents and raised in New Jersey, Patricia now lives in Miami.

Amina Gautier is the author of the short-story collections *At-Risk* (*2011*), which won the Flannery O'Connor Award for Short Fiction, and *Now We Will Be Happy* (2014), which won the Prairie Schooner Book Prize in Fiction. Her stories have been honored with the Crazyhorse Fiction Prize, the Danahy Prize, the Jack Dyer Prize, the Lamar York Prize, the Schlafly Microfiction Award, and the William Richey Award as well as fellowships from the American Antiquarian Society, the Bread Loaf Writers' Conference, the Prairie Center of the Arts, the Sewanee Writers' Conference, and the Ucross Foundation, and artist grants from the Illinois Arts Council and the Pennsylvania Council on the Arts.

Manjula Menon's stories have appeared in *Nimrod*, *North American Review*, *Santa Monica Review*, *Pleiades*, *Southern Humanities Review*, *Tampa Review*, and *Ego Magazine*, among others. She was awarded residencies at Yaddo and the Vermont Studio Center and has been a waiter at the Bread Loaf Writers' Conference.

Chinelo Okparanta was born in Port Harcourt, Nigeria. She is the author of *Happiness, Like Water*, a 2013 *New York Times Sunday Book Review* Editors' Choice, and one of the *Guardian*'s Best African Fiction of 2013. A 2014 NYPL Young Lions Award Finalist, and a Rolex Mentors and Protégés Finalist in Literature, Okparanta has been nominated for a United States Artists Fellowship in Literature, long-listed for the Frank O'Connor International Short Story Award, and short-listed for the Caine Prize for African Writing.

Jina Ortiz holds an MFA in creative writing/poetry from the Solstice Creative Writing Program at Pine Manor College in Chestnut Hill, Massachusetts. She is an adjunct professor of English at Quinsigamond Community College. Her writings have been published in the *Afro-Hispanic Review*, *Calabash*, *Green Mountains Review*, *Worcester Review*, the *Caribbean Writer*, and *Solstice Literary Magazine*, among others. She has received residency fellowships from Art Omi at Ledig House, the Virginia Center for the Creative Arts (VCCA), the Vermont Studio Center, Can Serrat in Barcelona, Spain, and others. She also received grants from the Worcester Cultural Commission and the Highlights Foundation.

ZZ Packer was born in Chicago, Illinois, and raised in Atlanta, Georgia, and Louisville, Kentucky. She currently lives in Austin, Texas. Her stories have appeared in the *New Yorker*, *Harper's*, *Story*, *Ploughshares*, *Zoetrope All-Story*, *Best American Short Stories 2000*, *Best American Short Stories 2003*, and NPR's Selected Shorts series. Her nonfiction has appeared in the *New York Times Magazine*, *Essence*, *O Magazine*, and the *New York Times Book Review*. She is a recipient of a Rona Jaffe Foundation Writers' Award, a Whiting Award, and a Guggenheim Fellowship. Her book *Drinking Coffee Elsewhere* (2003) won the

Commonwealth First Fiction Award and an Alex Award. It became a finalist for the PEN/Faulkner Award for Fiction and was selected for the Today Show Book Club by John Updike. She is currently at work on a novel about the Buffalo Soldiers, titled "The Thousands," an excerpt of which appeared in the *New Yorker*'s "20 Under 40" fiction issue under the title "Dayward."

Princess Joy L. Perry is a senior lecturer of composition, American literature, and creative writing at Old Dominion University in Norfolk, Virginia. A 2010 Pushcart Prize nominee, her fiction has appeared in *Kweli Journal*, *Harrington Gay Men's Literary Quarterly*, and twice in *African American Review*. In 2011 she was a Tobias Wolff Award in Fiction finalist and garnered an honorable mention from the *Common Review*'s first annual Short Story Prize in the summer of 2010. She is a past recipient of a Virginia Commission for the Arts Fellowship and a winner of the Zora Neale Hurston/Richard Wright Award.

Toni Margarita Plummer is a winner of the Miguel Mármol Prize and a finalist for the Mariposa Award. She is the author of *The Bolero of Andi Rowe* (2011), a story collection set in her hometown of South El Monte, California. Her fiction has appeared in *Thema*, *PALABRA*, and *Kweli Journal*, and she is a contributor to the anthology *Wise Latinas: Writers on Higher Education*. Plummer attended the University of Notre Dame and earned a Master of Professional Writing from USC. An editor at a major publisher, Plummer lives with her husband in New York.

Emily Raboteau is the author of a work of creative nonfiction, *Searching for Zion: The Quest for Home in the African Diaspora* (2013), and a novel, *The Professor's Daughter* (2005). Her fiction and essays have been widely published and anthologized in such places as *Best American Short Stories*, *Best African American Fiction*, *Best American Nonrequired Reading*, the *Believer*, *Tin House*, the *Guardian*, and *Guernica*. As an associate professor of creative writing at the City College of New York, she lives in New York City with her husband and two kids, both of whom were born at home under water.

Ivelisse Rodriguez has published work in the *Boston Review*, the *Quercus Review*, *Ragazine*, *Vandal*, *Asterix*, and *Kweli*. In December 2010 she was nominated for two Pushcart Prizes for her fiction. She holds a PhD in English–creative writing from the University of Illinois at Chicago and an MFA in creative writing from Emerson College. She is an assistant professor of English at Borough of Manhattan Community College in New York City. She has finished a collection of short stories titled "Love War Stories," and is working on a novel about the African diaspora and a novella about salsa music.

Metta Sáma is the author of *Nocturne Trio* (2012) and *South of Here* (2005, published under her legal name, Lydia Melvin). Her poems, fiction, creative nonfiction, and book reviews have been published or are forthcoming in *Blackbird, bluestem, Drunken Boat,* the *Drunken Boat, Esque, Her Circle* magazine, *Jubilat, Kweli Journal,* the *Owls, Pebble Lake Review, Pyrta, Reverie, Sententia,* and *Vinyl,* among others. She is an assistant professor of creative writing and the director of the Center for Women Writers at Salem College.

Joshunda Sanders is a writer and journalist whose work has been widely anthologized, and her essays have appeared in the *San Francisco Chronicle, Gawker, Huizache, Salon,* and the *Week*. Her reporting and writing has also appeared in the *UTNE Reader*, the *Dallas Morning News, Bitch* magazine, *Kirkus Reviews,* and *Publishers Weekly*. "Sirens" first appeared in the *Bellevue Literary Review*. She blogs at www.joshunda.com.

Renee Simms's stories and essays have appeared in *North American Review, Hawai'i Review, Salon, Brain, Child: The Magazine for Thinking Mothers,* and elsewhere. A Michigan native, she currently lives in Washington, where she teaches writing and African American literature at the University of Puget Sound. She has received fellowships, contributorships, honors, and prizes from *storySouth, Inkwell Journal,* the PEN Center, the Kimbilio Center for African American Fiction, the Bread Loaf Writers' Conference, the Arizona Humanities Council, the Voices of Our Nations Arts Foundation, and Cave Canem. She currently lives in Washington and teaches writing and African American studies at the University of Puget Sound.

Rochelle Spencer's work appears in several publications including *Mosaic Literary Magazine, Callaloo,* the *African American Review, Publishers Weekly, Poets & Writers,* the *Rumpus,* and *Crab Creek Review,* which nominated her nonfiction for an Editor's Choice Award and a Pushcart Prize. Rochelle has taught at Spelman College, New York University, LaGuardia Community College, and the College of New Rochelle, and she is a board member of the Hurston-Wright Foundation, a founding member of the Harlem Works Collective, and a member of the Wintergreen Writers Collective and the National Book Critics Circle. Rochelle is currently coauthoring a nonfiction book about the members of the Dark Room Collective and completing a doctorate on Afro-surrealist texts. For more information, visit www.rochelle spencer.com or www.twitter.com/rochellespencer.

Mecca Jamilah Sullivan's fiction has appeared in *Callaloo*, *Best New Writing*, *The Best Unpublished Stories by Emerging Writers* (*American Fiction*, vol. 12, 2012), *Crab Orchard Review*, *Robert Olen Butler Fiction Prize Stories*, *BLOOM*, *TriQuarterly*, *Prairie Schooner*, and others. She is a winner of the Charles Johnson Fiction Award and the James Baldwin Memorial Playwriting Award, and has earned honors from the National Endowment for the Arts, the Bread Loaf Writers' Conference, Yaddo, Hedgebrook, *American Short Fiction*, and the Center for Fiction in New York City, where she was awarded the 2011 Emerging Writer Fellowship. She is currently an assistant professor of women, gender, and sexuality studies at the University of Massachusetts at Amherst, where her research focuses on poetics and identity in women's literature of the African diaspora. Her short-story collection, *Blue Talk and Love*, will be published in 2014.

Hope Wabuke is a mom and writer who runs a communications company called TheWriteSmiths. She is also the director of media and communications for the Kimbilio Center for African American Fiction and a blogger for *Ms. Magazine*. Her work has been featured in the *Daily Beast*, *Salon*, *Gawker*, *Ms. Magazine* online, the *Feminist Wire*, and *Kalyani Magazine*, among others. A New York Times Foundation Fellow, Hope has also received fellowships from the Voices of our Nations Arts Foundation and from Cave Canem.

Xu Xi 許素細 is the author of nine books of fiction and essays. The most recent titles are *Access Thirteen Tales* (2011); the novel *Habit of a Foreign Sky* (2010), a finalist for the inaugural Man Asian Literary Prize; and an essay collection, *Evanescent Isles* (2008). She is currently Writer-in-Residence at City University of Hong Kong's Department of English, where she established and directs Asia's first, international low-residency MFA in creative writing that also focuses on writing of, from, and out of Asia. For more information, visit www.xuxiwriter.com, www.facebook.com/XuXiWriter, or @xuxiwriter.

Ashley Young is a black queer feminist writer and poet working as an editor in New York City. She received her BA from Hampshire College, where she studied education and theater and is earning a certification in copyediting at New York University. She is a 2010 Voices of Our Nations Art Foundation Poetry Fellow and a 2011 Lambda Literary Foundation Creative Nonfiction Fellow. Her feminist poetry and prose have been published in *Elixher* magazine, *Rkvry Quarterly Literary Journal*, *Autostraddle*, *Her Circle* magazine, and more. She authored a chapter in *Hot & Heavy: Fierce Fat Girls on Life, Love & Fashion* (2012) and is working on her first novel, an Audre Lorde–inspired biomythography.